SURGEON'S CH

SURGEON'S CHOICE

A Novel of
Medicine Tomorrow

FRANK G. SLAUGHTER

Doubleday & Company, Inc.

GARDEN CITY, NEW YORK

All the characters in this book are fictitious, and any resemblance
to actual persons, living or dead, is purely coincidental.

SURGEON'S CHOICE

1

Greg Alexander was perspiring freely by the time the red warning light went off in the small air lock of the hyperbaric chamber, indicating that, with the pressures now equal, he could open the main door between them without danger of lowering the vital concentration of air in the larger compartment. Through the small glass port, or window, set into the steel wall of the air lock, he could see one of the group of ex-Navy divers who operated the chamber from outside. And when the technician held up his hand with thumb and forefinger joined in the circle that was a universal sign of approval, Greg turned the latch opening the inner door and stepped into the brightly lit main compartment.

A highly sophisticated adaptation of the old-style pressure tank used to prevent—or treat—the "bends," which had so often crippled caisson workers years ago, the hyperbaric—literally "high pressure" —chamber had been devised for medical use, where the high oxygen concentrations it made possible were of considerable value in many special surgical procedures, as well as in diseases where air pressure was important.

Compressing air into the metal cylinder—not much larger than the buried tanks of large service stations—also concentrated the heat inside that air, so the temperature always rose rapidly during the initial period of pressure rise. Greg had undergone just such a rapid compression inside the cramped space of the air lock, hence the fine layer of perspiration that now covered his body and his sudden shiver when he encountered the cooler air inside the chamber itself.

Essentially a steel tank with glass ports through which the technicians outside could maintain a constant watch on those inside and pumps for controlling the pressure of air inside the chamber, as well as gauges reading constantly the temperature, humidity and other important factors, the chamber was a self-contained unit, with its own power source, in case of an electrical failure. Set into the side was a smaller air lock for the insertion of necessary instruments and medications, or the removal of tissue specimens for immediate pathological study, without disturbing the pressure level within the main part of the chamber. At one end stood a small compact laboratory cabinet and sink, allowing immediate emergency chemical procedures to be carried on inside the chamber.

The scene that met Greg Alexander's eyes was a familiar one: he might almost have been looking into a mirror, for, in hundreds of operations, he had himself occupied the central position at the narrow operating table. Hans Werner, the grizzled caretaker-technician for the Laboratory of Experimental Surgery, was in his usual place at the table's head but Dr. Jack Smith, professor of veterinary medicine at the nearby university veterinary school, occupied Greg's usual position beside it, holding up his rubber-gloved hands so their sterility would not be lost. The star of this little tableau, upon whose staging was centered tonight the entire life-preserving facilities of one of the two or three finest clinics in the world, was a brown and white spaniel lying quietly in the cone of brilliant light cast by a lamp in the ceiling.

Like everything else inside the hyperbaric chamber, the lamp was elaborately protected from any possibility of a short circuit or spark, which, because of the high concentrations of oxygen often used in hyperbaric medicine, could convert the entire inside of the tank into an inferno. Even the pumps that activated the suction apparatus for surgery and the drills, saw and other mechanical tools were all operated by air pressure through metal tubes brought in from outside—designed to remove any danger of spark.

The old Austrian technician was crooning a lullaby to the dog as she breathed oxygen through a special mask. Trained to tolerate the mask without struggling, she was breathing easily as she lay there, her belly swollen with pregnancy and the long white scar of a healed surgical incision across her chest in sharp contrast under the bright light to the sleek brown of her coat. The dog's eyes were bright with interest—and with trust—for she had lain on this same table several times before.

"No action yet?" Greg asked.

"Not so far, but the contractions are rhythmic, so it could come at any time," said the veterinarian. "Sorry I had to keep you from the symphony, but you did ask to be called when things got going and Hans said you would want to be here."

"Hans knows I skip the symphony whenever I can find an excuse." Greg smiled as he moved up to the table and reached across the old technician's shoulder to scratch the dog's ear, while her tail thumped against the cushion of the operating table in an acknowledgment of the gesture of friendship. "Maybe Letty does, too, and chose tonight just to help me."

"You must learn to enjoy music, Dr. Alexander." Hans Werner's voice still had a guttural accent even after more than twenty years in the United States, all spent in the animal house and experimental laboratory. "Ach! If you could only have been in Vienna in the old days, you would have heard music that was music."

"I'll go there when I retire, Hans," Greg promised.

"On a stretcher that will be," said the Austrian. "Or a bier."

When he'd stepped into the chamber from the air lock, Greg Alexander's swift glance had noted that the preparations he had ordered for Letty's accouchement were all made, as he'd been sure they would be. The large sterile tray at the far end, covered with a greenish tinted sterile sheet from the main operating room suite, was ready in case an emergency Caesarean section became necessary. Everything seemed well under control, however, so he allowed himself to relax.

Hans was Greg's right hand in the laboratory, where he spent as much of his time as could be taken from his duties as chief surgeon of The Clinic: he depended on the old Austrian, not only during the experimental surgery, from which had come the most advanced operative procedures in heart and lung transplant in the world, but for the care of the animals, which, like Letty, became quite as much individuals as any human patients—with the added ingredient of love. The animals early learned to love and trust their keepers and so the element of fear, so often a deciding factor in the outcome of delicate and dangerous surgery, was absent with them, making animal surgery usually more successful than operations on humans.

"Letty's enjoying this." Conscious for the first time in a long and busy day of being bone tired, Greg pulled up a stool beside Hans. "She knows she's the prima donna tonight."

"How long ago is it since she was your first successful heart-lung transplant case?" Dr. Smith asked.

"About seven months. Now she's racking up another first by having pups."

Letty whimpered softly as a contraction gripped her uterus, then relaxed again.

"She's about to go into high gear," said the veterinarian. "We could give her Nembutal but I'd rather not. Sometimes the puppies are so sleepy afterwards you have trouble making them breathe."

"Dogs knew about natural childbirth long before people did," said Hans Werner. "Don't vorry. Letty will take care of herself when the time comes."

"While we're waiting," the veterinarian said to Greg Alexander, "would you mind cluing me in on this hyperbaric technique? We horse doctors don't have such modern equipment in our business."

"A lot of clinics wouldn't call this rusty old tank very modern," Greg admitted wryly. "Down at Duke they've got a triple chamber that makes ours look like the one-horse shay."

"Still it vorks," said Hans Werner. "What you have accomplished in the old laboratory, Dr. Alexander, a lot of new schools, with all that steel and glass, will never do so well."

"We're now under only two atmospheres of pressure, and that's just a precautionary measure for Letty's safety, to take all the load we can off her heart during delivery," said Greg, going back to Dr. Smith's question. "I don't imagine you've noticed much of an effect from it at all."

"Nothing except an acute exacerbation of my normal claustrophobia, and a sudden sweat right after they closed the outside doors."

"We all have that experience," said Greg. "When you pump a lot of air into a small space, you pump a lot of heat in with it. This is a small chamber and the air conditioning isn't very effective. I

4

had a larger chamber in the new laboratory I planned two years ago."

"The one the Board of Trustees wouldn't approve?"

"Yes. Just between us, I'm glad they didn't, because it wouldn't have been adequate for our needs. Hospital construction is changing so fast that what I wanted to build two years ago would have been antiquated by now. This time I'm going to shoot for twin chambers, with an air lock between, maybe even one of those wet tanks like they have at Duke for simulating deep-sea dives."

"I don't see how you're going to be able to anticipate future developments if medicine is changing as fast as you say it is," Dr. Smith observed.

"We can't anticipate everything. But since the National Institute of Health gave me the funds to build this small chamber, we've —at least learned what we'll really need later on."

"I still don't understand completely how it works," the veterinarian said.

"Fundamentally, all we have here is a tank and a pump for compressing air into it," said Greg. "The air inside the chamber now is under twice the pressure we normally breathe outside, but you're not conscious of it because it's both inside and outside our bodies. The only reason for using pressure with Letty is to put more oxygen into her blood and thus ease the load on her heart— or rather the one we gave her at operation seven months ago."

"That's the part that really bugs me," Dr. Smith admitted. "When I studied physiology, we were taught that the hemoglobin in the red blood cells is saturated with O-two in the lungs and can't carry any more."

"That's true."

"Then how can raising the pressure in the chamber or breathing pure oxygen—or even both, as Letty's doing now—get more oxygen into the body?"

"The fluid part of the blood—the plasma—carries the extra oxygen to the tissues," Greg explained. "With normal breathing at atmospheric pressure, the red cell hemoglobin carries roughly nineteen or twenty cubic centimeters of oxygen for every hundred cc. of blood, but only three tenths of a cc. is dissolved in every hundred of plasma."

5

"That would have a negligible effect as far as the supply of oxygen to the body cells is concerned."

"Exactly. Even breathing pure O-two at atmospheric pressure only puts about two cc. of oxygen into each hundred cc. of plasma. But raise the pressure to three atmospheres while breathing pure oxygen and the amount dissolved in the plasma jumps three times."

"That's quite a change."

"At five times atmospheric pressure, we've been able to keep dogs alive in this chamber with no real blood in their circulations at all, using only a substitute that contains no red cells or hemoglobin. You can see what that would mean with a severe case of hemorrhage, for example."

"What about other uses?"

"We're in pretty much new territory there, although new work is being published all the time," Greg admitted. "The main argument I used to get the grant for this chamber from the National Institute of Health was that with it we can keep an organ we're going to transplant into another body alive and healthy a lot longer than we'd ordinarily be able to do. Hyperbaric oxygen is also pretty effective in early anerobic infections, but we've had only a few opportunities to treat those yet."

"For transplanting in humans, I can see that you could use the double chamber you mentioned," said Dr. Smith. "Think you can convince the board of that?"

The dog whined into the oxygen mask before Greg could answer. "I think they come now," said Hans Werner, and Greg looked quickly at the electronic monitor tube at the end of the chamber. The pattern of Letty's heartbeat was being shown there in a steady progression of moving lines across the face of the tube, and was also being recorded permanently by a sensitive stylus upon a moving strip of electrocardiographic tracing paper.

"The beat is steady and regular, with no sign of fibrillation," he said on a note of quiet satisfaction. "I think we're going to make it O.K." He leaned over to scratch the dog's ear again. "Stay with it, Letty, you're the only one of your kind in the world tonight."

Four puppies were shortly delivered in rapid succession. Afterward the veterinarian kneaded the dog's belly gently until the placenta was expelled.

6

"I don't believe her pulse varied a beat during the entire delivery." Greg's voice was quietly exultant. "This should be the final proof, Hans."

"For me," the old Austrian said with a shrug, "it was proved already."

"Any idea when you'll do your first human heart-lung transplant?" Dr. Smith asked as he and Greg paused in the air lock for the very brief period of decompression necessary after an exposure of two atmospheres.

"That's in the lap of the gods. We've had a number of successful transplants of the heart alone, but for both the heart and the lungs, even closer selection is required. It might be next week—or next year."

"I'm flattered that I could play a small part in tonight's triumph." Dr. Smith shivered as the temperature in the air lock rapidly declined with the loss of pressure, the reverse of what had happened when the huge steel tank had been inflated. "How long will it take us to decompress?"

"Actually, you and I could step out now with no danger of getting the bends," said Greg. "But it's just as well not to rush things."

"I've done a little scuba diving and this high oxygen pressure business intrigues me," said the veterinarian. "Do you mind if I look in on your experimental work from time to time?"

"I'll be disappointed if you don't," Greg assured him. "If we're lucky enough to get approval from the trustees for a set of chambers like they have at Duke, we hope to study what happens to skin-divers who keep going down, even after they pass the point of safe return."

Outside the building, Greg turned up the collar of his tweed jacket. The February wind was whipping up from the harbor, as only that of a Baltimore winter could do, and there was a threat of snow in the lowering sky.

"You can see how much the board thinks of the Laboratory of Experimental Surgery," he said wryly as they crossed to the main enclosed corridor of the hospital by way of an open walkway. "They didn't even give us a covered passage to it."

"It doesn't seem right," said the veterinarian. "Some of the most

7

important work on organ transplant has been done here—but only because you persevered in spite of all the handicaps."

"Many of medicine's most valuable discoveries have been made under similar conditions," said Greg, "so I suppose I've got no real cause to complain. Doctors are lousy money raisers, so we need a few millionaires on our boards—"

"As stubborn ones as Sam Hunter?"

"Don't forget that he's got as much money as the rest of them put together."

"I'm not forgetting it," said Dr. Smith. "But is he likely to let you forget it? If I had anything to do with it, the board would vote you a medal when it meets Saturday morning. Instead, they'll probably kick your teeth in, if the way they've treated the most important department of the whole clinic in the past is any example."

ii

Just off the rotunda of the central building that alone had housed the original clinic, a doctors' call-board was set against the back wall of the main corridor. The light behind Greg's name was still on, showing that he was in the hospital, and he pushed the button beside it, turning off the light behind his name there and also on a similar board before the telephone operators in an alcove off the hospital foyer.

Above the call-board was a bronze plaque with the raised letters across the top: "THE CLINIC FOUNDATION AND HOSPITAL IN THE CITY OF BALTIMORE." Beneath it, a group of other letters, smaller in size, spelled out: "An Institution for the Care of the Sick, Operated Not for Profit by a Board of Trustees Elected by the Members of The Clinic."

Conceived and brilliantly executed in a day when group medical practice was almost unheard of, The Clinic—as its founder had insisted upon calling it—had been the dream of one man, Dr. Henry Anders. Fifty years later on this February afternoon, the soul of Henry Anders was still a vigorous current flowing through every part of the great institution. Moreover, the "Members of The Clinic," composed not only of its staff but also of those who, as

8

Fellows, had honed their medical and surgical skills to a fine point during two years devoted to postgraduate study here, contained within its ranks more famous medical and surgical names throughout the world than any other institution could boast.

In the rotunda, Greg Alexander paused in the shadows beside the marble figure of Christ, which, two stories high, dominated the entire entrance foyer. It had been a long day for The Clinic's chief surgeon, beginning with morning rounds in the surgical building, then a clinical demonstration in the old surgical lecture room with its steeply rising rows of seats filled with students and Fellows, followed by a quick lunch in the hospital cafeteria before the usual afternoon of work in the Laboratory of Experimental Surgery.

Finally had come the conference, lasting far longer than planned, with Keith Jackson, the brilliant Harvard-trained architect who was in the final stage of planning a projected new hospital and diagnostic clinic building complex to replace the old, and long since outgrown, brownstone buildings of the original clinic and hospital.

Although a continuous tide of humanity ebbed and flowed through the hospital foyer only yards away from the statue, it was quiet here in the shadows behind it, and Greg felt an almost physical force holding him back from stepping out into the flow, which would, in a sense, rejoin him to the rest of the world.

The conference with Keith Jackson plus Letty's delivery had made him late again in getting home, a fact which, he knew, would only increase the wall of tension that had been growing between him and Jeanne these past months.

Or was it years?

The change had been so gradual that, coming home dead tired each night from his work as executive head of The Clinic—although Dr. Henry Anders II, son of the founder, held the nominal title of director—he could not tell when it had actually begun.

Twenty years ago, when Greg had first come to The Clinic as a young Fellow in Surgery, with four years of medical school at Johns Hopkins and a two-year internship there behind him, he had met Jeanne for their first date "at the feet of Jesus," in the parlance of the young doctors and nurses. For an instant now, as he stood in the shadows, he was startled to see her appear—as

9

she had then—from the other side of the great statue, the fluted cap of a senior student nurse upon her golden hair and the blue cape hanging from shoulders, which, after all these years, were just as proud and lovely as they had been then.

Then the girl said, "Good evening, Dr. Alexander," and he realized that his imagination had been playing him tricks again, obeying a deep inner wish that he and Jeanne could both go back to that long lost first meeting here and recapture some of the years of happiness and loving companionship which had followed.

The spell broken, Greg came out of the shadows into the brighter light of the foyer and the ebb and flow of the human tide through it. As he was pulling up the collar of his jacket again, preparing for the cold outside the double doors, a tall young doctor in a white coat came through and stopped at the sight of him.

"I guess you could shoot me, Dr. Alexander." Bob Johnson's tone was rueful. "I went out to the delicatessen to get some salami and while I was gone the call came from Hans. Did you have to go into the chamber?"

"It was no trouble at all, Bob." Greg was very fond of the Senior Fellow in Vascular Surgery, who was his right hand. "Your friend Keith Jackson kept me over here until nearly eight anyway and all I had to do was stop by and congratulate Letty."

"She came through all right then?"

"Not so much as an extrasystole. Four puppies and all beauties. Maybe Hans will let you have one of them for your boy."

"Were you pleased—with what Keith showed you—sir?"

"More than pleased. Have you seen it?"

Bob Johnson shook his head. "Keith's been acting very mysterious lately and Mary's hardly been able to get him out of his drawing room for meals. Well, good night, sir. I promise that you won't be disturbed any more tonight. You must be worn out."

"I'm a little bushed but a drink and some food will take care of that. Going home?"

"Not just yet. I want to recheck everything for the heart-lung transplant demonstration we're doing for the convocation. We can't have anything go wrong with all that medical brass watching. See you in the morning, sir."

On the steps outside, looking down the curving driveway to the broad street in front called The Parkway, Greg paused while a delivery truck passed. A couple of inches less than six feet, he was of medium build and, at forty-five, beginning to thicken a little around the middle because he rarely had time for any physical exercise except his work. His iron-gray hair was thinning a bit at the front but he still refused to wear a hat, even in winter, largely because he knew he'd never be able to remember where he'd left it last. The eyes beneath slightly bushy brows had lost none of their keenness, or kindliness, during the years, though some of the merriment that had twinkled at their corners, when he was younger, had been erased since he'd begun to worry so much about Jeanne.

When he'd been a Senior Fellow like Bob Johnson nearly twenty years ago, Greg and Jeanne had moved as newlyweds into an apartment in one of the brownstone-front, common-walled houses that had lined the other side of The Parkway then. Now they occupied an apartment in almost the same spot, one of several penthouse units that made up the top floor of the tall building which, with the adjoining Clinic Inn, more than a decade ago had replaced the older houses with their white marble steps that had once lined the south side of the thoroughfare. Buildings housing married Fellows and residents and the Nursing Home for the hospital completed a two-block front now. And compared to these modern structures, the brownstone of the rotunda which had housed the original clinic, and the two hospital wings on either side, only a few years less aged, were now relics of the past.

"Paper, Doctor?" When a newsboy thrust a copy of the evening paper before Greg Alexander's eyes, he saw across the top the heavy black headline:

MURDERER THOUGHT TO BE IN BALTIMORE AREA

From his pocket he fished out a dime and shoved the paper beneath his arm as he started down the walkway past the sundial in the center of the grassplot bounded by the curving drive. As he paused at the booth by the gate to acknowledge the greeting of the guard—part of whose aorta he had replaced with a tube of nylon mesh five years before—he could see a line of expensive-

11

looking automobiles lined up under the marquee of the Clinic Inn next door to his apartment house.

Friends and former Fellows would be gathering in the Falstaff Room already for drinks and rehashing of old times, he knew, and it would be pleasant to sip a tall drink with them but he resolutely put temptation aside. Things had become strained between him and Jeanne since that day two years ago, when he had come from the trustees' meeting that was always held at the end of a Convocation of the Members of The Clinic with the news that his plans for a new building complex had been summarily defeated. But he was loyal enough to her, and to what they'd had together, not to take the easy way out and avoid facing her anger at his being late by stopping for a more pleasant hour at the Inn.

Thinking of Jeanne, Greg glanced up to one of the two balconies fronting upon the street atop the Clinic Apartments, marking the location of the two penthouses. In summer, she'd often waved to him from the height, as he crossed The Parkway, but tonight the balcony was empty. He didn't notice the quick movement back into the shadows of the man who had been leaning over the rail of the adjoining balcony to watch him. But when Dr. Henry Anders II, director of The Clinic and only son of its founder, opened the door leading into the adjoining penthouse to Greg's, there was a smile of vast satisfaction on his somewhat overly handsome face.

iii

On another—and smaller—terrace, well below the penthouse level, Keith Jackson lit a cigarette as he studied, for perhaps the hundredth time, the buildings sprawled upon rising ground across The Parkway. He wasn't seeing the ugliness of the brownstone front, the windows filmed with pollutants that fouled the atmosphere or the rounded dome of the rotunda, however. Instead, his mind's eye had captured a vision, a soaring tower of twenty stories with two more underground, a temple of healing epitomizing the vastly complicated medical science of tomorrow, with, flanking it at half that height, two hospital wings that would provide adjunct service and double the capacity of the institution.

Inside the tower itself would be concentrated facilities for several hundred patients, postoperative, cardiac, severe infections—any conditions requiring constant watching and intensive treatment. With no patient more than fifty feet from centrally located nursing stations upon each floor and each room under constant watch by means of monitor tubes fed by closed-circuit TV cameras anchored near the ceiling, a patient need never feel that he was alone.

With a wealth of information about pulse, temperature, respiration, the electrocardiographic tracing—shortened in hospital shorthand to ECG—the oxygen level of the blood and a dozen other factors which could strongly influence the often delicate balance between living and dying continually being watched by sensors developed for monitoring astronauts in orbit hundreds of miles above the earth, and programmed through a master computer to sound a strident warning of any deviation from normal, the sick patient could be far more closely watched than if a skilled nurse were actually standing by the bedside. Most important of all, the double load of patients the Intensive Care Tower allowed would require little additional hospital personnel, an extremely important factor in a day when the supply of highly trained nurses did not even equal half the demand.

It was a magnificent dream, one that had been forming slowly in Keith Jackson's creative mind ever since Greg Alexander had invited him two years earlier to submit preliminary drawings for new clinic and hospital buildings to replace the now thoroughly antiquated ones across the street. The limitations imposed then by the trustees—and carefully detailed for him several months before by Greg Alexander, when Keith had asked about submitting plans again—had been like a blanket upon any creative action, however, and he hadn't even considered submitting sketches—until Henry Anders had brought the magazine article to him hardly a week ago. Nothing else had been needed to release the creative flow after that, and, working all night at the drawing boards he kept in the apartment, Keith had captured in the lines, angles and shadows of preliminary sketches, the essential substance of the dream before it could flit away.

When he'd showed the sketches to Greg Alexander for the first time earlier that afternoon, he'd been ready to do battle for his concept and for its execution in place of the more humdrum, conventional sort of building complex which a staid architectural firm downtown had already designed and which awaited only the approval of the trustees to begin its execution in steel, brick, mortar and stone.

The eyes of The Clinic's surgeon-in-chief had lit up the moment he saw that soaring tower and the graceful wings supporting it, and he'd nodded approval again and again while Keith pointed out the many advantages of the design.

Later Greg Alexander had added suggestions here and there, filling out from his vast experience the picture the architect was sketching. The surgeon himself had suggested a more full use of the master computer to marshal the flow of information from patients to the central storage center and also to execute the tremendously complex orders which were so important in the modern-day treatment of the desperately ill. The first frown had come to Greg Alexander's brow when Keith had mentioned an estimated cost of twenty-eight million dollars.

"The plans we already have would cost barely two thirds of that," he protested. "Fifteen to eighteen million according to the architect's estimate."

"But look at the difference in efficiency and the number of patients you could handle, Doctor," Keith had protested. "Your skilled nursing staff need not be any larger than with the first plant, perhaps even smaller, yet you can care for half again as many acutely ill patients as you do now. And by utilizing the somewhat newer buildings behind the original structure for ambulatory and convalescing patients, as well as those being examined for pre-admission studies, the capacity of the diagnostic clinic can easily be doubled, as well as the number of patients in the hospital itself."

"Would you be able to run a time-study analysis before the trustees' meeting Saturday morning?" Greg Alexander asked.

"It may take some doing," said Keith. "But a friend of mine is an assistant analyst for TRW. I've already talked to him about this project and the company has been pioneering in medical automation, so it may be that he can run a few studies for us between now and then."

"I'll need that when the Board of Trustees meets on Saturday after the convocation, along with as detailed preliminary sketches as you're able to give me."

"You'll have them," Keith had promised, and only now, when he thought of the work he had to get done before Saturday, did the young architect become a little scared.

After he left Greg's office, Keith had remembered his brief talk with Dr. Henry Anders II and wondered whether he should mention it. But there had been no reason not to believe Dr. Anders' explanation of his visit to the architect's office a week earlier, for who could have a greater interest than the son of the founder in seeing a monument to his father's genius rise above the old clinic.

A tapping sounded on the door behind him and through the glass Keith Jackson saw his wife, Mary, beckoning him inside to dinner. The apartment was one of the smaller ones in the building, with two bedrooms, a den which he used as an at-home office, a living room with a dining area, kitchen and bath.

"I met Dr. Alexander just now as I was going out to the delicatessen at the corner," she told him when he came inside. "He said your preliminary sketches are truly inspiring."

"The sketches are fine; I'm a good enough architect to know that without Dr. Alexander's approval." Keith pulled out a chair for Mary at the small table. "But I still don't understand why Dr. Anders brought the idea to me."

"Perhaps he remembered your plans from two years ago!"

"Not when he was a leader in the faction that torpedoed Dr. Alexander's ideas. By the way," he added, "I saw Dr. Anders come into the building as I was parking my car in the garage. Do you suppose Dr. Alexander called him about the project?"

"Really, darling," said Mary. "Don't you ever see anything but a drawing board?"

"What have I done now?"

"Dr. Anders has been sneaking into the apartment house through the garage for more than six months now."

"Why?"

"He's sleeping with Dr. Helen Foucald. No, I guess sleeping is the wrong word. He never stays more than a couple of hours."

"Two hours! What is he? Superman?"

"Just about that—from what I hear."

"Where do you get all this stuff?"

"Don't forget that I was a nurse across the street. Everybody over there knows Dr. Anders will make a pass at anything in skirts that looks promising—and go even farther when he finds one with enough curiosity."

"Curiosity about what?"

"Really, darling." Mary had the grace to blush. "Don't you ever listen to gossip?"

"Why should I—when you'll tell me eventually?"

"Let's just say that Dr. Henry Anders II is said to be bigger than life."

"But Dr. Foucald's such a prim thing—more like an old-maid schoolteacher."

Mary leaned over and kissed him.

"Thanks," he said. "What was that for?"

"For not really seeing Dr. Foucald. She makes a pregnant wife look like something the cat dragged in—with those Paris clothes of hers and that figure. But what makes you think there's any funny business about Dr. Anders wanting you to do the new plans?"

"I don't know—except that it's no secret how he and some others on the board fought Dr. Alexander to a standstill when he wanted to build a modern hospital two years ago. The main reason I wasn't even going to submit a plan this time was because the conditions were too rigid. Now suddenly, the sky's the limit."

"Don't look the gift horse too deep in the mouth. Have you figured what six per cent commission is on twenty-eight million dollars?"

"I still can't help wondering if Dr. Anders is trying to steal a march on Dr. Alexander."

"You mean like claiming he thought of the new plan first?"

"Maybe. He made me promise not to tell Dr. Alexander about his part in it, but he also insisted that I show the sketches to Dr. Alexander no later than today."

"Did he say why?"

"Only that if Dr. Alexander knew about his part in it he might be prejudiced against the plan."

"Dr. Alexander's not that sort of person," said Mary. "Besides, he's responsible for the whole convocation—"

"I thought they only had those at universities for graduations. Or when they give an honorary degree to a big shot who might donate a lot of money."

"Old Dr. Anders called the first meeting a convocation and the name stuck," Mary explained. "Former Fellows who have made some spectacular accomplishment through research or a new discovery are asked to present their findings before the group. If it's a new operation, the surgeon who worked it out usually does one as a demonstration, like the heart-lung transplant Dr. Alexander's going to do Thursday afternoon on a dog."

"How did you know about that?"

"Bob Johnson's the Senior Fellow in Vascular Surgery and Dr. Alexander's assistant, remember? Harriet was telling me about it in the laundromat this morning."

"That reminds me," said Keith. "The clinical laboratory is a pretty important part of an automated setup like the one I'm planning. Maybe I ought to spend some time with Dr. Foucald discussing the details."

"See that you spend that time in the lab then," Mary warned darkly. "With plenty of people around you."

2

Standing beside Ted as they waited for their entrance cue for the evening performance, Vivian Tarentino Hunter was a pocket Venus in her white nylon tights. The youngest daughter of an Italian circus family, born in Sarasota and reared there, Vivian had gone on the road at twelve with the one-ring Tarentino Circus her father had inherited from his father. Leaving the sawdust ring to go to college, she had met Ted at Florida State University, where he was already a member of the famed college circus troupe, and quickly earned a berth for herself with the flying trapeze act of which Ted was already a part.

The second son of Sam Hunter, the multimillionaire oil man and corporation stealer, Ted had gone to Tallahassee instead of following the traditional Hunter course of a B.A. degree at Austin, a year in Europe and an M.B.A. at the Harvard Business School. Actually, old Sam hadn't looked with particular favor upon his son being a circus performer, but since it was a college affair and Ted's grades were excellent, his bellow of protest had been somewhat muted. But when Ted announced just before graduation that he and Vivian had been married for three months, old Sam had hit the ceiling and disinherited his second son, refusing even to meet his daughter-in-law or see Ted receive his diploma at Tallahassee.

Ted and Vivian had been a double act during his last year at F.S.U., so it had been natural for them to take their talents to the ailing Tarentino Circus, traveling by truck from small town to small town, playing in large high-school auditoriums or whatever they could find. But with cataracts and retinal degeneration slowly cutting off his vision, Papa Gus Tarentino was about ready to throw in the towel at the end of the present season. Vivian had been taking a correspondence school business course so she could work as a secretary when Ted went to graduate school in the fall to get the M.B.A. his father had wanted him to get in the first place —but with the difference that if he won the coveted Harvard degree now, he'd be under no obligation to anyone.

Ted's left arm was around Vivian as they waited beside the exit from the auditorium floor for the elephant act which preceded their own to clear the ring. When he saw the line of elephants suddenly veer toward them, he quickly swept Vivian to safety behind him and, in the same movement, seized a stick lying on the ground close beside him. As he whacked the lead elephant on the snout, driving it back into the line, he could see the cause of the elephant's sudden fright, a mouse that had scampered across its path. And swinging the stick like a golf club, he knocked the tiny rodent out of the path of the other animals, saving the whole herd from stampeding.

"Quick thinking, fellow," said Joe Califino, the swarthy roustabout and elephant handler, as he passed them at the end of the animal queue. "Another minute and this lousy circus would have been spread all over the walls."

"You hurt your hand, Ted." Vivian's cry of concern directed his attention to a drop of blood on his right hand where a splinter from the stick he'd picked up protruded perhaps a quarter of an inch from the skin. Just then, however, the calliope—in the Tarentino Circus it took the place of a band—sounded the opening bars of the music introducing their act. So, reaching across with his left hand, he seized the end of the splinter between thumb and forefinger and jerked it out before falling into step behind Vivian for the march into the ring.

"Nothing but a splinter," he told her. "I pulled it out."

The "Ahh" of admiration that went up from the audience when Vivian poised at the edge of the ring in the glare of the spotlight always gave Ted a thrill of appreciation, even though muted by the small size of the small-town crowd tonight. Once or twice, as he climbed hand over hand up to the trapeze while Vivian was being hauled up by the roustabout who watched their ropes, Ted felt a slight pricking in the web between the forefinger and thumb of his right hand where the splinter had gone in when he'd whacked the elephant a few moments before. But he had forgotten about it by the time he reached the trapeze bar to stand beside Vivian.

As the music of the calliope changed to a rock-and-roll rhythm, they swung into the routine they had worked out during their final year at F.S.U. and had taken on the annual tour of the college circus, including a swing through Europe that summer. In time with the throbbing beat, the two of them performed like a single being, going through the intricate evolutions of their act without a net, high above the heads of the spectators, while Papa Gus and Joe Califino watched from below, ready to throw their own bodies into the path of a fall, should either of the performers slip.

In preparation for the climax of the act, Ted gripped between his teeth a rubber guard to which a shorter trapeze bar was attached by means of a carefully looped nylon rope. Swinging down into the catching position of the trapeze performer, he anchored himself firmly while Vivian stood upon the bar above him, swinging in an arc.

When Ted was securely fixed in the catching position, she unhooked the short bar attached by the looped rope to the rubber guard he held with his teeth. For three swings she balanced without support upon the longer bar, then suddenly pitched forward in a somersault at the end of an arc, diving into the semi-darkness while the spot followed her progress. A gasp came from the audience as she flew through the air like a lovely white bird, plunging for a distance of more than two thirds of the space between the trapeze and the floor of the arena, while the carefully looped nylon rope attaching her to the rubber guard held between Ted's teeth uncoiled itself. Ted had seized the rope between his hands to take some of the shock of impact from his teeth. When he felt the slight jerk at the end of her fall, he gave the rope a twisting motion and removed his hands to leave her body spinning below him at the end of a tether, supported only by the rubber guard he held in his teeth and the nylon rope.

For three full swings across the ring, Vivian spun like a top at the end of a string. Then the watching roustabout flipped the ascent rope across her path so she could catch it with her leg and release her grip upon the trapeze. Ted, too, seized the rope above her and, clamping his legs about it, slid to the floor to stand beside Vivian, bowing to the applause of the audience before they stepped into the clogs they had left at the edge of the ring and started to their quarters.

"Your old man's picture's in the afternoon paper, Ted." The roustabout thrust a newspaper at him as they passed the area where the trucks were being loaded for tonight's move to another small Maryland town. "Send him a ticket to the show tomorrow night and maybe he'll buy the circus."

"Fat chance of his coming." Ted managed to smile, but more and more lately he'd felt sad at the long separation from the proud old man; and the sight of Sam Hunter's face in the newspaper picture only made it more acute now.

The Tarentino Circus traveled upon trucks, several of which had been converted into mobile homes for the performers and crew. Ted and Vivian had their own tiny compact compartment at the back of a truck driven by Joe, the elephant handler. It was parked on the lot behind the auditorium now, ready to move as soon as the performance ended and the rest of the equipment had been loaded aboard. Inside their mobile apartment, Ted lifted Vivian's short blond pony tail to kiss the back of her neck.

"They loved you tonight, hon," he said.

"What there was of them," said Vivian. "What did Joe say to you outside just now?"

"Dad's picture is in the paper." He opened the afternoon edition to reveal a four-column cut of Sam Hunter stepping down from his private jet.

"Why would he come to Baltimore now?"

"Dad's been a trustee of The Clinic ever since old Dr. Anders operated on mother over ten years ago and saved her life. Every two years they have a convention there toward the end of February. The trustees meet right afterwards and dad always comes up to Baltimore then to have his checkup before the meeting."

"He looks a lot older than the last picture I saw of him. Do you suppose he knows you're this close by?"

"He knows all right."

"Then maybe he'll—"

"Not yet," said Ted. "If either of us goes to the other now, it would look like giving in. I guess we're both a little stiff-necked; we're that much alike. But when I can hand him a diploma from the Harvard Business School, I'm sure we'll all be together again."

ii

The sixth sense that tells a performer the temper of an audience, even through the closed doors of a dressing room, warned Georgia Merchant when the change came in the club itself. The first catcall was in the middle of Guy's favorite song, the imitation he did of Harry Richmond, complete with top hat and cane, and Georgia was on her feet at the raucous sound, heading for the door. By the time she reached the wings of the small stage of the sleazy Baltimore Street nightclub, however, almost the entire audience was beginning to boo.

Both the scene and the sound were all too familiar and Georgia was glad she had taken the precaution of getting dressed a little early, unconsciously, she realized now, as a precaution against just such an eventuality as this. With a quick glance, she checked the zippers on the several layers of fabric that covered her final costume, iridescent pasties over each of her nipples, and the briefest of G-strings, made of the same material. A second glance at the mirror beside the wing exit told her that, at forty-five, she was still as lush of form as she had been at thirty, when she and Guy were married. Only the face had begun to show the ravages of worry about him and the strain of the nightly grinds in smoky bottle clubs. Fortunately those lines could still be covered by the expertise she'd developed in makeup as the toll of years had left deeper and deeper marks.

True to the tradition into which he had been born, Guy was still trying to go on with the song, but when he turned toward the wings, the look in his face warned Georgia that something far deeper was wrong than the displeasure of a largely drunken audience at a failing comic. The grayness of his cheeks and the look of pain—physical, not mental—in his eyes, even as he sought to carry on his act and keep up the front, told her he was having another of his now periodic attacks.

"Get him off, Georgia!" Aaron Schwartz, the pudgy nightclub manager, was chewing nervously on the stump of his cigar. "A Teamster local's out there on a binge. They'll start tearing the place apart any minute now."

"My music, Gus," Georgia called to the piano player who led the four-piece band. "Loud and fast."

The drummer caught the words and stamped down hard on the pedal that pounded the bass drum. Guy looked startled, but, when he saw Georgia strutting out from the wings with the slinky stride of a stripper, as only she could do, the look of relief on his face almost made her cry.

"Go lie down, honey." She spoke out of the corner of her mouth as she passed him, and the light man mercifully darkened the stage, leaving only a bright spot on Georgia and giving Guy time to slink off without being conspicuous.

"Take it off, baby!" A voice shouted good-naturedly from the back of the crowd, and, when laughter swept the room, Georgia knew the immediate emergency was over. Over, that was, as far as the club's being torn apart by the patrons was concerned, but probably far from over for Guy, if this attack followed the pattern set by the others.

Anxious to finish her act and get back to Guy, Georgia signaled to the drummer to step up the tempo of the bumps and grinds for which she was famous, and the rest of the band had no choice except to follow the lead of the pounding beat. Being the featured performer, she normally didn't start the real strip until the act was half finished, dragging it out with flip asides to the audience, while she slowly peeled off long gloves and toyed with a feather boa, a technique she'd perfected long ago on the burlesque stage in a happier and more prosperous era. But now she wasted no time and the layers began to come off in fairly rapid succession.

At first the audience loved it, but, as the flimsy draperies that made up her outer costume followed each other to the floor, she sensed that they had begun to realize they were being cheated of the full measure.

"For God's sake, take it easy, Georgia," the manager pleaded when she paused in the wings after stripping down to the net bra that covered the pasties and the outer—and larger—of her two G-strings.

"How's Guy?" she asked as the audience began to shout for her return.

"He's having pain; we sent for a doc."

The roar of the audience was an animal sound now and heavy feet had begun to stamp in rhythm with the music. As Georgia hesitated, torn between the need to go to Guy and the knowledge of what would happen if the audience got any uglier, the manager gave her a shove that sent her stumbling back onto the stage and into the spotlight.

Baffled and angry, she stood stock-still for a moment, glaring at the impatient drinkers. Then, as the drummer began the beat, she deliberately put her hands behind her head and, squatting almost upon her heels in the classic pose, began a slow and sinuous rise to her full height, ending with a thunderous bump, as the drummer hit both cymbals at once with a mighty crash.

The audience roared its approval once again and she went into a fast routine that was one of her specialties, crossing the stage rapidly from one side to the other until, on the final round, she tossed the net bra and the outer G-string at the audience.

She was running through the wings toward her dressing room when the manager barred her way, forcing her to stop as the roar from the crowd followed her, a tangible force demanding that she return.

"For God's sake, give them another round, Georgia," he begged. "They'll tear the place apart if you don't."

"But, Aaron—"

"The doc's on his way and Guy's better now. Get out there, please."

"I'll stop them this time." Her lips set on a tight line. "Get me a wrapper for when I come off, Aaron."

At the first beat of the drum, she seized each of the flimsy pasties, half-dollar-sized bits of fabric covering her nipples, and tore them off to the thunderous approval of the audience. Lifting her arms and clenching her fists so her breasts stood out, she began a rhythmic march across the floor, while the men stood on their

his move. The two joints he'd smoked an hour ago hadn't even taken the edge off the craving for heroin that was torturing his body. But with dollars in his pocket and an automobile, he knew where he could find a pusher on Baltimore Street to supply what he needed. And fifteen minutes later he'd be floating on Cloud Nine.

Tuesday wasn't a good business night for a tavern like this one, he knew, so he couldn't expect the cash register to be exactly running over. But there was sure to be enough to get the fix and get away before the cops could find him. And somewhere in the next city there'd be a savings and loan office in the suburbs waiting to be robbed, another motel and a cheap broad, until the time came to rob, and kill, again, if anyone tried to get in his way.

The sixth car in the row he was casing proved to be everything he was looking for, a maroon Mustang like thousands of others on the road at all hours, with the keys hanging in the lock, where a kid had left them when he'd rushed his girl inside to get her properly high before renting a room in the motel. Lifting the keys, Frank Lawson put them in the side pocket of his jacket and settled his hand over the pistol already there.

Crossing the lot, he entered the tavern, noting in one quick glance that it was like a thousand others he had visited, many of them for the same purpose as tonight. Along one wall of the small entryway was a glass-fronted cabinet containing cigarettes, candy and cigars. The cash register was opposite the door, with rows of package goods on shelves at the back. To the right was an archway giving access to the usual dim-lit smoke-filled room, its walls lined with booths.

A small platform occupied one corner of the room, with a post-age-stamp dance floor where a young couple—probably the very one who'd been in the Mustang—was swaying in a close embrace. Two men were on the stools before the bar nursing glasses of beer while they talked to the bartender, but less than half of the booths were filled.

"Can I help you, sir?" He hadn't seen the blonde in the short skirt and long black sheer stockings, who appeared to be doubling as waitress and cashier, until she appeared from the other room. He saw now that tables were in there, too—for those, he presumed, who weren't interested in the music—which meant that the take might be better than he'd hoped.

"I need some change for the cigarette machine, please," he told her.

"Certainly, sir." She went behind the counter and rang up "No Sale" on the cash register. As the drawer opened, she reached out to him for the bill but, when Frank Lawson's hand came out of his pocket, the pistol was in it instead.

"Keep quiet and you won't get hurt, sister," he said in a low voice. "Understand?"

The blonde nodded, just as they always did. Even if she'd tried to yell, he knew nothing would come out but maybe a squeak that wouldn't have been heard above the blare of the music.

"Hand me the bills," he directed, and she scrambled nervously in the slotted money tray for a small handful of money, most of it in lower-denomination notes.

"Now the bigger ones—under the tray," he ordered, but her hands trembled so that she could hardly lift out the tray, and, reaching over, he grabbed the pile of tens and twenties, shoving them into his pocket. Luck was with him tonight; the manager must have been too lazy to go to the bank that morning.

"Now walk out with me," he directed the girl. "And be quick."

She was shaking and so pale he thought she was going to faint. But she managed to emerge from behind the cash register and made no resistance when he seized her arm with his left hand and propelled her through the door. She shivered when the cold outside struck her in her skimpy costume. But it also seemed to stimulate her, for she walked on steadier legs as he guided her along the side of the building in the shadows. When he came to a niche where several garbage cans stood, he stopped her and lifted the gun in his right hand.

"No, please," she whimpered, but he didn't let the plea deter him from expertly bludgeoning her back of the ear with the butt of the pistol. As she started to crumple like a rag doll, he gave her body a shove, causing it to fall into the dark niche behind the cans. It would be awhile before she was found there, and, with the combo drowning out the voice of anyone who called for her inside, he might gain an extra fifteen minutes, if he were lucky, before someone discovered what had happened and called the police.

Moving swiftly to the Mustang, he got in, slipped the ignition key into the lock and started the motor. It was one of the high-powered ones, he noted with satisfaction, and felt a momentary regret that he would have to ditch it so soon to throw the cops off his trail. Driving out of the parking lot at the usual rate of speed, he turned into the street outside and stepped on the gas gradually, feeling the powerful motor seize the small car and move it forward.

Two blocks ahead, he saw an expressway overpass and, when a ramp appeared on the right, turned up it, for the expressway could get him across town in a few minutes to the fix he needed so badly. Still thinking about the way his body would start to float in the air once the needle entered the vein and the plunger of the syringe was driven home, he failed to notice the DO NOT ENTER sign at the foot of the ramp. And by the time he got to the top and realized he'd come up a "Down" ramp by mistake, it was too late to stop the car before it was out on the expressway itself.

As he wrestled frantically with the four-in-the-floor gearshift, trying to put it into reverse and send the car back down the ramp, Frank Lawson's eyes suddenly dilated with horror at the sight of the heavy truck bearing down upon him. An instant later the little car was scooped up by the behemoth and sent hurtling off the overpass bridge to the street below.

But long before it struck, Frank Lawson was unconscious.

3

"What did you see out there?" Helen Foucald spoke from the sofa, where she was pouring martinis from a silver shaker, already frosted from the ice inside, into two glasses of exquisitely cut crystal.

"What do you mean?" Doctor Henry Anders II, at forty-five, had the build of an athlete, from tennis and golf, and the aristocratically handsome features bequeathed to him by his father—though little of that great surgeon's understanding and compassion for the people who came to him for help.

"You look like the cat who's just lapped up the cream, but there's nothing out there except a Baltimore February night. And nobody could be very happy about one of them."

Helen Foucald had taken off the tailored skirt and blouse which, with a long-skirted laboratory coat, was her daily uniform in The Clinic. As chief of the clinical laboratories and a highly skilled biochemist and hematologist, with a Ph.D. in her own right, she was severely businesslike by day. But now, in a long hostess gown belted about her slender waist, and with her surprisingly full breasts unbrassiered, she was softly feminine. The change even involved her face, softening her features and making them seem a little more full. But her eyes had lost none of their directness and the long-fingered hands were as skillfully efficient pouring the martinis as they were twisting the fine-focusing controls of a binocular microscope.

"It never ceases to amaze me how you change like a chameleon merely by crossing the street." Henry Anders leaned back comfortably upon the sofa and enjoyed his martini.

"Of late it's getting harder and harder to change back," Helen admitted. "Those damned estrogen pills I have to take so you can have your way with me—as the Victorians used to put it—must be responsible. Five years ago I looked like a boy and had to fight off more than one loving female, but lately I've had to take some of the padding out of my bra."

She swallowed half the martini in a single luxurious gulp, flicked her tongue voluptuously into the glass and skillfully transferred the olive to a position between her teeth, crunching it as she reached for the shaker to fill her glass again. The action never failed to excite Henry, which she very well knew, as well as annoy him.

"How many times have I told you it's plebian to eat the olive?" he demanded.

"But I *am* plebian," she insisted. "My ancestors were treading grapes in France to make wine when yours were holed up in New York with General Howe while Washington and his men were starving at Valley Forge."

"I still say America would have been better off if England had won."

"Don't forget that if my ancestors hadn't helped Washington, England probably would have." She looked at him reflectively. "You're something of a prig, Henry. I often wonder how anybody with so many inhibitions manages to shed most of them with his pants."

"Don't be vulgar, Helen. It doesn't become you."

"Why can't you understand that I'm two people who live on different sides of the street, Henry? If the Southside-of-The-Parkway me ever took my place on the Northside, my laboratory would be so full of young males breaking beakers and test tubes, there'd never be any work done." She finished her martini and put down the glass. "Where will you be seen with the charming Mrs. Claire Anders tonight?"

"At the symphony. We're patrons, you know."

Helen glanced at her watch. "Patrons are supposed to be late, I know. But if you're going to make your usual entrance just before intermission, you'd better get along with your chores."

Jeanne Alexander was in the living room of the apartment, nursing a highball glass morosely, when Greg let himself in. One look at her flushed face and glittering eyes told him it was not her first drink, and probably not her second.

"Hello, darling." He leaned down to kiss her but she turned her head and his lips touched only her hair. "I'm sorry I was late."

"It's nothing new," she said dully.

"After the meeting of the board on Saturday, I should be able to let up a little. We could run down to White Sulphur or the Homestead for a few days. Or we might even go to Florida; it's been too long since we've had a weekend away to ourselves."

She only nursed her drink without answering, and he felt a twinge of pain at the memory of the gay and laughing person she had been only a few years ago. The slender figure hadn't changed it was true. She could still wear the same size she'd worn when they were married nearly twenty years ago, too, and her face was unlined, although, with all its customary animation gone now, her features were almost like a mask.

She had never drunk much before the past year, usually a dilute bourbon highball nursed all evening whenever they went to a cocktail party. But he'd come home many an evening lately to find her like this, and the small bar off the living room was always well stocked, although he rarely had time for a purchase. Going to it now, he poured himself a generous measure of bourbon, splashed soda into it and dropped in two ice cubes.

"Did you fix yourself a sandwich?" he asked.

"I don't want anything. There's ham and salad dressing in the refrigerator; and bread in the breadbox with potato chips."

"Want me to make one for you?"

"I said I don't want anything."

He took his time about making the sandwich and sat eating it at the small table in the kitchen where they'd always had breakfast —until lately. The more he thought about the changes in Jeanne this past year, the more frustrated and utterly baffled he felt. Nothing he could say seemed to reach her any more. The small endearments that had once made them so close, hands touched in passing, a light kiss on her hair, still golden and soft like an aureole about her head, her small hand groping for his as they waited in line at the theater, the warmth of her body as she leaned against him, the casual exploring touch of their tongues as they kissed, promising a greater intimacy later—all these were gone, and missing them brought again the feeling of a band constricting his heart, a band that must be burst asunder before it was too late.

Or was it already too late?

Jeanne's footsteps behind him made him turn his head. She was standing in the kitchen doorway, holding an open medical journal in her hand, and the fire of anger in her eyes brought at least a little animation to her features.

"The new issue of *Surgeon* came today," she said. "Why did you let Henry Anders steal credit for your work?"

He didn't need to look at the journal to know what she meant; The Clinic librarian had placed a copy on his desk earlier that day with a bookmark between the pages where the article began. He could recall the heading once again without effort—but not without a sense of shame.

"Experimental Transplantation of the Canine Heart and Lungs, by Henry Anders II, M.D., Gregory Alexander, M.D., and Robert Johnson, M.D.; Report of Ten Successful Cases." Jeanne read the title, her voice hot with anger, and closed the journal.

"Did Henry do any of the work?" she demanded.

"No."

"Did he do the operations you described in the article?"

"He took out the heart and lungs in the first few cases."

"The ones that failed?"

"Y—yes."

"Then why—?" She choked on her anger and couldn't go on, but even then, he was thankful. For the fact of her being angry could only mean that the interest she'd always had in his work and his career wasn't entirely gone. And as long as even a spark remained, there was still hope that she would regain the zest for life which had always been her most notable characteristic.

"Henry's director of The Clinic," he said.

33

"While you do all the work."

"He does routine surgery, leaving me time for work in the experimental laboratory."

"Like this heart-lung transplant operation you devised."

"That—and others."

"If you had stood up for your rights when Henry's father died, you'd be director, not Henry."

"This is the way old Dr. Anders wanted it—so does Henry."

"You mean he asked you to let him share the credit?"

"Well—yes."

"And you were spineless enough to do it?"

Greg flushed at the accusation and wondered whether there was really any point in trying to explain—when he couldn't even think about the article himself without a twinge of guilt and shame.

"Don't bother to answer." The contempt in her voice lashed him like a whip. "It's written in your face."

"You don't understand," Greg protested. "Henry made it plain that putting his name on the article was the price of his support, when I present the new hospital plans to the trustees at the end of the week."

"And you sold your finest piece of work for that?" She threw the journal at him and he was forced to dodge in order to keep from being hit in the face. "You've been under Henry Anders' heel so long, it's the only place you deserve to be—like any other worm."

"Jeanne, I—" But she had gone back into the living room, leaving him with his mouth open and his protest unvoiced. After a moment, he began to eat his sandwich again, but he might as well have been chewing on a piece of soggy paper towel.

How to explain that the elder Dr. Anders had been the only real father he'd ever known? And what that had meant to a boy who had grown up in a Carolina orphanage, working half the day and going to school the other half, earning a scholarship to Chapel Hill by being valedictorian of his high-school graduating class when he was fifteen years old, managing a fraternity boarding house dining room at Johns Hopkins and working summers as a substitute intern at the Baltimore City Hospital to earn pin money. Even then, he probably wouldn't have been able to finish medical school for lack of money if Dr. Henry Anders hadn't taken an interest in him when he had accurately diagnosed a rare case in the junior year surgical clinic, and lent him money enough for tuition and the precious books that cost almost as much.

The new buildings were to be a monument to the memory of The Clinic's founder on its fiftieth anniversary, now only a few days away. If he had to buy the support of the founder's son by giving him credit for work he hadn't done, who was hurt save himself? He could bear that hurt, as he had borne the rejection of his plans two years ago, but he was beginning to wonder whether he could bear what it was doing to Jeanne, and his marriage.

Greg finished his sandwich, drank a glass of milk, rinsed the dishes and put them into the dishwasher. When he went back into the living room, Jeanne and her glass had vanished, but the closed door of the bedroom into which she had moved almost six months ago was mute testimony that nothing between them had changed. In fact, it had only become worse.

Beset by the sense of loneliness the closed door of the bedroom always caused, Greg went into their bathroom and brushed his teeth. Jeanne's wet bathing suit hung on the towel rod, for she still swam daily in the indoor pool that served both the apartment house and the adjacent motor hotel, owned by the same firm. It was almost the only activity, except the reflex ones of living, eating and sleeping, she hadn't given up, however, and he had come to dread the time when he would find the black nylon bathing suit dry. Remembering her slim loveliness in the brief black suit, he reached up to press the damp fabric to his cheek, then used it to wipe away the moisture that had come into his eyes.

"Jeanne!" He knocked on the closed door of the bedroom. "Please listen to me at least."

But there was no answer, and, after knocking and calling again, he gave up—as he had done so many times before—oppressed by the invisible wall that separated them even more than did the closed door, a wall he could neither penetrate with his love nor climb by force.

iii

Helen Foucald was taking a TV dinner out of the oven when the telephone rang. She answered it on the kitchen extension and was startled to hear Claire Anders' New England twang.

"Helen, darling," said Henry Anders' wife. "Is Henry still there?"

"What makes you think he would be?" Helen asked guardedly.

"Henry hates the symphony, so I was sure he would stop by your apartment to salvage at least some pleasure from the evening."

"You have an almost uncanny way of knowing what's going on, Claire. Could it be that you have ESP? Or do you bribe the doorman of my apartment house?"

"Perhaps the ESP—certainly not the doorman. Actually, I don't know anybody I'd rather have my husband fornicating with than you."

"I'm glad you're so broad-minded, Claire."

"Really, darling, I'm only being practical." Claire blithely ignored the thrust. "Half of Henry is quite enough for me—at the moment." Helen didn't miss the implications of the words—or the threat. "Really it's a pity so few men are as potent as they think they are, isn't it?" Claire continued. "If Henry keeps on slipping the way he has been lately, he soon won't be enough for two women any longer."

"Why don't we have lunch together one day and flip a coin for him?" said Helen.

"What a perfectly exciting suggestion! And how civilized! But I'm afraid Henry wouldn't like that; his ego is really so fragile. Give the dear boy his dues though; nothing's small about him except his mind. Well, the symphony is about to begin; I'm calling from a booth in the lobby. Thanks for sending Henry home. I imagine he'll make it just before intermission as usual."

"You're welcome, Claire."

"By the way, darling. Have you noticed that he's been behaving a bit oddly the last week?"

"What do you mean?"

"He's been acting like my brothers used to do when they'd

36

hidden a dead mouse in my bed—as if he's put something over on somebody."

"Come to think of it, he has been a little smug," Helen admitted. "Are you worried that he may be seeing another woman?"

"Oh, nothing like that; between us, we're quite able to keep him in line. After all, what man of Henry's potency has a wife *and* a mistress who can stay with him all the way?"

"If that's a compliment—"

"But it is, darling. It is. I'm sure Henry knows how lucky he is. Oh well, I imagine he's up to some sort of skullduggery in connection with The Clinic. He's always playing politics over there, you know."

"That must be it," Helen agreed. "Good night, Claire."

"Good night, Helen. We really must get together sometime and exchange experiences. It should be exciting, and, you being French and all, maybe I can learn something."

"I doubt that," said Helen. "No offense, of course."

"But of course." The click of the phone sounded in Helen's ear as Claire hung up, but her face was thoughtful as she replaced the receiver on the hook. Come to think of it, Henry had been acting rather differently lately, as if excited about something he was keeping secret. But that sort of excitement always made him an even more prodigious lover than was ordinarily the case, so she'd not bothered to examine its sources, knowing he couldn't resist very long the urge to boast of whatever small triumph he had accomplished.

Removing the TV dinner from the oven, Helen put it on a tray with a glass and bottle of *vin rouge* and carried it to her bed. Arranging herself comfortably among the pillows, she flicked on the TV set with the remote control; it was attached to the wall some six feet above the floor at just the right height for viewing from bed without having to crane one's neck forward in order to bring the screen into view. When the usual situation comedy with its carefully spaced inanities and periodic spattering of canned applause came on, she began to eat slowly and reflectively. But after a moment the screen and its words faded from both vision and hearing, although her other senses were quite alert.

Only the demanding urgency in her loins had been soothed by

Henry Anders' expert love-making; in spite of what marriage manuals called "postcoital lassitude," Helen's mind was operating as accurately as the small computer in her laboratory across the street. Henry was slowing up; there was no question about it. If Claire had noticed it, perhaps it was more than Helen herself had realized, and that, she admitted, could pose a serious problem for her.

In spite of their idle persiflage about tossing a coin for Henry, Helen knew perfectly well that Henry Anders' wife had no intention of sharing him if the time came when there was really not enough to share any more. The son of The Clinic's founder was about as hidebound an individual as Helen had ever known, except in the one particular of his sexual prowess. And with that beginning to wane, Henry Anders II, Symphony Patron, Senior Warden of the Episcopal Cathedral, Rotary District Governor, member of this and that board and supporter of this and that charity, would become what he really was, a dull and boring man who would grow more so as he grew older.

Understanding her own passionate nature, as well as its source— a drive to excel in all she did, not only by outperforming the men with whom she worked by day but also bringing them to heel, so to speak, at night—Helen realized fully how difficult it would be to find a satisfactory substitute for Henry Anders. The fact that under other circumstances she could hardly have stood him at all was in itself a protection against a love that might leave her defenseless by shattering, in its demands for giving rather than taking, the protective shield she'd built around the one weakness that could destroy all she had accomplished through the years—the fact that sometimes the demands of her body were stronger than her will.

iv

It had taken Georgia Merchant only a few minutes to dress and get the old car from the parking lot behind the dingy downtown hotel where she and Guy were living during the Baltimore engagement. She didn't even take time to remove her makeup but drove rapidly to the hospital. Even so, when she inquired at the nursing desk of the emergency room at The Clinic, she was told that Guy had been taken directly to the intensive care unit for immediate admission.

It was somewhat of a shock to see how old and bedraggled looking the buildings of the hospital were and for a moment she was troubled by the thought that the medical care here might be on a par with them. But then she remembered that this was actually one of the most famous medical institutions in the country, perhaps even the world, and took what small comfort she could from the thought.

The intensive care unit—the ICU in hospital shorthand—was in a remodeled portion of one floor, a dozen rooms partitioned off from what had been obviously a large waiting room at one time. The nurse's desk was in the center, where, merely by turning in her chair, she could scan the electronic monitor tubes grouped in banks on either side of her. But this arrangement, too, was far more antiquated—in appearance at least—than had been the hospitals in St. Louis, Detroit and Chicago to which Georgia had rushed Guy after attacks similar to the one tonight.

By now she knew what the monitor tubes in the nursing station were for. The bottom row gave a continuous visual record of the heartbeat, the blood pressure, the respiration and other functions, while the one just above it was connected to a closed-circuit TV camera inside each room. As she approached the nursing station, Georgia could see Guy on one of the monitor tubes; a doctor in a white coat was listening to his heart while a nurse adjusted the flow of oxygen through a nasal catheter into his lungs.

"I'm Mrs. Merchant," she told the nurse at the station. "My husband was just brought in."

"The doctor who phoned said Mr. Merchant was a coronary case, so he was brought directly up here," said the girl. "Dr. McNeal is examining him now but you can give me some information for the admitting office."

"You move quickly here, don't you?" said Georgia.

"We're not quite so antiquated as we look, Mrs. Merchant," the nurse said with a smile. "Besides, the cardiology service is one of the most active in the hospital."

39

By the time Georgia had finished giving the nurse the information she needed for the records, a black-haired young doctor in a white coat came out of Guy's room, carrying a chart in his hand. He spoke briefly to the nurse, wrote some orders, then came over to a small lounge overlooking the street, where Georgia was sitting. If he noticed anything odd in the fact that she was still heavily made up for her performance, he didn't mention it.

"Your husband's feeling much better, Mrs. Merchant," he said. "I gave him another hypodermic when he arrived."

"Thank you, Doctor."

"He tells me that he has been admitted to several other hospitals for a similar condition."

"The first time was in St. Louis nearly two years ago," said Georgia. "We're in show business, so we travel around a lot."

"Do you know what the diagnosis was there?"

"Coronary thrombosis. He was in the hospital a month and wasn't able to work for another three months."

"What kind of work does your husband do?" the young doctor asked.

"He's a song and dance man, though he hasn't done much dancing lately. I guess you wouldn't even remember vaudeville?"

"Only what I see on the tube," he said with a smile.

"Guy was a headliner in his day. You know—songs, dances and nifty patter. But lately—" She didn't finish the sentence.

"Did he have much pain before the first coronary attack?"

"He complained of feeling uncomfortable at times for maybe six months, but he thought it was indigestion. The doctor who sent him in tonight thought this might be another coronary."

"We can't be absolutely sure," said Dr. McNeal. "But from the looks of the electrocardiographic tracing on the monitor, it doesn't appear that he has an actual thrombosis. Do you understand the difference?"

"I'm not sure."

The young heart specialist turned over a sheet on the clipboard he was carrying and quickly sketched in the outline of a human heart. Upon it he drew heavier lines in two branching patterns, very much like trees with the trunks beginning near the top of the heart and gradually spreading out to cover its whole structure with an interlacing pattern of branches.

"The dark pattern I've drawn in here represents the coronary arteries," he explained. "They come off the aorta—the large artery that carries blood to much of the body—just after it leaves the heart. The coronaries supply blood to the heart muscle itself but, as people grow older, they often tend to thicken—"

"They told me in Detroit that Guy had hardening of the arteries."

"I could see the changes in the vessels inside his eyes with the ophthalmoscope," said Dr. McNeal. "In this case, the major cause of the trouble is a gradual thickening of the inner lining of the coronary arteries. Sometimes a clot—what we call a thrombus—blocks a major branch of one artery. If the block is large enough, the blood is cut off to a considerable section of the heart muscle and death is often instantaneous. But if the area involved is smaller, the damaged muscle heals slowly and a scar forms. That's probably what happened with your husband's first attack in St. Louis."

"And you think this one is less severe?"

"From present appearances, yes. The fact that he was subject to anginal pain from time to time shows that the lining of his coronary vessels has gradually thickened, decreasing the amount of blood reaching the heart muscle. The pain of angina is actually a warning of an insufficient blood supply to the heart but the pain causes spasm, too, and that makes the condition worse, unless medication like nitroglycerin is given immediately to dilate the arteries. This attack apparently started out as angina pectoris—the medical term is coronary insufficiency—and doesn't seem to have gone beyond that yet."

"Does that make any difference—as far as Guy is concerned?"

"My guess is that recovery should be fairly rapid," he told her. "That is, if there has been no real blocking of the coronary arteries."

"How soon will you know?"

"Possibly in no more than twelve to twenty-four hours—but only as far as this attack is concerned. You understand that, don't you?"

"We've been living with this for over two years now, Doctor," said Georgia. "It worries Guy that he can't carry his share of the load any longer and I guess that doesn't help his heart either."

"Emotional tension always makes heart disease worse."

"There are less and less bookings for men in the kind of show business we're in; most shows don't have comics any more, so Guy can't even get work as a straight man feeding lines to them. He's a proud man, Dr. McNeal. You might not think it now, but he really was good once; played the top English music halls when he was hardly out of his teens." Georgia's shoulders had drooped momentarily but she was past feeling sorry for herself long, or for Guy, and faced up to reality. "So what's to be done?"

"Until a few years ago—nothing."

"And now?" She wondered whether she dared grasp at the hope his words seemed to imply.

"Various operations have been devised in recent years to increase the blood flow to damaged hearts, though not all of them are as successful as we would like them to be," said the young doctor. "Lately, Dr. Gregory Alexander here at The Clinic has been removing the thickened lining of the coronary vessels from some cases with very good results."

"You mean he can actually go inside the arteries?"

"The technique is rather difficult to explain. Actually, a small jet of gas is used to strip out the inner layer of the vessel wall."

"Could that get Guy back on his feet?"

"I don't want to raise false hopes, Mrs. Merchant. Even if Dr. Alexander accepts your husband for surgery, I must warn you that it is not without considerable danger and only selected cases are helped at all."

"I've learned enough about heart disease these past few years to know that what's happening to Guy almost every day now isn't without considerable danger either," said Georgia. "So any way you look at it, we don't have much to lose."

"That's the sensible attitude to take," Dr. McNeal agreed. "I'll ask Dr. Alexander to see your husband in the morning but it will probably be several days before we can tell you just what to expect."

"You've given me hope, Doctor," Georgia said gratefully. "For folks like me and Guy, that's been in short supply for a long time."

4

Dr. Herbert Partridge, Senior Fellow in Neurosurgery, looked up when Bob Johnson came into Operating Room 16.

"Sorry I had to call you, Bob," he said. "This fellow—what's his name, Lew?" He spoke to the anesthesiologist, who was partly hidden behind the tent of draperies separating him from the operating field where Partridge was working, assisted by the resident on the neurosurgical service.

"Frank Lawson—at least that's the name the police gave us."

"He's got some broken ribs but they don't seem to have caused any air leak into his chest," said the neurosurgeon. "We've put in a tracheostomy tube to keep a clear airway and the chest X-ray is over there on the viewbox. See if you think anything needs to be done about those ribs, Bob."

Bob Johnson went over to the bank of ground-glass viewboxes attached to the wall of the operating theater and flipped the small switch at the bottom of the nearest box. The outline of a man's chest came into view, the rib fractures plainly visible. They were clean, however, without the bone splinters which could have penetrated the lung and caused an air leak into the chest cavity, squeezing down the softer lung tissue with its accumulated pressure and decreasing the respiratory function until death by suffocation occurred.

"Looks clean enough to me, Herb," he said. "I don't see any sign of pneumothorax."

"Take a look at the other pictures; you won't see anything like this very often."

The films on the two adjoining viewboxes were of the upper

vertebral column and skull; when he saw the neck vertebrae, Bob Johnson whistled softly in amazement. Two of the lowermost cervical vertebrae, as the neck section of the spine was called, looked as if they had been crushed by a hammer. Bone fragments were scattered in the surrounding tissues and the bones themselves were fragmented badly.

"Looks like somebody tried to guillotine him with a dull blade—and quit half through," said the chest surgeon.

"It was almost that," Partridge agreed. "Lawson held up a tavern tonight and was escaping in a stolen Mustang when he took the wrong ramp and came up on the expressway facing the traffic. A big truck tossed that Mustang over the guard rail of an overpass like I'd kick aside one of my kid's Match Box trucks he's always leaving on the living room floor. With two vertebrae crushed and the spinal cord severed in the lower cervical region, the poor devil might as well be one of those frogs we used to pith in physiology class in medical school to study reflexes. Anything below his neck that doesn't operate mechanically by reflex action is just about out of the picture now."

"How about the respiration?"

"He wasn't breathing when they got him to the emergency room," said the anesthesiologist. "But the duty intern was on the ball and put him on a Mark IV respirator before he did anything else. I'm carrying him on the respirator now through the tracheostomy tube."

"Do me a favor and stop by the emergency room on your way out, Bob," said Herbert Partridge. "I promised to send a preliminary report down to a couple of policemen who are waiting there."

"What do you expect to be able to do?"

"Nothing but clean up the wound and put on some kind of a support to keep Lawson's head from wobbling like a rag doll. He sure doesn't have anything else to hold it up."

"How long do you think he'll last?"

"Maybe an hour, maybe a week. He might as well be dead either way. Even if he recovers consciousness, which I doubt, he'll have to be in an iron lung or on a Mark IV for the rest of his life."

Downstairs, Bob Johnson found two policemen drinking coffee

in the small automatic canteen off the corridor leading from the emergency room into the main part of the hospital. There was a small lounge there with a telephone for the convenience of the police and reporters.

"Dr. Partridge is going to be tied up in surgery for another hour at least," he told the officers. "He asked me to give you a preliminary report for him."

"What's Lawson's condition, Doctor?" The older of the police officers took out a notebook. "The intern in the emergency room doesn't seem to think he has much to go on."

"The spinal cord was severed in the lower neck region, which means he'll be a paraplegic for the rest of his life—if he lives," said Bob. "He'll probably be an iron lung case, too. Have you notified his family?"

"Don't even know whether he has one yet," said the second officer. "We only managed to identify him from some cards that were in his wallet. He's Frank Lawson, bank robber, ex-con, murderer and heroin addict. Stuck up a bank a few days ago and shot a teller, then killed a salesman who gave him a lift. I'd like to see him get out of the hospital, so he can at least walk to the electric chair."

"If Lawson had gone a little farther across the expressway, the truck that hit him would have been forced to swerve down that ramp," said the first policeman. "With a rig that size coming down out of control, God only knows how many homes would have been smashed—and the people inside them. Do the state a favor, Doctor, and let Lawson die."

"We're not allowed to make that decision yet," Bob Johnson said. "His relatives still have to be notified. Will you take care of it?"

"Lawson's got a police record a mile long; if anybody ever admitted they were kin to him, it will be in the FBI files," said the older officer. "We'll wire Washington first thing in the morning to notify the relatives—if any. But either way, he has to be a case for the medical examiner."

At the big call-board off the main lobby, Bob Johnson punched the button that clicked off the light behind his name. As he was turning away from the call-board, Dr. James McNeal came up and pushed the button, turning off the light behind his name.

"What's got you out so late tonight, Jim?" Bob asked as they started through the foyer toward the front door.

"Just admitted a severe case of coronary insufficiency on ICU," said the Senior Fellow in Cardiology. "He may be a candidate for one of those gas-jet jobs."

"So?" Bob Johnson's eyes brightened. "Just let us get this heart-lung transplant demonstration Dr. Alexander's going to do for the convocation Wednesday afternoon out of the way, and we'll be ready for him."

"It'll take a day or two to evaluate his condition," said the cardiologist. "Got time for a beer in the Falstaff Room across the street?"

"Sure. What's the occasion?"

"A lot of the old boys will be over there bragging tonight, and it might be nice to sit around and listen to them. Give you some idea of the plush life that could be waiting for us when we leave these hallowed—if somewhat dingy—halls."

"You wouldn't be looking for some prospective employer, would you?"

The cardiologist shook his head. "You'll never get me to practice outside a university hospital, or at least a large clinic like this!"

"In spite of the poor pay?"

"The pay'll be good enough—as long as you're not greedy. The private clinic setups most medical schools have now for their faculties takes the financial sting out of teaching. You still headed for Walter Reed?"

"The first of July. Dr. Alexander's already lined me up as assistant chief of the thoracic and vascular section over there. When my two years with the Army are over, I hope to come back and work with him here."

"More power to you," said Jim McNeal. "I'm going to head farther south; these Baltimore winters are beginning to get me down."

Since midafternoon, expensive cars had been stopping under the marquee of the Clinic Inn across The Parkway from the hospital and diagnostic clinic complex. Cadillacs, Continentals, Eldorados, Mercedes, Jaguars, Porsches, a couple of Rolls-Royces—all exhibited the traditional M.D. emblem with the staff and serpent of the caduceus upon it.

The bar and adjoining dining room of the Falstaff Tavern were now swarming with prosperous-looking men and their expensively dressed women having dinner. The scientific program of the biennial Convocation of the Members of The Clinic would not start until Wednesday afternoon, but the evening before and the morning preceding its beginning gave the Members an opportunity to renew old acquaintances and enjoy the social atmosphere, which was even more important than the professional side of the alternate-year get-togethers.

Since a full-dress meeting of the Board of Trustees that governed Clinic and hospital administration was also held on Saturday following a convocation, political currents sometimes ran so swiftly that they swept everything else aside. Medical politics was the subject under discussion by a group at a table in the corner of the lounge, when Bill Remick, a roentgenologist from Washington who was also on the building committee of the board came into the tavern.

"Hey, Bill," he was hailed by Joe Palentino, a New York internist sitting with two other Members at one of the tables. "Over here."

Remick gave his order to a passing waitress and made his way across the room, stopping to shake hands with a half dozen friends on the way.

"You know Abe Lantz from Cincinnati and Jim Paynter from Miami, don't you, Bill?" Joe Palentino said as the X-ray man took the empty chair at the table.

"Sure," said Remick, shaking hands with the others.

"Where's Amy?" Abe Lantz asked.

"She couldn't make it; a new grandchild takes precedence over a convocation any day."

"Makes you feel old though," said Lantz. "I thought my wife would have a fit when she heard we were to be grandparents, but now she's as doting as they all are."

"You're close to Greg Alexander, Bill," said Joe Palentino. "How about a preview of his plans for the new hospital and clinic buildings to replace the old monstrosity?" He nodded toward the window where the lights of the dark massif of The Clinic across the street were visible. "We've been hearing some strange rumors."

"Don't write off what you call a monstrosity yet, Joe," said Bill Remick. "Fifty years ago, when that was built, it was the last word in hospital architecture."

"And anybody who has lived in one of those cells up there on the second floor off that rotunda won't ever get over feeling a little nostalgia at the thought of its passing," said Abe Lantz.

"Yet it's got to go," said Jim Paynter, putting into words what they had all been thinking.

"Not if Sam Hunter has his say," said Joe Palentino. "I hear he's just as stubborn about any change as he was two years ago, when he led the stampede that destroyed Greg's plans for a really modern hospital and diagnostic clinic."

"What I don't understand is why Greg took it lying down," said Abe Lantz. "A dozen medical schools would be glad to have him as professor of surgery. He could pick up and leave here any time he wants to at probably twice the money."

"It happens that The Clinic is Greg's life," said Remick. "He's never told me—and I wouldn't ask him—but I'd be willing to bet that, before he died, Dr. Anders made him swear to stay on here and keep the place going the way the old doc intended for it to go."

"But Greg wasn't even kin to old Dr. Anders," said Abe Lantz. "Why was the mantle passed on to him?"

"Because there wasn't anybody else to pass it to," said Joe Palentino. "Not many sons turn out the way their fathers would like them to—and Henry II, least of all."

"Do you think Greg has come up this time with a compromise plan Sam Hunter is liable to accept?" Jim Paynter asked the X-ray man. "Old Sam has quite a faction of die-hards behind him on the board. If Greg doesn't knuckle under, he'll get steam-rollered again."

"Don't ask me," Bill Remick said. "You all know how I tried to get Greg to stand up and fight Sam Hunter two years ago."

"And maybe lose everything?" Jim Paynter asked.

"The Clinic is something very special," said the roentgenologist. "It's been an example to doctors all over the world for fifty years and I don't see us settling for second-rate buildings just because Sam Hunter has half the oil wells and money in the world besides being a stubborn old goat."

"What would be your idea then?" Joe Palentino asked.

"Personally, I'd like to see the new hospital begin where the one that's just been built at the Georgetown Medical Center in Washington leaves off as far as automation is concerned."

"Automation's a dirty word in the vocabulary of a lot of doctors, Bill," said Abe Lantz. "You and I know what it promises for the future because we've seen it at work. But the average doctor sees himself as possibly one day being replaced by a data processing machine."

"That's absurd!"

"Of course it is, but there's the bogey-man just the same."

"Look what's happened since the sulfonamides and Penicillin were discovered nearly forty years ago," said Bill Remick. "A lot of people said then that doctors would soon be doing nothing but writing prescriptions for pills, but look what happened. The drugs quickly became tools that let us broaden the scope of our work and the same thing will be true in an automated setup. I say anything a computer can do for me, let it do it; that way, I'll have more time to study real problems without wasting so much time on routine matters."

"Besides getting a couple of extra afternoons off a week for golf," said Jim Paynter. "One thing is for sure: the young men coming out of medical schools now are looking for positions with group clinics; most of 'em aren't even interested in slogging to build an individual reputation for themselves the way we did."

"More power to them if they can see two patients in the time it used to take us to see one," said Bill Remick. "God knows there aren't enough doctors to go around now, and even with automation things are bound to get a lot worse before they get better—if ever."

In O.R. 16, Herbert Partridge finished applying the plaster cast that would hold Frank Lawson's head in an arched or hyperextended position and pulled off his gloves. The respirator clicked on with mathematical regularity; it was adjusted to send a pulse of oxygen through the tube in the patient's windpipe approximately sixteen times a minute, inflating the lungs and simulating breathing. So sensitive were the control valves of the machine that even the slightest attempt at spontaneous breathing would trigger the pressure control mechanism of the respirator, changing the rhythm of the softly clicking valves.

"Any sign of respiratory movement, Lew?" Herb Partridge asked the anesthesiologist.

"Nothing," said Dr. Gann. "He'll never breathe again without help."

"How about his heart?"

"As strong as yours or mine and the blood pressure's been well maintained all the way, too. If he ever wakes up, he'll be able to think—but for the rest of it, he might as well be a zombie."

"Sort of gets you, doesn't it?"

"No matter how many of these you see, you always have a feeling of helplessness with a paraplegic." Dr. Lewis Gann was an experienced older man who had seen most of the ills to which humans were subject. "Sever the spinal cord in the lower back and a man has at least half a body that functions; with arms that work, he can drag the other half around. But cut the upper cord—"

"This poor devil was a loser before he ever started," the young neurosurgeon agreed. "One of the cops who followed the ambulance told me he's spent more of his life in prison than he has out of it."

"He's still a human being—and entitled to live as long as we can keep his heart and brain functioning," said the anesthesiologist. "Which means a Mark IV or an iron lung."

Herb Partridge's eyes went to the monitor tube on the wall, where, picked up by the marvelously sensitive devices used to watch astronauts in flight thousands of miles away, the electronic pattern of the heartbeat was being registered in a flashing picture of rising and falling lines.

"Let's get a cup of coffee," he said. "This case is giving me the willies."

"Stay with him about an hour after you get to ICU," Dr. Gann told the nurse-anesthetist who had been assisting him. "The nurses up there ought to be able to take over then."

A small, brightly lit section of the staff dining room was half filled with nurses and house staff on night duty when they drew cups of coffee from an urn that bubbled constantly at one end of the serving counter. The younger doctor picked up two doughnuts from a tray nearby, but the older man passed it up.

"My cholesterol was up when I had my check last month," he said. "Maybe it's from too much animal fat like Dave Connor claims, but my guess is the real culprit's what I go through every time we take a patient off the heart-lung pump after Greg Alexander finishes one of those long jobs inside the heart. I tell you, Herb, if surgery gets any more complicated, it will soon be completely beyond the ability of ordinary men like me to stand the strain."

"Maybe somebody will build a robot to give the anesthetic." Herb Partridge was beginning to unwind after the tense two hours in the operating room.

"Years ago, about the time you were playing cops and robbers, people got all excited about what they called technocracy," said Dr. Gann. "A lot of 'em even convinced themselves that the machines were going to take over the world."

"Now it's computers."

"As long as it takes men to make the gadgets, I think we're safe." The older doctor dripped saccharin into his coffee cup from a plastic bottle, then carefully screwed the top back on and placed it in the pocket of his coat. "It's when the machines start making other machines on their own that we'll really have to worry."

"That may not be too far off. I was reading the other day that they've got computers programmed now to study the results of other computers and report on them."

"Maybe if the studiers find enough errors," said Dr. Gann, "they'll all get mad with each other and destroy themselves."

A nurse popped into the dining room, her eyes bright with excitement.

"Letty's had pups!" she announced, and a sudden spattering of applause swept the room. "Four of them!"

"Makes me feel good to know you can't keep an old dog down," said the anesthesiologist. "I guess it's a new day for medicine, too—when a dog with another dog's heart and lungs can still have pups."

iv

"Unhook me, Henry." Claire Anders dropped her mink coat upon a chair in their large bedroom. "I'm dying to hear what you're up to that's so mysterious."

"What do you mean?"

"When you came to the concert tonight at your usual time—just before intermission—you looked like a cat that's been lapping up the forbidden cream. That look always means you're up to some skulduggery."

Henry unhooked her dress at the top and ran the zipper down her back so she could shrug it off her shoulders and let it drop in a pile at her feet. She wore only the briefest of lingerie and a strapless support bra, which she unhooked with a deft motion before bending to loosen the garter belt that held up her stockings. Kicking off her shoes, she peeled them off, then unhooked the garter belt and stripped off both it and the briefs.

"I bet Helen doesn't look a bit better naked than I do," she said as she removed diamond clips from her ears.

"You're well preserved, Claire." Henry started taking the studs from his dress shirt. "For your age, of course."

Claire made a face at him and raised both hands to loosen the diamond beret in her hair, a movement that caused Henry

52

to miss one of the studs, although he'd seen her thus many thousands of times.

"Helen's only thirty-five but she hasn't had you all these years to keep her young, Henry," she said. "After all, there's nothing like a loving husband to keep a woman's endocrines functioning properly."

Claire walked over to her closet, passing close to him, and picked out a sheer negligee, which she slipped on. "You still haven't told me what you were so mysterious about," she reminded him as she went back to the dressing table.

"I've laid a trap for Greg." Henry stepped out of his pants and hung them over the chair. "He won't get out of this one."

"What is it?"

"When he presented the plans for a new clinic and hospital complex to the trustees two years ago, they sent them back to be modified into something less expensive. He's supposed to present that at the next meeting."

"The one on Saturday?" Claire was brushing her hair.

"Yes. I saw the plans of a new, way-out hotel in a magazine recently and remembered that a young architect named Keith Jackson had submitted a very original design for the hospital and clinic two years ago. When I took the magazine to Jackson and suggested that he draw something like it for The Clinic and show it to Greg, he took off like a rocket."

"Wasn't that rather obvious, dear?"

"I made Jackson promise not to tell Greg I had anything to do with it."

"Is it that good?"

"It's out of this world, Claire, but nobody could build it around that statue of Christ in the lobby. You remember the clause in father's will, don't you?"

"The one that said the statue must always be central and any changes in the existing buildings must be made on the same site?"

"Else the whole property reverts to me." Stepping out of his shorts, Henry scratched his hairy chest luxuriously. "Jackson's plan would cost so much that the board would never build it here on the old site. And if The Clinic is moved out on the Beltway, where a lot of the board already want it, the present property will revert to me and I'll be rich."

Claire had been removing her makeup with cleansing tissue; she had the sort of soft peaches-and-cream complexion that showed little sign of age. When she turned on the bench, her eyes suddenly widened and a pleased smile came over her face.

"Why, you're all excited about this, aren't you, darling?" Getting up, she dropped the negligee. "For goodness sake! Come to bed before you burst a blood vessel—or something."

5

The illuminated dial of the travel clock on the bedside table showed 5 A.M. when Sam Hunter awakened in one of the VIP suites of the Clinic Inn. His checkup at the laboratory was to begin with blood examinations at eight and the instruction sheet sent him in Dallas several days earlier had warned him neither to eat nor drink anything after midnight. His mouth felt dry and the headache that always lasted until after he'd had his morning coffee was in full throb now, but there was no point in waking Moto, his valet and chauffeur, who was sleeping in the other room.

Even ten years after Evelyn's death, old Sam still felt lonely when he waked in the morning and saw the other half of the bed empty. Young Sam hadn't produced a grandchild yet to comfort an old man during his declining years and with Ted gone, there really wasn't much left in life, even for one of the richest men in the world. Except to make more money—and lately that had even begun to lose its thrill for him.

If only Ted hadn't married that wop girl and run off with a circus, he thought, but even the old sense of resentment no longer burned with the same fire; there just wasn't enough energy left in him to ignite it fully. It wasn't that Sam Hunter particularly blamed his younger son for wanting a fling; God knows he'd had his at about the same age as Ted—and his father and grandfather before him. Ted's particular crime had been in bringing foreign blood into a line that went back to the Revolution, when the original Theodore Hunter had come over like many another Scotch-Irish adventurer to help the Colonies fight their battle for freedom and see what he could get out of it for himself.

The first Ted had recognized a good thing when he saw it; when the war was over, he'd moved with the tide of expansion southwestward, first into the Yazoo region, where he cannily bought land and sold it weeks before the bubble burst, then on to Louisiana and eventually to Texas. Texas land had been the real basis of the Hunter fortune, especially when it began to spout the black gold of oil. But now that Ted had spurned his overtures to drop the girl and once again resume the course his father had charted for him, clinging instead to the daughter of a man whose fleabag of a circus was barely able to keep moving, and with young Sam seemingly incapable of producing an heir, all the Hunters had striven to gain and hold through nearly two centuries must, it appeared, eventually go into a foundation. And that meant being doled out to hospitals and schools by trustees who had no appreciation for the fact that the largesse they handed over to others represented the blood, the guts and the sweat of a line of empire builders.

It was a depressing thought, a prospect that made Sam Hunter feel old beyond his sixty-eight years. But he knew he had to go on, if for no other reason than to keep alive the hope that one day Ted would admit his mistake, divorce his wife and come home to his rightful place.

Why does the damn clock have to run so slow? old Sam thought savagely when he saw that the long hand had moved only a quarter of the distance around the dial since he'd awakened.

Throwing the covers back, he padded to the bathroom in his bare feet and took his teeth out of the container where Moto had put them to soak in Polident. Rinsing them off, he stuck them in his mouth and clamped them down on the cigar without which he was hardly ever seen in public. But even the smoke of the expensive tobacco tasted like burning rope, and, after a few puffs, he ground it out in an ashtray and switched on the television set.

Only a farm program was on at this time of the morning, telling how to grow an early vegetable crop in Maryland. Which didn't mean a thing to an oil and cattle man from Texas, especially when he didn't believe half of what so-called agricultural experts tried to tell him anyway. Going to the window, Sam Hunter pulled

56

back the heavy drapes and looked out across The Parkway to the lights of The Clinic, for dawn had not yet begun to break.

He wasn't such a fool as not to realize the various pressures that were being applied to members of the Board of Trustees, or the maneuvering going on in preparation for the meeting at the end of the week. The old Clinic building had been good enough for Dr. Anders when he'd operated on Evelyn, so why did it have to be any different now? he asked himself. There was an assurance of stability, of permanence about the old brownstone buildings, a conviction that there was good in the past which needed to be preserved. And with old Dr. Anders dead, Sam Hunter felt that the trust of seeing that things were not changed had passed to him.

At almost that same moment, Ted Hunter awakened in the snug apartment located in the back of one of the circus trucks, which provided living quarters for him and Vivian. He felt a slight sticking pain in his right hand between the thumb and forefinger, where the splinter had gone in when he'd seized the stake to whack the elephant on the snout and prevent a stampede. But when he sucked on the spot for a moment, the pain went away.

Through the thin partition, he could hear Joe Califino snoring in the driver's cubbyhole just back of the cab, so he knew they had already reached their destination for tonight's performance, under the sponsorship of the inevitable local charity, and were parked somewhere, probably near the auditorium. Miraculously, the advance agent for the circus still seemed able to find bookings, even in a day when the big shows played for the most part in coliseums or large auditoriums and drew the lion's share of the customers. But a breakdown or a spell of bad weather could wreck a small show like this, so the number of circuses like the Tarentino outfit was growing smaller every year.

Feeling chilly, Ted reached down to the foot of the bed and pulled up a blanket, being careful not to disturb Vivian, who was sleeping like a lovely blond baby beside him. Unable to get to sleep again immediately, he lay with the blanket pulled up to his chin, still feeling the shivery sensation between his shoulder blades and dreading the cold outside, which he must face in a few hours when they began to move the circus equipment into the inevitable small-town auditorium. Everybody had to help in an outfit as small as the Tarentino Circus, but Ted would have worked beside the roustabouts anyway, for he was very fond of Papa Gus and knew well on what a narrow profit margin the outfit operated.

Down on the Rio Grande, where the Hunter family had large holdings, a rambling cottage stood on a rise overlooking the river. The sun was warm there even in winter and the oranges hung heavy on the trees, like the golden apples his mother had read about to him when he was a small boy. Ted felt a wave of nostalgia and his throat tightened at the memory of the days when he and Sam, Jr., had ridden over the rolling pasture lands, stopping to peel off their clothes and frolic in a waist-deep pool, where the languid flow of the creek had been halted for a time by a makeshift dam of fallen tree trunks from last year's hurricane.

Then, as if sensing his mood even in his sleep, Vivian moved against him and the reality of her loveliness, warm and fragrant in his arms, dispelled any other thought.

ii

At first, Guy Merchant wasn't sure what had awakened him, until it came again, the odd skipping beat of his heart he'd noticed many times before. Usually, it presaged the start of the pain and the terrible sense of impending disaster that accompanied a severe attack of angina. The pain could usually be assuaged—if he didn't wait too long—by slipping beneath his tongue one of the tiny tablets of nitroglycerin he always carried with him. He knew he could get the tablet now merely by pressing the bell beside his hand on the bed to call the nurse from her station just outside the door, but he held back.

More than once in the past year, knowing the burden he had become to Georgia, Guy had tried to keep her from realizing that one of the attacks of anginal pain was coming on, hoping he could hold off taking the nitroglycerin until the slow shutdown of blood to the heart could cause death and free her from the burden of him and his illness. But each time, the agony in his chest and left arm, plus the fear of impending death that went with it, had become so severe that his resolve had broken down and, driven by a compulsion beyond resistance, he'd reached for the blessed tablet.

As yet he felt no pain, however, and he lay there waiting, dreading it, yet hoping he'd have the strength to keep from pressing the call bell when the fire of agony lanced through his chest. When the odd little pause in the heartbeat came again, reaching consciousness only because it was like a familiar sound no longer heard and therefore noticed, he reached across with his right hand, and felt the pulse beating in his left wrist. The rhythm of the beat was somewhat irregular but that was nothing new; he'd noticed it many times, especially in the past three months, when he'd felt his pulse surreptitiously so as not to disturb Georgia with the knowledge of his concern.

It came once more, the pause that seemed endless, and for an instant Guy knew some of the apprehension that accompanied an anginal attack, though none of the pain, before he felt the throbbing pulse once again through the artery beneath his finger.

Perhaps ten beats followed in steady progression, then the pause began once more—but this time without an end. And realizing that his heart had stopped, Guy Merchant only had time before blackness engulfed him to pray that it would never beat again.

iii

Peter Carewe wasn't surprised when the tall stewardess with the red hair dropped into the vacant aisle seat beside him as the early morning plane from New York to Baltimore was taking off from La Guardia. He'd seen her eyeing him when he came aboard a few minutes earlier and had recognized the look; it was one he saw in one form or another in the eyes of more than half the women he met, the appraising glance, the unanswered question—although later he managed to answer quite a few of them.

The girl was worth considering, though he couldn't muster much enthusiasm this early in the morning. If it hadn't been for a UN secretary from Sweden, he would have been in Baltimore last night, instead of having to get up before dawn and whistle down a taxi in the almost deserted canyon of First Avenue, where the mammoth towers of the United Nations Plaza Apartments shot skyward on the bank of the East River.

"You're the doctor from WHO, aren't you?" the stewardess asked as she buckled her seat belt. The plane was nearly full and the aisle seat beside him had been one of the only empty ones in the front of the plane.

"Dr. Peter Carewe. Yes."

"I saw the TV special about you last week. Your work must be very exciting." The special had featured him as an example of the corps of doctors from the World Health Organization who ranged about the globe, fighting disease wherever they found it.

"Swatting flies isn't exactly the most glamorous occupation in the world." He relaxed and admired the redhead's legs in the short tunic that had become the uniform of the stewardess on almost every airline in the world.

"You're just being modest, Doctor. According to the TV special, you're oo-7 with an M.D. And *he* certainly got around."

"The trouble is you don't meet many glamorous women in the jungles I've been slogging through, hunting tsetse flies and the mites that carry strange fevers," he assured her. "I usually have better luck on airplanes."

The redhead accepted the ploy for what it was, just as he'd accepted her taking the seat beside him instead of the narrow bench back of the forward door provided for the stewardesses during takeoff and landing when all of the seats were filled.

"Are you on the way to The Clinic Convocation?" she asked.

"How did you guess?"

"The TV special said you were once a Fellow there. I took a year of nurse training at The Clinic, until the glamour wore off and I decided I wanted to live a little instead of marrying an intern and putting him through his residency."

"You may have turned down a good bet. Doctors who finish a fellowship at The Clinic go up pretty fast when they go out into practice."

"Unh unh!" said the stewardess. "I saw too many girls left behind with a divorce and a couple of kids to look after, while her ex married some gal from the Junior League who could help him build up a society practice. That's not for me."

"What is for you?"

"A chance to live a little and meet interesting people—like you."

As the plane moved down the runway at a rapidly increasing rate of speed, preparatory to becoming airborne, Peter Carewe took another look at the stewardess' legs and decided to stake out at least a tentative claim. If he took the professorship in the School of Public Health which had been offered him in Balitmore he would be doing a lot of traveling out of there and it might not be a bad idea to have a few irons in the fire. The girl appeared to be in her late twenties and although this would be a good twelve years less than his own age, he prided himself on being as fit—and as lusty—as he had been in his twenties.

"Are you based in Baltimore?" he asked casually.

"New York. Baltimore's a pretty dull town."

"I keep an apartment in the United Nations Plaza." The plane was airborne now and the stewardess had started to loosen her belt. "I'm in the telephone book and I'll be back in New York at the end of the week," he added. "Give me a ring and perhaps we can have a drink together."

"That will be nice." She stood up and smoothed down the white tunic. "Coffee, Doctor?"

"Please."

"We don't have time to serve breakfast between New York and Baltimore, but I can get you a sweet roll or a danish."

"Danish for me. I haven't started worrying yet about cholesterol."

The plane was banking now and through the oval window beside him Peter Carewe could see the sprawl of the United Nations buildings stretching along the East River, with the tower where his apartment was located nearby. Yesterday he'd sat in the office of the courtly Danish physician—himself a world authority in the field of public health—who directed the Western division of the network of men, women and facilities known as the World Health Organization, or, for short, WHO.

"We've had a protest from the office of the Russian delegate about that TV special NBC did on you last week, Peter," Dr. Nordstrom had said.

"On what grounds?"

"Our Soviet friends don't need grounds for their protests; they seem to have some sort of a machine that grinds them out merely by pressing a button."

"They must have cooked up something."

"On the program you implied that whenever a problem happens to lie in territory behind the Iron Curtain, WHO people are sometimes denied freedom of access to facilities we need in our work."

"Aren't we?"

"Of course. I just had to pass the protest on to you as a matter of record."

"You can tell the Russians where to shove it," Peter said bluntly. "Anything else I should know?"

"We may have another detection job for you. A batch of oral polio vaccine being used in California has been causing some rather severe reactions. It may be simply a contaminant, but I've sent a culture team from Los Angeles to look into it. How long will your meeting last in Baltimore?"

"I'm addressing the banquet on Thursday night and could leave right after that, if the matter became urgent."

"It isn't likely to develop that fast, so enjoy yourself," said the director. "But we can't let this thing out in California go too long without trying to find out what happened. If people start being afraid of the oral vaccine, we shall lose our most effective weapon against polio."

"I'm going to tell about the way we isolated and identified the monkey kidney virus in my address Thursday night," said Peter.

"Let's hope we can run this one down as quickly as you did that difficulty," said the director. "Confidently, I'm going to recommend you for a Nobel prize in health for that job."

"It wasn't that important," Peter protested.

"It was—and other people besides myself know it." The director picked up a letter on his desk and held it between his fingers. "Is there any truth to this rumor that the School of Public Health in Baltimore has offered you a professorship?"

"It's true; John Teague and I had dinner together a few nights ago. But I'm not sure I should accept."

"May I ask why?"

"Maybe I'm not ready to settle down yet."

"You'd be turning down one of the most prestigious chairs in the field."

"I still don't understand why it was offered to me."

The director smiled. "I think you're being unduly modest, Peter. After all, you're the nearest thing there is today to the sort of death detective Paul De Kruif used to write about. As dean of the School of Public Health in Baltimore, Dr. Teague might want to add some glamour to his faculty."

"You make me feel like a Hollywood movie idol," Peter protested.

"After that television special the other night, you could be just that."

"Actually, I've been approached. One of those Oxford gray rabbits who inhabit the warrens of Madison Avenue called the day after the broadcast and suggested that I consider a series on TV with the same title, 'The Doctor from WHO.'"

"It might be good public relations for our profession."

"Maybe. But I wouldn't want to be tied down to a weekly job."

"Then you've turned down the Baltimore offer?"

"Not finally. I promised John Teague to come by and talk to him about it while I'm down there. But there's a thrill to running down something like that monkey kidney virus, a feeling of adventure and accomplishment I'm afraid I wouldn't find as a professor. Maybe in another ten years I'll be ready for it—when I'm fifty and beginning to slow down a little."

iv

Flight 216 had been four hours late leaving Atlanta, having encountered bad weather. Fortunately for Dr. Ed McDougal, one of the airport bars stayed open all night to accommodate the nocturnal flow of travelers, so by the time the big four-engined jet was airborne shortly before dawn, he was pleasantly lubricated and quite ready to forgive the airline for the delay.

Not so Hannah McDougal, however. She had matched Ed drink for drink while they waited, but the liquor only made her more than normally quarrelsome. When the trim stewardess set a breakfast tray before her, she eyed the food disdainfully—but not Ed.

"Boy! This looks good!" He tucked the corner of his napkin into his shirt front just beneath the collar and tore off the end of a small envelope package of sugar, letting it trickle into the steaming cup of coffee a second stewardess had just poured from a vacuum flask.

"Do you have to eat like a farmhand?" Forced to fight continually a tendency to accumulate weight around the hips, seeing anyone else enjoy food always irritated Hannah.

"That's what I started out as." Ed was feeling too good to let Hannah and her chronically bad temper spoil his day. "Might go back to it, too—after I make my pile."

"Don't count on my being with you."

"Suit yourself." The big surgeon with the shock of graying red hair buttered a piece of toast and popped it whole into his mouth.

"You wouldn't miss me at all." Hannah's tone was petulant.

"Oh, I'd miss your bitchin'." He tackled the scrambled eggs and sausage. "Nothing makes a man work harder than knowin' his wife will give him hell when he gets home. That way he's got a good reason to stay at the office and make money."

"Then at least I'm worth something to you."

"Just admitted it, didn't I? Of course, you used to be good in the hay—"

"Do you have to broadcast it to the world?" she hissed.

"Lettin' a thing like that get around never hurts a woman, hon. You were really something before we were married. Remember that time we went to the house party on the Severn? Man oh man!"

The memory was pleasant—and poignant—enough to silence even Hannah McDougal's acid tongue for the moment.

"Champagne?" A stewardess stood beside them, a bottle poised.

"Champagne for breakfast! This is the life!" Ed picked up Hannah's empty glass with his own and held them while the girl filled them both, then handed Hannah's to her.

"To the old days, dear." He touched his glass to hers and emptied it in one swallow, holding it out for the stewardess to refill when she turned from serving those on the opposite side of the aisle.

"Do you have to be such a pig?" Hannah said furiously under her breath as the girl moved down the aisle. "The way you embarrass me."

"Don't mean to, hon. Don't mean to. It's just my way."

Hannah nibbled at the breakfast resentfully, unwilling to dull the remaining glow of the whiskey and the added one from the champagne with food. Most of the time she felt dead inside; only the stimulus of alcohol or Benzedrine could bring her to life for a while. And even then, the letdown afterward was worst of all.

"Bet when I asked you for a date that day at the stenographic pool, you never dreamed you'd wind up the wife of one of the most successful surgeons in Texas." As usual, Ed was talking with his mouth full, chewing vigorously between the words. "We've come a long way from those days, hon; never had a chance to really think how far, until Greg invited me to talk on pancreatic surgery at the convocation."

"Just be sure you're sober enough to do it right."

"I never mix alcohol and surgery. You ought to know that."

Proof of what Ed had said about his success was hanging in the clothing rack at the front of the airplane, a full-length ermine coat that had cost close to $10,000 at Neiman-Marcus.

He'd never been niggardly with her, once he'd begun to make some money, Hannah admitted to herself as she lay back in the seat and closed her eyes. The big diamond on her finger was ten times the carats of the one he'd given her when they were married. And the matching wedding ring was a far cry from the dime-store band he'd slipped on her finger before the Bowling Green justice of the peace who had married them one summer night.

They'd barely had enough money between them to pay for the motel near Annapolis, where they'd spent their honeymoon, and the bottle of whiskey Ed had bought, along with crackers and cheese for the wedding feast. But it had been as close to paradise as Hannah had ever come—before or since.

Dear God. What has happened in the years between? she asked

65

silently, without realizing that this was the first time she had prayed in years.

How could Ed have been a big, boisterously happy Fellow in Surgery in those long-ago days, charming every woman he met with his Texas drawl and his red-headed, handsome exuberance, a catch any girl would have been proud of—and then turn into a pig who smacked his lips over a glass of free champagne, ate with his napkin tucked in his shirt and talked like a rustic.

What did I do to deserve this? Could the Lord possibly be punishing me for deliberately trapping Ed into marriage?

She'd known he wanted her for a long time before the house party on the Severn that summer. Just as she'd known she had to yield soon or see him lured away by some of the other girls, who were willing to go with him anywhere he wanted—and as far as he wished. But in yielding she had to make sure of marriage, and that had taken some planning.

The opportunity she'd been waiting for had come several months after their first date. Four girls from the secretarial pool had rented the cottage that summer and word of it had quickly spread through The Clinic. Invited by one of the four to a weekend house party, Hannah had asked Ed and they had driven down in his old Buick on Saturday afternoon.

The festivities were already in full swing when they arrived. Everybody was frolicking in the lazy tidal river, an arm of the Chesapeake, sailing the small catboats that went with the cottage or just drinking up the considerable supply of liquor brought by the male guests. After a couple of drinks to catch up, Ed and Hannah had danced awhile to the music of the portable record player that was blaring out in one corner of the big living room, then had gone swimming with the rest.

When someone challenged Ed as a Texan to take care of cooking the steaks on an outdoor fireplace in the late afternoon, he'd agreed enthusiastically and Hannah had been given no opportunity to protest, though she would much rather have spent the rest of the afternoon playing the game of amatory hide-and-seek she had planned in preparation for the evening.

She had been sitting alone on the dock after supper in the warm August darkness, morosely watching the play of lights from the cottages along the river on the surface of the slow tidal stream and the bright glow of the moon just beginning to rise in the east where the river emptied into the Chesapeake Bay, when Ed plumped himself down beside her and handed her a filled glass.

"Been hunting for you for ten minutes, sweetie," he said. "Nobody seemed to know where you were."

"You were busy," she said a little acidly. "So I came out here."

"Had to take charge of the steaks or somebody would have messed 'em all up. I guess nobody 'cept a Texan really knows how to cook steaks out of doors. Drink up. We've got us some lovin' to do."

"Suppose I don't want to."

"You were hot enough a couple of hours ago. Man, I'm still panting from that kiss you gave me when I came down from putting on my trunks in the boathouse."

She'd taken a long drink from the glass before answering deliberately, "Maybe that's as far as you're going to get."

"Now, don't say that, sugar," he protested. "If I thought you'd gone to all the trouble of bringing me here to this nice romantic spot just for a little pettin', I'd be downright disappointed."

She couldn't help laughing at his tone, but her pulse had already begun to beat faster from the warmth of the alcohol in her veins. To hide her reaction from him, she drank another third of the potent mixture in her glass, adding further fuel to the fire.

"What made you think there'd be anything else?"

"Oh, a guy can tell." His arm slipped about her and she had to fight against yielding immediately to the fierce, demanding possessiveness of his kiss. Finally, she pushed herself away, for it wasn't part of her careful plan to let him think she was quite the pushover she fully intended to be—in time.

"Let's finish our drinks," she said a little breathlessly.

"Sure." Ed emptied his glass. "All the time I was cooking the steaks I was thinking about how warm and loving you can be. The hotter the steaks got, the hotter I got."

"You certainly didn't show it."

"Depends on where you were looking." He handed her glass to her. "Finish this and let's take ourselves a little swim."

"My suit's wet."

"Who said anything about suits?" He was unbuttoning his sport shirt as he spoke and pulling it over his head. "We're going to take us a swim Texas style."

"Not right here," she gasped. "Everybody can see with the moon coming up."

"Me, I don't care." He was stripping off his slacks as he spoke and she looked away instinctively. "If you insist on being modest, step inside the boathouse. I'll swim in there in a minute and hang my clothes on a nail."

Inside the boathouse, it had taken her only a moment to step out of the playsuit she was wearing and the briefs and bra under it. There wasn't any use kidding herself about what was going to happen—or that she didn't want it to happen and hadn't intended for it to happen.

For perhaps the dozenth time since her friends had invited her down to the Severn for the weekend, Hannah had made a quick mental calculation—with the same answer. She was as regular as a clock and this was the fourteenth day of her cycle, probably the very day of ovulation, so the odds in favor of pregnancy were higher than at any other day of the month.

She had lowered herself into the warm water by the time Ed came swimming into the boathouse, lying on his back and holding his clothing up in a compact bundle while he propelled himself by kicking. He found a ladder that extended down into the water from the boathouse above and climbed it, looking like a dripping Greek god in the pale gleam of the moonlight as he hung his clothing on a nail and then, with a barely audible splash, slid under the surface and disappeared.

The water inside the boathouse barely came to her shoulders as Hannah searched it for the phosphorescence that would betray Ed's presence. But he had turned to swim behind her and, when his head broke water, his hands went around her body to cup her breasts in his palms. With a gasp of pleasure, she leaned back against him and reached up to take his head between her hands, turning her face so he could reach her lips as he stood holding her body against his.

She felt the proudness of him thrusting against her as his mouth

68

opened to her kiss, then his hands sliding down over her hips to the cleft in her loins, parting the soft flesh so she could settle upon him with a deep shuddering sigh. For a single moment she lost consciousness at the height of her own release until his voice brought her back to the present.

"Do you need to do anything?" he asked. "I mean, to keep from getting pregnant. The Clinic doesn't look with favor on its Fellows knocking up secretaries."

"I don't think this is the right time," she lied.

"Good. There's a room upstairs over this boathouse. When I changed up there this afternoon, I figured we could use it later."

"Suppose somebody finds us."

"Everybody came here tonight with the same idea in mind. We just happened to get started earlier than the rest, which puts us one up on them."

She giggled. "You can say that again."

Hours later, as they lay in each other's arms with all passion sated, he'd said: "One of these days we've got to get ourselves married, sugar—when I get a weekend off."

"Do you really want to?"

"How could anybody not want something like you around every night when he gets home. You're the most, baby."

And she did love him, she'd told herself as she responded to his skilled caresses. Besides, he'd mentioned marriage himself, so she hadn't really conned him into it or anything.

When the stewardess took their trays away, Hannah moved a little closer to Ed in the comfortable first-class seat, letting her shoulder touch his. He was relaxed and happy, smoking one of the thin cigars he'd taken up instead of cigarettes after removing the first lung from a patient for cancer over ten years ago.

Almost twenty years had made a difference—in both of them—but the toll on Ed had been remarkably light. A sprinkle of gray showed in his red hair, but the salt and pepper effect made him look distinguished, where before he had been merely handsome. He kept himself fit, too; but not with the lazy games of golf most doctors favored, riding from green to green in an electric cart. Four days at noon he played a fast game of handball in the YMCA near his office, and he was still club champion in his class. His waistline was the same as it had been when they were married and he had the same zest for life and for love.

Not that she'd let her own figure go either, Hannah assured herself. Tennis at the club several afternoons a week still kept the muscles in tone, even if two quick scotch and sodas were needed afterward to recapture the momentary zest of competing and winning.

What had happened between her and Ed wasn't physical, though inevitably it had its physical side. The trouble was that somewhere along the line, especially since the boys had grown up and gone to Yale, the zest and ardor which some older people—and a precious few, when she thought about it—seemed to find in life had somehow escaped her.

It hadn't seemed to escape Ed though; he was as affectionate as ever, in spite of what he called her bitching. For a moment she experienced a surge of affection for him, something she'd felt only rarely for a long time. But when a gentle snore escaped from his lips, her own tightened with annoyance and the old feeling of futility and depression seized her once again.

v

For the convocation, the regular staff of The Clinic had been assigned to various committees. In addition to the building committee, where Helen Foucald had asked to be placed in order to safeguard the interests of her laboratory, Greg had put her on the welcoming committee, charged with meeting various dignitaries and their wives and making certain that they were transported to the Clinic Inn, where rooms had been reserved for them. She was still in bed, though awake, when Greg Alexander telephoned.

"I hope you weren't asleep, Helen," he said.

"I was just waking. I like to take a while at it."

"Could you shorten the process a bit this morning?"

"Of course, Greg. Is anything wrong?"

"Almost everything's right, as a matter of fact. Letty had pups during the night."

"That's wonderful."

"I want to see her before I start making final preparations for the heart-lung transplant I'm doing tomorrow for the convocation, but I'd also planned to meet Peter Carewe's plane this morning. Could you do that for me?"

"When does he arrive?"

"There's an early jet out of La Guardia. He wired me last night that he'd been held over in New York and would take that flight."

"I sometimes take it myself when I go to New York for the weekend," she said. "I'll have plenty of time to meet the plane."

"Thanks. Since Peter's our dinner speaker, I thought we ought to give him a little VIP treatment."

"Especially when he's an authentic VIP. Congratulate Letty for me; she certainly made history last night."

The morning traffic made the trip to the airport somewhat longer than Helen had counted on. As she hurried into the terminal, the announcement of Flight 26's arrival was just coming over the loudspeakers and she had only time for a reassuring glance into her compact mirror before she spied the tall form of Dr. Peter Carewe coming off the plane.

She had no trouble recognizing him; he was just as handsome as he had been on TV a week before. She saw his eyes scanning the crowd and knew he was looking for Greg Alexander. But when they reached her, they stopped dead center and a warm glow came into them. Conscious that she must be blushing at the uninhibited admiration in his gaze, she stepped forward.

"Dr. Carewe?" she asked—quite unnecessarily.

"Yes." He came over to her in three quick strides. "You saved my life."

"H—how?"

"When I saw you standing there, I said to myself, 'Peter, my boy, you're not going to leave this airport until you know who that beautiful woman is.' You saved me the risk of getting slapped for speaking to you—or maybe getting punched in the nose by an irate husband."

She laughed. "Not many I see around here would dare try that. I'm Dr. Helen Foucald. Greg Alexander sent me to meet you."

"Good old Greg," he said. "I hope you haven't had breakfast."

71

"N—no, I haven't."

"The best I could get on the plane was a cup of coffee and a danish and I'm starved." He signaled a passing skycap and handed him a baggage check and a dollar. "Claim this for me, will you," he said. "I'll pick it up outside after breakfast."

"I hope Greg didn't break a leg or anything," Peter said when they were seated in the airport restaurant.

"Oh no. Letty had pups during the night."

"That's what I always liked most about Greg. He'd pay as much attention to a sick dog in the experimental lab as he would to the chairman of the Board of Trustees."

"Letty's something special," Helen explained. "Greg did a heart-lung transplant on her over six months ago; and for her to have pups just in time to be reported at the convocation is more than any of us hoped for."

"I take it you're on Greg's side in this battle I've been hearing about for a new clinic."

"I certainly am," she said. "If you could see how antiquated my department is—"

"Your department?"

"I've been chief of laboratories for three years now."

"That's why I haven't seen you before. It's been over five years since I've been back for one of the convocations."

"I came here from the Lahey Clinic in Boston," she explained. "I was a Fellow there for two years after I got my degree from the Sorbonne."

"I did some work at the Sorbonne before I went out to Japan to study tsutsugamushi fever," he said. "It's even more antiquated than The Clinic."

"I read your report on that work," she told him. "It's too bad they couldn't go into it in more detail on 'The Doctor from WHO' the other night on TV."

"That program was mainly a public relations ploy for the World Health Organization. I just happened to be chosen for it."

"For the very good reason that you're the most glamorous man in the entire organization."

"Glamour doesn't count for much when you're trying to drain a malaria swamp in Kenya, or spraying for tsetse flies in the Congo."

The waiter came and he ordered for them. "But enough about me. Tell me about yourself."

"Mainly I'm a hematologist, but I'd had some experience running a laboratory in Paris and Dr. Anders selected me for the job here."

"Is Henry still the same conniving bastard he always was?"

"I—I don't know what you mean," she said, startled by his amazingly accurate description of Henry Anders.

"You must have been steering clear of him then. How do he and Greg get along?"

"All right, I suppose. Why?"

"Henry has hated Greg Alexander ever since the old doc practically disinherited Henry by making The Clinic a foundation so Greg could keep it going the way the old man intended for it to go."

"They seem to get along all right." If Peter Carewe noticed anything wrong in her voice, he didn't make it known, but attacked the ham, eggs and coffee, which had just arrived, with the same vigor he'd put into a campaign to control an epidemic of cholera.

"Henry knows Greg is the real genius behind The Clinic's continued success, so he wouldn't let it come to a showdown between them and risk being slapped down by the trustees," he said over the second cup of coffee. "Henry's way would be to try to discredit Greg somehow so he'd resign. The thing I can't understand is how Greg has managed to stand it this long—or Jeanne."

"I don't know her too well."

"Jeanne's brother, George, was a classmate of mine at Hopkins. We used to have dinner with Greg and Jeanne every now and then when Greg was still a Fellow." He sat back in his chair and wiped his mouth with a napkin. "Nothing's better than ham and eggs for breakfast—with a beautiful woman across the table."

The implication in his voice made Helen blush again and she wondered whether he would think her an inexperienced old maid. "It's a wonder you haven't married then," she said.

"Never found a woman who could improve on room service—for the ham and eggs. I didn't see a wedding ring on your finger, perchance, did I?"

"No. I'm too busy running a laboratory."

"Not too busy to have dinner with me tonight, I hope."

"Do you always move this fast?" she asked with a smile.

"Only in special situations. Actually, I may not have but two days here; some trouble is brewing in a batch of oral polio vaccine on the West Coast. If the people we have working on it don't run down the culprit soon, I'll have to fly out there and start looking into it."

"Since you're off to the wars, so to speak, I couldn't well refuse you, could I?" said Helen. "I live in the Clinic Apartments."

"Good," he said. "Anybody as beautiful as you are this early in the morning must be a real knockout by candlelight around midnight."

"You might be disappointed."

"I picked you out of the crowd just now."

"But I was looking for you then—and that attracted your attention."

"You would have attracted my attention if you'd been facing the wall," he assured her, and Helen decided it was time to change the subject.

"Is there any truth to the rumor that you may settle down and become a professor?" she asked.

"Now that I have seen you, maybe yes. Tell me, can you cook ham and eggs?"

"I once took a course in cooking at the Cordon Bleu." Then her eyes twinkled. "But I thought you preferred room service."

6

The clock in the lobby of the hospital read eight when Greg Alexander crossed it and took a right-hand corridor that joined the diagnostic section of The Clinic to the surgical building. Just off the corridor was a self-service canteen for the convenience of the staff and visitors, with banks of machines that dispensed food and drinks merely by dropping a coin into waiting slots.

He hadn't awakened Jeanne when he'd left the apartment that morning; in fact, he could hardly remember when they'd had breakfast together. She'd been sleeping poorly in the early part of the night, he knew, because he had often heard her small TV set after midnight.

He was stirring a steaming cup of coffee from one of the vending machines when Dr. David Connor, the staff cardiologist, came in and went to the coffee machine. As he turned with a cup in his hand, the somewhat pudgy heart specialist saw the surgeon and came over to sit beside him.

"You look sort of peaked, Dave," said Greg. "Everything all right?"

"I went to the symphony last night."

"We missed it; I was late getting home."

"You didn't miss anything. Pozl was waving his arms and his hair as usual. Haven't seen you eating here often. Thought you preferred the staff dining room to this kind of food."

"I do. Letty had pups during the night and I'm going by to see her."

"Heard about it already," said the cardiologist. "Congratulations."

"Thanks—for Letty. What brings you out so early, Dave?"

75

"Jim McNeal admitted a heart case last night, a broken-down vaudeville hoofer named Guy Merchant."

A bell rang somewhere deep down in Greg Alexander's brain. "Gentleman Guy?"

"Could be. Friend of yours?"

"I saw him in a show downtown when I was a student at Hopkins. He was the headliner then."

"Not any more, I imagine. Jim said he was brought in from one of those joints down on Baltimore Street."

"I guess hoofing is on the skids these days, along with vaudeville and burlesque."

"Merchant almost skidded out this morning," said the cardiologist. "He had a cessation a couple of hours ago but the nurse on ICU was watching the monitor tube and saw the heart pattern flatten out. She had the Pacemaker on him in less than a minute and by the time Jim got there he was ticking again."

"You've got that resuscitation routine worked out well."

"Provided it happens in the intensive care unit. If this fellow had been on one of the regular floors, we might never have gotten his heart started again in time to save him from being a vegetable the rest of his life because of brain damage due to lack of oxygen."

A thought raced through Greg Alexander's brain. Dave Connor was the hospital gossip, a bachelor who loved nothing better than feeding information into the grapevine that connected every department without wires or other means of transmission, an invisible network over which a rumor could travel from the furnace room to the superintendent's office in less time than it took to walk the distance. This might just be the place to launch a trial balloon in preparation for the showdown with the trustees later on in the week, he decided, knowing the information about his plans would be sped faster by Dave than in any other way.

"There's a way of making certain that it does," he said casually.

"Does what?" Dave Connor was munching on a danish pastry.

"You were talking about cessation of the heart—in the intensive care unit. There's a way of concentrating patients who are likely to have that sort of a thing happen to them where facilities for

76

resuscitation will always be available. I was talking to Keith Jackson—"

"Seems like I've heard that name before. Who's he?"

"A young architect who lives in one of the apartments below me. You probably remember the sketches he submitted for the new buildings two years ago."

"That could be it. They were way out, weren't they?"

"For then, I guess some people might say they were, but not today. Anyway, Keith has an idea for a new approach to building what we need."

"I thought you fought that out two years ago, when the trustees turned down your first proposal."

"I wasn't thinking far enough ahead then, so maybe it's just as well they did turn me down," the surgeon admitted. "Keith has come up with an idea for what will probably be the most highly automated hospital in the world—and also the most advanced."

"As I remember it, that was the trouble with your first plan— particularly where Sam Hunter was concerned," Dave Connor demurred. "He claimed that the impersonal care such a hospital would generate wasn't in keeping with what Henry Anders intended when he founded this place."

"Sam Hunter's wrong, Dave. The more I look into this question, the more I'm convinced that the future of medical care lies in a high degree of automation. You knew Dr. Anders well, so you know this is exactly the sort of a thing he would like to see here on The Clinic site today."

"Maybe. But you don't expect to change Sam Hunter, do you?"

"As well try to put a smile on one of those faces on Mount Rushmore," Greg Alexander said. "But he's not the only trustee."

"He's the only one worth five hundred million dollars," said the cardiologist. "Which means that when the chips are down, whatever Sam Hunter wants built is what will be built—and it'll be put where he wants it. Don't go butting your head against a wall again, Greg. You got squashed once—"

"Perhaps because in my heart I knew what I was proposing wasn't what The Clinic really needed. This time, I'm convinced we've got the answer."

"Powerful forces are against you this time, too, maybe more powerful than before, from all I hear. I'd hate to see Henry Anders get you into a position where you'd have no choice except to leave—and wreck whatever future this place does have."

ii

Henry Anders II smiled when he saw the systems analyst with his clipboard and pocket calculator checking the traffic through the main corridor of the diagnostic building as he came in shortly before nine o'clock. It proved that the bee he had planted in Keith Jackson's bonnet a few days earlier was already buzzing, in ample time to stir up enough talk in the hospital for some of it to spill over to the Board of Trustees well in advance of the Saturday meeting.

The Clinic's director was feeling a little fagged, but pleased—with everything. Not only was his plan moving smoothly but the latter part of the evening with Claire had been quite rewarding. She was quite a woman when she wanted to be, and last night she had wanted to be. The thought that he was doubly blessed in this respect perked him up a little, particularly when he saw Helen Foucald hurrying through the lobby after dropping Peter Carewe off at the Clinic Inn.

"Why so fast?" he asked as he fell into step beside her.

"I'm late. Greg asked me to run out to the airport and pick up Dr. Peter Carewe."

"The boy wonder of the mosquitoes? I could never stand him when we were students."

"I found him rather charming. We had breakfast together at the airport."

"Watch out for that fellow, Helen. He's up to no good where women are concerned."

"What are you up to, Henry?" She was surprised at her instant reaction to his criticism of Peter Carewe.

"What do you mean?"

"Claire called me last night—before you got home."

"She told me about that. It wasn't my idea."

78

"I suggested that we have lunch together some day—to compare notes on your prowess as a lover."

"For God's sake, Helen! Do you have to speak of me as if I were a stud?"

"That's what you really are, aren't you, Henry? I suppose all your women eventually learn they have to pay some sort of a fee."

"This is no place for public discussion of such a subject," Henry said stiffly. "We can talk about it tonight."

"I can't see you tonight. Peter Carewe invited me to have dinner with him."

"Maybe he wouldn't be so anxious if I told him—" He broke off at the sudden look of contempt in her eyes.

"You'd do it, too, wouldn't you?" she said icily.

"Of course not. I was just—"

"If I become interested enough in Peter Carewe, I'll tell him about us and a few others, Henry. But *I'll* do the talking."

She was at the door of the lab now and paused with her hand upon the knob. "Do you understand?"

"Well, I—"

"Do you understand, Henry?"

"You can depend on me, Helen."

"I hope so." She turned the knob and opened the door.

"Wait a minute," he protested. "How about tomorrow—?"

"I'll see you at the first session of the convocation this afternoon, Doctor." She was suddenly brisk for the benefit of the technicians in the busy laboratory visible through the open door. "Perhaps we can discuss that case in more detail then."

iii

"Miss Jeanne!" The heavy knocking on the bedroom door and the sound of her own name finally brought Jeanne Alexander from the drugged sleep she had achieved by taking a Nembutal sometime after midnight. At first, she thought it was Greg calling to her, as he had done after she had shut herself up last night and locked the door. But then she recognized the voice of Ethel, the maid, and went to unlock it.

"Miss Jeanne, you ought not to lock yourself in like that," Ethel said indignantly. She had been with them for many years and had her own key to the apartment.

"I'm sorry, Ethel. What time is it?"

"Pretty near nine o'clock." The maid's tone indicated her disapproval of anyone's sleeping that late. "I've been here 'bout an hour but, when I didn't hear no breathin' from your room, I got worried. S'pose somethin' happened to you in there. We'd have to break the door down."

"I'm sorry, Ethel."

"You orta be, Miss Jeanne. I met the doctor leavin' as I was comin' in, and tried to get him to let me fix him some breakfast. Imagine an important man like him not havin' nothin' but coffee and them stale danish pastries they sell at the canteen."

"He usually eats in the hospital cafeteria," Jeanne protested.

"Lately I've been findin' them cellophane wrappers off the pastries in his coat pockets, when I go through 'em before sending 'em to the cleaners. The way he's been workin' I bet he don't even take time to go to no cafeteria. I tell you, Miss Jeanne, that man's killin' hisself for sure."

"Was he—did he seem to be all right?"

"He was in a hurry—and all excited 'bout a dog named Letty havin' pups last night. But it don't make no sense."

The maid broke off when Jeanne laughed on a note of hysteria. "You all right, Miss Jeanne?"

"Yes, Ethel. I wasn't laughing at you."

"You can fire me for sayin' so if you want to, Miss Jeanne, but it ain't nothin' to laugh about when a fine man like the doctor has to sleep by hisself every night. I been noticin' the way things are in this house and it just ain't right. Seems to me you should be thankful you ain't got no worse competition than a dog."

"I think you're right, Ethel," Jeanne said, suddenly sober. "Thank you for reminding me."

"What do you want for breakfast?"

"I'll step across to the motel coffee shop." A rooftop passageway connected the two buildings. "A lot of people I know will probably be over there."

"Do you good to get out," the maid approved. "You been staying too much to yourself lately."

In her bedroom, Jeanne pulled the nightgown over her head in front of the full-length mirror on the bathroom door and studied her body in the glass. She could find little fault with it, even at forty. Daily swimming in the enclosed pool atop the motel next-door had kept her slim and her weight was within ounces of what it had been when she and Greg were married almost twenty years ago. She could still wear a size fourteen dress, too, without alterations.

The trouble couldn't be the menopause, she told herself as she stepped into the shower and turned it on; she was still as regular as a clock. Or the Doctor's Wife Syndrome that was being talked about so much nowadays. Until two years ago, she had considered herself a vital part of Greg's life, sharing his troubles and his triumphs, with no feeling of being shut away from anything that concerned him.

The shutting away had been her own action, she admitted now, and, at the sudden wave of depression that swept over her, she deliberately turned the shower control to "Cold" and stood gasping in the needle-sharp stream, hoping the shock would drive it away.

It did help and before depression could grip her again, she dressed hurriedly and took the elevator down to the sixth-floor level, where the enclosed crosswalk connected the apartment house and the adjoining inn. She had intended having breakfast at the coffee shop on the first floor, but the rooftop dining room was half full because of the convocation, so she turned in there instead.

"Good morning, Mrs. Alexander," the hostess greeted her warmly. "Any place you'd prefer to eat?"

Jeanne's first impulse was to choose a corner away from the crowd that partially filled the dining room, many of them former Fellows and their wives back for the convocation. But she deliberately put down the urge to hide and answered the hostess' greeting with a smile.

"Over near the window will do, thank you."

A glass wall of sliding doors, closed now, separated the restaurant from the patio and pool. The hostess pulled out a chair at a table where the sun shone through a window and placed a menu before her. Almost instantly, a smiling young waitress brought ice water and filled a cup beside her place with coffee.

"I'll take soft scrambled eggs, sausage and wheat toast buttered," she told the girl, and leaned back in her chair. Recognizing several former students of Greg's she acknowledged their greetings with a nod and a smile but was glad when no one came to the table. Then, across the restaurant she saw a woman in an ermine coat enter and stand beside the hostess, obviously surveying the room to see whether or not she knew anyone there. In the instant that Jeanne recognized Hannah McDougal, Hannah saw her too, and started across the room, followed by the hostess.

"Jeanne, darling!" Hannah bent to kiss her cheek. "Mind if I have a cup of coffee and something with you?"

"Of course not, Hannah. Sit down."

Jeanne had never been really close to the other woman, but their husbands had been in the same class of Fellows at The Clinic and she had seen Hannah a number of times at medical conventions. Ed McDougal was known to be quite a comer, she knew, both in practice and in medical politics in Texas, and Hannah's coat further testified to his success.

"Did you just get in?" Jeanne asked.

"A few minutes ago—almost twelve hours late." Hannah dropped her coat across a chair and took a seat at Jeanne's elbow. "The plane was late and the food was lousy—as usual. The only thing good was the liquor."

"Where's Ed?"

"Across the street. Sam Hunter's having a checkup this morning and Ed wanted to see him between examinations. Confidentially, Ed's afraid Greg may con Sam out of a lot of money for The Clinic here and get him to cut down on what we're supposed to get for the university medical school down in our town."

"I thought that battle was fought out a couple of years ago at the trustees' meeting—when Greg lost."

"Ed refuses to believe Greg will give up that easy." Hannah reached for a saccharin pack from the sugar bowl. "Now that Sam Hunter has disinherited his younger son, Ted, there'll be an even larger bequest when the old man dies, and it doesn't make sense for him to leave it here. Really, Jeanne, you don't spend millions of dollars on a new hospital in a place like this. How do you stand living around here anyway?"

Jeanne had asked herself that same question more than once during the past year. Now she felt called upon to defend The Clinic, if only because she had never particularly liked Hannah McDougal.

"The Clinic Apartments are very nice," she said. "And it's convenient to Greg's work."

"I guess it does come in handy for your husband to be able to get his breakfast at the hospital dining room—particularly when there's been a party the night before and you don't feel like getting up," Hannah conceded. "Thank God we've got a good housekeeper. She's been with us more than ten years and I just leave the running of the house to her."

Jeanne's breakfast arrived and Hannah's eyebrows lifted at the sight of the plate and the pile of toast beside it on the saucer.

"How do you manage to stay so trim and eat like that?" she demanded. "I eat practically nothing and still have to keep my behind girdled up until I feel like I'm wearing armor. Fortunately, Ed likes me a little plump; he's the bouncing kind."

"Just bring me some eggs without any toast," Hannah said to the waitress who poured her coffee, and turned back to Jeanne. "You still didn't tell me how you stay so slim."

"I don't eat like this every morning," Jeanne admitted. "Almost every day I swim in the pool here on the rooftop, too."

"Our pool's back of the house but we can't use it in winter. I think I'll get Ed to enclose it." Hannah looked around the room, nodded to several people, then turned back to Jeanne. "Well, what's the dirt?"

"Dirt?"

"You know—the dope about the old crowd. Whose wife has left him since the last convocation and who's sleeping with whom."

"Really, Hannah. I don't keep up with things like that. Greg works late most of the time, so we don't see much of the old crowd."

"Not having children, you wouldn't and maybe you're better off at that," said Hannah. "Ed, Junior, knocked up a Mexican girl a few months ago and we had a hell of a time paying her off. The price these abortionists get nowadays is terrible."

Hannah's eggs arrived and she attacked them as if she were

famished. "I saw Peter Carewe across the airport when we came off the plane," she said when her plate was clean. "He was with a woman, so we didn't get to speak to him."

"Peter and my brother George were good friends," said Jeanne. "We used to see a lot of him when they were students."

"I sure would like a romp in the hay with him," Hannah confided. "Did you see him on the Doctor from WHO program?"

"I'm afraid not."

"You missed something. They tell me women practically mob him everywhere he goes, like a movie star."

"That must be a new experience for a doctor."

"Don't kid yourself, dear. Women are always after 'em." Hannah started to light a cigarette, but her hand shook so much that she had to steady the lighter with the other one.

"Are you all right?" Jeanne asked.

"Of course I'm all right. Why?"

"You seem nervous."

"Show me a woman forty-two years old married to a handsome and lusty man who makes a hundred thousand dollars a year that isn't nervous."

"But why?"

"When he's surrounded all day long by young women in white uniforms, or else naked under an examining sheet? Don't tell me you don't worry?"

"I never have."

"Maybe you don't need to, being married to Greg."

"What does that mean?"

"Only that he's one in a million. Out in practice, all the doctors are busy climbing over the others to get ahead and kicking the other fellow in the face for good measure while they're going up."

"That's Greg's only weakness," said Jeanne. "He's so married to his work he lets other people take advantage of him."

"Believe me, having a husband who's married to his work is a lot better than having one whose eye's always roving. Ed McDougal will lay anything that wears a skirt, if he gets a chance."

"Then why do you put up with him?"

"The biggest reason I suppose is habit; you get to expect certain things when you're married to a go-getter—like this coat. When I come into a restaurant wearing it, every woman in there envies me. Me"—she gave a short bark of a laugh—"Hannah Shultz who was a thirty-five-dollar-a-week secretary until I managed to snag Ed. Now I get a new Continental every two years and my clothes come from Neiman-Marcus or Bergdorf Goodman."

"They're certainly smart."

"The best always are. Besides, Ed's still pretty vigorous and if you've got to have a man panting over you several times a week, it might as well be somebody who can make you pant a little, too."

Jeanne suddenly realized that she couldn't remember when she and Greg had last made love. He'd been staying at the hospital a lot these last few months but it had never occurred to her even to suspect another woman—nor did she now.

"I always liked you, Jeanne. You're not like that bitch Claire." Hannah's voice brought Jeanne out of her reverie. "Persuade Greg to play ball with Ed and Henry on this deal to move The Clinic, and he can get rich enough overnight to buy you a coat like mine."

Somewhere in Jeanne's brain a warning bell suddenly rang. "Why would anybody want to move it?" she asked.

"To get out of this lousy neighborhood, for one thing," said Hannah, and leaned closer, dropping her voice to a more confidential tone. "Ed and Henry have got a way all worked out to develop the property across the street after The Clinic is moved to the new location that's been proposed on the Beltway at the edge of town. If Greg gave up his opposition to it, they'd let him have a piece of the syndicate cheap."

"Syndicate?"

"That's as much as I can tell you now." The other woman's manner was suddenly guarded, as if she realized she had said too much. "But you always treated me nice and I'd like to see both you and Greg get ahead. If he plays ball with Ed and Henry, he can get enough of old Sam's money to build a new clinic and still line his own pockets." Hannah stood up and reached for the coat.

"I'm going upstairs and get me some sleep," she said. "That damn plane had the most uncomfortable seats I was ever in and Ed snored all the way—when he wasn't watching the stewardess' legs. I tell you, if they get those uniforms any shorter, they can just

85

let the girls take the place of in-flight movies as far as the men are concerned."

When Hannah was gone, Jeanne sat looking out the window, but not really seeing the dull February day outside, while she rehearsed the conversation again in her mind. She didn't consider for a moment suggesting to Greg that he take up Hannah's idea of joining Henry Anders and Ed McDougal in whatever it was they were planning. What did concern her was how she might find out more about it and possibly help Greg, as the first step toward curing the illness of her own marriage and keeping it from becoming like that of Hannah and Ed. For, in spite of the ermine coat and the diamonds, Hannah McDougal was obviously a desperately unhappy woman.

The trouble between her and Greg dated back, she decided, to the night two years ago when he had come home from the post-convocation meeting of the Board of Trustees, dejected after the plan he'd worked so hard on had been turned down summarily, following a savage attack by Sam Hunter. Easygoing though Greg was, compromise where a principle was concerned wasn't part of his nature; which, she realized now, was probably why his agreeing to develop another set of plans had both surprised and disappointed her.

Disappointment—that was the key, she was sure. Since the day when she'd first seen him in the hospital, she had put her whole life into Greg and his career. And his agreeing to the sort of pedestrian structure the board seemed to have in mind, instead of the real hospital of the future she knew he wanted to build, had caused a wave of bitterness to sweep over her, bitterness at him for seeming to yield on a matter of principle, where he had never yielded before.

Now she suspected that his apparent yielding had been merely a regrouping of his energies to approach the problem from another point of view. But disappointed as she had been then, she had treated him unfairly at a time when he was carrying more burdens than any man should be required to carry.

The experimental work in heart-lung transplantation had been his main concern even then, for without new facilities to carry it on, the whole thing was certain to be crippled. Yet in her dis-

86

turbed condition, she realized now that she'd seen even it as a rival, a place where he buried himself because he couldn't face her scorn at his having failed her. But if Greg had been willing to share credit for his pioneering work with Henry Anders—who deserved no credit—then he must have wanted the additional facilities a new clinic and hospital would give him more desperately than he had ever wanted anything else in his life.

It was sobering to realize how much her failure to understand and to help must have hurt him. And how the hurt must have increased almost from day to day, as she had shut him ever more completely out of her life. She felt a moment of sudden panic now, a touch of the fear she had experienced momentarily less than an hour ago, when Ethel had told her how excited Greg had been when he left for the hospital that morning. But with it went a sudden rush of gratitude that there was still time—as long as her only competition was a dog. Somehow she had to help Greg, and, in the process, save her marriage and regain her own self-respect.

But where to begin?

Then a name came into her mind, a name he'd mentioned last night when he'd come home all excited about some new plan, but which she'd ignored in her anger over the surgical journal article. Now she got up and went to the cashier's desk, paid her bill and returned to the apartment building. In the elevator, however, she didn't punch the button for the penthouse floor, but descended to the lobby. Searching the rows of mailboxes, she finally came upon a name that rang a bell in her mind, and, noting the apartment number 8-A above the mailbox, returned to the elevator and pressed the button for that floor.

iv

Georgia Merchant had been asleep just before dawn, when the sudden stoppage of Guy's heartbeat had created the gravest emergency a hospital can face. The ensuing swift and purposeful action by the hospital staff had awakened her, but Guy's room was filled with people, so she could no longer follow closely what was happening upon the closed-circuit television monitor tube above the nurse's desk. From long hours spent in similar ICUs about the country, however, she knew where to look for what medical people called the "vital signs."

Watching the monitor tube where Guy's heartbeat had been registered, she had seen the flashing beam of the electrocardiograph reappear after a few moments, indicating that his heart had begun to function again. And as she watched the tenuous flicker of motion upon the glass front of the monitor, she found herself praying silently that these capable people would fail in their endeavors and that the existence which had become practically intolerable for him might cease without causing him any more pain.

Her prayer was not answered, however. And watching Dr. McNeal approach the waiting room some ten minutes later, she had felt a surge of anger against the efficient hospital staff, a reaction to her own guilt at having allowed herself to wish even for a moment that Guy's heart would not start again.

"Your husband's heart is beating again, Mrs. Merchant." The young doctor sat down in a chair across the small coffee table from her, with its pile of old and dog-eared magazines. "I'm sorry I couldn't take time to tell you what was happening, but we had only minutes to get it started again before his brain would have been damaged from lack of oxygen."

"I think he would rather you hadn't started it, Doctor."

"Patients with anginal pain often feel that way."

"And I think I agree with him."

"That's understandable, too, Mrs. Merchant. But we have no choice."

"Why not, when you know there's no hope?" she burst out. "Why couldn't you just let him die in peace?"

Dr. McNeal looked at her with eyes that were tolerant and understanding. "You love your husband, so in the final analysis you, next to him, are best equipped to decide whether he lives or dies. Are you ready to take that responsibility upon yourself?"

Faced with the question, Georgia could only shake her head; there was no evading his logic.

"Can you tell what happened yet?" she asked.

"The heart rhythm is only just now being established, but from the look of the ECG pattern on the monitor he must have had a massive thrombosis, probably involving a major branch of one of the coronary arteries."

"That's very bad, isn't it?"

"Unless there's another cessation—the term we use to describe a stoppage of the heart—the next forty-eight hours should tell us whether the immediate damage from the thrombosis will be more than his heart is able to cope with."

"And if it is?"

"Then he will no longer be able to maintain enough circulation to keep vital functions such as kidney action going and the blood will start backing up in the lungs, causing congestion along with other symptoms—the picture we call heart failure."

"Do you think that's likely to happen, Doctor?"

Dr. McNeal nodded slowly. "His heart was barely maintaining the circulation before the last attack, so I don't expect it to be able to cope with a large thrombosis like this one. But you can never be sure in these cases."

"Last night you spoke of a possible operation," she reminded him.

"That was before this new crisis. I have asked Dr. Connor, The Clinic's cardiologist, to see your husband this morning and Dr. Alexander, the surgeon, will see him, too, for consultation. By that time we may be able to give you a more definite prognosis."

Dr. Connor, whom Dr. McNeal introduced to Georgia as the heart specialist, gave her no encouragement, however, when he saw Greg later. One of the nurses showed her the location of the hospital canteen, where she obtained coffee, but, when she returned to the ICU and again began to watch the pattern of Guy's heartbeat being recorded by the flashing point of light that moved steadily across the glass front of the tube to the opposite side, then was resumed again on the left, even she could see that the peaks and valleys of the ECG record were gradually contracting.

Which could only mean that Guy's heart was failing, as Dr. McNeal had implied that it almost certainly would.

7

Sam Hunter was finishing his glucose tolerance test when Helen Foucald came into her office. Through the door leading to the main laboratory, she could see that a blood specimen was being taken from his veins by one of the technicians and was shocked at the change that had come over the old man in the nearly two years since the last convocation.

At that time, old Sam had been full of vigor, dominating the trustees' meeting and riding roughshod over Greg's plan, until in the end the matter had been deferred to give him and his committee a chance to plan another building that might fulfill the provision in the will of The Clinic's founder that the statue of Christ in the administration rotunda must always be a central feature and at the same time would be within the cost limits Sam Hunter himself had insisted upon.

Helen went into the main laboratory while the technician was placing a small dressing over the puncture wound in Sam Hunter's arm where she had withdrawn the blood. Picking up his routing sheet, she noted that this was the last test requiring fasting that morning.

"Would you like to come into my office, Mr. Hunter?" she asked. "I'll have someone bring you coffee and toast there."

The idea of food perked the old man up somewhat. As he followed her into the office, he pulled one of his stogies from his pocket and bit off the tip before lighting it with a match from an old-fashioned matchbox.

"When you're used to ham and eggs at seven o'clock, you can get pretty hungry by ten," he grumbled.

"Sorry I can't find the ham and eggs." Helen took the seat behind the desk while the old man sprawled in a chair beside it. "But I'm beginning to understand your preference for them."

"Don't tell me the French have taken up that American habit."

"I just had breakfast at the airport. Dr. Alexander asked me to meet the banquet speaker for the convocation."

"The fellow from the World Health Organization?"

"Yes, Dr. Peter Carewe."

"That UN business is another waste of money. Spending it on people that don't have the gumption to try and help themselves is like pouring dollars down a rathole."

"Part of what is spent for the WHO is for your own protection, Mr. Hunter." Having defended Peter against Henry, Helen now found herself playing the same role against the Texas multimillionaire. "If we keep down disease in other countries, we'll have less of it coming in here—including a disease called communism."

"The money could be better used in Red-hunting and quarantine measures."

"Like keeping Mexicans from crossing the border?" Helen asked innocently, and the old man gave her a sharp look.

"As smart as you're good-looking, aren't you?" He sighed. "Wish I were forty years younger."

"That's the nicest compliment I've had in a long time. What are you going to do about a new clinic and hospital at the trustees' meeting on Saturday, Mr. Hunter?"

"Don't see any reason to change my mind from what we voted for two years ago," he said. "What's the sense of pouring out all the money Dr. Alexander wants to put into this location when people are living like pigs all around it?"

"They are the ones who need help the most, Mr. Hunter."

"You mean they're the ones that need to help themselves. When Henry Anders built The Clinic, this section was populated with working people. Women got out every morning to scrub the stone steps until they shone and it was a pleasure just to walk down The Parkway. Now what do you have? Slop and filth everywhere, bringing disease."

"Poverty's at the base of it, Mr. Hunter. Don't forget that."

"Haven't you heard? The government's outlawed that. All they're doing is throwing good money after bad and that's what I'm trying to keep from happening to this hospital. Rebuild it here and you'll have the same people flocking in for free medical care who've been putting the place in the red lately. Relocate it out in the suburbs and it will attract people that can help support it, the kind it ought to attract."

"The finest doctors in the country still apply for fellowships here," Helen reminded him. "Because they know they'll get the best training and experience in what you call a rathole that they can get anywhere."

"Maybe. But if the work here didn't have to be cluttered up with taking care of so many people from the slums, it would be more efficient."

"I've been told that the first Dr. Anders decided to build here because he wanted to provide a place where poor people could come without too much hardship."

"That was when the people in the neighborhood were honest working folks who took pride in what they were doing, not a bunch of loafers." The toast and coffee arrived just then and Sam Hunter tackled it with some of his vigor. "That's the trouble now, Doctor, people want everything handed to them on a silver platter without working to get it. Anything worth having is worth working for."

"But sometimes disease doesn't wait."

"Oh, some soft-hearted do-gooder is always around to bleed over people. Most of those who live around here could work if they were willing to get a little dirt on their hands. What has all the money the poverty program's been dumping into places like this done anyway? Paying high-school dropouts sixty-five dollars a week to finish school so they can become typists that don't even know how to spell cat? Or training waitresses to spill soup and leave tables dirty?"

"The slum dwellers could be taught new technical skills."

"Taught! You can't teach them anything."

"Perhaps nobody has tried hard enough."

"It's not the place of The Clinic Foundation to do that. How can I go to my business friends and tell them I want money to build a new hospital in the middle of a neighborhood that's practically a pigsty? They'd laugh in my face."

"Slums can be changed. I could show you where it's already beginning to happen, Mr. Hunter, if you'll take the time to go with me."

"To some block where OEO—if that's what you call it—has poured in a million dollars to create a showplace?"

"The OEO financed several health centers but the people have done the rest themselves—the people and the landlords."

"I read about that, too."

When Sam Hunter jumped from his chair and went to the window, Helen wondered for a moment if she had baited him too far. Not only might his opposition to Greg Alexander be heightened by her arguments, but he could have a stroke, too, judging by the angry pulsing of the torturous artery in his left temple.

"What's that building down there?" he asked suddenly, and Helen came over to the window to join him.

"Where?"

"What looks like a new addition to the experimental laboratory. We haven't authorized building anything here since the last trustees' meeting."

"That's the new hyperbaric chamber—part of the setup for experimental surgery."

"Hyperbaric?" The old man frowned. "Isn't that some foolishness about pumping up an operating room like a tire?"

"The word means 'high pressure,' Mr. Hunter. Dr. Alexander is very—"

"Did he have that building put up when we already turned down a plan of his that included one of those things two years ago?"

"The building was erected last year; I believe it was financed by a grant from the National Institute of Health."

"The government?"

"Yes. But I understand that Greg—Dr. Alexander—paid for much of the equipment himself."

"I'm going to call a special meeting of the board Friday afternoon to look into his actions," the old man snapped. "If he wants to remain an employee of The Clinic—"

"I'm sure Greg Alexander does want to remain an employee—as you so quaintly put it—of The Clinic, Mr. Hunter." Helen's voice was biting. "But if he knuckles under, don't think it's because he's afraid of you or the board. It will only be because he wants to keep a top-flight medical institution where the people who need it most live. If you had known the first Dr. Anders as well as you claim to, you'd know that was his dream, too."

ii

Dr. David Connor did his job well. By ten o'clock bets were being taken in the quarters of the resident house staff on Greg Alexander's chances of selling his new plan for an automated hospital and clinic to the trustees at the end of the week. Odds on Greg dropped sharply when the grapevine also carried the news that Sam Hunter, looking more dour than ever while having his annual regular checkup, had stormed angrily out of Helen Foucald's office earlier that morning, and was demanding a special meeting of the Board of Trustees to censure Greg.

As for the subject of the wagers, Greg was showing Peter Carewe, who had come over to the hospital to say hello, the effects in experimental animals of the high concentrations of oxygen achieved in the hyperbaric chamber, after experimental infection with anerobic—oxygen-hating—bacteria, as opposed to ordinary organisms which thrived in an atmosphere of oxygen. Earlier experiments had given striking results but he had insisted on running a second series to verify the first.

In the Laboratory of Experimental Surgery adjoining the old surgical building, Greg looked across the small table where Bob Johnson was autopsying a rabbit which had been used in the experiment. The animal had been killed moments before, painlessly with an injection of Sodium Pentothal.

"You can see that hyperventilation with oxygen under pressure inhibits bacterial growth *in vivo* as well as it does *in vitro*," he told Peter Carewe. *In vivo* meant inside the living body, while *in vitro* meant in laboratory cultures or in chemical experiments.

"A series of one case?" The doctor from WHO raised his eyebrows slightly; it was a standing joke in medical schools that students often came to weighty conclusions on insufficient evidence.

"An omen perhaps. Naturally, we'll repeat the experiment until we know for sure."

"Helen was telling me about your heart-lung transplant case having pups," said Peter. "Congratulations, Greg."

"We got in that murderer who was almost killed on the express-way last night, Dr. Alexander," said Bob Johnson. "Herb Partridge asked me to see him about an hour or so after Letty had her pups, but there was nothing vascular or thoracic involved."

"I didn't even see the papers or hear the news this morning," said Greg. "What happened?"

"This guy had already killed a couple of times and was making his getaway after holding up a tavern when he took the wrong ramp. The police say he's been in prison most of his life and was headed for the gas chamber before he escaped."

"Was he badly injured?" There was a sudden intensity in Greg's voice.

"Almost decapitated, according to the paper," said Peter Carewe.

"Herb Partridge did a laminectomy last night," Bob Johnson added. "Two cervical vertebrae were destroyed and the spinal cord was severed. About the only things functioning in him are the brain and the heart, but they're pretty well cut off from any nerve connection to the rest of the body."

"Did you say the cervical cord was severed?" Both of the men noticed the excitement in Greg's voice now.

"Cut clean in two in the lower cervical region," said the younger surgeon. "He's on a Mark IV respirator and Herb doesn't know whether or not he'll regain consciousness. But his heart is pumping away just like nothing had happened—" Bob dropped the scissors he was holding as the full import of what he was saying struck him.

"If he's going to die one way or another, he may be just what we're looking for," said Greg.

"What do you mean, Greg?" Peter asked.

"As a donor—for a transplant."

"But can you possibly find anyone in the time we have who's far enough gone to be the recipient?" said Bob.

"An ideal case may be in the hospital already," said Greg. "Dave Connor was telling me about him at breakfast, a man who's had several coronaries and almost went out with a cessation early this morning."

"That must be the one Jim McNeal was talking about for a gas-jet dissection last night," said Bob. "But Jim told me at breakfast that he'd had a cessation and if the nurse on ICU hadn't happened to be watching his monitor when the ECG curve flattened out and got a Pacemaker on him in time, he'd have been gone for sure. Jim says he's real rocky still and his heart's failing."

"Which makes him all the more urgently in need of a new one," said Greg.

"If he lives as long as this spinal case does," Bob agreed. "But from what Jim said, it will be touch and go."

"As soon as you finish here, Bob, have the heart-lung pump checked out." Greg spoke from the doorway of the laboratory and Peter Carewe was close behind him.

"What about the heart-lung transplant you'd scheduled for tomorrow?" he asked. "I've been looking forward to that."

"Wouldn't you rather see a human transplant instead?"

"Of course."

"Maybe we can arrange that but we've got to work fast. I'm going to see Dave Connor; he's got to be convinced first."

iii

The door of apartment 8-A was opened by a pregnant young woman in a smock.

"I'm Mrs. Alexander from upstairs," said Jeanne. "May I come in for a moment, Mrs. Jackson?"

"Oh yes, Mrs. Alexander." The girl's smile was warm. "Please call me Mary—and don't look at this apartment. Little Keith is walking, so everything's topsy-turvy. My husband worships yours —but then I guess almost everybody does."

Everybody except me, Jeanne thought. *I only pray I'm not too late!*

The small living room was tastefully, though sparsely, furnished, as was the dining room visible through an archway.

"Keith's too much of a visionary for us ever to be rich," Mary Jackson apologized. "But I do try to buy nice things."

"I imagine vision is worth a lot to a creative person."

"Oh yes. I wouldn't want him anyway else—just as I'm sure you wouldn't want Dr. Alexander to change. All the nurses worship him."

"You were a nurse?"

"A supervisor across the street—until I got too big to get between the beds and the walls. Harriet and Bob Johnson talk about Dr. Alexander all the time. Bob says he's the finest surgeon in the world and Keith is just overjoyed to be working with him on the new Clinic plans."

"My husband has been busy and I haven't wanted to bother him, so I haven't seen them," said Jeanne. "Do you suppose your husband has a sketch around here?"

"They've been all over the place for a week—ever since Dr. Anders suggested the idea to him."

"Dr. Anders?" Jeanne asked, startled.

"Oh, my goodness!" Mary Jackson put her hand over her mouth. "That's supposed to be a secret, particularly from your husband."

"I'll keep the secret," Jeanne promised. "It's just that I didn't know Henry Anders was involved in this particular project."

"Dr. Anders saw this article about a new hotel in Atlanta; there's been a lot about it in some of the news magazines. They say it's all glass and just like outdoors, except that it's still closed in. Anyway, he thought something like that in the new Clinic would be a fine monument to his father and remembered that Keith had submitted some sketches two years ago." She smiled deprecatingly. "I'm afraid those were pretty far out, though; Keith was in a sort of avant-garde phase then. But when Dr. Anders brought the article to him, along with some other material about new trends in hospital construction, Keith took off like a rocket."

"Did Dr. Anders give any reason why he brought the sketches to your husband, instead of going through the building committee?" Jeanne asked.

"He said there was some tension between him and Dr. Alexander about the new hospital and he wasn't sure Dr. Alexander would look with favor on it if he knew the idea had been suggested by him." She gave Jeanne a quick look. "Is anything wrong, Mrs. Alexander?"

"I don't know. Did you say you have some sketches here in the apartment?"

"They're in the den; Keith uses it as a sort of studio here at home." She led Jeanne down a short hall to the door at the end. It opened into a smaller room containing a drawing table; sheets of drawing paper were scattered all over the place.

"This place is a mess, but I don't dare touch anything," Mary Jackson said. "Keith calls these fragmentary sketches his seeds."

The ideas represented by what had been called "fragmentary sketches" were brilliantly conceived, even daring, Jeanne saw; yet, for all their soaring grace, there was a practicality about them, too. Mary leafed through a pile of larger drawings on the table by the window and pulled one out. Placing it on the table, she switched on the overhead light to bathe it in brilliance.

What Jeanne saw there almost took her breath away.

Where others had sought to enclose the giant statue of Christ that was the central figure in the rotunda, Keith Jackson had some-how managed to create the illusion of separating it from all earthly attachments. Massive steel pillars at the corners supported the entire structure of a central tower composing the very heart of the building. The intensive care floors were arranged in the form of a U, with the open end facing The Parkway. Inside the U stood the statue, with floodlights bathing it from below and above, a visible symbol of everything The Clinic had stood for since its founder first conceived it.

"The central section, where the statue is located, has a glass roof three stories high," Mary Jackson explained. "The operating theaters, the admitting areas where the patients are brought in the night before surgery and the main laboratories are all underground. There are two floors of them, with the emergency entrance by way of a tunnel at the back."

"It's beautiful!" Jeanne cried. "Simply beautiful."

"Keith says Dr. Alexander flipped the first time he saw it. You can't see the floor detail too well in these sketches, but each wing is a separate unit with its own nursing station on every floor. That way, all sixteen rooms in each unit are visible from the nursing station, besides having their own closed-circuit television and the monitors that are used now for watching the vital functions. Being

98

a nurse, I guess I'm more enthusiastic about this than some other people might be."

"I was a nurse, too," said Jeanne, "though it's been quite a while ago."

"Then you can see how efficient this arrangement is compared to most hospitals. Keith says it's ten years ahead of the times."

"It may be more than that."

"The hospital wings where patients go after they leave the ICU tower are structured to give them the greatest freedom in looking after themselves, so much less personnel will be needed," Mary explained. "Keith hasn't worked out the details of that part yet, but they'll be very simple—actually, more like hotels. The central ICU tower is the one that caught his fancy."

"And mine," Jeanne agreed. "I've never seen anything like it."

"There's never been anything like it, Mrs. Alexander—at least not in hospital construction. Keith thinks that when it's finished, it's bound to upgrade the character of the whole neighborhood. He says even a slum landlord won't be able to look at that tower without wanting to make his own buildings better places for people to live."

"When you see it there in the sketch, you can believe he's right. Is this the drawing my husband saw?"

"It's the basic plan, but more of the details are drawn in on the sketch Dr. Alexander has in his office. He was so enthusiastic about it that he asked Keith to get a friend of his to run some traffic study patterns, so a few changes may have to be made later on. But this is so close to being final that whatever changes have to be made won't make any real difference in the eventual appearance of the structure."

"Then this plan is the one my husband will show to the trustees on Saturday?"

"We certainly hope so; Keith's been working night and day to get the drawings ready. He's even hired two extra draftsmen and he'll be a walking zombie himself by then from lack of sleep, but the whole thing should be in a form that will capture even a trustee's imagination."

"I hope so," Jeanne said fervently. "Thank you for showing it to me, Mary. You've been very kind."

99

"Surely Dr. Alexander must have spoken to you about it," said the architect's wife. "Keith says he never saw such a look of awe on a man's face as was on your husband's when he saw the sketches for the first time."

"I can understand that, now that I've seen it myself. Good-by."

"You won't mention Dr. Anders' connection with it?"

"I promise."

But as she was walking back to the elevator, Jeanne decided that nothing in her promise to Mary Jackson prevented her from finding out, from whatever source she could, just what mischief Henry Anders was up to now.

8

"You're out of your mind, Greg," said Dave Connor when the surgeon told him what he hoped to do for Guy Merchant.

"We've done more than a hundred dogs, Dave, most of them both heart and lungs. As Hans has said more than once, what difference is there between transplanting organs into dogs and putting new ones into human beings?"

"There's a helluva lot of difference." The cardiologist's voice always rose when he got excited. "A man's got a soul and a dog hasn't."

"Got any proof of that?"

"For Christ's sake, Greg, this is no place for theological discussions. I just don't think it's right to kill this poor devil before his time comes."

"How long will that be, the way he is now?"

Dave Connor shrugged. "A few days at most. He was already on the ragged edge when he had the attack of angina while he was doing his act last night in that joint where he and his wife were working."

"What does she do?"

"She's a stripper and still somewhat of a looker. Used to play the top houses in burlesque before they degenerated into the sort of grind houses they are today."

"She stayed with him then?"

"You never saw two more devoted people."

"And, therefore, more worth saving as two, not one."

"Don't try to sway me with sentiment!" Dave Connor snapped irritably. "I'm looking at the thing from the viewpoint of what's best for you."

"That's what I want you to forget, Dave."

"Have you even considered what undertaking a heart-lung transplant in an unsuitable case can do to your chances of getting the kind of new clinic and hospital you want out of that bunch of hard-headed businessmen who control the trustees?"

"Frankly, no."

"They'll say you only did it to impress them and that, if you don't have any better sense than to accept a poor risk and give The Clinic a bad name, you've got no business being in charge at all."

"I'm not in charge, you know."

"I don't know any such damn thing! Henry's only a front; without you, this place would fall apart. And right now a spectacular failure by you might be all that's needed."

"The Clinic survived old Dr. Anders' death."

"Only because you were here to carry on what he started."

"You're forgetting something important, Dave."

"What?"

"We all took an oath in our last year of medical school. Part of it says: *'So far as power and discernment shall be mine, I will carry out regimen for the benefit of the sick and will keep them from harm and wrong.'*"

Dave Connor flushed. "How many doctors today live strictly by those precepts?"

"You and I do. That's why you can't deny this man the chance to live that I may be able to give him, just because you're afraid I'm going to be blamed if I fail."

"But does it have to be now? When so many of your enemies are here at one time?"

"Lots of my friends are here, too? Don't forget that."

The cardiologist shrugged. "All right—as long as you understand what you're risking. What do you need to know in order to evaluate him for surgery?"

"Everything."

"Guy Merchant has had at least four coronary attacks and God knows how many episodes of anginal pain. Which means that his heart circulation hasn't been keeping up for probably more than a year and a lot of the muscle has been replaced by scar tissue. Last night he had a severe anginal attack but fortunately there was a doctor in the audience, with a medical bag in his car parked close to the theater. He gave Merchant Demerol and a vasodilator, so he escaped an actual block of the coronary vessels that time. But to show you what a ragged edge he travels on, this morning he had a real coronary."

"With the cessation?"

"Yes; even the monitor shows it now. Merchant's heart is in early failure, his liver is already starting to enlarge and we can hear some moisture at his lung bases. We're giving him the works, of course, to help his heart keep up the circulation. But our measures aren't taking hold, which means there just isn't much reserve left."

"Making him an ideal case for a transplant."

"Except for one thing."

"What's that?"

"He's got an advanced case of emphysema, too; been a heavy smoker practically all of his life. Right now we can hardly get enough oxygen into his lungs to keep him alive, because his vital capacity is curtailed from the emphysema. Maybe you can give him a new heart, if you can find one—"

"We may have one; that's what gave me the idea."

"Who?"

"The convict who was injured last night. He's a perfect physical specimen below his neck and all we need are his heart and lungs."

"But are you ready for an operation of that magnitude on a human being? There have been plenty of heart transplants, and a lot of failures. But the heart and the lungs—"

"I've got ten living dogs whose heart and lungs came from others in one piece, Dave. One had pups last night and we've even swapped from one dog to another and back again. Actually, the technique of heart-lung transplant is simpler than putting in the heart alone, because you have less blood vessels to suture."

"It's going to be a hell of a job explaining to Merchant's wife what you propose to do."

"We can't just stop with the wife; both of them have to know," said Greg. "Can Merchant stand it?"

"I guess so; he's sedated, but conscious. Do you want to talk to them now?"

"There's no point in arousing their hopes before I have permission to use the convict's organs when he dies. Will you go to them with me after I get the legal details straightened out?"

"Can't you just get permission from this convict?"

"Herb Partridge doesn't think Lawson will ever regain consciousness and the police still haven't been able to find any family. Which means I've got to go to court first."

"You're going way out on a limb, Greg," Dave Connor said doubtfully. "I wonder if I'm not a fool for going out there with you."

"Answer me one question: would you want me out on that limb if you were in Merchant's place?"

"Hell yes!"

"Then it's settled. I'll be in touch."

ii

Ed McDougal was sitting in Henry Anders' office when he came back from making rounds on his private patients about eleven o'clock. Henry didn't bother to see those on the open wards oftener than a couple of times a week. Bob Johnson and the other Senior Fellows on surgery could be counted on to take care of any patient who got into trouble. And by putting in an appearance on the wards two or three times a week, Henry could defend himself, if he had to, at the monthly review of cases during the regular staff meetings.

"Henry, old boy!" Ed pumped his hand. "How the hell are you?"

"Fine, Ed. How are things in Texas?"

"Couldn't be better."

"Getting rich, I suppose?"

"I'm getting my share—and not complaining. Who was that looker in the white coat I saw you talking to in the corridor just a bit ago?"

"You must mean Helen Foucald. She's head of our clinical laboratory."

"Been doing some experiments with her lately, Henry?"

"You know we've always been heavy on research here, Ed." Henry Anders smiled knowingly as he reached for a cigar.

"You're a dog, Henry! I don't know how you do it." Ed McDougal's voice became businesslike. "I was planning to get here last night and see Sam Hunter before he started his checkup, but the plane was late. Have you seen him yet?"

"No. I was planning to drop in on him at the Inn before I go home tonight."

"We'd better not let all that dough be going around without a guard," said the Texas surgeon. "Sam's not himself these days. Ted's marrying that wop girl from the circus shook him up."

"Did he really disinherit the boy?"

"Threw him out in the cold, I hear. Swears he's leaving every dime of Ted's inheritance to our new medical school down home and your Clinic. Now's the time for us to make our play, boy."

"What good will it do me? Dad's will expressly stated that I get the property, but only if The Clinic moves to another location."

"Then we'll move it. You still want my help with that little deal you were telling me about at the Southern Medical, don't you?"

"Of course."

"Well, I've been doing my part. You'll be surprised how many of the board I've talked to since then—and how many I've convinced that the new Clinic needs to be out on the Beltway." Ed leaned forward and jabbed his finger at the other surgeon. "What have you been doing, Henry?"

"I've got some pretty important people lined up for the syndicate to develop the property." Henry took a paper from his pocket and handed it to the Texas surgeon. "Take a look at this."

Ed McDougal read the list and nodded approval. "Between us, we'll put this thing through, Henry—and make ourselves rich into the bargain."

"We haven't settled how Sam Hunter's money is to be divided yet," said Henry Anders, and Ed McDougal gave the other surgeon a quick, suspicious glance.

"You wouldn't double-cross old Ed, would you, Henry? Maybe with some ploy of your own?"

"I've already got the ploy. The only question is how we divide what we can wangle out of Sam Hunter now."

"Building a new medical school costs a lot of money."

"So does building a new Clinic."

"How about a third for you and two thirds for my school?"

"That sounds fair." Henry had been hoping for a fourth.

"So what is this plan of yours?"

Henry Anders quickly sketched the stratagem upon which he had embarked by showing the hotel pictures to Keith Jackson. When he finished, Ed's eyes gleamed with frank admiration.

"It's perfect, Henry boy," he said. "Old Sam will be against the new plan simply because Greg wants it and that should be enough to torpedo the whole project by convincing the board that it can never be built without Sam's money. By the way, how much would the one Greg's planning now cost?"

"Keith Jackson's rough estimate is about twenty-eight million."

Ed McDougal whistled softly. "Built here, of course?"

"Yes."

"Out on the Beltway, where the land has already been offered, you wouldn't have the expense of tearing down the present buildings, or building around any of them to keep operating. That could lop off a couple of million, I would imagine."

"Nearly three, I've been told."

"Then old Sam's got plenty for both of us and some to spare." Ed held out his hand. "Check, partner, we're in business."

Henry Anders withheld his hand. "With one provision."

"What's that?"

"Greg Alexander is out."

"That may not be easy," Ed McDougal warned. "Greg's got a fine reputation—not just here but in the country at large."

"So make him professor of surgery in your new school."

"I've got that job sewed up for myself. Besides, you know as well as I do that he's turned down a half dozen professorships already."

"Then give him an endowed department of experimental surgery. You must have some millionaire friend in Texas who would like to have his name on such an institute."

"I could arrange that." Ed McDougal nodded slowly. "And Greg might bite—after he's slapped down hard by the trustees on Saturday."

"Make him bite," Henry Anders said bluntly. "Make him bite, or it's no deal."

"Why are you so anxious to get rid of Greg?"

"He robbed me of my birthright by persuading my father to leave The Clinic to a charitable foundation and I swore then to get even with him some day. This is my opportunity."

"It's a deal, but you'd better talk to that architect and make sure he doesn't get cold feet and compromise on his plan if Greg suggests cutting costs. Somewhere along the line, Greg's bound to realize he might have a chance to put the plan through by decreasing the cost, especially if it's as good as your description."

"I've got Jackson so sold on the idea of the new buildings as a monument to my dad that I don't think he'll accept any sort of compromise, even if Greg suggests it," Henry Anders assured the other surgeon. "Architects are creative people, like artists and writers. Jackson will fight for his brain child."

"We're both going to have to depend on that." Ed McDougal stood up. "I'll go out and find old Sam and see how he feels. What about his checkup?"

"It was due to begin here this morning, a couple of hours or so ago."

"That means he didn't have any breakfast."

"What difference does that make?"

"About all the pleasure left in life for Sam comes from eating. Just about now he should be fit to be tied, so I'll go drop a few hints that Greg is giving him the run-around. That should have about the same effect as a small atomic bomb."

iii

Jeanne Alexander and Claire Anders had agreed to have lunch in the motel coffee shop at noon to make final plans for the luncheon on Thursday for the wives of the Members attending the convocation. A leading dress shop was putting on a fashion show for the affair, fully cognizant that the wives of prosperous doctors were always a lucrative market for their merchandise.

"I've snagged something else that ought to interest these girls," Claire said over a salad and coffee.

"What's that?"

"A clinic on how to be a widow."

Jeanne started to laugh, then saw that Claire was serious. "Whatever gave you that idea?"

"A lot of 'em are going to be widows before many more years. Let's face it, my dear: our husbands have one of the highest death rates as a group in the male population."

"It still seems sort of disloyal to be anticipating it."

"Not disloyal, realistic. Most of these gals have a considerable vested interest in their husbands' careers. After all, a lot of them supported their men through residencies and fellowships."

"I did—they were some of the happiest years of our marriage."

"You're entitled to more than memories now and so are two thirds of those who'll be at the luncheon," said Claire. "Do you know that successful doctors and their wives have one of the highest divorce rates of any upper income group?"

"Maybe a divorce lawyer would be more appropriate for your clinic then."

"You've got a point there; the only trouble is that it's the husbands who jump over the traces. Did you hear about the Smiths?"

"No."

"A few months ago, Ed took up with this filly who's only nineteen—and him fifty-five if he's a day. He divorced Millicent and is shacked up with this child in an apartment, but one of these days he's going to get a hell of a shock when they're in bed together and she looks at him half asleep and says 'Daddy!'"

"Why, that's incestuous."

"Whatever that means, I guess it is—but getting back to this widow business, I've asked the trust officer of a bank I've got some stock in to give a clinic on widows. He's a handsome fellow and puts on a good show. Most of these women are going to outlive their husbands by ten years or so, if they escape a divorce, so they might as well go first class either way."

"You have a point there," Jeanne admitted.

"Think of all the medical marriages we know. How many women are suffering from the Doctor's Wife Syndrome?"

"You don't have to look far," said Jeanne soberly. "I've been a victim of it myself for some time now."

"Was that the trouble? I thought it might be the menopause."

"The pill would have taken care of that."

"But what do you have to feel unwanted about, Jeanne? Greg's the nicest man I know and everybody knows he's never looked at another woman. While Henry—well, surely you must have seen him coming and going from Helen Foucald's apartment."

"Well—"

"It's a very satisfactory arrangement—as I was telling Helen last night."

"You talked to her about it?" Jeanne was horrified.

"Why not? You'd better be glad you didn't marry Henry that time he was so hot after you."

"We only had a few dates," Jeanne protested. "Henry introduced me to Greg on one of them and after that I couldn't see anybody else."

"I guess that's another reason why Henry hates Greg so; I thought it was all because the old man liked Greg so much."

"You really thinks he hates Greg?"

"My husband is an easy hater," said Claire. "I talked to Henry's old nurse once and she said that even as a child he'd never let anyone else play with his marbles."

"Aren't you being hard on him?"

"I know Henry better than anybody else could. You see, Dr. Anders wanted more out of his son than Henry could provide, things like intelligence and the sort of dedication that drove him to establish The Clinic. Greg has all of that, so Henry has to hate him."

"You ought to be a psychiatrist."

"Oh, Henry's not hard to figure out. He even hates me, because I've got things he knows he'll never have—money, breeding and class. But he likes having a woman with all those things, so he'll hang on to me."

"Did you know he's trying to drive Greg out of The Clinic?"

The startled look in Claire's eyes told Jeanne she had no part in whatever Henry Anders was plotting. "Even Henry wouldn't be dumb enough to try that," said Claire. "Whatever gave you that idea?"

"I think he hopes to get the trustees to vote down Greg's plans for The Clinic a second time on Saturday. After that sort of a slap in the face, even Greg would have to react, probably by leaving The Clinic."

"That would be almost the only way Henry could attack him," Claire said thoughtfully. "What I can't understand is why Henry would be such a fool. He always was a little paranoiac, it's true, but this could really be serious. If he drives Greg out, The Clinic will begin to fall apart. Half the staff would resign in less than six months."

"Maybe that's what he wants. Then the property will be his under the terms of his father's will."

"The conniving bastard!" said Claire. "He started to tell me something last night about Greg, but he was all excited and something else came up." She lowered her voice. "But if this new plan is everything you say it is, the trustees might just be as taken with Keith Jackson's sketches as Greg and you apparently are, which would solve the problem."

"Sam Hunter's apparently the key to the whole thing," Jeanne explained. "Ed McDougal's up here to keep Sam Hunter's money for his medical school. He's joined forces with Henry."

"How did you learn all this?"

"Hannah and I had breakfast together this morning—accidentally."

"How is Neiman-Marcus' favorite customer?"

"Jittery, if you ask me. I think she's afraid Ed may divorce her for another woman; at least she talked about it almost all the time we were together."

"The Doctor's Wife Phobia," said Claire. "As I remember Ed, Hannah's got good reason to worry. He always was a woman-chaser and, with those black Irish good looks of his, plenty of them are willing to be caught."

"I don't think it's Ed that Hannah's worried about. It's losing the income and position he's given her. I gather that he lets her spend money like water."

"Hannah's a fine-looking broad and a man like Ed McDougal

would get a lot of satisfaction out of seeing his wife in the best. But how did she happen to let on about the Sam Hunter business?"

"Apparently she thinks Greg has lost already and felt sorry for me. My guess is she thought I might warn him in time to accept defeat gracefully."

"Which he'd never do, so Henry thinks he'll win either way." Claire was dead serious now. "If the trustees decide to move The Clinic at Saturday's meeting, Henry will be rich and independent of me. And if they leave it here and turn down Greg's plan, he'll be rid of your husband. Either way, we've got to stop him."

"You really don't have to get involved, Claire."

"I'm involved already. Once Henry's rich, I could be replaced by a young filly. It isn't a very pleasant thought, Jeanne."

"I'm sorry to be the one who gave it to you."

"You did me a favor," Claire said briskly. "If Henry and I were divorced, I would have to find myself a younger man and that's never satisfactory for very long. Henry would be in the same fix, though you couldn't get him to admit it. One woman isn't enough for him yet, so he'd take a young girl right away. But once his age starts to catch up with him—and it's already beginning—she'd probably shed him, too, and take him to the cleaners in the process."

Claire got to her feet and began to gather up purse and gloves. "Henry and I are good for each other and I guess, at that, we're more honest than a lot of married couples, who just go on hating until one of them gets enough worked up to have a fatal heart attack. Thank God it's usually the man."

iv

It was past noon when Greg Alexander and Dr. Philip Dennison, the country medical examiner, were ushered by a secretary into the chambers of Judge Paul Sutler. The judge was a handsome man in his sixties, and an old friend of Greg's.

"You gentlemen are making me have a sandwich and a glass of milk for lunch during the noon recess of court." He gestured to the tray the secretary had just put down on his desk. "What is so important that you want me to get indigestion?"

"Dr. Alexander came to me this morning with a request, sir," said the medical examiner. "I don't feel that I can honor it without an order from you."

"What is the request, Greg?" the judge asked.

"I want your authority to remove the heart and lungs from a dead man."

"Couldn't Phil do that at autopsy? I take it that this is a coroner's case."

"It's Frank Lawson, the man injured in the expressway accident last night."

"The escaped prisoner who murdered the salesman during his getaway?"

"Yes."

"Then he's dead?"

"Not yet—but none of us at the hospital think he can last very long with a severe head injury and the spinal cord severed in the lower neck region."

"I suppose you want to do a transplant?"

"Yes—a double one."

"What's that?" the judge asked with a frown.

"The heart and lungs in one operation."

"Sounds like a large order. Who's the patient?"

"His name is Guy Merchant. He's had a number of coronary attacks, the last one this morning, and his heart is slowly failing. Dave Connor doesn't think he can live more than a few days longer—"

"Without a new heart and lungs?"

"Yes."

"This is a tricky legal problem." Judge Sutler rubbed his chin thoughtfully. "Have you tried to get permission from Lawson?"

"He hasn't regained consciousness and our neurosurgeons don't believe he will."

"What about relatives?"

"The police haven't been able to locate any," said Dr. Dennison. "Apparently Lawson was a loner."

"And a condemned criminal who has been identified twice as a murderer," Greg said.

"That's the trickiest point of all," said the judge. "Undoubtedly, the state would put Lawson in the gas chamber, if he could ever be brought to trial."

"I'm afraid that's never going to happen," said Greg.

"I'm dealing only in hypothesis now," Judge Sutler explained. "Until Lawson's in prison and a death order has been signed, we have no right to become his executioner."

"This isn't an execution," Greg protested. "I fully intend to take measures to keep him alive as long as possible."

"Won't that defeat your purpose, if the patient you're trying to help is going downhill?"

"It's a risk we shall have to take," said Greg. "In organ transplantation there are two major problems: first, preserving the donor organs until they can be connected up to the circulation of the recipient. And second, overcoming the tendency of the body to reject any tissue that isn't its own."

"Can you be sure this won't happen with Lawson's heart?"

"Not entirely," Greg admitted. "But his blood is type O—the universal donor—which is in our favor. We're running some other tests now and should have at least preliminary results by the latter part of the afternoon, but we also have ways of combating the rejection phenomenon, if it does occur."

"How about the technical difficulties of the operation?"

"My assistant and I have already done more than a hundred transplants in dogs, nearly half of them involving both heart and lungs. Most of them are doing well. One of our first cases had pups last night."

"It's an impressive record."

"We're not worrying about the surgical technique," Greg assured him. "All we ask is that the heart and lungs we use are in the best possible condition, which seems to be true with Lawson."

"Greg and I have discussed the question of what standards to use in determining death, sir," said the medical examiner. "We both agree that the three usual criteria—absence of heartbeat, absence of respiration and absence of brain activity, must be observed."

"I wonder if they're enough from the moral viewpoint," said Judge Sutler. "What worries me is that, if you can take Lawson's heart out of his body, put it into someone else, and start it to beating again, it couldn't possibly have been dead in the first place."

"We know that tissues die at different rates," said the medical examiner. "But with the heart no longer functioning, death of all tissue is inevitable. Greg and I agree that absence of any evidence of brain activity, as determined by the electroencephalograph, should be the ultimate test in this case."

"Suppose the heart stops first? Won't you lose valuable time while you wait for the electroencephalograph to tell you the brain is dead?"

"We can get around that by connecting a pump-oxygenator, such as we use to maintain circulation during open-heart operations, to Lawson's heart immediately after it stops beating," Greg explained. "That way, we can keep the blood flowing and maintain an adequate supply to the heart through the coronary arteries."

"In other words, you would be keeping part of a dead man alive until you could transfer that part to another person?"

"That's it exactly," said Greg.

"And even though Lawson will be legally dead before you remove his heart and lungs, you will take every measure to see that those particular organs still live?"

"Yes."

"That's what I mean by a moral question," said the judge. "If you can take a living vital organ from a man's body, aren't you in essence committing murder?"

"Not when the organ you remove is the only part of him that could be considered alive," Greg argued. "Actually, though, I believe the moral question solves itself."

"How?"

"My obligation as a physician is to keep a human being alive as long as my abilities and the resources at my disposal will allow. In this case, I shall be going one step farther than is ordinarily the case by keeping Lawson's heart alive even after the rest of his body is dead."

"There's a nice point of something there," the judge admitted wryly, "but I'm not quite sure what it is."

"As a criminal, Lawson's life belongs to the state," said Greg. "Surely, if the state has a right to *take* his life, it also has a right to *give* part of it to save another life."

"You've got an eloquent argument there. Let me think about

this for an hour or two and telephone you my decision. Can you wait that long?"

"I think so."

"Call me earlier if things start moving too fast."

v

It was past one o'clock when Greg Alexander came to the intensive care unit following his meeting with Judge Sutler and Dr. Dennison. He examined Guy Merchant carefully, studied the chart for some time, then came over to where Georgia Merchant was sitting. She had seen him briefly that morning when he had first examined Guy, but he had not talked to her then. Now he sat down beside her.

"I'm Dr. Alexander, Mrs. Merchant," he said.

"The heart surgeon?"

"I do the cardiac surgery here—as well as other things."

"There's no hope for Guy, is there, Dr. Alexander? I mean, he's beyond being helped by an operation?"

"On the contrary," said Greg. "If you'll take a walk with me, I think I can show you something you'll be interested in seeing."

Outside the building, he guided her to the Laboratory of Experimental Surgery and the animal house in its attached building beside the newly built hyperbaric chamber. It was feeding time when they entered, and the barking of dogs anticipating the meal greeted them.

"They sound happy," said Georgia doubtfully.

"Contrary to what you might have heard, they are treated very well."

"Is this where—you experiment?"

"This is the Laboratory of Experimental Surgery. I want you to see a special case over here in the corner."

Letty lay quietly with her puppies nestling against her, nursing happily. "This is our prima donna, Letty," he said. "Last night she gave birth to these puppies."

"They're adorable."

"Would you believe that six months ago Letty received a transplant of both a new heart and a new set of lungs?"

115

Georgia caught her breath suddenly, for his purpose in bringing her here had become apparent. "But the operation has never—"

"Half the dogs here have had successful heart-lung transplants—some more than once—Mrs. Merchant. You can see for yourself how healthy they are."

"But that's different from humans."

"Not as far as the technique of the operation is concerned. We worked it out here on dogs and our rate of success is surprisingly high."

"I—" Georgia suddenly felt a little faint. "I think we'd better go outside."

"Of course," he said. "I had no wish to upset you, but I thought it might help you to see Letty."

Outside the building, Georgia took a cigarette from her bag. When her hand trembled so she couldn't get the lighter to work, Greg held it for her and after a few moments, she was composed again.

"Are you asking my permission to experiment on my husband, Dr. Alexander?" she asked.

"We're no longer experimenting, Mrs. Merchant." Greg opened the door to the corridor and the elevator leading to the intensive care unit. "My assistants and I have been doing heart-lung transplants successfully for more than two years now."

"But only on dogs."

"The technician who looks after our laboratory animals says the *real* pioneering was with dogs. When we operate on our first human, we will merely be repeating a procedure we have done many times before."

"But it still wouldn't be the same."

"I'm not going to tell you that operating upon a human being will not be more of a strain than upon an animal, even an animal for whom you have a great deal of affection, as we have for Letty and the others. But the actual technique of the operation is the same; the only difference is that in dogs we have been able to work out and solve many of the problems that caused some of the earlier heart transplants to fail."

"But operating on a dog must be simpler than on a human."

"Actually, it's more difficult. The organs of a dog are much smaller and its tissues, much thinner."

"Has the rejection problem really been solved, Doctor?"

"Not completely, but we've come a long way with that, too, in the past several years."

"Surely transplanting both the heart and the lungs is much more difficult than the heart alone."

"Strangely enough, it isn't," he said. "You see, the lungs have a circulation of their own: a large artery carries blood from the right side of the heart to the lungs and a similar vein brings it back to the left side of the heart. In a heart transplant, we connect the heart to the body circulation and also to the lungs, but when transplanting both heart and lungs, we don't disturb the circulation of the lungs at all. This cuts the actual suturing almost in half."

"I suppose you have a donor, or you wouldn't even consider surgery for Guy."

"We do have—an ideal one in fact."

"May I ask who it is?"

"An accident case that was admitted last night. He was seriously injured when a truck struck his car on the expressway."

"Has he given permission?"

"This patient is expected to remain unconscious; that's why I couldn't talk to you earlier. An hour ago, I made application to Judge Sutler for permission to use his organs. The judge has promised to give me his decision this afternoon."

"Why from a judge?"

"The man is Frank Lawson."

"The murderer?" Her eyes filled with horror.

"He's a fine physical specimen—and young."

"You're very sure of yourself, aren't you, Dr. Alexander?" Georgia's voice was not without a tinge of bitterness. "Arranging for the transplant before you consulted me."

"I was considering your feelings and those of your husband, Mrs. Merchant. If I had told you when I was here earlier that I was ready to transplant as soon as a suitable donor was found—and you had agreed—the period of waiting could have been very hard on you. Especially since your husband's condition has already begun to deteriorate."

Georgia drew a deep breath; it was hard to believe this whole thing wasn't really a nightmare. "This decision is a heavy responsibility for me, Doctor."

"Nobody knows that better than I do," said Greg. "I make decisions almost like it nearly every day."

"But not for the person who is dearest to you in the world."

"No. That would make a considerable difference."

"If Guy is deteriorating already, how do you know he will live until the operation can be performed?"

"We don't know," he admitted. "But when the time comes to act, there will be no time for indecision, so I must have all the details arranged beforehand."

Georgia turned to look out the window, but saw nothing of the chill February sky outside. Every instinct urged her to leave matters entirely in the hands of this quiet surgeon, who was so courteous, considerate and confidence-inspiring. Her indecision came not so much from any doubt of his ability or his evaluation of Guy's condition, as from her own guilt over the feeling she had experienced that morning, when, even while the desperate battle for Guy's life had been going on in the room, her prayer had been that those efforts might fail.

If she gave her permission and the operation succeeded, she knew she could never forget that, had her prayer been answered, she would have condemned Guy to his death. Then it suddenly occurred to her that Greg Alexander himself might be the answer to her prayer, for, in a way, he possessed in his skilled fingers the power to turn death into life. Turning to face him, she asked, "What chance does Guy really have of your operation being a success? Fifty-fifty?"

"With luck, more than that. Our mortality with dogs is now down to around twenty-five per cent."

"And without the operation?"

"Dr. Connor and Dr. McNeal tell me death is certain in a few days, perhaps sooner. But even if it wasn't, the emphysema in your husband's lungs wouldn't allow him to live very much longer. The time would come soon when he would need oxygen continuously."

"I don't have the right to decide!" she cried. "You'll have to ask Guy."

"I was going to do that in any event."

"Don't try to high-pressure him, please, Dr. Alexander. Just tell him what the situation is and let him make the decision for himself."

"Why don't you come into the room with me? Then your conscience can't hurt you, no matter what happens."

"I might break down and upset Guy," she said doubtfully.

"I'm a pretty good judge of character, Mrs. Merchant. Shall we go in?"

"Hello, ducks!" Guy greeted her with the English term of endearment that had meant so much to them through the years. "Are you all right?"

"I'm fine, darling," said Georgia. "Dr. Alexander has something to talk to you about."

Guy Merchant listened silently while Greg summarized in a few words the procedure he proposed to follow with the heart-lung transplant.

"I've known ever since I felt my pulse stop this morning that only a miracle could help me, Doctor," he said when Greg finished. "Perhaps you're that miracle."

"I can't guarantee it," Greg warned.

"It's an all-or-none shot, so I've got nothing to lose. Georgia will sign the permit."

"We shall move you to the operating room sometime before the surgery actually begins," Greg told him. "So don't be alarmed when they come for you."

Guy smiled. "I already know what it is to die, Dr. Alexander. And it's not half as bad as you might think."

vi

Ed McDougal caught Sam Hunter as the oilman was having his last X-ray around one o'clock. The two picked up Henry Anders at his office and were lunching at a corner table in the motel restaurant across the street from The Clinic.

"Why didn't you let me know Dr. Alexander had built that new building, Henry?" Sam Hunter demanded.

"It didn't cost us anything." Henry Anders flushed, for the older man's tone was that of a parent reprimanding a child.

"What building is this?" Ed McDougal asked.

"Greg managed to wheedle enough funds out of the National Institute of Health to build a hyperbaric chamber," Henry explained.

"Without permission from the board?" Ed was quick to recognize a possible break.

"No outlay from Clinic funds was required," said Henry. "Apparently Greg didn't seem to think it was necessary to get permission."

"I never could see any use in wasting money operating on dogs anyway," said Sam Hunter. "Isn't the budget for the laboratory going to rise with all that new equipment in operation?"

Henry Anders tried to remember some details of the budget but couldn't; he'd always left such things to Greg. Sensing that Henry didn't know the answer to the question, Ed McDougal stepped into the breach.

"Operating a hyperbaric chamber is bound to cost money," he assured the oilman.

"Do you have one at your hospital down home, Ed?"

"We looked into it some time ago and decided against it."

"Why?"

"Cost, mainly." It wasn't the truth, but he couldn't let the opportunity go by to prejudice Sam Hunter further against Greg. "Besides, oxygen under pressure hasn't turned out to be the panacea a lot of people predicted it would be when they first started using it abroad."

"You mean Dr. Alexander has been experimenting with something that's not accepted medically—something foreign?" Sam Hunter rose to the bait, just as Ed had hoped he would.

"It's not exactly that," he temporized.

"What is it then?"

"In some experiments"—he was careful to emphasize the word— "enough good results have been shown to justify the expense."

"What percentage?" Sam Hunter insisted.

"I can't give you the exact figures, sir, but I do know the results have been disappointing in many cases."

"You should have stopped Alexander before he spent all that money, Henry," said Sam Hunter.

"But it was government funds, sir."

"And whose pockets did they come from?" The old man pushed his coffee cup aside and bit off the end of a cigar. "That's the trouble with the country now: everybody wants a handout from the federal government. And the damned fools we send to Congress are always ready to give it to them to get votes."

"It's got to stop somewhere; you're right about that, sir." Ed McDougal carefully fueled Sam Hunter's anger.

"It's going to stop here, as far as this particular thing is concerned," the old man snapped. "Do either of you have any idea how much it takes each year to run that experimental laboratory?"

"I don't remember the exact cost, but it's considerable," said Henry Anders.

"Enough to put The Clinic in the black if it was out of the budget?"

"Possibly." Following the lead Ed had given him, Henry wasn't letting a chance slip by to prejudice Sam Hunter further against Greg.

"We'll have to stop that waste, too!" The old man banged his fist on the table so hard that a cup bounced off to the floor. "You can bet the trustees will have something to say about it."

Bill Remick, the Washington roentgenologist, had been watching the three from a table not far away. And since Sam Hunter made no particular attempt to lower his voice, a good portion of their conversation had come to his ears.

"From what I can hear, Ed and Henry are doing a hatchet job on Greg over there," he said to Abe Lantz, who was with him.

"It's no secret that Ed wants to corral a lot of old Sam's dough to build a medical school in his own hometown, where there's a small university," said the internist. "And of course Henry opposes Greg whenever he gets a chance—for a lot of reasons."

"Don't the damn fools know this place would fall apart without Greg?"

"Henry would probably like to see that happen. Then The Clinic property would go to him under the old man's will and there are rumors of a new condominium project that would make Henry a millionaire."

"Where did you hear all this?"

"The rumors have been floating around for some time. You can't pin anybody down, but I'd be willing to bet that a lot of our brother Aesculapians here in Baltimore are in on the deal."

"Trustees, too?"

"Could be. They're as hungry as anybody else for a fast buck."

"Then it's time somebody defended Greg." Bill Remick got to his feet. "Pay the check when it comes, Abe. I'll fix it with you later."

"What are you going to do?"

"Ed and Henry have been working old Sam over from one side. It looks to me like it's time to give him a little going over from the other."

"He'll slap you down—hard."

"Sam Hunter may have a billion dollars, but his colon's as full of diverticula as everybody else's," said the roentgenologist. "When you see them in the fluoroscope the way I do, you can't tell a millionaire from a pauper."

"Hello, Mr. Hunter," Bill Remick said cordially as he approached the other table. "Couldn't help hearing you discussing the fine work Greg Alexander has been doing here with the hyperbaric chamber."

"What are you talking about, Bill?" Ed McDougal demanded.

"You must know how valuable oxygen under pressure is, Ed," said the X-ray man. "Or Henry should, if you don't. Some of the major work in that field has been done right here by Greg Alexander."

"I let the section heads run their services pretty much by themselves, as long as everything is satisfactory," said Henry.

"Glad to hear you approve of Greg's results then," said Remick blandly. "I really didn't believe the rumors I've been hearing of friction between you two."

Remick turned to the oilman. "I don't imagine you read medical journals, Mr. Hunter, so you wouldn't realize that Greg Alexander has made The Clinic the most important center for research in heart and lung transplantation in the country. I happen to know he has less trouble getting National Institute of Health grants for his work than any other clinic in the country."

"From what I hear, he's wasting money," Sam Hunter growled.

"Then you haven't been listening to people who are knowledgeable in the field of heart surgery." Remick's voice was suddenly sharp.

"What do you know about it, Bill?" Ed McDougal demanded. "Your field is X-ray."

"As it happens, I've been working with the National Institute of Health on cineradiography," said the roentgenologist. "That's X-ray motion pictures, mainly of the circulation, Mr. Hunter. And I know that nobody is more respected at NIH than Greg Alexander, especially considering the difficulties he works under."

"What do you mean—difficulties?" Sam Hunter asked.

"Surely Henry told you Greg runs the experimental laboratory with the smallest budget of any department in the hospital. Most of the money for his work actually comes from federal grants and private gifts from people who realize how important it is."

"What about this new building?"

"The hyperbaric chamber?"

"Yes."

"I helped get National Institute of Health funds for that—after the Board of Trustees was so short-sighted as to vote down the plans for the new buildings including it two years ago."

"But it's no good."

"Who told you that?" Bill Remick asked.

"Henry here—and Ed."

"Really, Henry." Bill Remick's eyebrows were raised in mock surprise. "Do you mean to tell me you let Mr. Hunter believe Greg's managing to build the hyperbaric chamber isn't the most important thing that's happened at The Clinic lately? Even you"—Remick's voice suddenly cut like a surgeon's scalpel—"must know how important it can be in transplant operations to have the donor organ saturated with oxygen. Some people believe this technique alone is going to open up an entirely new field of surgery."

"He still didn't get the approval of the trustees," Sam Hunter said doggedly.

"Board action isn't required for expenditures where other sources of funds are available—and they were here," said Bill Remick. "I think you're being sold a bill of goods, Mr. Hunter. If you ran your business this way, you wouldn't have those millions of yours very long."

9

Greg was scheduled to open the program of the first professional meeting of the Convocation of the Members of The Clinic at three o'clock Wednesday afternoon with a paper on hospital automation. At fifteen minutes before the hour, he, Bob Johnson, Herb Partridge, the neurosurgeon, and Dave Connor stopped by the room in the intensive care unit where Frank Lawson had been taken from the operating suite the night before. The respirator was clicking along steadily, inflating the wounded man's lungs sixteen times a minute with oxygen from a large tank beside the bed.

"His pulse is ninety to a hundred," the nurse who had been sitting beside the bed reported. "Blood pressure's one hundred over sixty."

"No spontaneous respiratory movements?" Greg asked.

"None at all, Dr. Alexander."

Dave Connor listened to the unconscious man's heart, then took the tips of the stethoscope from his ears, folded up the tubing and stuck it in the side pocket of his long white coat.

"The heart's functioning well," he said. "Probably too well for your purposes, Greg."

"Especially with Merchant going into heart failure."

"What do you think will cause death here eventually, Dr. Connor?" Bob Johnson asked.

"There's no reason for his heart to stop beating, unless something outside the heart itself makes it stop," said the cardiologist. "That's all I can tell you."

"I think death will come from the brain," said Herb Partridge. "It must have been pretty badly damaged for him to remain unconscious so long. Besides, I had to ligate both vertebral arteries,

125

so the cerebral blood supply is lessened. And with spinal fluid leaking from the neck wound, there's always the probability of an ascending infection around the upper cord to the brain itself."

"Merchant can't last very long, either," said the cardiologist. "His liver is enlarging steadily and the moisture at the bases of his lungs is increasing, which means that his heart is waging a losing battle in spite of all the help we're giving it with digitalis and oxygen. He could use a new heart right now, Greg. Too bad you can't give him this one."

A high-pitched beep came from the small pocket sentinel which, like all of the hospital staff, Greg carried in the breast pocket of his long-skirted white coat. He moved at once to the nurse's desk and picked up the telephone.

"There's an outside call for you, Dr. Alexander," said the operator. "Just a moment, please."

Judge Sutler's voice came on the line. "You can go ahead in the Lawson case, Greg," he said, "but I must insist that the medical examiner be present to certify death."

"I'll call Dr. Dennison as soon as we take Merchant to the operating room," Greg promised. "Thank you for your promptness, sir."

"I'm dictating an official order for your protection. We'll mail it to you tonight. How is your patient?"

"He's losing ground, sir. I don't know whether he will outlast Lawson or not."

"I hope he does. Good luck with the operation."

"The judge has given his permission for us to use Lawson's organs," Greg told Bob Johnson and the others when he came back into Frank Lawson's room. "It's almost three o'clock, so I'd better get down to the lecture hall to open the convocation. Have you got the slides, Bob?"

"Right in my pocket, sir," said the younger surgeon. "I'll go down and check out the projector before the convocation officially begins."

A stream of doctors was pouring across The Parkway from the motel to the hospital entrance for the opening session of the convocation when Bill Remick spotted Peter Carewe's tall form among them. He called to the public health man to wait for him; the two had been friends during the fellowship days but had rarely seen each other since.

"How do you stand on this question of moving The Clinic, Bill?" Peter asked.

"I'm agin it," said the roentgenologist. "Who's been propagandizing you?"

"John Teague mentioned it when I had dinner with him in New York last week and I spoke to Jeanne Alexander on the phone for a few minutes before I left the motel. She thinks a movement is underway to dump Greg at the same time, but that's hard to believe."

"I've been telling Greg that ever since the trustees' meeting two years ago." Bill Remick's voice was grim. "But you know how hard it is for Greg to think ill of anybody."

As they were entering the hospital, Peter Carewe glanced up at the massive statue in the rotunda. "I guess if you had to pass that statue twice a day going and coming, it might influence your thinking."

"Particularly if you thought that way in the beginning," Bill Remick agreed as they turned into the corridor leading to the surgical lecture hall.

When the surgical section of the hospital had been built originally, some fifty years earlier, the main lecture room had been placed between two of the largest operating theaters for a definite reason. According to the custom prevalent at that time, cases presented to students at clinical sessions in the lecture room were then wheeled directly into one of the operating theaters. Merely by filing from the lecture hall into rows of seats arranged on one side of the operating theater, the students were then able to watch the actual operative procedure and witness the verification of the diagnosis made during the lecture presentation just preceding, or enjoy the discomfiture of the surgeon when his predictions turned out to be wrong.

The evolution of more sterile techniques, and particularly the rise in hospital infections, had completely changed the pattern of procedure, but had not changed the arrangement of the lecture room. The south wall still featured the tall windows originally designed to provide a maximum of sunlight for the examining area, a strip of open floor twenty feet wide across the end of the room beneath the windows, with a door on either side, which had originally opened into one of the two main operating theaters.

In the lecture hall itself, the seats rose in a steep incline until the back row was on a level with the third floor of the surgical building, enabling the occupants to look down directly upon the lecture area with only the limitations of their vision affecting their ability to observe the cases under discussion. Doors at the top of the incline gave access from above to the upper tiers of seats, while two passageways on either side led to the first-floor corridor.

More recently, the doors opening directly into the operating theaters had been blocked off and closed in order to prevent traffic through the area. But the doctors' lounge and scrub rooms for each of the main theaters still occupied the space underneath the incline where the seats were located.

In order to make the activities going on in the operating rooms visible to observers, small enclosed observation galleries had been built at the second-floor level in each of the two main operating theaters. But since they could contain only a few observers, closed-circuit television cameras had been installed more recently, at Greg's insistence, looking down upon the center of each of the two theaters. The activities there during surgery could thus be photographed by the cameras and carried to screens set well up on the walls on either side of the center podium. And merely by switching on the closed-circuit cameras, those in the lecture hall could watch closely the surgery being performed in either or both of the main operating theaters with no danger of contaminating the patients.

The lecture hall was almost filled with Members of The Clinic and staff, plus a few students, when Peter Carewe and Bill Remick came in and found seats. Around them the buzz of voices filled the room but, as yet, the space on the ground level contained only a podium with a microphone for the speakers and a desk and chair for the presiding officer. Above the desk and against the wall, was a screen so arranged that it could be raised or lowered by means of a switch beside the projector set into the middle of the second row of seats.

About five minutes before three, Henry Anders and Ed Mc-Dougal came in from one of the lower floors. Since he was going to preside at the opening session of the convocation, Henry went to the desk at the front while Ed climbed to a spot high up, calling greetings to friends as he sought a seat.

"Those two are working hand and glove," said Peter Carewe to Bill Remick. "And from the looks on their faces, they must think the world's their oyster."

"This particular oyster may not have the pearl they're expecting to find in it." Bill Remick surveyed the now almost packed rows with a swift glance before settling back in his seat. "A lot of the most famous names in American medicine are here and between them they can influence people with considerable amounts of money. If Greg can come up with the right sort of a structure to replace these old buildings and preserve the spirit of The Clinic, most Members will support him. It might just be that Ed Mc-Dougal and Henry Anders are betting on the wrong horse with Sam Hunter."

iii

At two minutes before three, Hans Werner pushed a wheeled cart into the open space at one side of the lecture room. On the cart, the brown and white spaniel named Letty lay upon a blanket; beside her was a carton loosely covered with a towel. Bob Johnson was checking out the projector, and, as he flipped the switch beside it, the screen slowly descended upon the wall behind the podium.

The clock on the back wall said one minute to three when Greg Alexander came in and took a seat near where Hans Werner was standing patiently beside the cart, soothing the dog lying upon it by scratching her head at the base of her ears. When the hands of the clock showed three, Henry Anders banged on the table sharply with a gavel and the room became silent.

"It is my pleasant task to welcome the Members of The Clinic to the twentieth biennial convocation," he announced. "I want to tell you how pleasant it is to see so many familiar faces once again. If my father were alive, I know it would have given him great pleasure to greet each of you personally, as I hope to do before the convocation ends at noon on Friday.

"I have been asked to invite all of you and your wives, sweethearts—or secretaries"—he waited for a guffaw of laughter to sweep the room—"to a cocktail party being given by Claire and myself with Hannah and Ed McDougal in the Falstaff Room at the Clinic Inn from five to seven this evening."

A wave of applause greeted the announcement.

"Believing that all work and no play may make jack, but also makes Jack a dull boy"—he paused briefly for the titter of appreciation—"we have scheduled no night sessions for the convocation, allowing each of you to entertain himself in whatever manner he chooses."

"Got any good telephone numbers, Henry?" somebody asked, and there was another round of laughter.

"I am pleased to announce that registration for the twentieth convocation has already exceeded any previous one, with more undoubtedly still to come," Henry continued. "Members of the Board of Trustees are reminded of our regular meeting on Saturday morning. Also, one member of the board has requested that the trustees meet on Friday at four P.M. to consider a special matter which will be placed before them by this trustee."

"So the battle begins," said Bill Remick to Peter Carewe. "They're not wasting any time."

Henry Anders paused, apparently waiting for some reaction to the announcement. When none came, he glanced at Greg, as if he expected an objection from him, but Greg was looking at his notes. Flushing angrily Henry whacked his gavel on the table to still the stir of conversation.

"The first paper on the program is by Dr. Gregory Alexander," he announced. "The subject is hospital and clinic automation."

Greg moved to the podium and, placing a folder he was carrying upon it, faced the audience.

"Before I start discussing the topic assigned to me," he said, "I wish to announce a change in the printed program sent to each of you in advance. Originally, we had scheduled an operative clinic tomorrow afternoon in which my assistant and I planned to transplant the heart and both lungs from one dog to another. In our hands, this procedure has now been successful a number of times, and one of our patients has been alive for more than a year. She shows every sign of good health, as I think you can see."

At his words, Hans Werner gently lifted the leash around Letty's neck and the spaniel stood up, wagging her tail.

"Actually," Greg added, "Letty went what might be called the second mile last night and produced even more convincing evidence that the heart and lungs we transplanted into her chest over a year ago are now functioning well." Reaching into the carton, he lifted two of the puppies in his hands and held them up, while Hans Werner took out two more as a ground swell of applause swept the room.

"Last night, two human patients were admitted to the hospital whose presence has caused me to change the program somewhat from that which had been announced." Greg handed the puppies to Hans, who put them into the carton and wheeled the cart from the room. "One is now in progressive heart failure from a severely damaged heart; the other is unconscious with a lacerated cervical cord and a severe brain injury. All of us are agreed that he cannot live, and, since he has no known relatives and is an habitual criminal known to have murdered a man during a recent robbery, I petitioned the court this morning for permission to remove his heart and lungs immediately after death and transplant them into the body of the coronary patient I mentioned—if he lives long enough for this to be possible. Until the decision is made one way or another, however, I must keep two operating teams in a constant state of readiness, so I have been forced to cancel the operative clinic previously scheduled for tomorrow afternoon."

The room was silent now, gripped by the drama in his words, as he continued: "We cannot, of course, tell just when, or if, it will be possible for us to perform this transplant. However, should it become possible, we have made arrangements to notify all of you at the Inn who might be interested in watching the procedure, which will be presented on closed-circuit television in this same room."

As calmly as if he had not just made the most dramatic announcement of the entire convocation, Greg opened the folder that held his paper. He did not notice when, high up near the top row of seats, a tall man with graying hair and heavy horn-rimmed glasses, who had been rapidly making notes on a stenographic pad, hurriedly left the room and headed for a booth outside the emergency room containing a phone marked: "Reserved for Police and Press."

iv

"My discussion of hospital and clinic automation will of necessity be rather brief," Greg began. "Most of the information was accumulated while preparing plans for a possible new set of clinic and hospital buildings as chairman of the building committee of the Board of Trustees. Two of the most advanced hospital plants being built today are undoubtedly those at the Georgetown University Medical Center in Washington and the University of Alberta in Canada. Together they represent a distillation of what is known about automation in hospital and clinic procedure throughout the world, at the moment. The subject is widening so rapidly, however, that what is new today may already be superseded tomorrow, so I shall therefore give you only a brief sketch of some of the salient points."

His audience was fully attentive, for not one among them was not conscious of his own stake in the course medicine took in the future, or that automation would largely determine that course.

"The problem can be stated very quickly," said Greg. "The cost of medical services, according to authentic reports, is now rising at about three times the rate of other living costs, judged by the consumer index. In nineteen sixty-seven, the cost of an average hospital room was fifty-five dollars per day; it will reach one hundred by nineteen seventy-five, while the total national health bill will rise from fifty-four billion dollars, representing six per cent of the GNP for nineteen sixty-seven, to one hundred billion and eight per cent in the same period. Health as an industry will likewise rise to where one and a half million doctors and nurses and four and a half million hospital workers will be needed by nineteen seventy-five.

"Remember that I said 'needed.'" He pointed to the screen where Bob Johnson had projected the stark figures by means of the slide projector. "None of us, of course, is obtuse enough to believe that the number of people required will be found, which means that something else must take the place of human hands. That something can only be machines, medical robots, if you please.

"The statistics I have given you represent what is needed merely to maintain the status quo, but just what is that status quo actually worth? Books could be written, and have been, about the dismal failure of what we like to consider the finest medical system in the world to provide an adequate level of health to the American people. I shall give you only a few examples of just how dismal that failure really is:

"The United States now ranks thirteenth among nations in infant mortality, with countries like Japan and Finland well ahead of us, although their standards of living cannot compare with ours. During the most prosperous twenty years in United States history, when we sent rockets soaring into space toward the moon and other planets, we actually dropped seven places in such a vital statistic as the infant mortality rate.

"Our low quality of health cannot be blamed on poverty when we are the richest nation in the world's history, for even when the sick man gets to a hospital today, he has no assurance that the care he receives will be comparable in any way to the wealth of the nation. Not long ago, the Columbia University School of Public Health reported that forty-three per cent of the nation's five thousand, two hundred general hospitals gave care that can only be called 'poor to fair.' In fact, a recent study of general practitioners in a southern state suggested that the average patient who consulted them might be almost as well off if he had gone to a witch doctor."

There was a murmur of indignation among the listeners, but

he ignored it as he continued: "These are facts we must not only face but correct. With the United States dropping to ninth place among nations in the standard indices of health, we of the medical profession can no longer face the public in our practices and claim to be guardians of their welfare, when we have failed in our task. It is true that the greatest cause of cost increase in medical care is the rising expense of hospital operation, an expense which can largely be charged to inefficiency. But although the medical profession rarely supervises the day-to-day operation of a hospital, the fact remains that we are deeply concerned with its administration because its failure reflects on us in the minds of the public. If we only use it, our influence upon hospital planners and administrators can be very great, and we must not hesitate to do so in the future.

"Since labor is the greatest problem, doctors must take the lead in insisting that labor-saving procedures be introduced into hospital and clinic care. When a single machine now being manufactured in Sweden can process three thousand blood samples an hour, while performing eighteen different tests on each sample, the individual laboratory technician is already largely outmoded, except as supervisor of the machine. What is more, such machines can be connected to computers which will print out the result faster than human hands can possibly write, without the one error in every six determinations that now results from human laboratory operations.

"Diagnosis, too, can be computerized and automated to a great extent, as is being demonstrated by research in many parts of the country and by the number of papers on medical automation appearing in such a widely circulated medical publication as the *Journal of the American Medical Association*. Merely by having a patient sit in a special chair, it is now possible to determine and record simultaneously heart action, pulse, respiratory rate, blood pressure and even the emotional state, printing the results on computer tape and sounding a warning when abnormal findings are discovered. What is popularly called an 'electronic nurse' can give the doctor in his hospital office at any moment the temperature, heart rate, blood pressure, electrocardiographic tracing and respiration of a patient in a distant part of the hospital or even in another building. Our sensitive monitors in the operating room, many of them developed for watching astronauts far out in space, now tell us the condition of the patient at every stage of the operation merely at a glance. The same can be done in the intensive care units, which are a central feature in every really modern hospital being constructed today.

"Even in the business office, automation can cut costs remarkably," he continued. "Doctors' orders, pharmacy requests, X-ray requisitions and many other items can be handled automatically by a computer, cutting down the same three hundred out of every thousand dollars of hospital expense, as determined by a recent study, chargeable to handling costs and records, a really inexcusable expense when methods are readily available to prevent them.

"Two years ago I was charged by the Board of Trustees with the task of planning a modern hospital and diagnostic clinic to replace this outmoded structure which we all love, but which is now unprofitable and even dangerous to operate. On Saturday, I shall present to the board a complete plan for the most highly computerized hospital in the world today, as well as the most beautiful. Fifty years ago the present Clinic was in a modestly prosperous district of middle-class homes; today it is the center of a slum whose inhabitants rarely earn enough to be classed above the accepted guidelines for the determination of poverty. When this hospital and clinic were built, Dr. Anders wished to show how they could serve a community, as well as the world; the fact that the community has deteriorated along with the physical plant of the hospital does not change, in my opinion, the purpose for which it was built. With a modern plant, we can still render a service to people who need it much more now than did those in this area fifty years ago. On Saturday, I shall present to the Board of Trustees for their consideration, the preliminary architectural drawings for such a modern hospital-clinic complex, one that will be a truly fitting tribute to the man whose vision made possible the founding of this clinic a half century ago."

Greg closed his folder and stepped back from the podium as a wave of applause spread through the audience. Before anyone could ask a question, Henry Anders hurriedly announced: "Because of the shortness of time, there will be no discussion of this paper. None of you, I am sure, want to be late for the party, so we will go on to the next speaker, Dr. Abraham Lantz. His topic: 'The Early Diagnosis of Pulmonary Embolism.'"

v

Bob Johnson joined Greg outside the lecture hall. "Did you see Jud Templeton there this afternoon?" he asked.

"Are you sure?" Greg understood at once the significance of the name, since Jud Templeton was a roving reporter for both the morning and afternoon newspapers, and a legendary figure in Baltimore journalism.

"No doubt about it. I recognized him from the emergency room. He was at the back of the hall, taking notes like mad. When you announced your plans for the transplant, he fairly bolted from the room."

Greg glanced at his watch. "That means he'll make the final editions of the afternoon paper. Now the fat's really in the fire."

"Why, sir? It seems to me that the publicity will help the cause."

"The other side is sure to claim I released the story to the press."

"Who do you suppose did invite Templeton here?" Bob asked. "A big shot like him wouldn't ordinarily cover just a medical meeting. The paper would send a stringer."

"I don't know."

"Do you suppose *they* did it?" Greg didn't pretend not to understand whom Bob meant by *they*.

"My guess is that I was expected to object to the announcement of the special meeting of the board," he said. "If I had, the reason would have been made public, putting me in a bad light early in the session."

"Then you know the reason for the special meeting?"

"Dr. Foucald told me this morning that Mr. Hunter is going to demand an investigation of my building the hyperbaric chamber."

"But it was constructed with government funds."

"That doesn't make any difference to Sam Hunter. He's got a feud going with the government, too."

"Do you plan to put Lawson in the chamber when the time comes for the transplant?"

"I don't think so," said Greg. "We'd have to raise the pressure to at least three atmospheres and we might lose more than we gain, because of the time it would take to decompress. Besides, I suspect our greatest problem is going to be keeping Merchant alive until Frank Lawson dies."

"It would be nice if we had two chambers connected together."

"Keith Jackson has included them in the new plans, with a connecting air lock so we can use each chamber separately, or move freely from one to another without decompression," said Greg. "I asked him to do it when he started to make up the detail drawings."

"But if they're already squawking about the chamber we have—"

"Sometimes a man has to 'dream the impossible dream' as the songwriters put it. We might as well give them something to really squawk about."

10

Taking advantage of the momentary stir while Abe Lantz came forward to start presenting his paper, Helen Foucald slipped out of the lecture hall. Peter Carewe had been watching her and followed; in the corridor outside, he overtook her easily with his longer stride.

"Where are you going in such a hurry?" he asked.

"Back to the laboratory to check on some tests we're running."

"I was hoping we could have a cup of coffee together somewhere."

"There's a small coffee shop off the corridor just outside the laboratory if you don't mind stopping by there with me first to see how the tests are going."

"What's so important in the lab at this time of day?"

"Greg asked me to run some cell compatibility tests between Mr. Merchant, the heart case he mentioned, and the donor."

"I'm not familiar with the technique," he said. "You can bring me up to date on it."

"The original tests were devised by some French investigators," she explained as they entered the laboratory and went over to where a technician was working at a table by the window. From the rack in front of the technician, Helen took a small tube containing a bottom sediment of a dark red solid, a middle section that was yellowish in color and a short column of whiter material floating on top.

"This is heparinized blood from the donor," she said. "The dark sediment at the bottom is composed mainly of red cells, the clear section in the center is serum and a pedicle of white cells is floating at the top."

Putting that tube back into the rack, she moved on to another one. "After sedimentation, the pedicle was strained off through a nylon filter and a suspension made containing several dilutions. As near as we could, we divided it into concentrations of one, two and four million cells. The part that came to the surface was then separated after being put through the centrifuge to get as pure a preparation of lymphocytes as possible."

"Ingenious."

"Has Dr. Johnson made the intradermal injections?" Helen asked the technician.

"We gave him the preparations from both Merchant and Lawson," said the girl. "He injected them about an hour ago."

"Isn't this like a test for allergens?" Peter asked.

"It's very much the same," Helen agreed. "By injecting several dilutions of a preparation of the donor's lymphocytes into the skin of the recipient, and vice versa, we should be able to tell by the skin reaction around the injection within twenty-four hours just how much each will react to the other."

"I wonder if there'll be that much time. Greg said just now that the recipient is already in heart failure."

"We're running a second set of tests for that very reason, checking for lymphocyte agglutination. The results won't be ready for another hour, though."

"Meanwhile, we can be having that cup of coffee," said Peter, and they left the laboratory for the vending area nearby.

"In a way I feel responsible for the special meeting Henry announced just now," Helen said when Peter set two cups of coffee down upon the small table she had selected in the busy shop.

"Why?"

"Sam Hunter didn't know about the hyperbaric laboratory until he saw it through a window of my office this morning. I guess I spilled the beans."

"Are you sure that's the reason he called the session?"

"It must be; he was furious. I warned Greg right away, but there doesn't seem to be anything he can do."

"Surely Greg couldn't have expected to hide anything as large as a building."

"Since it was financed with an NIH grant, and Bill Remick

helped arrange it, I guess Greg just forgot to notify the other members of the board. Mr. Hunter got very angry when I tried to defend Greg and I'm afraid I only made things worse by arguing with him."

"After hearing Greg speak this afternoon, I've got an idea he will land on his feet. By the way, what are you wearing for dinner tonight?"

"A pale blue dress. Why?"

"An orchid should go well with that, worn in your hair."

"Why there?"

"In the South Seas, a girl wears a flower behind her ear, signifying whether she's willing to be courted—according to the color of the flower."

"The trouble is, I don't know what color indicates what."

"Red's my favorite," he said promptly. "It stands for—"

"Availability?"

"Something like that."

"Do you want me to wear red?"

"I'm not quite sure yet." The bantering note had gone out of his voice. "Are you?"

She shook her head, wondering how many more hours would pass before someone told him she was known throughout the hospital grapevine system to be the mistress of Henry Anders.

"Promise me one thing," she said quickly. "However it ends, there must be no regrets."

"I'm the one who's supposed to say that," he protested. "You've got our roles reversed."

ii

Guy Merchant was asleep when Greg came into his room with Bob Johnson and Dr. James McNeal, Senior Fellow in Cardiology. Folding back the sheet over the sick man's feet, Greg pressed his finger into the puffy skin over his right ankle and studied the pit in the waterlogged tissue left when he removed it.

"The edema's increasing," he said softly, so as not to awaken the sleeping man.

"We've stepped up the oxygen to ten." The heart specialist

140

nodded toward the bottle attached to the large oxygen tank beside the bed. Through it, the gas was bubbling rapidly, churning into a froth the water that half filled the bottle. "He's breathing practically pure oxygen but his ear lobes are still dusty from cyanosis."

"Obviously the vital capacity is very low," said Greg.

The amount of air the lungs could contain between full inspiration and full expiration was a fairly accurate index of those organs' efficiency. But in the type of emphysema caused by smoking, where the lungs largely lost their capacity to expand and contract with breathing, the vital capacity was always sharply limited.

"Even without the damage to his heart, he would have gotten into trouble soon from emphysema," said Dr. McNeal. "Now the congestion from cardiac insufficiency has curtailed his breathing capacity even more."

"How much longer?" Greg asked as they moved on to Frank Lawson's room.

"My guess would be no more than twelve hours," said the cardiologist, but they both knew that no actual limit could be set, for entirely too many factors were involved.

The click-click of the respirator attached to the tube in Frank Lawson's windpipe greeted them when they opened the door of his room. Greg leafed through the top pages of the chart handed him by the nurse who had been watching to see that the tracheostomy tube didn't become clogged.

"His temperature has been rising slightly for the past several hours," she reported. "Dr. Partridge ordered chloramphenicol intramuscularly."

Bob Johnson raised his eyebrows; a powerful antibiotic, the drug would tend to combat any infection that might shorten Frank Lawson's life.

"Herb has no alternative," Greg reminded the younger surgeon. "Lawson's his patient and he has to keep him alive as long as he can."

"X-ray did a portable film of the lungs right after lunch," said the nurse. "The report may already be at the desk outside."

"See if it is, please." While she was gone, Greg moved closer to the bed to study Frank Lawson's face, which was puffed and swollen from the trauma that had almost sliced off his head. When he lifted one of the injured man's eyelids, he saw that the pupils were dilated and did not contract from the light that entered them, a sure sign of brain damage.

"The lung X-ray is clear, Doctor," the nurse reported.

"Thank you," said Greg. "How does his condition appear to you, Miss Strong?"

"He's losing ground," she said without hesitation. "Dr. Partridge thinks the rise in temperature may be from an ascending infection around the temperature center or a slowly spreading hemorrhage."

The temperature center was located in a small, but vital, area of the brain that controlled most of the body functions absolutely necessary for life. If either hemorrhage or an infection were approaching it, Frank Lawson's hours of life might be shortened considerably, but with no way to look inside the brain and see, they could only wait.

When the doctors came into the small waiting room, Georgia Merchant looked up from the magazine she had been staring at for the last half hour without really seeing either the words or the photographs in it.

"Guy's worse, isn't he, Dr. Alexander?" she asked.

"I'm afraid so."

"Maybe it's better this way. He wants to die and you'll be saved the loss of a patient."

"I would hope not to lose him, Mrs. Merchant."

"We both appreciate your being willing to gamble your own reputation on a case as far advanced as Guy's," she said. "I think he might have kept that attack from coming on this morning if he'd called for nitroglycerin."

"Are you saying he deliberately tried to bring about his own death?" Bob Johnson asked.

"He's tried before by holding off the medicine," said Georgia. "This time he might have made it if the nurse hadn't been so quick. That's why, when Dr. Alexander offered him the operation, he jumped at it as a way of doing what he wasn't able to do for himself."

Surprised at how quickly Guy Merchant had agreed to such drastic and dangerous surgery, Greg, too, had come to much the same conclusion.

"What about you?" he asked her. "Can we do anything to help you?"

"Everybody is more than kind," she assured him. "I've been praying that, if you can't save him the way you'd like to do, he doesn't come out from under the anesthetic at all. But he's going so fast now, you're not likely to even be able to operate, are you?"

"The situation doesn't look promising."

"It's strange the way things work out. Anybody in show business will tell you that Guy has been a decent and honorable man all his life, while Lawson's been a criminal since he was a boy. The one way Lawson might be able to atone for some of his sins before he dies would be to make it possible for Guy to go on living, at least for a while. Maybe if he were conscious and knew the sort of future he would have, not being able to use his arms and legs and living in a respirator in prison, he would want Guy to have his heart."

"Not many people have the generosity and the courage to die for others," Greg reminded her.

"I suppose so," she said. "I don't even feel exactly right about praying for Guy to get well, when I'm really praying for somebody else to die."

iii

In his office, Greg asked his secretary to get Jud Templeton on the phone at the newspaper office downtown but she reported that he was still at the hospital.

"Try that telephone off the emergency room where reporters sometimes phone in their stories," he said. "If Mr. Templeton is there, please ask him to come up."

It was no more than ten minutes before the newspaperman was ushered into Greg's office by the secretary. "Thank you for coming up, Mr. Templeton," he said. "I'm pretty busy or I would have come down to see you."

"This is *your* castle, Doctor. What can I do for you?"

143

"I'm more concerned about what you can do *to* me. If I'd known you were in the lecture hall this afternoon, I would have asked you to leave before I made the announcement about the transplant."

"Your front office invited us to send a reporter to cover the convocation proceedings, Doctor."

"I'm still surprised that it would be a reporter of your caliber, Mr. Templeton."

"I'm here by special invitation. Didn't you know?"

"I'm afraid not."

"A special press card was sent to the office about noon by messenger, admitting me to all sessions of the convocation."

"By whose authority?"

Jud Templeton took a press card from his pocket and put it on Greg's desk blotter. It was made out in the reporter's name— and signed by Henry Anders II.

"You seem surprised," he said when Greg handed him back the card. "Is anything wrong?"

Greg shook his head. "Your invitation is in good order. But I still think it would have been better not to publicize the transplant so early."

"If you're hinting that you would like to have the story killed, it's already in the presses for the Wall Street Final."

"You didn't lose any time."

"The public has a right to know you're on the verge of making medical history, Dr. Alexander."

"There have been other transplants."

"But not from a murderer to a burlesque straight man. There's a particular name for that kind of story—it's 'human interest.'"

"Did it occur to you that your premature publicity may have jeopardized my chances of being able to operate at all?"

"Georgia Merchant's not going to object and neither is Guy. They're the Lunt and Fontanne of the burlesque world and too attached to each other for either one of them to deprive the other of a chance to live."

"You seem to know them well."

"I used to be a candy butcher in the old Gayety Theater back in the thirties. I don't know anybody I'd rather give a break to

144

than Georgia and Guy. Whichever way this operation ends, Doctor, I'm going to do a feature on her that ought to put her back in the big time."

"Don't you realize that as soon as your story comes out, thousands of people will be pulling for Frank Lawson to die?"

"It couldn't happen to a lousier guy—and the sooner the better."

"The medical examiner and I have to determine when Lawson is legally dead, Mr. Templeton. And with all this publicity, I might unconsciously be more careful to be sure he's dead, before I start to remove his heart and lungs, than I would ordinarily be. That could jeopardize the success of the operation."

"The Doctor's Dilemma? That's an angle I hadn't thought of."

"I'm sorry I mentioned it."

"Oh, I would have thought of it eventually, you can be sure of that. But the more I do think of it, the better this story is turning out to be. When do you think you'll operate?"

"Maybe not at all—after Judge Sutler reads your story."

"You don't have to worry on that score."

"Why?"

"Along with the routine request for reporters to cover the convocation, we also got a tip that something dramatic would be announced."

"When was this?"

"Before noon—when my card came."

Greg frowned. "Do you have any idea why?"

"My guess is somebody wanted us to report the special meeting of the Board of Trustees that was announced in the lecture room. I heard some whispering down there that you're about to be given the shaft."

"That wasn't worth a visit from the star reporter for both papers."

"You're a more important man than you think, Doctor, but this time you're right," said Templeton. "We also had a tip from the judge's office and a copy of his order releasing Frank Lawson's body to you as soon as the medical examiner pronounces him dead. Judge Sutler knows a good story when he sees it, even if you don't."

"You could at least have asked me about it first."

"And have you kill the story?"

145

"There isn't any story yet, Mr. Templeton. Nothing has actually been done except to make the decision to operate, if circumstances work out so I can."

"Right after the six o'clock news goes on the air tonight, thousands of people will be rooting for Guy Merchant and praying for Frank Lawson to die. You doctors have been worrying about where you can get a supply of hearts and other organs for transplant. Why not from condemned criminals like Frank Lawson?"

"That's a ghoulish idea."

"But still a good one. Judge Sutler told me on the telephone not an hour ago that he was finally persuaded to let you have Lawson's body because you said that, if the state assumed the right to *take* a man's life, it should also assume the right to *give* that life to another."

"That's another time I should have kept my mouth shut," Greg said wryly.

"Why—when you spoke a profound truth? Before you take Frank Lawson's heart out, you're going to have to put him on a heart-lung pump, aren't you?"

"Possibly—for a few minutes at least."

"And when you've taken his heart and lungs out, you'll shut off the pump, won't you?"

"Yes."

"What's the difference between sending five thousand volts of electricity through a man's body and simply throwing the switch on the heart-lung pump so it will stop? That's certainly a lot less barbarous way to execute somebody than with the electric chair or the gas chamber, to say nothing of that civilized custom we call hanging."

The newspaper man pointed to a painting on the wall, a reproduction of Rembrandt's famous *Anatomy Lesson.* "Didn't the early anatomists learn a lot about the body by dissecting living criminals?"

"That's what the medical histories say."

"Why not let some of these punks who start riots and kill innocent bystanders know they'll be taken apart alive with forceps and scalpel if they get caught. It might even make them have second thoughts."

"Really, Mr. Templeton, I'm sincere."

"Believe me, I couldn't be more serious about anything, Doctor. I got mugged one night last year when I was on an assignment. This is a sore subject with me."

"What I'm trying to tell you is that a matter of ethics is involved in your printing the story of my announcement to the convocation."

"You mean there's not supposed to be any cult of the personality among doctors?"

"That's one way of putting it—yes."

"You'd better tell that to the headline-grabbers of your profession. We reporters know better."

"Such publicity wouldn't do The Clinic any good either."

"That's where you're wrong, Dr. Alexander." Jud Templeton's voice was entirely serious now. "I grew up in this town and I know how proud it has always been of The Clinic. But there still has to be a man at the top, a captain of the team, and he's the guy the public wants to know about. That's been lacking here since old Dr. Anders died."

"We wanted it that way."

"Maybe you did; I'll give you credit for really believing the guff about ethics that so few doctors really practice any more. But publicity is damned important for The Clinic right now, if not for you. Every time you pick up a magazine these days there's an article in it about the high cost of medical care or the mistakes doctors and hospitals make. Hardly a week passes without another book attacking the medical profession, and the way you're all getting rich."

"I'm a teacher. Don't put me in that class."

"I'm familiar with the setup here and with your work, Doctor. In fact, I could come pretty close to naming your salary. The public needs to know at least one clinic in the country doesn't worry about whether or not you can put up a dime when you're sick."

"There are a lot of others like ours."

"They're not the ones you read about in the books and articles that try to run down American medicine. Put a new heart and lungs into Guy Merchant even for a week, Doctor, and you'll have a line of people a mile long waiting to get into the hospital."

"That's partly what I'm afraid of," Greg admitted. "We already have more than we can handle."

"But not more than you *could* handle, if the facilities and money were available. I know all about the battle that's going on over whether to move The Clinic. I had my appendix out ten years ago in your private ward and it was antiquated even then, so something's got to be done. Once this story breaks, a howl of objection to moving it will go up; in fact, I might just be able to help you get the money you need to rebuild this beloved monstrosity."

"Are you saying we should work together?"

"We could both do worse, Doctor. Maybe I was a bit underhanded today in breaking the Merchant-Lawson story without telling you, but you wouldn't have given it to me otherwise, so I didn't have any choice. From now on, though, we can both profit by co-operation."

"How?"

"You see that I'm kept informed as the Merchant-Lawson story breaks and I'll see that The Clinic gets the full benefit of the publicity."

"I'll have to think about that."

The newspaperman smiled. "Just getting you to admit that much means I'm ahead of where I was when I came in this afternoon and you had planned to chew me out. Believe me, Doctor, we both have the same goals. I'm sure we can do a lot more working together than pulling separately."

iv

A few moments after Jud Templeton left, the telephone in Greg's office rang. It was Helen Foucald.

"I've got the results on those agglutination tests you asked me to run, Greg," she said. "Do you have time to come down to the lab and look at them?"

"I'll be right there."

At the laboratory he found Helen and a technician in one corner, jotting down the results from a bank of test tubes which had been set up in front of a strong light. "Here on the left is the normal lymphocyte transfer test," she explained. "As you can see, there's no agglutination."

"That's even more than we had hoped for," said Greg.

"Over here we have the leuko-agglutination test, which is also negative. The irradiated hamster test and the histocompatibility tests can hardly be read accurately before tomorrow noon."

"I've got an idea that won't do us much good. Merchant's failing rapidly."

"What about Lawson?"

"He's showing a change, but as yet we're not sure exactly what's happening."

"Can I do anything else?" she asked.

"No, you've helped me a lot, Helen. I see you found Peter Carewe all right this morning?"

"I didn't find him, he found me." Greg didn't miss her blush.

"I'm sure Peter was much happier having you meet him than he would have been with me."

"He didn't seem to be displeased." Helen smiled. "We had breakfast together at the airport restaurant."

"Peter's quite a boy," said Greg. "And he's doing a wonderful job in his field."

"We're having dinner tonight—unless you're liable to need me."

"Could you make it at the Inn, where I can reach you? If we operate, we'll need a lot of blood-gas determinations in a hurry."

"Of course," she said. "We'll be going to the cocktail party first, anyway, so it will be simple to stay on."

When he returned to his office, Greg was surprised to see Jeanne sitting in the chair beside his desk. Her smile was a bit tremulous until he closed the door and pulled her out of the chair into his arms for a long kiss.

"I know doctors' wives should stay out of their husbands' offices," she said, "but I need to talk to you."

"No more than I needed your being here. Is anything wrong?"

"Not with me any more—I hope."

"That's the best news I could possibly have, darling."

"I visited Mary Jackson in her apartment this morning and she showed me some of Keith's preliminary sketches for the new Clinic. I understand now how you feel about them."

"They're breath-taking, aren't they?"

"Yes. I—Greg, can you ever forgive me?"

"There's nothing to forgive."

"But the way I've acted lately—and last night. Throwing that medical journal at you was unforgivable."

"I had time to think about that afterward, and you were entirely right," he told her. "I should never have tried to compromise with Henry and the faction that's fighting me. It's only made them stronger and lost me some support."

"Are they strong enough to defeat your new plan?"

"Possibly, but I'm not giving in. If the trustees don't want the kind of Clinic I'm going to offer them, they can do without it—and me."

"You can take that chair in experimental surgery at California any time you wish," she reminded him.

"If it comes to that, we will," he said. "I'm not going to let my work be hampered any longer by inadequate facilities, but we'll cross that bridge when we come to it. Right now, I'm too happy to have you back from that far country you've been living in to care about anything else. Do I dare ask what brought you back?"

"I'll tell you later," she said. "Will you be able to go to Ed and Hannah McDougal's cocktail party?"

"I'm afraid not, darling. Bob Johnson and I hope to do a human heart-lung transplant sometime tonight."

"Is this the time for that?" she asked quickly, and he knew what was worrying her—the same thing that had made Dave Connor reluctant to approve the transplant.

"You don't choose the time," he said. "It just happens, like the conjunction of two planets that produced the Star of Bethlehem. But it's the man who's waiting for a new heart and lungs I'm worried about—not the effect my failure might have on the board."

"I didn't mean that."

"I know. You're right, of course; whatever happens, it's bound to influence them one way or another."

"When do you think you can come home?"

"Certainly not until this operation is settled, which means probably tomorrow morning. Bob and I have two operating rooms set up and waiting now."

"I don't think what I have to tell you can wait that long," she said. "Hannah McDougal and I had breakfast together."

"I didn't know you liked Hannah that much."

"I don't. But when I saw in her what I was in danger of becoming, I knew she'd done me a great favor. Did you know Ed is trying to get Sam Hunter's money for a new medical school in Texas?"

"Yes."

"He's up here doing everything he can to keep The Clinic from getting more than a small amount of it."

"That makes sense from Ed's viewpoint. After all, Mr. Hunter's a Texan, too."

"That isn't all. He and Henry Anders are working to drive you out of The Clinic."

"Did Hannah tell you that?"

"No—Claire. We had lunch together."

"Claire's a smart girl, but why would she go against Henry?"

"She has the money in the family now, so she can hold the reins on him. I think she believes a triumphant Henry would be insufferable."

Greg chuckled. "When did you become such a psychiatrist?"

"Since this morning—when I realized Ed McDougal was trying to sabotage you and your work. Is there any way to fight them, Greg?"

"The only way I know is to make the transplant succeed. You can do one thing for me, though."

"Anything I can—you know that."

"Go on to the cocktail party this evening without me and see what you can learn."

"If you want me to."

"I do. And darling—"

"Yes?"

"As soon as this case is finished and the board meeting's out of the way, we're really going to have that trip I've been promising you—a sort of second honeymoon."

"Aren't we a bit old for that?"

"We'll give it the old college try just the same. By the way, take a look at the final edition of the afternoon paper before you go to the party. I didn't intend it this way, but I think we'll be exploding a small bomb under Ed and Henry just about the time the party starts. Excuse me, my phone's ringing." He picked up the receiver as the light started flicking upon the base of the telephone.

"I'm up in intensive care, Greg." Dave Connor's voice on the telephone was urgent. "You'd better come up here right away."

11

When he stepped off the elevator at the ICU floor, Greg realized at once what was happening, for Guy Merchant's labored breathing could be heard yards away, along with the ominous rattle in his chest. Taken together, they could only mean his failing heart had almost reached the point of no return. Because it was no longer able to pump blood satisfactorily into the rest of the body, fluid was now seeping through the walls of the lung air sacs, causing a congestion that could quickly result in the critical state called pulmonary edema.

"We've put in a catheter and I've just injected fifty milligrams of ethacrynic acid intravenously." Dave Connor was completing an injection when Greg came in. "Unless his kidney function is shot, too, we ought to start extracting fluid from the bloodstream and the lungs within fifteen minutes or less and take some of the load off his heart."

"Don't you think a tracheostomy is indicated?" Greg asked. "He needs as clear an airway as he can get."

"That's why I called," said the cardiologist. "Do you want to do it up here?"

"We can work better in one of the anesthetic rooms, where Lew Gann can watch him and use suction to remove fluid from the airway," said Greg. He didn't add that Guy Merchant would be ready then for the transplant, for it didn't seem likely that there would be one.

"He's all yours," said Dave Connor. "Good luck."

Greg rang the operating room supervisor from the nurse's station on the ICU. "Please set up for a tracheostomy right away, Miss

White, and call Dr. Johnson," he said. "I'm bringing down Mr. Merchant; we can do it in the anesthetic room for O.R. 2."

ii

It was nearly an hour before Greg returned to his office on the top floor of the surgical building. Somewhere during that time he remembered the beeper in his pocket giving its strident summons, and, when he asked the operating room supervisor to take the message, her report that Dr. Edward McDougal was waiting to see him. But too much had to be done at the moment for him to take time out to see the Texan.

The tracheostomy had been skillfully performed by Bob Johnson. A small operation carried out through an incision in the neck and the wall of the windpipe just below the Adam's apple, it allowed a curved tube to be inserted and left in place, giving a direct airway to the lungs and making breathing much easier for patients with congestion and moisture in the respiratory passage. After that, he had talked briefly to Georgia Merchant, explaining why the small surgery had been necessary, and had then visited Frank Lawson, confirming the fact that he, too, was going downhill, though, unless the treatment being given Guy Merchant was far more effective than they could expect it to be, not fast enough to allow completion of the transplant.

Greg found Ed McDougal pacing up and down in his office. The beefy surgeon's face was flushed with anger and annoyance.

"Where the hell have you been?" he demanded. "I called for you an hour ago."

"I've been supervising a tracheostomy."

"On the heart patient?"

"Yes." Greg dropped into the chair behind his desk, suddenly conscious of a weariness that extended into his very bones. "What's bothering you, Ed?"

"That grandstand play you pulled downstairs at the convocation this afternoon. What else?"

"It was just a simple announcement."

"You know damn well you can't transplant the heart and lungs

154

successfully from one human being to another who's so far gone in heart failure that you have to do a tracheostomy."

"I've done it enough times experimentally to prove you're wrong, Ed."

"But dogs aren't people. The problems aren't the same."

"I didn't know you were doing experimental surgery."

"Me experiment?" The other surgeon gave a bark of a laugh. "Hell, man! There's no money in that."

"I wasn't working for money."

"I know what you're doing. You're trying to make a big splash to impress the board." The Texas surgeon thrust his head forward belligerently. "Do you deny that your patient's dying?"

"I wouldn't plan to operate on him if he weren't. What is it you want from me, Ed? I've got work to do."

"Call this grandstand play off. You can always say the patient's too far gone to stand the operation, and this time you'd be telling the truth."

"Merchant has improved considerably since we did the tracheostomy," said Greg.

"Dave Connor says he's still failing."

"How do you know that?"

"Henry called Dave."

"You didn't worry about ethics, did you?" Greg's voice was like a whip and the other surgeon flushed.

"Henry's director of The Clinic. He can go wherever he likes."

"But *you* can't come here telling me what I can and cannot do. If Henry wants to forbid me to operate, let him do it himself."

"You know Henry." The Texas surgeon threw up his hands in disgust.

"I know his way is to work underhandedly. What's your way, Ed—a knife in the back?"

The other man flushed. "You don't have to be insulting."

"What else are you when you come in here and try to browbeat me? Or when you rushed to the hospital as soon as you got here this morning and corralled Sam Hunter to influence him against the plans I have for the new hospital?"

"How did you know that?"

"Jeanne and Hannah had breakfast together."

155

"That loud-mouthed bitch! If she—"

"Hannah didn't tell Jeanne anything I didn't already know, so don't blame her. Just blame yourself for conniving—"

"But—"

"And don't think I don't know you and Henry have joined forces to try and force me out of The Clinic."

The statement brought Ed McDougal up short. "Believe me, Greg, that wasn't my idea," he protested.

"But you agreed to join forces with Henry just the same. You've got your nerve, Ed, coming up here and giving me the devil when you and Henry are busy doing everything you can to destroy me. For your information, I plan to operate on Guy Merchant, if organs become available in time. And nothing you or Henry can do will dissuade me."

"We'll ruin you in the board meeting—"

"Go ahead and try. I'm through with compromise; it wasn't worth the trouble anyway."

"What do you mean?"

"I had worked out a plan for rebuilding that was so conservative even someone as blind to what's really needed here as Sam Hunter and his followers are, would get behind it. But I'm not even going to present it now."

"Then the rumors are true that you've got a way-out plan under wraps?"

"I told the Members this afternoon that I'm going to present such a plan to the board."

"We don't have to be enemies, Greg." Ed McDougal's tone was suddenly conciliatory and Greg gave him a suspicious look.

"Why the milk and honey?" he demanded. "You want Sam Hunter's money for your new medical school and I want it for The Clinic. Right now, I'll admit your chances look a lot better than mine, but a lot can happen between now and Saturday."

"If neither of us asks for too much, we might both come out ahead," the Texan suggested.

"What about your agreement with Henry?"

"I told you I wasn't for that."

"Maybe you're telling the truth, Ed; I don't know. But when Henry joined forces with you, I'll bet he stipulated that I must be a casualty of whatever finally emerges. Now you come offering to make a deal behind Henry's back, so how do either of us know you won't double-cross us both when the time comes?"

The Texan shot up out of his chair, his face fiery red with anger. "I came here to give you a chance because I didn't really want to go along with Henry's plan to force you out," he snapped. "But now I feel no obligation to help you keep your job."

"I'd like to think you have enough love for The Clinic's welfare not to leave us out in the cold when it comes to Sam Hunter's money, Ed." Greg went to the door and opened it. "And because I give you that much credit, I'm going to tell you something you don't know—though you will in a little while anyway. There was a reporter at the opening session of the convocation this afternoon."

"Why you son of a—!"

"I didn't have anything to do with his being there."

"The hell you didn't!"

"I think you'd better leave, Ed."

"I'm not going until I tell you what I think of you."

"You've already done that, so why waste your breath? Henry invited Jud Templeton, the newspaperman I was talking about."

"How do you know that?"

"Templeton told me after he'd filed the story. I saw his press card—signed by Henry."

"Why would Henry do that?"

"You mean he didn't confide in you?"

"The last thing any of us want is for this controversy to get into the newspapers. You should know that."

"Well it's there already. Henry did it deliberately."

"But why?"

"He's working with you, not me; why don't you ask him? My guess is he wanted the announcement of the special session of the board to be made public, figuring that I'd demand to know why. Then he could reveal that Sam Hunter wants to censure me for building the hyperbaric laboratory. Anything Sam Hunter does is news, so it would have worked—if I'd been fool enough to ask why the meeting was being called."

"Of all the damn fools—"

"That's our Henry, but you should have expected something like it when you teamed up with him to knife me in the back." Greg shook his head. "I've had about all of you and Henry I can take for one day, Ed. Better go, or you'll be late for your party."

When the Texas surgeon was gone, Greg dropped into the chair behind his desk and began to shuffle through some papers upon it. But the words printed there faded into black scrawls on the white paper and presently he pushed the sheets aside and picked up the phone.

"Can you ring the telephone the reporters and the police use just outside the emergency room?" he asked the operator.

"Yes, Doctor. It's a pay station but I have the number."

"Please ask Mr. Jud Templeton to come to my office."

"Of course, Dr. Alexander. I'll do it right away."

When he put down the phone, Greg sat back in the chair and studied the medical school diploma framed on the wall. The words were in Latin, but he could remember as well as if it had been only yesterday the voice of the commencement speaker long ago quoting Robert Louis Stevenson's famous tribute to physicians in general:

"There are men and classes of men that stand above the common herd: the soldier, the sailor, and the shepherd not infrequently; the artist rarely, rarelier still, the clergyman; the physician almost as a rule . . . Generosity he has, such as is possible to those who practice an art, never to those who drive a trade; discretion, tested by a hundred secrets; tact, tried in a thousand embarrassments; and what are more important, Heraclean cheerfulness and courage."

Courage, he had, Greg decided; it had certainly taken that to tackle one of the last frontiers of surgery, replacing failing organs with strong ones from those who could not use them any more. And, most of all, to confine his work to those most complicated, yet most important of organs, the heart and the lungs.

Generosity, he was sure he had shown in trying to win over those who opposed him, seeking to understand their unwillingness to take a step which they were afraid might damage The Clinic, whose welfare they were sworn to guard as trustees. Actually he'd been generous to a fault—and almost lost Jeanne in the process, but there was a limit to which generosity could go. And when a man carried the spirit of compromise so far as almost to alienate his wife, when he saw his enemies working to blemish his reputation publicly and, what was more important, sabotage the work by which he hoped to save lives that were otherwise doomed, it was time to fight those who fought him with their own weapons.

iii

"Come in, please, Mr. Templeton," Greg said when the secretary opened the door for the newspaperman.

"I must say, I wasn't expecting a call this soon, Doctor."

"I've been thinking about your offer to help me."

"You could certainly use it," said Templeton. "A lot of people are after Sam Hunter's money and each one is willing to cut the other one's throat to get it. It doesn't speak well for the quality of charity St. Paul wrote about, does it?"

"Most authorities translate charity there as love."

"Or that either. The Hippocratic oath is undoubtedly one of the purest ethical statements ever propounded, but, like almost everything else in the way of ideals in times like these, it's honored in the breach as much as in fulfillment. Where do we start, Doctor?"

"Perhaps here." Greg took a small key from his pocket and unlocked the center drawer of his desk. From inside it, he removed a sheet of draftsman's tracing paper, which he handed to Jud Templeton.

The journalist studied the soaring lines and angles, the shadows and sharply etched dramatic highlights for a long moment.

"Are you releasing this now?" A note of awe was in his voice.

Greg shook his head. "Hardly anybody except myself and the architect has seen it. This drawing will not be released publicly until after the trustees meet on Saturday."

"When it may be as dead as a doornail! This could be your biggest gun, Doctor. Let me run a cut of it in tomorrow afternoon's paper and people will be bombarding your Board of Trustees with thousands of calls and letters demanding that it be built as

159

a fitting monument to old Dr. Anders and to that statue over there in the rotunda."

"I promised to present plans to the trustees."

"These aren't your first, are they? I remember hearing something about another set being drawn by a firm of architects downtown."

"I first saw that sketch less than a week ago," Greg told him. "Keith Jackson's been working night and day since then to make the preliminary drawings for me to show to the board."

"Do you think an ossified mind like Sam Hunter's can appreciate the beauty of a structure like this? I've seen that office building of his in Dallas and a more thoroughly uninspired piece of architecture was never built."

"Mr. Hunter's not the only member of the board."

"Let's not kid ourselves, Doctor. Most of the members expect him to put up the money for the new building, whether The Clinic is built here or out on the Beltway, so they'll vote with him."

"Where would you rather see it go?"

"I live just off the Beltway, so I'd like to have it where my daughter-in-law can rush my grandchildren to it if they get the bellyache. What's more important, she can be sure some knife-happy surgeon isn't going to operate for appendicitis when all the kid has is that thing where the lymph glands in the belly become swollen because of a respiratory infection."

"Acute mesenteric lymphadenitis."

"A family I know of had three kids operated on for appendix in as many days—until the father got suspicious and demanded a consultation with a young professor of pediatrics from the university medical school. Three kids operated on for appendicitis in forty-eight hours! Do you know what the odds are against that happening?"

"It would take a computer to figure it."

"But only a cheap adding machine to calculate what it cost that couple in surgeon's fees and hospital bills. So however much I'd like to have The Clinic in my own backyard, I can see that it's needed more right here in the worst slum in the city."

"Will you help me keep it here?"

"I can damn sure try," said Templeton. "I've got an interview set up tomorrow morning with Dr. Peter Carewe. He impresses me as being the kind of a guy who won't weasel on anything I ask him, and, if I use the right kind of questions, he'll probably come through with the right answers. Ever since that TV program the other night, people would listen if he recited 'Gunga Din' through his nose." He picked up the sketch again. "This must be the plan Dr. Anders spoke about when he called me this morning and invited me to sit in on the first session of the convocation."

"You didn't say anything about that before," Greg said quickly.

"I only thought of it after I left here, and you've been tied up ever since."

"Just what did Henry Anders tell you?"

"He said some sort of dramatic announcement would be made. And he also said a new plan is in the offing and implied that there would be a hell of a fight in the board over it."

"Of which he would furnish you with the details?"

"That was the size of it." Jud Templeton's gray eyes studied him quizzically. "You seemed surprised, Doctor. Wasn't Dr. Anders in on the secret?"

"Frankly, no."

"That sort of puts a different aspect on things, doesn't it?"

"Quite different."

"Do you suppose somebody could be setting you up, Doctor?"

"Setting me up?"

"As a patsy, to be knocked off at the right time. Keith Jackson's got the reputation around town of being brilliant but sort of way out—you know, almost avant-garde. And with all that conservative element on the board, it might just be that someone is trying to give you and Jackson enough rope to hang yourselves."

"That sounds rather far-fetched."

"Maybe yes and maybe no. Let's not forget that Dr. Anders knew all about this plan when he called me this morning, in spite of the fact that you say only you and Jackson have seen it. Did Keith Jackson even mention him to you?"

"No."

"You're sure?"

"Absolutely."

"What shape were these sketches in when Jackson first showed them to you?"

"That's one of them you have now."

Jud Templeton picked up the sketch and held it up to the light once again. "Notice how much detail he has here; this is hardly the sort of rough sketch an architect would knock out just because he was struck by an idea in the middle of the night."

"I can see that now," said Greg. "But you can't deny that it's inspired."

"No doubt about that, but men are inspired by a lot of things. Just because there may have been an ulterior motive behind the original inspiration doesn't alter the fact that a work of art often comes out of it."

Greg Alexander ran his fingers down the row of tabs on a telephone-number index beside the phone on his desk. When he came to J, he pressed down a tab and the top flew up, revealing Keith Jackson's office and house numbers, along with others. Picking up the phone, he dialed nine for the outside connection and then the number; Keith himself answered the second ring.

"This is Dr. Alexander," said Greg. "How's everything going?"

"Fine, Doctor—except for sleep."

"One of the trustees has requested a special meeting Friday afternoon at four o'clock and I have an idea there'll be a demand then for the preliminary plans. Could you possibly make it?"

"There goes *another* night's sleep—but we'll have something ready for you."

"I'm going to ask you a question, Keith," said Greg. "And I need a frank answer."

"What is it, Doctor?"

"When you first brought your sketches to my attention a couple of weeks ago, had anyone else suggested the idea to you?"

There was a moment's pause, then the architect said, "I think I told you the idea originally came from an article—I believe it was in *Life* or *Look*—about that new hotel in Atlanta. It showed a possible way to handle the problem of the statue."

"Do you remember who brought the article to your attention?"

"I promised not to mention it."

"This is pretty important, Keith. The success of the whole project may hinge on your answer."

"It was Dr. Henry Anders, sir. He said he thought something like the Atlanta hotel theme would be a fitting memorial to his father, but he didn't want me to mention his part in it to you."

"Did he say why?"

"He was afraid you might be prejudiced against the idea because it came from him. I didn't know you very well then, Doctor, so I accepted his explanation. Lately, though, it's been troubling me and I'm really glad you asked about it."

"Thanks, Keith."

"Is anything wrong, Dr. Alexander?"

"No. I think everything is going to work out all right."

"Then I'd better get back to my work. Good-by."

"You were right, I've been booby-trapped," Greg told Templeton when he hung up the phone. "Those who don't want The Clinic rebuilt here suggested that idea to Keith Jackson, figuring I might fall for it and present the trustees with a radical design most of them wouldn't go along with."

He picked up the sketch again and studied it for a moment, then handed it to the newspaperman. "Take another look and tell me what you think?"

"I've already made up my mind," said Jud Templeton. "Whoever's behind all this—and I think I could name names if I had to—has outsmarted himself. When do I get a chance to run the sketch in the newspaper?"

"How about the Friday afternoon edition?"

"Fine. But I'll need it well before that. Making a cut takes time."

"Take it with you now. I'm trusting you that the newspaper piece won't come out until Friday afternoon."

Greg handed Jud Templeton the sketch and he put it in his writing case, handling it as carefully as if it had been a precious jewel. "I'll do my piece at home telling about the heroic struggle to keep greedy profiteers from destroying the greatest medical institution in the world," he promised. "And I'll have an engraver friend make the cut outside the paper so nobody will have an inkling of it until I hand the whole thing to the city editor Friday morning."

"You're being very helpful," said Greg. "I'm indebted to you."

"There was a price involved, don't forget that. You're to keep me up to date on the progress of the Merchant-Lawson operation." Jud Templeton glanced at his watch. "The paper owns a TV and radio station; we've got the six o'clock spot covered already but I'll need two or three lines on the case for the eleven o'clock news."

"I've an idea the whole thing will be settled by then—probably against us. We almost lost Merchant less than two hours ago in an acute heart failure."

"What about Lawson?"

"He's losing ground."

"But not fast enough?"

"That's about it."

"How's Georgia taking it?"

"Very well."

"She's a trouper," said Templeton. "Do you mind if I talk to her? She's always good for a feature and the slant of a wife on this sort of a situation might be very interesting right now."

"Not if she doesn't object."

"One other thing. Can I do a feature about you?"

"NO!"

"I knew you'd say that, but what a story it would make. Imagine thumbing your nose at one of the richest men in the world to further the dream of a man who wasn't even related to you."

12

The afternoon session of the convocation was almost over when Greg looked in through a door that gave access to the upper row of seats in the lecture room. Henry Anders was no longer presiding and Greg was not able to see Ed McDougal anywhere. A change of speakers was taking place just then and a number of doctors were leaving, among them, Helen Foucald.

"If you're looking for Henry," she said, "he gave the task of presiding to Dr. Remick as soon as that Texan came back at the end of the coffee break. I imagine they're out plotting against you."

"Well, at least it's nice to know they're consistent."

"Greg."

"Yes."

"There's something you ought to know. I learned it accidentally."

"You don't have to betray any confidences, Helen."

"Maybe the time has come to burn a few bridges."

"It might turn out that you backed the losing team. We're playing in a very fast league."

"That's why I want my part of the game to be on the level," she said. "Henry's cooking up some sort of a scheme to get you out on a limb so he can saw you off at the right moment. I don't know the details but—"

"I know them already, Helen, so don't burn your bridges yet."

"But how?"

Greg looked at his watch. "Just about now the Wall Street Final editions of the afternoon paper will be hitting the newsstands. Henry invited a reporter to be at the opening session so he and Ed McDougal could publicize the fact that the Board of Trustees will probably try to censure me Friday afternoon. But they didn't figure on my announcing the transplant and it's such startling news that their little plan got pushed out of the way."

"Henry must be fit to be tied."

"Ed McDougal came to my office during the coffee break this afternoon. He offered to back me—up to a limit—and split Sam Hunter's money with me."

"Poor old man, so narrow-minded and so convinced that he's right."

"Paranoia in a mild form is an occupational disease of both age and big business," said Greg. "Old Sam is no worse than a lot of others; when he sees the facts, he usually does what's right."

"I take it that you didn't accept Dr. McDougal's offer."

"No."

"Could you have still built The Clinic here if you had?"

"Possibly. But if I had taken the bait, the first chance Ed got he'd double-cross me, just as he was willing to double-cross Henry."

"Poor Henry," she said. "He does so much want to be a really big man but he never is, except when he's making love. I guess you could call him a human phallic symbol."

ii

When Greg came back to where Guy Merchant lay upon a table in one of the anesthetic rooms, he found a nurse-anesthetist watching the patient while Dr. Lewis Gann smoked his pipe in the adjoining lounge and dressing room for the surgical staff.

"What do you think of Merchant's condition now, Lew?" the surgeon asked.

"He's still losing ground, but a lot more slowly than before Bob did the tracheostomy. How about Lawson?"

"Herb Partridge thinks there's a slow hemorrhage into the deep centers of the brain. We'll have to wait and see."

"I heard your announcement about the new automated hospital," said the anesthesiologist. "What is my department going to be like?"

"You'll be working underground most of the time. I can tell you that much."

"Then your setup will be somewhat like the one at George-town?"

"Keith Jackson hasn't worked out the details yet, but the principle will be the same. Patients for surgery will be admitted to the operative section the night before and go directly from their own rooms on the lower levels to the O.R. by the shortest possible route the next morning. Every precaution will be taken to avoid any possibility of contamination and cut down the incidence of post-operative infection."

"No interns scurrying in and out at the last minute taking histories and doing preoperative physicals?"

"All of that will be done in the diagnostic clinic—except for acute emergencies. The patient's record will be stored in the data proc-essing system and printed out as it is needed by the computer."

"Do you have in mind letting a computer take the history—like they're experimenting with out in Minnesota and some other places?"

"If we can get the money for it—yes."

"You're thinking big, boy." Dr. Gann shook his head admiringly. "Real big."

"The heart of the whole project is a twelve-story high-rise ICU built where the present rotunda stands, with the statue of Christ at its base surrounded by glass. And we'll have full-sized twin hyperbaric chambers underground, placed so we can go from one to the other for transplantations without having to be decom-pressed."

"Still not interested in artificial hearts?"

"Other people are working on that," said Greg. "My job is to make heart-lung transplants feasible, and, with the surgical tech-nique worked out, we can concentrate on problems of rejection. The only way to do that is to perform transplant operations as often as we can and then fight the rejection battle as it arises, using what we've already learned from dogs and from the patients we operate on as the basis for future progress."

"Suppose Ed McDougal and his crowd succeed in blocking you? I've got some money on you in the hospital pool."

"If I can't have what I need here, I'll go somewhere else. Maybe you'd better go out and hedge that bet, Lew."

"If you can lay a career on the line, I guess I can risk five bucks," said the anesthesiologist.

One of the Junior Fellows in surgery burst into the lounge, carrying a newspaper in his hand. "This just hit the newsstands," he said excitedly. "You're all over the front page, Dr. Alexander."

Jud Templeton had been as good as his word, Greg saw. Blazing across the top of the front page was a headline in bold black type:

CLINIC SURGEON TO PERFORM HEART-LUNG TRANSPLANT

Beneath it, under Jud Templeton's by-line and with a two-column cut of Greg was the story:

> A startled Convocation of former Fellows of The Clinic and staff doctors today heard one of their number, Dr. Gregory Alexander, announce at the opening session of their biennial convocation his intention to make surgical history. Probably while the group is still in session for their meeting, Dr. Alexander plans to transplant the heart and lungs of a convicted murderer into the body of a patient dying of heart failure. Guy Merchant, the prospective recipient, is a well-known musical comedy figure of former years. The proposed donor, Frank Lawson, is a four-time loser who may have a chance before the day is over to fulfill the well-known Shakespearean adage that *"Nothing in his life became him like the leaving of it."*

There was more: brief summaries of Greg's experimental work, as described in previous newspaper accounts, and a biographical sketch of him, Guy Merchant and Frank Lawson. Greg handed the newspaper back to the excited young doctor, who left immediately to spread the news throughout the hospital.

"Somehow I don't get the impression that you were surprised by those headlines," said Dr. Gann.

"Jud Templeton warned me this afternoon after he'd sent the story to the copy room."

"I was hoping you'd stolen a march on Henry and his motley crew by getting in touch with Templeton yourself."

"Henry did that for me," said Greg. "He invited Templeton to cover the convocation, thinking I would object to the Friday special session of the board and sentiment would build up against me when it was learned that I will probably be censured. But I accidentally stole a march on him by announcing that I had canceled the dog transplant operation scheduled for tomorrow in order to keep the operating teams free for the one we hope to do this afternoon or evening. As it turned out, nobody paid much attention to the special board meeting; I didn't even see any reference to it in the newspaper."

"So Henry and Ed got the shaft—on their own petards? It couldn't happen to a more deserving pair. Can you stay here for ten minutes or so, in case the nurse watching Merchant needs help?"

"Sure. What's your hurry?"

"I want to get some more money down on you before news of this gets out and the odds start changing."

iii

The final edition of the afternoon newspaper hit The Clinic and its environs like an exploding bomb. Those who had been attending the convocation first saw it when the afternoon session broke up for the McDougal-Anders cocktail party, shortly before five o'clock. Even before the party started in the Falstaff Room of the Clinic Inn, however, it was a major topic of conversation for the Members.

Henry Anders and Ed McDougal saw the newspaper as they were crossing The Parkway for a conference of war. Henry turned a little pale at the sight of the bold black headlines and poured himself a drink as soon as they reached the suite Ed had rented as headquarters for his political maneuvering. Only after a gin and tonic, did Henry's normally florid face regain some of its color.

"A lot of Members aren't going to like this publicity," he ventured. "I guess Greg hung himself with the rope we gave him by having that reporter there."

"Don't be a fool!" said Ed McDougal. "Greg would never have allowed premature publicity about the transplant if he'd had anything to say about it. This is the best break he possibly could have had—and you gave it to him."

"But you said he talked to Templeton."

"Only after the story was written. Templeton didn't want to risk having Greg use whatever influence he had with the publisher to call off the story."

"I still don't see—"

"Then you'd damn sure better start looking," the Texan said savagely. "You and I know the experimental work that will make this transplant succeed—if it does—was done with a budget of peanuts. Much of that came out of Greg's own pocket, too, so now he can argue to the board that, if he's able to do what he's doing with so little money, he could accomplish a lot more if he really had some funds."

"He'll never convince Sam Hunter of that."

"Sam's not the only one on the board, remember? For five years or so The Clinic's been coasting on the reputation it built up during your father's lifetime and what Greg has been able to do. This transplant business could be just the shot in the arm it needs to be back on top professionally, and, if that happens, Greg can thumb his nose at Sam Hunter and the rest of us with a campaign to raise funds and rebuild the way he wants to do. But it would be Greg's clinic then—don't forget that it doesn't even have your father's name on it—and you'd be out on your fat behind."

Henry Anders poured a second gin and tonic and drank half of it in one gulp. He was sweating, although the room was not excessively warm.

"Wh—what do we do?"

"First we'll try to undo the mess you made by tipping off that reporter, starting with Sam Hunter," said the Texas surgeon. "But let me do the talking. I know how to handle the old man; all you'll do is to put your foot in your mouth again."

Moto, Sam Hunter's valet, let them into the millionaire's suite. "Mr. Hunter has been sleeping, Dr. McDougal," he said. "He was very tired when he finished the examinations this morning and he has more tests tomorrow."

"We won't be long, Moto," Ed promised. "Just a couple of things we wanted to ask Mr. Hunter about." He looked around the sitting room of the suite. "You don't have the afternoon paper yet?"

"Mr. Hunter reads only the morning Dallas *News* and, of course, the *Wall Street Journal.*"

"Moto!" Sam Hunter called from the bedroom. "Who's out there?"

"Dr. McDougal and Dr. Anders, sir."

"Tell them I'll be out in a minute."

"Make yourselves comfortable, gentlemen," said the valet, and vanished into the bedroom. Sam Hunter came out a few minutes later, wearing a silk dressing gown.

"I was getting ready for that party," he said. "Why aren't both of you downstairs being hosts?"

"We thought you should see something first." Ed McDougal handed him the newspaper, folded so the bold headlines were the first thing he saw. The old man skimmed through the story, the half glasses he usually wore, perched low on his nose, then gave it back.

"I thought doctors were supposed to avoid publicity," he said. "Isn't there something about that in your code of ethics?"

"This is certainly a breach of ethics, sir." Ed seized the opening gambit the old man seemed to have given him. "From what I learned in the hospital this afternoon, there's no chance of the man who's supposed to receive the new heart even living long enough to be operated on."

"Alexander's no fool," said the oil baron. "If I were losing, I guess I'd try some sort of a grandstand play like this, too."

"It does appear to be an act of desperation, sir," said Ed. "But it's also deceitful, don't you think, to imply that you plan to save a man's life when you know perfectly well you've got no chance of doing it?"

"I'd call it smart. Didn't know Alexander was that good a poker player."

"Are you going to let him get by with it, sir? Surely this grandstand play won't change your mind."

"Nothing changes my mind until I get ready to change it. You ought to know, Ed, since you're so determined to get a lot of money out of me for that medical school of yours down in Texas."

"But, sir—"

"You're a good poker player, too, so I'm surprised that you'd try to put over something as obvious as this scheme of yours to discredit Dr. Alexander," the old man added. "As far as I'm concerned, this business about avoiding publicity you doctors make so much fuss about is a lot of hokum. You criticize other doctors who make the headlines, but you still grab every chance to make them yourselves."

"I don't think you're being quite fair, Mr. Hunter." Ed McDougal had lost some of his assurance. Like Henry Anders, he was beginning to sweat.

"I used to own some movie theaters down in Texas before the war," said Sam Hunter. "As a courtesy to doctors, we would accept messages for them while they were in the theater, and flash telephone numbers for them to call on the screen. I got sort of suspicious after some of the managers reported the same doctors seemed to be getting calls all the time. When we checked at the box office to see who came through, we discovered that most of the ones who were always being paged in our theaters weren't even there, so we stopped the free advertising."

"That sort of thing is frowned on by the medical societies," Ed protested.

"But doctors still go on doing it just the same. I had a chance to think things over while I was trying to go to sleep this afternoon. It seems to me like some of you fellows are pushing me sort of hard on this Clinic thing." He turned to Henry Anders. "That's a right smart woman doctor you have there in the laboratory, Henry. She's lock, stock and barrel for Dr. Alexander, so maybe there's more to him than I thought. Anyway, I'm going to talk to her some more and maybe to him, too, before I make up my mind about what I'll do at the board meeting. What chance does he have with this heart transplant idea of his, by the way?"

"None at all, sir," Ed McDougal said quickly.

"I didn't ask you, Ed. You've been so busy getting rich down in Texas, you wouldn't know anything about it anyway. What do you say, Henry?"

"He's never done the operation on a human being, sir."

"How about dogs? Dr. Foucald said something about that and so did that X-ray fellow."

Henry Anders took a deep breath. He didn't want to admit Greg Alexander's success, yet he knew he couldn't fool the old man very long.

"Speak up!" Sam Hunter barked. "Or don't you know what's going on in your own clinic—like Dr. Remick said today?"

"Greg—Dr. Alexander has transplanted both heart and lungs in a number of dogs, sir. I don't know how many are alive but one of them did have pups last night."

"It looks like somebody's been trying to make a fool of Old Sam." The millionaire nodded slowly. "I don't know anything about medicine, but the last man that tried it with oil down in Texas wound up in the poorhouse. Now get out of here and let me get ready for the party. Is that handsome wife of yours going to be there, Henry?"

"Oh yes, sir. Claire's looking forward to seeing you again."

"She's a better man than you are," said Sam Hunter bluntly. "See you downstairs, gentlemen."

Outside, Henry Anders took a handkerchief from his pocket and wiped the sweat from his face. "The old coot is on to us, Ed," he said. "What are you going to do?"

"I'm going to drop a few hints among the trustees that this newspaper article was planted by Greg," the Texas surgeon told him. "How well do you know Dr. Foucald?"

"Rather well." Henry began to perk up somewhat.

"Been layin' her regularly?"

"Well—yes."

"I thought so, from the look on your face when I saw you together in the hospital this morning. How is she in the hay?"

"Neither of us have complained." Henry was regaining some of the assurance he'd lost under Sam Hunter's lashing tongue.

"Wish I had time to try a little jousting there myself, but that dough of Sam Hunter's is too important to my plans. Does she live in the apartment building next-door?"

"Yes. In one of the penthouses."

"Why don't you go up there and lay down the law to her, so she'll know what to say if the old man talks to her again?"

"That's a good idea." Henry Anders brightened perceptibly. "Tell Claire I've been delayed at the hospital for a little while."

"Make it a quick one; we need to talk to a lot of people. This is the only chance we'll have to get them all together, except the dinner Thursday night, and it may be too late by then."

iv

Peter Carewe hadn't noticed Helen leave the lecture room during the afternoon session. When it was over, he looked for her among the departing crowd, and, not finding her, went to the laboratory. There he was told by her secretary that she had left early to dress for the cocktail party.

"Do you know her home telephone number?" he asked.

"I'll get her on the phone for you, Dr. Carewe. You can take it in her office." When the phone rang, Helen was on the line.

"My secretary said that gorgeous doctor from the WHO wanted to speak to me." At the lilt in her voice he felt a sense of happiness perfuse his entire body. "Most of my technicians are women, so be careful how you wander around there or the laboratory results for the rest of the afternoon will all be in error."

"I looked for you at the end of the clinical session," he said. "Thought we might have a quick drink before the cocktail party."

"I'm afraid I'm not dressed."

"In that case, I'd better come up there."

"That will be nice," she said. "I'll leave the door on the latch."

He was there in less than ten minutes. As she had said, the door was unlatched and he let himself in, closing it behind him.

"That you, Peter?" Helen called from the bedroom.

"It had better be."

174

"I'll be out in a minute. Make yourself comfortable."

When she came out of the bedroom, she was flushed from the bath, and from his presence—like a schoolgirl, she thought, on her first date. Her dress was deceptively simple, of yellow linen, with a gored skirt that flared out as she turned for his inspection.

"You're the one who's gorgeous." He took her hands, leading her toward the sofa, but she deftly guided him to a love seat on the other side of the room instead. The sofa was a reminder of too many things she'd just as soon forget at the moment.

"Ever since we had coffee together I've been thinking about when I'd see you again," he said. "I wanted to tell you about the dinner I'm going to order—"

"It will have to be at the Inn. Greg wants me to stay in touch, in case he does the transplant."

"This is the first time I ever hated Greg in my life," he said. "But maybe we can find a corner to ourselves. We'll take hours eating and more hours afterward over brandy in my suite, enjoying the miracle of digestion."

"You must have had a French ancestor. Only a Frenchman could appreciate that sort of an evening."

"My mother was French."

"And mine, American."

"No wonder you have so little accent. We're really two citizens of the world, aren't we?"

"Oh, my experience can't begin to equal yours. Father was a correspondent for the old Paris edition of the *Herald Tribune* and mother was a fashion editor. We lived in a village outside the city, until they sent me to an American preparatory school inside Paris."

"Are they there now?"

"My parents were killed in an airplane crash in the Alps just as I was getting ready to go to college."

"That's the best way to go—together."

"The insurance they left took me through the Sorbonne and a Ph.D. I was embarked on a career in hematology until I decided to come to the United States instead."

"To Boston—you told me about it this morning."

She laughed. "You swept me off my feet so completely, I can't even remember what I did or said."

"Neither can I, except that when I saw you there in the airport this morning, I knew I'd found my heart's desire. Doesn't that sound corny?"

"Not if it isn't what you call a line."

"Would I use a phrase like that as part of a line?" He threw up his hands in mock horror. "It could only come from the heart."

"Really, Peter, you're delightful." She leaned forward to kiss him, but when he put his arm about her and crushed her mouth beneath his own, what she had intended to be a light caress turned into the almost blinding heat of desire. Suddenly helpless before the hot tide of passion that swept over her, and feeling the swift stirrings of his own surging desire, she knew that in another instant he would lift her and carry her to the bedroom—and willed with all the surge of passion flowing through her that he would.

Perhaps no sound could have intruded so completely into the fierce rush of desire that gripped them both as the grate of a key in the lock. Helen heard it first and, pushing Peter away, was halfway to the door of the apartment when it opened to reveal Henry Anders standing there gaping at them.

"Why, Henry!" Helen's voice was a little shrill and the intruder could not have been such a fool as not to have realized the nature of the scene he had interrupted. "Did I forget to lock my door? I must be more careful."

"I guess I must have pushed it open when I was getting ready to knock," Henry Anders mumbled.

Peter Carewe's glance went quickly to the lovely flushed woman standing between him and Henry's bulk, then to Henry's embarrassed face. He didn't miss the shrillness in Helen's tone, or Henry's bumbling embarrassment—and both sent a chill through him.

"Thought you'd be at the party, Henry," he said to help cover up the awkwardness of the situation. "You're one of the hosts, aren't you?"

"Claire sent me up to tell Helen she won't need the"—Henry's eyes raced quickly around the apartment until they lit upon a lovely antique silver coffee service in a glass-fronted cabinet—"the coffee service. Turns out that the Inn has one, so there's no need for you to bring yours, Helen."

"Thank you, Henry." Helen's voice was calm now. "Peter and I are coming down in a few moments."

"I'll see you there then." Henry backed out of the room, closing the door.

For a moment after the latch clicked, there was a silence; then Helen said, a little too brightly: "Where were we?"

"I was about to sweep you off your feet, I believe is the cliché that expresses the situation," said Peter, and her heart contracted at the note of pain in his voice. "But that would be a little anticlimactic now, wouldn't it?"

"I'll get a wrap," she said. "You're the celebrity of this occasion, so I shouldn't be monopolizing you."

13

"Back so soon, darling?" Claire asked when Henry, looking baffled and angry, appeared in the Falstaff Room, where the Members of The Clinic and their wives had begun to gather for the cocktail party. "I gather Helen wasn't in the mood."

"Didn't Ed tell you I had to see a patient in the hospital?" he demanded shortly.

"Come now, darling. It's your loyal and devoted wife you're talking to, somebody who knows you never let duty interfere with pleasure."

"Can you say anything but the same about yourself?" he snapped, but Claire had already turned to greet a doctor from Minneapolis and his somewhat dumpy wife.

"How nice to see you," she said warmly to the guests. "Do have a drink. Hannah and Ed McDougal are a little late."

"Where the hell are our co-hosts, anyway?" Claire spoke to Henry again as the couple from Minneapolis moved on. "Ed came in here, told me you'd be late and ran away. And Hannah hasn't shown up at all."

"All hell has broken loose." Henry plucked a glass from the tray of a passing waiter. "Haven't you seen the afternoon paper?"

"I've been busy here, seeing that everything was ready for the party."

"Jud Templeton was at the convocation this afternoon when Greg announced that he expects to do a human heart-lung transplant before morning. It's all over the front page."

"So?" Claire's eyebrows lifted. "It would seem that Greg stole a march on you two."

Henry exploded into an oath that startled some of those nearby and emptied his glass hurriedly. "On top of that, Sam Hunter is acting up."

"You should have better sense than to get into these situations without consulting me, darling," Claire told him sweetly. "And to tie yourself up with Ed McDougal of all people; he'll double-cross you the moment your back is turned. Ah! Here come our co-hosts now. Looks like they're having a snit."

Ed McDougal and Hannah had come into the room and Claire moved over to greet them. "I was beginning to be afraid you two had forgotten your own party, darlings," she said.

"Sorry we're late, Claire," said the Texas surgeon. "I had to change clothes."

"You're so efficient, Claire," said Hannah. "And since the guests are almost all men, I knew you'd have everything under control."

"Now that you're here, I'm sure we can handle them," said Claire. "You always do things on such a big scale down in Texas, darlings. I feel like we ought to barbecue a bull or something, so you'll feel at home."

"Break it up, Claire," said Henry. "Sam Hunter just came in."

"Aren't you afraid to let all that money go unprotected, Ed?" Claire asked. "I thought you and Henry would be guarding him on either side, like the men from Brinks—with Hannah bringing up the rear. After all, somebody might talk Mr. Hunter into giving a buck or two to their favorite charity." She left the others and moved across the room to greet the old financier, who was standing alone in the door, looking over the people there.

"Mr. Hunter!" she said warmly. "How nice to see you!" Leaning forward, she let the old man kiss her cheek.

"You're about the only one here who could say that and really make me believe it, Claire," he said. "You're wearing well."

"That's because I vary my diet. Wouldn't you like a drink?"

"Some bourbon and branch water, if you have such things here."

"Of course we do." Claire signaled a waiter. "Bourbon and water for the gentleman—I'll have the same."

"You're quite a woman, Claire," the old millionaire said admiringly. "If I were thirty years younger, I'd do my best to put horns on Henry."

"Confidentially, you'd do it, too," Claire assured him. "You must have been quite a rounder in your day—and I'll bet that day isn't far behind you."

"I'm complimented, Claire, but it's a lost cause." Sam Hunter took the glass the waiter handed him and stared at the pale amber contents morosely. "Nothing much to live for any more except making money and browbeating everybody I can. And that's a damn poor excuse for anybody's existence."

"Are you going to let them move The Clinic outside the city?" Claire lowered her voice as she guided him toward a corner table.

"I don't know yet." The old man studied her over his glass. "You know Henry will be rich if I do, don't you?"

"I'm not sure I want him rich."

"Why not?"

"We're an ideal couple as it is. I've got money and Henry's got— shall we say—an unusual capability of pleasing a woman."

"So these rumors I've been hearing about him are true?"

"They're true, Mr. Hunter. Remarkably so, in fact."

"I knew there must be some reason besides his charming personality why women seem to like him so much," said the old man. "I gather you think that if Henry had money, you might have to share him with others."

"I already share him; right now he's more than one woman has a right to expect. But things will change. And as long as I have the money, I can keep him from roving."

Sam Hunter smiled. "They call us Texans wheelers and dealers but a smart woman can put it over us any day. I'll think about what you've been saying, Claire. Go on now and entertain your other guests."

"Are you sure I can't do anything to make your stay here more pleasant?" she asked.

"Not any longer, my dear," said Sam Hunter sadly. "Not any longer."

ii

There was a stir of interest when Peter Carewe came in with Helen Foucald. Helen saw Claire and Sam Hunter together and deftly guided Peter across the room to where the two were standing.

"Hello, Claire," she said. "You look ravishing tonight."

"It's mutual," said Claire.

"Good evening, Mr. Hunter," said Helen.

The old magnate bowed gallantly and Claire said, "I presume this is Dr. Carewe. I'm Claire Anders."

"Our hostess!" said Peter warmly.

"One of them. The other one is conferring with my husband and her husband over there in the corner of the room, planning some sort of skulduggery. She's the one flaunting the ermine collar and the deep V."

"I want to apologize for my behavior in my office this morning, Mr. Hunter," said Helen. "I'm afraid I was very rude to you."

"You held up your end of it very well, Doctor. I always admire anybody who puts up a good fight—even against me."

"There's Jeanne Alexander and the Pucketts," said Claire. "Excuse me while I go and speak to them. Why don't you three take one of the tables?"

"You seem to have an exciting life, young man," said Sam Hunter when they had seated themselves and a waiter brought drinks for Helen and Peter.

"I stay busy."

"Spending American money on naked savages who go back to eating each other as soon as they use up what you give them?"

"You've got the WHO mixed up with UNESCO, Mr. Hunter. I'm busy making the world safe for capitalism by stamping out disease so industry can move into undeveloped lands and exploit native labor."

"Humph!" said the old man, but there was a gleam of amusement in his eyes. Sam Hunter could respect a worthy antagonist; in fact, one reason he'd come to Baltimore prepared to face down Greg Alexander and the plan for a new Clinic was because Greg had given in at the board meeting two years ago and agreed to accept a compromise. The surgeon had, however, risen sharply in the old man's opinion since he'd learned of the newspaper article that afternoon.

"I saved one of your own drilling outfits from having to shut down in the Persian Gulf just last year, Mr. Hunter," said Peter.

"How's that?"

"Some Anopheles gambiae mosquitoes—the kind that carry malignant malaria—had been brought into the area on company planes. We found them in baggage loaded in Ghana and for a few months the whole operation was about to be stalled by malignant malaria—"

"So you went about swatting mosquitoes?"

"No." Peter grinned. "We used the human approach—killed them with sex."

"What a happy way to die." Claire Anders had just joined the group again with Jeanne. "I'd like you to meet Jeanne Alexander, Sam. I'm trying to convince her you're not an ogre at all but a very nice man."

Sam Hunter greeted Jeanne with courtly grace and Peter Carewe kissed her. "It's been too long since I've had one of those dinners you used to cook when I was a senior medical student, Jeanne."

"None of us had any money," he explained to the others, "so Jeanne would make a big pot of sauerkraut and wieners and ask us over. Where's Greg?"

"I talked to him a little while ago on the phone," she said. "He has to stay close to the operating room until the question of the transplant is decided."

"Nobody's talking about anything else, and Ed and Henry are fit to be tied," said Claire. "Confidentially, they planned this whole affair to impress you, Sam, and now Greg's stolen their thunder. But don't let me interrupt whatever you were discussing."

"I was telling Mr. Hunter how we stopped an epidemic of malignant malaria in the Persian Gulf last year, when Anopholes gambiae mosquitoes carrying the disease, were brought in by plane," said Peter. "You see, we'd learned how to record the mating call of the female mosquito on a tape recorder, so all we had to do was to play the tapes close to open flames from a kerosene burner. Then when the males came flying in, they were incinerated."

"That's cruel," said Claire in mock horror. "Did the females incinerate themselves, too, like the Indian wives used to do—what do they call that?"

"Suttee!" said Sam Hunter. "I saw it happen once in India when I was traveling there a long time ago."

"How terribly romantic," said Claire. "Like something the Bronte sisters might have written."

"Life doesn't happen that way," said Peter. "In the Persian Gulf, the female gambiae soon took up with other mosquitoes, but fortunately they didn't breed true. Pretty soon all the carriers of malignant malaria died off and so did the epidemic."

"The eternal adaptability of the female," said Helen. "Sometimes I think it's the only thing that has kept the human race alive."

"Are you a philosopher, Doctor?" Sam Hunter asked.

"My work usually deals with the smallest unit of the human body, the single cell," she explained. "When you study life in a microcosm, everything boils down to simple principles of growth and survival."

"Monotonous, isn't it?" said Claire. "I'm glad humans vary the pattern."

"As I watch a culture of cells, every now and then one of them begins to vary beyond the ordinary limits established by genetics, as we know it," said Helen. "When that happens, a predator is loosed upon the rest of the growth and the destruction is almost beyond belief."

"Are you implying that those of us who succeed in business are predators who prey upon ordinary little people?" Sam Hunter asked.

"Not necessarily," she said. "But do you deny that strong men usually succeed because of the failure of many weak ones?"

"If all were of the same strength, no one would get ahead."

"I still say that orderliness is admirable," she insisted. "That way the entire life cycle of a single cell is predictable, along with the nature of its offspring."

"It's a lot more fun to have a little variety," said Claire. "Fortunately, the pill has taken care of that situation."

"With everybody so busy enjoying themselves, they'll stop bothering to raise children," Jeanne objected. "Then the birth rate will fall off even more sharply than it has already and we'll be overrun by more fertile races. I think it was Will Durant who said in one of his lectures that the final determining factor in the rise and fall of any civilization is the birth rate. As it becomes more and more highly developed, the rate tends to fall—"

"The American birth rate has been dropping steadily, except for the brief period of upsurge produced by the war babies," said Helen.

"Exactly," Jeanne agreed. "While at the same time, the population of the less highly civilized areas—according to our standards —is increasing faster than the food supply. Eventually they'll overrun the more highly developed nations and then the cycle will start all over again."

"What the more highly civilized nations need to realize," said Peter, "is that by helping others learn to look after themselves through measures like birth control and raising more food, they're actually protecting their own cultures. What really destroys an advanced civilization is selfishness, their refusal to share with others the bounty their own intelligence produces."

"You're leaving out one important factor, Doctor," said Sam Hunter.

"What's that, sir?"

"Hard work. If the 'have nots' you're so busy bleeding about would get out and work, they'd pretty soon rise out of their own ruts into the higher level of the 'haves.'"

"You can't work very hard when the tapeworms, hookworms, or filariae in your body use up your food faster than you do, Mr. Hunter," said Peter. "And it's hard to be energetic when your blood's so pale from anemia that it doesn't even look like blood at all. As a doctor, the world is my practice and I can't see much sense in the American government paying farmers not to plant wheat and corn when everybody concerned would be a lot better off if they were allowed to plant all they could and sell it for use abroad. The only countries I've seen where communism has made any real inroads lately are those where the people were so hungry and sick they'd turn to anything. That's why we in the UN are working so hard to find cheap sources of food, like wheat and rice strains that produce twice as much grain as the ones we have now."

"The answer may be somewhere else," said Helen. "In our laboratory, we've managed to create a few mutations by exposing algae to X-ray. Some of them have bred true for many generations."

"What do you mean, Doctor?" Sam Hunter asked.

"A mutation is a new individual that doesn't follow the pattern of the parent cell or, with more complicated growths, the pattern of the species," she explained. "We're studying the green growths called algae that accumulate in water everywhere, hoping to find a mutation that will grow so rapidly it piles up cells and eventually forms a source of food."

"But algae need food, too, don't they?" Jeanne asked.

"They *do*," said Helen, "but there's an almost inexhaustible supply in organic waste that's now thrown away or destroyed. By growing algae selectively, so to speak, we hope to find a food source whose proportions of protein, carbohydrates and even fats can be regulated by controlling the area in which they grow. A highly concentrated protein food material that's cheap to produce is the one thing most hungry people in the world need more than anything else."

"So you'll feed them up to where they're strong enough to destroy us, eh, Doctor?" said Sam Hunter.

"I don't think that's a valid argument, Mr. Hunter," she protested. "The course of history has been that, as a people become better fed and more civilized, they tend to lose many of their more aggressive characteristics."

"Fat and lazy?"

"Which would you rather have, Mr. Hunter?" Peter Carewe asked. "Fat and lazy Chinamen enjoying the good things of life, or a hungry horde waiting to pour down into the rice bowl of Asia and seize control of half the world?"

"There's a weakness in your theory, Dr. Foucald," said the oilman. "The Germans are one of the most highly industrialized civilizations of the world and have been for a long time. They eat well and heavily, yet they've started two wars in my lifetime."

"I think the danger is that people who are prosperous can get so fat and lazy they don't bother to control the few individuals who turn into predators in order to achieve positions of power for themselves," said Jeanne Alexander. "That's what happened in

Germany, but I still think a nation hungry for food is more of a danger to the world than a few individuals hungry for power."

"Especially if the rest of the world watches out for the development of such megalomaniacs, and controls them," said Peter Carewe.

"And how do you propose to do that, Doctor?" the oilman asked.

"That's the function of the United Nations, sir."

"Humph!" The old man expressed his opinion of the world organization in the single expletive. "What have they done? A lot of talk and nothing else."

"Perhaps that's just where the UN has actually accomplished most," Peter Carewe insisted. "It's true that there has been a lot of talk, but with our modern means of communication, the whole world has been able to hear, and many of them see, who's really trying to keep peace and who's doing everything they can to set men against each other. If it hadn't accomplished anything else except that, I think the United Nations would have amply justified itself, but the really important work of the United Nations is being done in health centers throughout the world, trying to relieve disease, improve health, decrease suffering and cut down birth rates that keep people so poor they can't provide for the children they're so busy producing."

"Hear! Hear!" said Claire Anders. "Now, why don't you beautiful and intelligent people stop monopolizing each other and start mingling with the guests. This is supposed to be a social get-together and not a forum for deciding the problems of the world."

iii

"You do have a way of corralling the most handsome men, Claire," Hannah McDougal said when Claire came over to where she was standing in the corner with a glass in her hand, talking to Henry. Hannah's face was flushed and a slight slurring of words betrayed the fact that she had been drinking steadily since she had come into the room—to say nothing of before.

"I wouldn't say that, darling," said Claire. "Where's Ed?"

"Off somewhere having a council of war."

186

"Why aren't you with him, Henry?" Claire asked. "Or have they excluded you from the highest councils?"

"Damn it, Claire—"

"Please—no profanity before our guests. Excuse me, Hannah, I quite forgot that you're a hostess."

"You're welcome to forget it when the time comes to pay the bar bill," Hannah told her. "The way these people are swilling down expensive liquor is enough to make you shudder."

"I still think we should have had a barbecue," said Claire as she moved away to speak to other guests.

Hannah gave Henry an appraising look and, conscious of it, he preened himself a little. "This party's getting pretty dull," she said. "What say we cut and run?"

He looked around to see if anyone could have heard, but they were alone at the moment. "What about Ed?"

"Oh, he'll be gabbing with those cronies of his until the small hours. It always happens this way when we go to a convention, so I've learned to look after myself." The implication was obvious enough even for Henry Anders to understand.

"Ed deserves anything that happens for running off and leaving us alone." Hannah moved a little closer so her body casually touched Henry's. "Why don't we have a drink together in my suite upstairs. The liquor's better and I'm sure there are a lot of things we need to talk about."

"How soon?" Henry wet his lips with his tongue.

"Maybe half an hour. People will be drifting out to dinner by then."

"Henry's about to make his play," Claire observed *sotto voce* to Jeanne Alexander when she saw Hannah McDougal drift casually toward the door, stopping to speak to several people on the way.

"Don't you even mind?"

"If it wasn't Hannah, it would be Helen Foucald, though I have an idea that arrangement is due for a shake-up, judging by the look of those two yonder in the bar." Claire nodded toward where Helen and Peter had been joined by the dean of the School of Public Health. "It would take a lot stronger woman than Helen— or me—to resist a man like that Peter Carewe. I think she's gone off the deep end for him."

"I still can't help being a little shocked by all this," Jeanne confessed. "Maybe I'm too old-fashioned for today."

"Stay the way you are and shelter what you already have in the love of a good man," Claire advised. "You'd be surprised to know how infrequently that happens."

14

Dr. Herbert Partridge was halfway down the corridor to the lobby, intending to cross The Parkway to the Inn, in case the party was still in progress, when the pager in the pocket of his white coat beeped sharply. He turned aside immediately to the nearest telephone—in the office of the pediatric section.

"Dr. Partridge."

"Intensive care wants you, Doctor. The nurse said right away."

"Tell Dr. Johnson and Dr. Alexander I'm going there and will report as soon as I find out the situation." The neurosurgeon knew Frank Lawson's heart was still beating, for, if it had stopped, the Code One alert would have been flashed on the entire hospital paging system.

Code One automatically sent teams trained in all phases of cardiac resuscitation to the area of emergency, including those specially skilled in using the new closed-chest method, where the heart was literally massaged between the breastbone and the spine by pressure upon the chest. It also alerted a team for open-chest surgery, if that became necessary, but between the new closed-chest method and the cardiac Pacemaker that could jolt a stopped heart into action with repeated minute currents of electricity, open-chest surgery was rarely ever used any more for this greatest of complications.

Herbert Partridge found the intern assigned to intensive care beside Frank Lawson's bed. Across from him was a nurse who had also been watching the slowly dying man; no patient with a tracheostomy tube in place was ever left unwatched, because of the possibility that the tube might be blocked by coughed-up secretions and cause immediate suffocation.

One look at Frank Lawson's face explained why the neurosurgeon had been called. As if amused by some macabre joke hidden deep within his brain, his features were twisted in a maniacal grin.

"He started doing that about five minutes ago," the nurse said with a shudder. "It's almost like he was laughing inside at something."

"*Risus sardonicus.*" Herb Partridge spoke the words that popped into his conscious mind from some deep store of memory, put away long ago in medical school and rarely used since.

"Doesn't that have something to do with poisoning?" the young intern asked.

"Strychnine causes convulsive spasms of the face and neck at first before it involves the whole body," said the neurosurgeon. "So does tetanus."

"He couldn't possibly have developed tetanus this early, I'm sure." The intern leafed through the chart quickly. "Besides, they gave him toxoid when he was brought in."

Herbert Partridge's trained mind was working like the computer it actually was, sorting wheat from chaff as it considered the possibilities represented by the symptom complex he was watching and seeking to reach one diagnosis that fitted the entire picture. Suddenly the whole pattern fell into place.

"He's gone into a convulsive state," he told the intern.

"But why?"

"The hemorrhage must have reached some of the vital centers of the brain. We had a warning of it earlier, when his temperature started to rise."

"Why is the convulsion limited to the upper neck and the face?"

"Actually, it isn't. If the rest of his body hadn't been disconnected from the brain when his spinal cord was severed, this would be a generalized spasm. And if that tracheostomy tube wasn't giving him a clear airway through the windpipe, we'd be fighting right now to keep his breathing from being shut off entirely by the contraction of his throat and chest muscles."

"I've never seen anything like this," said the intern in an awed voice.

"The only muscles actually receiving impulses from the brain and going into spasm are those connected to that part of the nervous system which is still intact," Herb Partridge explained. "That means the cranial nerves connected to the brain itself and those coming off the first few segments of the spinal cord above the point where it's severed. Everything below the spinal cord wound is disconnected and, therefore, cannot respond, so the rest of his body doesn't convulse."

"I'm glad of it," said the nurse. "This is scary enough."

The pocket pager in Herb Partridge's coat beeped again and he went to the phone at the nurses' station; it was Greg Alexander.

"Frank Lawson's in an almost continuous convulsive state," the neurosurgeon reported in answer to Greg's query. "It's the damnedest thing you ever saw. Only the face and upper neck muscles still connected to the nervous system are in spasm."

"How about the heart?"

"The rate has increased sharply, so the brain control by way of the autonomic nervous system is undoubtedly involved, too. Do you want me to bring him down to the O.R. suite so you'll be ready?"

"I'd appreciate it," said Greg. "Lew Gann and Bob Johnson went to get an early dinner in the cafeteria and I can't leave the area. You don't think Lawson's in any immediate danger of a heart stoppage, do you?"

"No. His pulse is still strong. What about Merchant?"

"The tracheostomy helped his breathing but his heart's weakening fast. I think this is going to be close, Herb—very close."

"I'll bring Lawson down to one of the anesthetic rooms and attach electroencephalographic terminals to his scalp so we can monitor the brain waves. From the looks of his condition right now, they should be skittering all over the tube."

"Is Mrs. Merchant still up there?" Greg asked.

"I think so. She was in the waiting room when I came up."

"Ask someone to show her down to the corridor outside the O.R. I think I'd better bring her up to date on what's happening."

A sofa had been placed at the end of the corridor beyond the line, plainly marked upon floor, walls and ceiling, where only authorized operating room personnel were allowed to go—and then only when wearing special shoes.

"What's happening, Doctor?" Georgia asked when Greg came down the first-floor corridor to where she waited. "Dr. Partridge said they're taking Frank Lawson to the operating room."

"He's begun to have convulsions and we want him where we can be ready in case there's any sudden change," he explained.

"What about Guy?"

"Putting the tube into his windpipe and giving him the special injection has helped some," said Greg. "But his lungs are beginning to fill up again, showing that his heart is still having trouble keeping up the circulation."

"Can you give him something else to remove the fluid?"

"We don't want to use the drug too often. It hits the kidneys pretty hard to make them remove extra fluid and we could damage them."

"Maybe it would be better to just let him go on and die."

"I couldn't do that, Mrs. Merchant, even if you asked me."

"I know," she said. "This morning when they were trying to start Guy's heart, I prayed for him to die. My conscience has been troubling me ever since."

"It shouldn't," he assured her. "You had no way of knowing then that we might have a chance to save him."

"The newspaperman who talked to me this afternoon said you're risking your own position here to give Guy a chance. Is that true?"

"What I'm risking isn't important, compared to being able to save a life that's doomed otherwise."

"But if you *should* fail, couldn't things be bad for you?"

"Doctors always hate to lose a patient—in spite of the jokes you hear about us."

"I got a glimpse of Frank Lawson's face as they were taking him to the operating room." She shuddered at the memory. "He's dying, isn't he?"

"Yes."

"And the sooner you operate on Guy, the better off he'll be?"

"No question about that."

"Then can't you hurry Lawson's going a little?"

"Even the court can't name me his executioner, Mrs. Merchant."

"Would you accept the responsibility if it did—in order to save the life of another?"

Greg shook his head. "Chronic hospital wards are filled with people dying from cancer and other incurable diseases. If we perfect the heart-lung transplant operation to where it's rather uniformly successful, there will be a lot of pressure from people doomed by heart disease to take the hearts of those who can't be saved and give them to those who can. But doctors shouldn't be forced to make the final decision."

"Why?"

"Taking another man's life is still murder, unless the state orders it; I'm not at all sure it still isn't murder, even then. My own conscience would make me wait until Frank Lawson is pronounced dead, even if the state gave permission to end his life earlier."

"It's all so complicated," she said. "I want to have Guy well and I know that's what you want, too. Just go ahead and do what you think needs to be done, Dr. Alexander. I'd rather not even know what's happening until it's over—one way or the other."

"That's the better way, I'm sure," he agreed. "Once we start operating, we won't be able to keep you posted on the course of events anyway. Don't you want me to order a sedative for you so you can get a little rest?"

"No, thank you. Guy and I always bore our share of the load, until he got to where he couldn't carry his any longer. It would be sort of disloyal to him if I let down now."

On his way back to the operating suite, Greg met Jud Templeton outside one of the first-floor doors leading to the surgical lecture room. "I'm keeping a weather eye on those closed-circuit TV screens in there," he said. "The emergency room intern says that, when you operate, the whole thing can be seen there."

"We do televise important operations," said Greg, and added pointedly—"For doctors."

Jud Templeton grinned. "I've got a special invitation—remember? Are you going to revoke it?"

"No."

"They tell me that Lawson's gone into a convulsive state. Is this the end?"

"The beginning of it."

"Couldn't happen to a more deserving fellow. Any repercussions on my story?"

"Not yet. I think it threw the enemy into a state of confusion, but they'll counterattack before long."

"If Lawson hurries up his dying, you may be able to deal them another body blow with a successful transplant. It's like an old-time Western—the beleaguered garrison, the Indians outside the wall and the relief column racing to the rescue. Only, this time, I guess the Indians are ahead."

"We haven't given up the fort," said Greg with a smile. "There may still be quite a battle."

ii

The announcement via the TV screen that both Guy Merchant and Frank Lawson were now in surgery exploded in the midst of the Anders-McDougal cocktail party in the Falstaff Room at the Clinic Inn. Peter Carewe and Helen Foucald saw it first in the bar, where they were having a drink before dinner.

"I'll have to be in the lab when the operation on Guy Merchant really starts," she said. "Sometimes emergency proceedings are needed in a hurry to determine blood gases and things like that."

"But we can still have dinner here while you're waiting."

"Why not?" She opened her bag and took out the small, cigarette-case-size pager. "When the time comes, the hospital operator can call me."

A general exodus from the room had followed the TV announcement. "Call me when the real action starts, will you, Bill?" Peter told Bill Remick, who was just leaving. "We'll be here in the dining room."

"Well, that ends the party." Claire Anders took a fresh drink for herself and moved over to where Sam Hunter was talking to Jeanne Alexander.

"Nothing's duller than the end of a dull party, when you have to stay on feet that already hurt, waiting for the last straggler to leave," she said. "Jeanne, why don't you and I take Mr. Hunter to dinner in the restaurant?"

"I wouldn't be able to eat anything until the transplant operation is settled," said Jeanne. "You and Mr. Hunter go on, Claire. I'll have milk and crackers or something in our apartment, where I can watch the TV screen. Good night, Mr. Hunter. I enjoyed talking to you."

"Good night, Mrs. Alexander," the old man said. "Your husband and I haven't always seen eye to eye lately, but I can still wish him well with his surgery."

"That's more than a lot of people are doing right now," said Claire. "Don't worry about the luncheon tomorrow, Jeanne. Everything's under control."

"Where's Henry?" Sam Hunter asked as he and Claire moved toward the dining room, where the head waiter greeted them obsequiously.

"Oh, he's occupied somewhere," Claire said airily. "Probably deep in the heart of Texas—to make a lousy pun."

"You're a very remarkable woman, Claire," said the old man as they were being seated at the table. "I've never known but one like you."

"Don't tell me she was a saloon keeper on the frontier. You know—the one with the heart of gold who's a pushover for the handsome gambler."

"She was a countess in Italy—Salerno, to place it exactly."

"I remember Salerno well." Claire's tone was suddenly faraway. "Henry and I went there on our honeymoon. What was she like— this *contessa* of yours?"

"Very lovely and very blue-blood—like you."

"But not gone to seed, like my family."

"You certainly haven't gone to seed, my dear," he said gallantly.

"Only because I'm what you Texans call a maverick. Even as a little girl, I wouldn't let mother put me in starched dresses and do my hair in pigtails. Instead, I played baseball with the rest of the boys, until I was around fourteen."

"What happened then?"

"The groceryman's son and I were wrestling one day and he accidentally found out I wasn't a boy. I discovered the same thing a few minutes later—and I've never been the same since."

Sam Hunter smiled. "How much of this sort of talk is a shell to hide your disappointment at being married to a windbag?"

"You're not supposed to know that," she protested. "Ed McDougal and his cronies are somewhere upstairs right now, planning how they're going to pull the strings to make you jump."

"What if I don't jump the way they want me to?"

Claire studied him for a moment—then smiled. "My guess is they're much more liable to jump the way *you* want them to. I'm sure you didn't get to be one of the richest men in the world by letting people like Ed and Henry run over you."

"I owed ten years of additional happiness with my wife to your husband's father," the old man said soberly. "If I go on now and let Dr. Alexander build this new hospital he's planning behind my back—"

"Greg Alexander never did a really underhanded thing in his life," said Claire. "My guess is that he's got an idea and thinks you'll buy it, if you see it in a really understandable form and not just as a fragment."

"If I go along with that idea, it would be a blow to Henry."

"And to Ed McDougal?"

"I've dealt with Ed's kind all my life, but I don't want to slap Henry down, even though right now I suspect I should take him across my knee and give him a good hiding."

"Do what you think is best according to your conscience; I'll take care of Henry," said Claire. "Now, tell me about this Italian contessa of yours. She sounds like somebody I'd like."

"She was very sophisticated and I was anything but—still am, for that matter. But when you've got half a billion, you can do as you damn please and the worst people will say about you is that you're eccentric. The contessa taught me that the relationship between a man and a woman who don't intend to marry can still be —I don't exactly know the word."

"Something more than tumbling a Mexican maid in the barn when your parents weren't looking."

"Why, yes. How did you know?"

"Women have their moments, too, but if they've got any sense, they soon realize that romantic love eventually burns itself out like a fever. So most of 'em end up marrying the boy their family approves of and living moderately happily ever after—on their memories. Dessert every meal can get pretty tiresome; you need some meat and potatoes for regular fare—until your hips start spreading and you have to cut them out. You'd be surprised how many of my friends spend most of their time going from doctor to doctor or knocking themselves out with tranquilizers because they're not willing to accept reality and make the best of it. What every woman really needs is a perfect husband and a perfect lover; it's too bad they're rarely ever found in the same person."

"The contessa said almost the same thing."

"It must be a wonderful fulfillment for a woman to know she will live on as a romantic image in the heart and mind of a man she was happy with, however briefly." Claire's tone was wistful. "I imagine it's a little like being immortalized in a painting, the way Goya did the Duchess of Alba."

"Aren't you happy with Henry, Claire?"

"Who's happy?" she said with a shrug. "Henry is a lousy husband but a superb lover. When he finishes love-making, he goes to sleep; and when he gets up in the morning, he goes to the hospital." Her smile was overly brilliant, her tone brittle, like a piece of fine china. "I have the best of Henry when I want it and only a little of the worst, so I'm very fortunate, wouldn't you say?"

"And yet you're afraid."

Claire Anders gave the old millionaire a startled look and for a moment the hard bright façade she presented to the world crumpled, like the false front of a Western movie set in a high wind. But it was only for an instant, then everything was in place again.

"Why do you say that?"

"Once in Salerno, I saw the contessa looking at a workman who was repairing a wall. There was the same sort of hunger in her eyes, just for an instant, that I'd seen in the eyes of a coyote caught in a fence on the range and starving. I knew then that it was time for me to go back to the States, while I still had some memories I wanted to keep."

He reached across the table and put his hand over Claire's in a gesture that was extraordinarily tender for a man who had broken powerful opponents on many occasions, ruthlessly and without compunction. "Whatever happens on Saturday, I won't let it be anything that would cause you pain."

"Thank you, Sam." She squeezed his hand. "But what about Greg's new building?"

"I'll cross that bridge when I come to it. To have earned the loyalty of so many people, I suspect Dr. Alexander is strong enough to take another disappointment—if he has to."

15

"I wonder what Claire and Sam Hunter are so busy talking about," Peter Carewe said as he and Helen were waiting for the steaks he had selected to be cooked. "I wouldn't have thought they had much in common."

"Claire's a rare sort of a bird—and so, I imagine, is Mr. Hunter."

"I don't know her very well."

"That's a condition she would have remedied by now—if I hadn't seen you first."

"I'm glad you did," he told her. "Now, tell me something about your work. I want to learn all about you between now and Friday."

Dear God, not everything, Helen thought, but deep in her heart she knew the prayer would be of no avail. She'd seen Peter's eyes when Henry Anders had burst into the apartment that evening; while he might not have jumped to any conclusions then, he was no fool and Henry's every action, when he found them together, had spoken the truth far louder than any words could have done.

"I've been working with Greg Alexander on the problems of automating the laboratory," she said.

"I enjoyed his paper this afternoon—but I was envious, too," said Peter. "In the jungle, we're lucky to have a microscope and enough material to do an elementary job of culturing bacteria."

"I've seen some of the machines Greg spoke about," she said. "They've even got one now that can take mass survey electrocardiograms, and sound a warning when the test shows something abnormal."

"A lot of mossbacks in the AMA aren't going to like anything that looks like production-line medicine," he warned. "They've been fighting it since the thirties."

"They'll have to accept automation. Progress is already passing them by."

"Shape up or ship out, eh?"

"Why not, when doctors are digging their own graves by sticking to the horse and buggy approach to medical care represented by the individual physician practicing alone in his own office? A whole new medical generation is coming out of the hospitals now. They know nothing except partially automated clinic medicine and that's enough to make them realize the handwriting's on the wall for the old ways. When they get out into practice and see patients running all over town from doctor to doctor, spending days getting a complete examination and laboratory checkup that could be done in one place in a tenth of the time and at half the cost, things are going to change—fast."

"There will still be opposition by the conservative wing," he warned. "Look what's happening here this week—in a clinic that's been one of the most advanced medical centers in the world for the past fifty years."

"If Greg wins out on the new building, we'll prove we're right."

"Whatever happens, you're safe," he assured her. "You could be a success in any field if you bring to it the same energy you put into your profession."

"The same is true of you."

"Oh no. I'm the doctor from WHO—medical playboy."

"I'll never believe that, not after the way you put Sam Hunter in his place when he started belittling your work tonight."

"It could cost me my job. That old man is powerful."

"Not as powerful as the Russians—and you coped with them."

"That was a labor of love. Speaking of love, I've known you about nine hours now and I'm more strongly attracted to you than I've been to any woman I've ever met."

"I guess it's entirely unmaidenly of me, but that goes for me, too."

"Then what stands between us?"

"In the first place, love at first sight doesn't happen—except in popular novels and in the movies."

"It happened to us—at least to me."

"But your feeling is physiological."

"What's wrong with physiology? We couldn't get along without it."

"It's all right for an affair—the more physiology and less real love you have then, the better off both parties are. But I'm not sure I want to have an affair with you, Peter."

"Surely you're not afraid?"

She shook her head. "I'm thirty-five years old and not exactly repulsive, so it stands to reason that I've slept in other beds than my own—and not alone."

"Spare me the details."

"That's one reason why I'm not sure I want an affair with you," she said. "Already, you aren't certain you could keep it at just that level, else it wouldn't make any difference to you how many men I've slept with. In fact, you'd hope, subconsciously at least, that the number was large."

"Wherever did you discover that kind of reasoning?"

"It's really rather elementary psychology. If I've had a lot of lovers, it stands to reason I'm pretty good in bed."

"We're talking about *you*," he said with a show of anger. "Not some streetwalker."

"I may not be far above those, either. You have no way of knowing."

"If I have good taste in anything, it's in women," he protested. "That's why I singled you out this morning the very first time I saw you."

"Your picking me out was a real compliment—and I appreciate it," she said. "You have quite a reputation as a connoisseur and practically every woman here tonight was wondering what it would be like to go to bed with you. A woman can make love with a man she doesn't respect and even enjoy herself—we're perverse creatures, you know. But to live with a man and be happy, she's got to respect him."

"Do I have to perform some feat of arms to convince you I'm sincere, like a knight of old vying for his lady fair?"

"Lancelot won Guinevere's love simply by being *le bel knight sans reproche* if I remember the French correctly."

"I'm not perfect enough for that." His tone was serious now. "I'll even admit to being a little vain and really enjoying the adulation that goes with my job."

"Plus the opportunities for—shall we say—amorous dalliance?"

"That too. After all, I'm a normal male animal."

"The phrase Claire Anders used was 'gorgeous male animal.'"

"But not gorgeous enough to sweep you off your feet?"

"I'm trying to tell you I'm not like those girls who've been throwing themselves at you. I have a career of my own, to which I am very dedicated."

"That needn't—"

"Two careers rarely fit into a marriage. Look what happens so often in the movie colony."

"As well compare hothouse orchids to cabbages."

"Nevertheless, the symptoms can be diagnosed," she insisted. "I'm a very competent woman who's been holding her own successfully for some time in a masculine world. Which means that I'm essentially masculine myself."

"Nobody could guess it to look at you."

"I'm talking about my essential drives, the forces that made me chief of laboratories here at The Clinic."

"Any woman who's active in spheres outside her home has the same drives you have, but that doesn't necessarily mean she has to leave home because of them. Claire Anders is a good example."

"Claire feeds her ego with her intellectual superiority over Henry —plus the fact that she's wealthy in her own right."

"What do you feed on?"

"My ability to hold my own in my field against all comers."

"Was that the reason you left France? Because French women are expected to stay at home and not play a large part in men's affairs?"

"That—and marriage."

"I wondered about that," he said. "Did you love him very much?"

"I thought I did. He was older, a professor, and I considered myself his intellectual inferior."

"I'll give odds that you learned better."

"It's no bet. I saw him at an international medical convention in Boston several years later. He'd turned into a little pouter pigeon of a man, all bombast and no substance."

"Do you really think he was any different then than when you thought he was your ideal?"

"I'm sure he hadn't changed a bit. But I had, and I wondered then what I had ever seen in him."

"Did you ever decide what it was?"

She nodded. "You may not like to hear this, but I'm being very honest with you. I suppose it's no accident that the great lovers of history are so often small men; they make up in other ways for their lack of height. He taught me not to be afraid of drives—the essential id, I suppose it should be called in Freudian terminology. I'd known they were there but I'd been suppressing them through fear."

"You know why you really broke off that affair, don't you?"

"I told you—"

"You were rationalizing then—to avoid admitting the real reason for your flight from France. Your relationship with this pouter pigeon was purely physical and, being a woman of strong urges, you were afraid his attraction for you might put your mind into servitude to him."

She didn't answer, but instead lifted her glass and looked at the amber liquid as if searching within it for some portent of the future. "Here we are, trying to be very modern, even flippant, about what's happened to us in the last nine hours," she said at last. "And neither of us succeeding very well, because I suspect that deep down inside us, we're both pretty old-fashioned."

"Don't let it get around. You'll ruin my reputation as a playboy."

"Would that be so bad?"

"That's what I'm trying to decide. I haven't had a chance to talk to you about it but John Teague has offered me something of a roving professorship, with two purposes. One is to use the glamour that has latched on to me to induce more young doctors to enter the public health field."

"I don't know anybody who could do it better."

"I wouldn't take the job for that reason alone, but John also wants me to help him sell a much larger concept."

"To whom?"

"This city, to start off with; then, using it as an example, to the rest of the country and perhaps the world—though that's too big a task at the moment. He calls it the 'Whole Man Concept.'"

"I heard him talk on it at one of the staff meetings," she said.

"Do you agree?"

"Absolutely. Greg is fighting for the same thing in trying to keep The Clinic where it's always been, instead of letting it be moved out on the Beltway."

"Until this morning, I didn't think much about John's offer. But since I met you, the idea of staying here has become pretty attractive."

"You mustn't be guided by that," she said quickly.

"Suppose I left the decision to you—what would it be?"

She looked away and he saw her fingers tighten on the stem of the wine glass until he wondered whether it might not snap.

"Don't rush the decision," he said, wanting to help her and conscious, too, that he needed to gain time for himself. "We'll talk about it again—at breakfast."

ii

As Herb Partridge had predicted, the pattern of Frank Lawson's electroencephalogram on the monitor appeared to have gone crazy. Through electrodes attached to his scalp, the tiny action currents of electricity accompanying all brain activity were led to the delicate machine, where they were amplified to enable them to be studied carefully. Small and large waves appeared helter-skelter on the tube of the monitor with practically no relationship to the pattern of wave motion characterizing normal brain action.

"I never saw anything like this before," said the neurosurgeon when Greg Alexander came in with Dr. Philip Dennison, the medical examiner. "His brain has practically gone wild."

"The blood pressure's beginning to fall a little, too," reported the nurse-anesthetist who was watching the patient. "It's one hundred now over seventy."

"As the pressure falls, the rate of hemorrhage into the brain itself will probably decrease," said Herb Partridge. "Which means dragging the whole thing out even farther."

"How do you plan to handle the organs for transplantation?" the medical examiner asked.

"My assistant, Bob Johnson, is standing by in the other operating room," Greg explained. "Merchant has been in there for the last several hours so we could have him near the main pump-oxygenator. When the time comes here, I'll make a quick incision and remove the heart and lungs. Meanwhile, Bob will be getting ready in the other room."

"Do you plan to attach Lawson's heart to a pump to maintain the coronary circulation?" Dr. Dennison asked.

"I think not—unless we have trouble preparing Merchant for the transplant," said Greg. "We discovered with our dogs that the time you take connecting the donor organs to the pump-oxygenator can be better spent in getting the transplant into place in the recipient and the blood vessels connected up so its circulation can function. Fortunately, we'll be transplanting both heart and lungs, so the problem of making the necessary blood vessel connections is not nearly so great."

"How's that?"

"By making a temporary coupling to the aorta first, we can circulate the recipient's blood through the donor's coronary arteries immediately," Greg explained. "That way, we can keep the heart alive while we're completing the other connections."

"Don't you still have the problem of keeping it alive during the transfer period?"

"If things work out as we hope they will, we should have ample time for that," said Greg. "While we're putting Merchant on the heart-lung pump we will be cooling his body rapidly to reduce the need for oxygen by the brain cells. As soon as we remove the donor's heart and lungs, we will place them in a container of Tyrode's solution and cool them rapidly, too. Once the tissues are cooled, their need for oxygen is reduced markedly, giving us more time to connect them to the body of the recipient. Of course, it would be better if we were able to place the donor in a hyperbaric chamber and saturate his heart and lungs with oxygen before removing them. But our chamber is located beside the

Laboratory of Experimental Surgery, so the disadvantages in carrying the organs to the operating theater and the time involved more than outweigh anything we'd gain."

"Wouldn't it be better if you had both patient and donor side by side in adjacent pressure chambers?"

"When the new hospital is built, that's the way it's going to be."

"When? Not if?"

"It will be built someday—even if I have to move on somewhere else to make it possible."

"Has it come to that?" Dr. Dennison asked.

"I hope not," said Greg. "But there are plenty of other places with laboratories where I can go on with my work."

"I watched an open-heart operation once," the medical examiner said. "Just seeing a patient lying on the table without the heart and lungs functioning, while a pump made of metal, plastic and rubber took over, gave me the willies. And when they started warming the heart at the end of the operation and it went crazy, that was too much for me."

"Ninety-five over sixty," the nurse-anesthetist reported. "The pulse is definitely weaker, too."

"Maybe Lawson will do one decent thing in his life and not waste time dying," said Herbert Partridge.

"Move him into the operating theater, Herb, and get things ready," Greg said quietly. "I'd appreciate your prepping him while I check on Merchant."

"Sure," said the neurosurgeon, and moved immediately through an adjoining door to the scrub room between the two main operating theaters, with its row of basins and, above each, a container of sterilized brushes.

"Those currents still look pretty strong to me." The medical examiner glanced at the monitor tube with the crazy pattern of brain waves registered there and shook his head doubtfully. "It could be quite a while yet."

"With the pressure dropping like it is, we can't afford to take any chances," said Greg. "If the hemorrhage in Lawson's brain hits a really vital center, he could die before we're ready."

"Dr. Alexander." The operating room supervisor spoke from the door, her voice urgent. "Dr. Johnson would like you to come to O.R. 2 right away, please. The patient's pulse is very weak."

iii

"It happened so quickly, I hardly had time to call you, sir," Bob Johnson said when Greg came into the adjoining theater. "He was knocking along just like he's been doing for the past several hours, when suddenly he gave a gasp and his pulse started fading."

Where before Guy Merchant's breathing had been regular, though shallow, the rate was varied now. The valve of the respirator would click rhythmically three or four times in a row, showing that the sick man was making no effort to breathe at all; then it would click rapidly as faint respiratory movements tripped the delicate controls and allowed breathing directly into the oxygen-filled breathing bag.

"Looks like he's had a pulmonary embolism," said Greg. "I should have anticipated it."

"Shall I start prepping him, sir?" Bob Johnson still wore the gown and gloves he'd worn while performing the tracheostomy and so did not need to scrub again. At Greg's nod, he changed swiftly into fresh sterile gown and gloves while the entire operating room staff moved into action like a well-kept machine.

"Make an incision over the femoral artery so we can get a cannula in there as quickly as possible," Greg directed as he moved to the scrub room. "Unless his condition improves in the next few minutes, I'm going to open his chest and put him on the pump-oxygenator."

It was a daring move, but the only choice if Guy Merchant were to be kept alive until the organs from Frank Lawson's body became available. In a case of severe coronary thrombosis, the danger was always present that clots would form inside the heart, where the blood supply to a portion of muscle had been shut down. Obviously this had happened and one of the clots had broken loose as an embolus floating in the bloodstream. Traveling through the pulmonary circulation from the right side of the heart, it had entered ever smaller arteries in the branching treelike pattern of the vessels in the lung, until finally one was reached through which it could not pass.

Trained to anticipate and cope with even the direst emergencies, the operating team went into action without panic or any lost motion. The fact that nobody knew just how long a patient could safely be carried on the pump-oxygenator with his heart and lungs practically stilled and his body in a state of what might be called suspended animation from cooling, was a problem they would face when it arose.

That the heart-lung pump could take over safely from the vital organs for which it substituted during the several hours often necessary to replace vital parts of the heart, such as valves, or to repair abnormal openings from faulty development, was well known. What Greg planned to do now, however, was to substitute the pump for Guy Merchant's heart and lungs while they waited for the substitute organs to become available. Thus every second Frank Lawson lived longer than the perhaps hundred and eighty minutes that it was known to be safe to keep the heart stilled, would take them that much farther into the unknown. And should Lawson's heart continue to beat for hours, the point might well come at which Greg would simply have to remove the pump connections, let Guy Merchant die and face the accusation that he had tried to keep him alive when death was inevitable so he could claim to be the first to transplant both heart and lungs, even in a hopeless case.

16

The announcement at the Anders-McDougal cocktail party that
the main actors in the critical heart-lung transplant were being
taken to the operating theaters had quickly emptied the Falstaff
Room in favor of the surgical lecture room. But when the closed-
circuit television screens at either side of the lecture hall remained
blank and no immediate word came of just when actual surgery
would begin, beyond the fact that both patients were ready, many
of the doctors who had rushed there with the first announcement
began to drift away.

When the screen on the left was suddenly illuminated with a
picture of the hurried preparations being made to put Guy Merchant on the heart-lung machine, the room was less than half
filled. Jud Templeton had been sitting on one of the back rows
of seats, catnapping while he waited for some action to begin.
At the sudden stir among the onlookers when the screen was
illuminated, he came wide awake and moved quickly a dozen
rows nearer the screen so he would be able to see better. At
the same time, he took from his pocket a small notebook and
a ball-point pen.

Jud had witnessed enough operations to be reasonably familiar
with what was going on, but some of the equipment was new.
A small plump man with a pince-nez was sitting two seats
away from him and, when he recognized Dr. Timothy Puckett, a
pediatrician who was also chairman of the Board of Trustees, he
moved to the seat beside him.

"Where is the heart-lung pump?" he asked.

The small doctor looked at him over the rim of his glasses.

"The pump-oxygenator is that machine you see at one side of the operating room, where the technicians are working," he said somewhat prissily. "First time you've ever seen open-heart surgery?"

Jud Templeton nodded, figuring that by remaining silent he was less likely to betray his lack of professional status. As he had hoped, Dr. Puckett seemed to have mistaken him for another doctor.

"The heart of the pump actually consists of those stainless steel discs inside the long plastic cylinder in the center; the one that's about a third filled with blood." Dr. Puckett evidently enjoyed showing off his knowledge. "A constant stream of oxygen pours through the long cylinder, and, when the metal discs revolve, they pick up a thin film of blood, exposing it to oxygen in the upper part of the tube, where it is absorbed by the hemoglobin of the blood. Carbon dioxide leaves the blood at the same time and is removed chemically before the oxygen is used again."

"It's certainly ingenious."

"And very efficient," said Dr. Puckett. "It takes the place of both the heart and the lungs by not only pumping blood through the body but supplying it with oxygen and removing the carbon dioxide at the same time."

"It hasn't been connected yet, has it?"

Dr. Puckett looked at him pityingly, as at one whose ignorance was beyond belief, but still did not appear to be suspicious.

"The patient's body is being cooled rapidly now to decrease the need for oxygen. At low temperatures, the metabolism of the body cells is slowed remarkably and they need very little oxygen in order to live, so the pump is able to supply it."

"Remarkable."

"When I was a Fellow here twenty years ago, none of this was even dreamed of."

"Isn't Dr. Alexander taking quite a chance?" Jud Templeton asked. "I mean, with a procedure that's still not fully established and all?"

"Working in a large clinic like this with a big charity population to draw from, Greg Alexander is able to do things that those of us in individual practice wouldn't dare to do," Dr. Puckett admitted.

"I guess a lot of doctors try to cut men like Alexander down because they don't have as much on the ball as he does," Jud Templeton observed. "Take this business about automating the hospital that he reported on this afternoon. Not many men would have the foresight or the courage to look that far ahead."

"There are arguments on both sides." The smaller man pursed his lips. "I've always believed in the biblical advice not to put new wine in old bottles."

"That was a practical matter a few thousand years ago; then bottles were made of skin, and, if the new wine hadn't finished fermenting, the gas might burst them." When Dr. Puckett looked disconcerted, he added, "I guess you use penicillin, don't you?"

"Of course."

"If you follow the same line of reasoning in your practice, you ought to feed your patients moldy bread instead."

"The inference seems rather far-fetched," Dr. Puckett said stiffly.

"That new wine-old bottle idea is like a lot of other adages," said the newspaperman. "Originally there was a very simple explanation for them, but people kept repeating them with an air of wisdom until finally they got so hoary with tradition that everybody lost sight of why they came about in the first place."

"You may be right. I never thought about it."

"You said just now that Dr. Alexander's a pioneer because, with such a large charity population in the area, he can do things other people might be afraid to do. Isn't that an argument against moving The Clinic?"

"Well—perhaps. But there are even stronger arguments in favor of it."

"Like what?"

Again Dr. Puckett shot him a suspicious look but seemed satisfied that the questioner was simply naïve. "There's the matter of access, for one thing. On the Beltway, paying patients from out of town could reach The Clinic much more easily."

"Dragging a sick kid a two-hour bus ride each way just so a few private patients can be comfortable doesn't sound like what old Dr. Anders had in mind when he built this hospital." Jud Templeton made no attempt to keep the contempt out of his voice. "I'll bet if the trustees decide to move it, the newspapers in this town will start raising hell. Poor people wouldn't be able to get to The Clinic any longer the way they do now, so nobody would gain, because then pioneers like Dr. Gregory Alexander wouldn't have the clinical material for important research and what The Clinic has meant to medicine for the last fifty years would be lost."

As the small doctor suddenly rose and started for the door, Jud Templeton grinned. Unless he was mistaken, Dr. Timothy Puckett would be busy preaching a new gospel to his fellow trustees between now and Friday's meeting.

ii

"How is he, Lew?" Greg asked the anesthesiologist as he reached for a sponge to push back the rubber fingers of his glove so they would fit snugly over the tips and not interfere with the sensitivity of his touch. Having prepped and draped both the chest and groin of the patient, Bob Johnson was now making an incision in the latter area.

"Blood pressure's barely perceptible," Dr. Gann said. "If you had decided to do this ten minutes later, you'd be operating on a man who's clinically dead."

"Finish getting the femoral cannula in, Bob, then cannulate the inferior vena cava," Greg directed. "I'm going to do a median sternotomy so I can compress the heart while you connect the pump."

Beside the operating table, the pump technicians were working swiftly and skillfully, completing the task of charging the vital machine with pooled blood of Guy Merchant's type from the hospital blood bank. The surface area of his body had been calculated that morning and the fact determined that he would need just less than four liters—each a thousand cubic centimeters on the metric scale and just over a quart—of blood circulating per minute to maintain life when the pump took over. Now the machine stood waiting.

The long cylinder where the shining steel discs would shortly start turning to expose the blood to oxygen, just as was normally done in the lungs, was closed. The sterile plastic tubes that would

212

connect it to Guy Merchant's body were filled and the ends were double-wrapped in bags of polyethylene to maintain sterility.

A resident surgeon was working on Guy Merchant's extended arm, exposing a small artery and vein in order to insert flexible plastic tubes called cannulae into them so the venous and arterial blood pressures could be constantly reported by lines moving across the face of the monitor that faithfully recorded all vital functions where they were instantly visible to the watching technicians, the surgeon and the anesthesiologist. Through a needle in Guy Merchant's foot vein, an anesthetic solution containing a muscle relaxant was slowly dripping into his body, while the respirator connected to his lungs by way of the tracheostomy tube and windpipe inflated them rhythmically sixteen times a minute.

Taking the scalpel handed him by the instrument nurse when he moved up to the table, Greg drew the blade the full length of Guy Merchant's breastbone, or sternum, splitting the skin and the tissues beneath it down to the bone in a single stroke. Inside a rubber bag beneath his body, an icy slush was being circulated meanwhile, rapidly lowering his body temperature.

"Oscillating saw," Greg said, and the instrument, protected by a sterile cover, came into his hands. The motor that drove the wedge-like blade, with its arc-shaped outer edge covered with teeth, began to whine and, as the blade vibrated rapidly back and forth, he lowered it to touch the whitish bone revealed in the depths of the incision.

The whine of the saw deepened as it bit into the bone and a spray of dust rose, to be dampened down as the resident, who had moved up to assist Greg now, sprayed sterile water upon the saw to keep it cool. Moving carefully so as to cut almost, but not quite, through the breastbone, because of possible damage to vital structures beneath it, Greg quickly sawed the length of the sternum. Then, with a heavy blade called a Lebsche knife, whose blunt, hoe-shaped foot protected anything beneath it from injury, he finished splitting the bone. Severing ligaments at its upper and lower end, he quickly spread the sternum apart, freeing the underside of the bone from the pericardial sac covering the heart.

"No perceptible pulse or spontaneous respiration," Dr. Lewis Gann reported.

"No pulsation in the radial cannula," the technician watching the electric monitor echoed.

As coolly as if he had not heard the reports indicating that Guy Merchant's heart action had ceased and he was now technically dead, Greg reached into the chest cavity through the narrow opening provided by the split breastbone and took the heart itself in his hand. At the same moment, Dr. Gann switched the respirator to a more strongly positive pressure in order to inflate the lungs and counteract the failure of Guy Merchant's respiration, which had occurred even before the heart had ceased to beat.

The heart was visible in Greg's hand now, lying immobile, with a wedge-shaped area of almost black muscle tissue indicating where the coronary artery had been blocked that morning by a thrombus, when Guy Merchant's first heart cessation of the day had occurred. Still keeping every movement deliberate and purposeful, for haste here could tear delicate structures and destroy any chance of success, Greg began to squeeze and release the heart rhythmically, simulating, with externally applied pressure by his own hand, the pumping effect normally achieved by each contraction of the heart.

The change in the patient's general condition from this maneuver was startling. With blood now being forced into the lungs and the rest of the body, the color of the tissues visible in the open wound improved remarkably as the normal exchange of oxygen in the lungs was resumed. The instrument nurse breathed an audible sigh at the success of this first step, but there was no relaxation of attention, for yet another critical action remained, the change from the pumping action of Guy's hand upon the exposed heart to that of the far more complicated pump-oxygenator.

"You're a pretty good heart substitute, Greg," said Dr. Lewis Gann. "If you can hold out."

For the first time, through a throat microphone beneath the collar of his gown connected to a jack in the floor, Greg spoke directly to the audience watching in the surgical lecture room by means of closed-circuit television.

"This patient went into *extremis* rather rapidly," he said, "so we had to act quickly in order to restore cardiac function until we are able to place him upon the pump-oxygenator. You can't see the change in the tissues without color, but we are maintaining a fairly adequate respiratory interchange by manual pressure alone."

While he was speaking, the resident assisting him had inserted a rib spreader, an instrument with blunt jaws which could be opened to any degree desired by means of its ratchet drive, into the incision. When the younger man turned the screw, the jaws of the instrument separated widely, opening the divided breastbone and giving Greg more room in which to continue his manipulation of the heart, as well as affording a complete view of the operative field for the onlookers.

Turning his head, Greg glanced at the small monitor screen back of Dr. Gann, where the TV picture being reproduced on a larger scale in the lecture room could be seen.

"I think you can see the area of darkened muscle here on the surface of the heart." With a blunt forceps from the instrument table, he traced the outline of the wedge-shaped area of damage with his free hand. "This is where the blood supply of the heart muscle was blocked early this morning due to an acute coronary thrombosis. When added to the chronic heart damage already present from hardened coronary arteries and previous episodes of thrombosis, this new insult brought on a state of heart failure which has progressed in spite of all measures to support the heart. The sudden emergency of the last few minutes, however, we believe to have been caused by an embolus to the lungs."

"Don't forget to remind them that you just brought a dead man back to life," Dr. Gann said *sotto voce*.

"As you know," Greg continued, "I propose at the earliest possible moment to transplant the heart and lungs of a healthy individual who is dying from an injury to the brain. Unfortunately, the progressively deteriorating condition of this patient made it necessary to intervene before the organs to be transplanted became available.

"My assistant, Dr. Robert Johnson, has just finished placing a cannula in the femoral artery through the small incision you may be able to see on your television screen in the right groin and upper thigh," he continued. "This will allow a return of arterial blood to the body after it has passed through the pump-oxygenator. He is now threading a perforated tube upward through the common femoral vein into the inferior vena cava to carry blood from the lower two thirds of the body to the pump before it can reach the heart.

"The pump, of course, is designed to maintain a steady flow of blood throughout the body, while at the same time supplying oxygen to this blood and removing carbon dioxide from it. The patient is also being cooled and I can already detect a marked lowering of temperature in the tissues around my hand. Once we are able to connect him to the heart-lung pump and inject previously cooled blood into his circulation, the rate of body cooling should increase very rapidly until we obtain a general temperature of about seventy-seven degrees Fahrenheit, the optimum for this sort of procedure."

Bob Johnson had finished placing the cannulas and two plastic tubes now led from the small wound in Guy Merchant's upper thigh to the heart-lung pump, with clamps in place to prevent circulation through them yet. Quickly, Bob changed gown and gloves and, slipping into the position Greg had been occupying, placed his hand around the heart and took up the rhythmic squeezing of the muscle without a beat being missed.

"We are now ready to connect the venous system of the patient to the pump-oxygenator, after which it will no longer be necessary to compress the heart or to operate the respirator," said Greg. "Fortunately, we shall not need to place special cannulas into the coronary arteries to maintain the heart's own circulation, as would be the case if we were repairing or replacing a valve or closing a defect."

While speaking, he had taken a forceps and gently picked up a portion of the thin-walled upper chamber, or atrium, on the right side of the heart. Using a needle threaded with tough black silk, he now began to sew a circular pattern called a pursestring suture around a portion of the wall about the size of a half dollar.

"If you remember your anatomy," Greg spoke into the microphone again for the benefit of the audience beyond the wall in the lecture room while he was placing the suture, working around Bob Johnson's hand, which still rhythmically squeezed the more muscular part of the heart comprising the ventricles, "the superior vena cava collects blood from the upper part of the body and the inferior vena cava does the same for the lower part. Both of them empty into the right upper chamber of the heart, the atrium, where I am now placing a purse-string suture preparatory to opening it. Early heart transplants were extremely difficult until a technique was developed for leaving a cuff of the atrium around the point where the two large veins enter it, making it necessary to suture only atrium to atrium, a far simpler and shorter method of reconnecting the right side of the heart."

He had finished placing the purse-string now, forming a pattern that looked very much like the mouth of an old-fashioned bag of Bull Durham tobacco used for rolling cigarettes.

"Since we plan to leave the larger portion of the right atrium in place when suturing the donor heart to it," he continued, "I shall put a tube into the superior vena cavae through this opening. Dr. Johnson has already cannulated the inferior vena cava through the common femoral vein."

As he spoke, he cut through the thin wall of the atrium with a pointed scalpel, controlling the spurt of blood by tightening the purse-string immediately and closing the opening. "Thus, we can leave the tubes in place while we suture the right side of Lawson's heart to Merchant's and keep the heart-lung pump running."

"Pump ready, Doctor." One of the pump technicians answered his unspoken question.

Skillfully, Greg placed loose snares of cotton tape around both the superior and the inferior vena cava outside the heart. Handing them to the resident, who was still acting as first assistant while Bob Johnson maintained the rhythmic pressure upon the heart itself, he picked up a plastic tube with a bulb-shaped end handed him by the instrument nurse. Loosening the purse-string suture momentarily, he pushed the tube gently through the atrium and into the opening of the superior vena cava, where the assistant immediately tightened the snare, forming a tight connection around the tube so no blood could leak by it. The second snare insured that no blood flowed through the lower vein and the entire volume of blood that normally returned to the right side of the heart could now be diverted to the pump.

The pump technicians had been watching Greg closely. As soon as the venous flow was under control, one of them threw the switch that started the metal discs spinning in their bath of blood inside the long plastic cylinder at the center of the machine. At the same moment, Greg reached down to remove the clamp closing the tube connected to the femoral artery in the thigh.

"Body clamps off," he said, warning the technicians that there was no block now between the heart-lung pump and Guy Merchant's circulatory system, save the valves of the machine itself.

"Line pressure, one hundred." The technician spoke as he watched the gauge, with one eye on the second hand of his watch.

Ordinarily, no longer than forty-five seconds was necessary to build up enough pressure to maintain the circulation. Having quickly reached the desired rate of revolution the pump was humming softly and already the reservoir of blood in the long cylinder was starting to turn a brighter red as oxygen was absorbed by the continuous film covering the upper part of the moving steel discs.

"Blood temperature ninety degrees," the second pump technician reported.

Since no blood was now flowing into the heart it lay flaccid and empty in Bob Johnson's hand.

"Respirator off," said Dr. Gann, and the sudden cessation of its rhythmic click-click—no longer needed with no blood flowing through the lungs—was louder *in absentia* than it had been while audible.

When the pump technician opened the valves connecting Guy Merchant's circulation with the machine itself, the line pressure dropped at once as blood flowed into his body. But the pump quickly raised it again to the needed level of about one hundred and eighty millimeters of mercury, corresponding roughly to a normal blood pressure.

Blood collected by way of the great veins and the two tubes inside them was now being carried to the pump, where, through the medium of the spinning discs, its oxygen supply was replenished and the waste carbon dioxide removed. A little higher concentration of the latter than normal was maintained in the blood being circulated by the pump, however, because the concentration of carbon dioxide regulated the flow of blood through the arteries of the brain, a flow which must be maintained at all costs, lest damage to that extremely sensitive organ occur during the period of shift from circulation by heart to circulation by pump. Leaving the pump, the blood now flowed under increased pressure into the groin artery, where Bob Johnson had placed the cannula at the beginning of the operation, back-flooding the entire arterial system of the body with freshly oxygenated blood.

Physiologically, every part of Guy Merchant's body, save the heart and lungs, was now functioning, though at considerably less than the normal rate because of the sharp lowering of all body processes by the steadily increasing cold. Not until the blood temperature reached thirty-five degrees on the Centigrade scale used in scientific work (roughly eighty-five on the more familiar Fahrenheit scale), would the pump technicians open the heat inlet on the pump heat exchanger and rewarm the blood slightly to make certain that it fell no lower than that level.

"Urine output one cc. per minute," reported a technician whose duty it was to watch that function. To the untrained observer, urinary flow might seem of little importance but actually it was a sensitive indicator of the adequacy of the arterial pressure, and therefore of the blood flow to the kidneys.

"The patient is now on the pump-oxygenator," Greg announced by way of the microphone. "His heart and lungs are no longer needed and all other body organs are functioning normally."

iii

"I've been in practice twenty-five years, but this sort of thing scares the hell out of me," said one of the older doctors watching the TV screen in the lecture room. "Imagine somebody just lying there, not breathing, his heart not beating, while a machine keeps him alive. It's enough to make you believe in robots."

"If you ask me, this automation business has already gone too far," another doctor said. "A little more of it and we'll be done away with altogether."

Neither noticed Jud Templeton quietly taking notes on a pad with a stubby pencil while they were talking.

"For my money," the first doctor said, "we ought to stop fighting Medicare and fight automation."

"I wouldn't want it to get around but I haven't done half bad at all with Medicare," a third man chimed in. "Take most of the old people who come into my office. I used to give them a quick glance and a prescription for a tranquilizer so I could get them out fast, knowing I was losing money every minute I wasted on them—"

"But not any more," the second doctor agreed. "I'm doing twice as much surgery on people over sixty-five as I did before Medicare—and getting paid for it. A lot of 'em have chronic gall bladders or diaphragmatic hernias that can be demonstrated in the X-ray. Before Medicare came along, I didn't want to X-ray them because I couldn't be sure I'd even get paid for that. Now I'm doing routine gall bladders and G.I. series and finding a lot of operable conditions."

"Why don't you vultures start treating the whole patient instead of some organ you can operate on and take the government for a big fee?" A stocky red-haired man who had been sitting in the second row smoking a pipe spoke in a tone of disgust. "If you'd take a decent history before ordering a gall bladder X-ray and finding a low-grade chronic condition that isn't causing any real trouble, you'd know a lot of these old people are just lonely because their children have left home and don't have time to bother with them any more. Nine times out of ten those digestive symptoms you use as an excuse for surgery are nothing but spasm of the G.I. tract a visit from the kids at Christmas could cure. Take a knife to them and they've got something physical to center their complaints on, which makes it twice as hard for us psychiatrists to get anywhere with them."

There was a moment of indignant silence, then the three who had been so busy with Medicare moved away, ignoring the red-headed doctor, who didn't seemed troubled at all by their attitude. Nothing was happening on the TV screen that looked exciting now, so Jud Templeton moved into a seat beside the psychiatrist.

"You certainly put them in their place," he said. "I couldn't help overhearing—and admiring."

"Who are you?"

"My name's Templeton."

"Jud Templeton?"

"Yes."

"Thought I recognized you. Who let you in?"

"I'm here by invitation." Jud handed him the press card. "Courtesy of the director."

"You just used a dirty word." The psychiatrist handed him back the card and held out his hand. "I'm Dr. Jake Stafford, a maverick from the psychiatric service. I was hoping Greg Alexander had finally realized Henry Anders is getting ready to take him to the cleaners and hired himself a press agent."

"I'm for free," said Templeton.

"Except the headlines you can get out of it?"

Jud shrugged. "You just heard what your friends had to say about Medicare, so what right has the medical profession to look down on newspapermen any more?"

"You've got a good point there," Stafford admitted. "As you may have guessed, I don't have a very high opinion of a lot of my medical confreres."

"Care to elucidate?"

"Not for publication—yet. I'm writing a book on what's happened to the medical profession in the twenty-five years since I finished school. We've gained more in knowledge and lost more in respect from the public than in any previous century in history."

"What's your diagnosis, Doctor?"

"Money—what else?"

"Everybody's got a right to make money."

"Nothing's wrong with making money—so long as it doesn't become your whole aim in life."

"I can see now why you named yourself a maverick," said Jud Templeton. "Were you always that way?"

"Maybe," said Stafford. "When I joined the Army in 'forty-two, medicine was still a calling. But when I came out in 'forty-six, it had become a trade."

"Would you care to risk a guess why?"

"I *know* why. Those of us who were in the service were thoroughly disgusted with the brown-nosing that got eagles for men who put the desire for power and position above the kind of service Hippocrates wrote about. We longed to get back in civilian practice the way the Israelites yearned for the Promised Land; the pastures were greener and there was plenty of water in the streams, so we came out expecting to find things the way they were before—only better."

"And they weren't?"

"Hell no. The minute we got out, we discovered that the guys who'd been smart enough to stay behind had gotten rich. While we'd been serving our glorious country in uniform, they'd been collecting ten-dollar bills for house calls and sticking them in the side pockets of their coats, until they could bury them somewhere so the Internal Revenue wouldn't know they'd ever collected them. Between calls, they'd been buying up property that was bound to zoom in value as soon as the war ended, taking advantage of every investment opportunity that came along for somebody who had a pocketful of money. Meanwhile, what was happening to us in uniform?"

"If you were as broke as I was, you were damn lucky to get enough to eat and pay your bar bill at the officers' club!"

"That's just about the size of it," said the psychiatrist. "A lot of us had to borrow money to pay our insurance so we could afford to be in uniform. When we got out, those debts came due pretty fast and who could blame us for trying to catch up to the ones who'd stayed behind and got rich?"

"Which made you as bad as they were."

"Maybe worse," Stafford admitted. "At least we had a choice of the way we would go, while, with patients flooding the doctors back home with money, they could hardly go but one way. The trouble is that, while we were getting rich in the years right after the war, we lost something pretty precious—our professional dedication. And when we no longer had that, we could hardly expect the next medical generation to find it suddenly."

Dr. Stafford examined his pipe and saw that it had indeed gone out while he was talking, then stuck it in the pocket of his tweed jacket. "Whenever I can, I come down here and watch Greg Alexander at work, but not because I particularly admire what he's trying to do," he continued. "Take that fellow he's carrying on the pump"—he gestured toward the screen—"while he frees the organs he hopes to remove and waits for the call from the operating room on the other side telling him this murderer—what's his name?"

"Frank Lawson."

"Telling him Frank Lawson is about to do the decent thing and die early. But what good is it all going to do?"

"A life may be saved."

"For what?"

"In his time, Guy Merchant had a lot to be proud of."

"His name was up in lights, yes, but you know how show business is. I doubt very seriously if Merchant even has the sixteen quarters of coverage he'll need to get more than the minimum under Social Security. So even if Greg Alexander does give him a new heart and lungs, what's it going to mean to him?"

"Life, for one thing."

"You can't cut out one man's heart and put it into another man without detaching the nervous control from the brain. The new heart has got to function on its own, which means it can't respond to the sight of a pretty girl walking down the street in a mini-skirt by stepping up its beat, whether the acceleration is going to be needed or not. If Merchant happens to exert a bit too much, his heart won't be able to respond to that either and the moment the amount of blood being pumped to his brain is less than what his brain needs, he'll keel over in a faint."

The psychiatrist shook his head vigorously. "I meant what I said to those three medical vultures just now, Mr. Templeton. One of the greatest tragedies in life is to be old and alone. I see the flotsam and jetsam of that tide floating up in my geriatric clinic every day and there's nothing I can do to make them feel wanted again. You can find foster parents for a cute little child with the certainty that it will be loved and wanted for itself. But who's going to adopt an old man who doesn't always make it to the bathroom before he wets his pants and goes to sleep before the TV set snoring so loud that nobody else can hear the program? The tyranny of the aged feeds on the guilt complexes of their children. When you're young, you hate your parents because of the authority they have over you. But when you're older, you're afraid to put them away—like the Indians did the oldsters back in their days—because you know your own kids might do the same thing to you."

"Wouldn't you say it would be worthwhile to save the brain of an Einstein by giving him a new heart?" Jud Templeton asked.

"Of course, but Einsteins are few and far apart. And who's to say what brains are worth saving and what shall be let die? There's a moral question here, too, you know."

"Would you have Dr. Alexander stop his work just because the moral side of it hasn't been solved yet?"

"Of course not." Dr. Jake Stafford grinned. "Who knows? I may want one of those transplants myself, when he gets so he can really make it work most of the time. Greg Alexander is so devoted to his work that he never lets other considerations trouble him and, whenever I get disgusted with my money-grabbing colleagues, the way I was with those three just now, I look to him to restore my spirits—and my faith. As long as men like him are around in medicine, I can believe that the sort of dedication we had twenty-five years ago still exists."

"Do you think Dr. Alexander will win out in his battle with the trustees for an automated hospital and diagnostic clinic?"

The psychiatrist looked at him quizzically. "You for or against?"

"For—all the way. Are you?"

"For, naturally, but I've got nothing to lose. They can't teach robots head-shrinking, and half the time we psychiatrists don't know what the hell we're doing ourselves." Then his voice took on a more sober note. "Just the same, I wish Greg Alexander hadn't spoken on automation today. It scares the daylights out of a lot of doctors—and with some reason."

"I don't see why."

"A doctor spends four years of college, four years of medical school, and maybe fifty thousand or so of his old man's money for the M.D.—plus five more years in hospital residencies if he wants to be certified. Naturally, the thought that he may be largely replaced by a diagnostic machine can tie his gut up in knots."

"So what's the answer?"

"The same one that coped with the Industrial Revolution in England a few hundred years ago. Making more goods available to people always creates more jobs and more need for what those jobs produce. With machines taking over the diagnostic chores and some of the treatment ones, too, doctors can give their patients a better grade of medical care. Which means more people living into old age to provide more work for more doctors. We're the only profession in the world, Mr. Templeton, whose idealism always pays off in dollars. And don't tell me that isn't the best of all rewards—doing good and getting paid for it, too."

"Please, Dr. Stafford." Jud Templeton held up his hand in mock protest. "You'll have me starting all over—in your field—when I've got a story to write."

"What's your lead?"

"The old tried and true, of course," said the newspaperman. "Today a man in white held back the angel of death with gloved hands. . . ."

17

Peter Carewe and Helen Foucald were just finishing their dessert when the beeper on the table beside them emitted its high-pitched, compelling sound. "Here's the end of a perfect evening," she said. "I've got to call the hospital operator."

"Greg has put the heart patient on the pump," she reported when she came back to the table. "We have to do frequent blood-gas determinations while the pump is operating to make sure the CO-two level doesn't get too low and cut down the blood flow to the brain, as well as watching the electrolyte balance."

"Can't somebody else in the lab do it?"

"Some of these determinations are a little intricate, so I usually have to read the instruments. We only have a couple of technicians on duty at night and they'll need help."

"Any idea how long you'll be?"

"The laboratory assistant I talked to said Frank Lawson is still alive, so it could go on for quite a while."

"I'll walk across with you," he offered.

"Please don't. Let's end the evening as it is now, with soft lights and brandy."

"You talk as if there won't be others."

"That's up to you. Tonight will give you a chance to think a little—and back out if you like."

"How about breakfast together?"

"I'd love it, but you may not want to get up as early as I do. I have to be in the laboratory by nine."

"In the bush, the day is half gone by nine o'clock," he told her as they walked to the door.

"I'll meet you in the restaurant here at eight-fifteen then?"

"No room service?"

"Let's not push our luck," she said quickly. "It's a long time till morning and I'll understand if you change your mind."

He stood watching her until she disappeared through the door of the restaurant and his expression was thoughtful as he moved to the long bar and took one of the stools there.

"Bourbon," he told the bartender, but when the glass was set before him, he sat looking at it for a long time without tasting it.

ii

"Keep watch on things here, Bob; I'm going across and take a look at Lawson." Greg stepped back from the operating table, where he had been carrying out some of the preliminary dissections preparing Guy Merchant for the time when he would remove the organs which were to be replaced. "How is he, Lew?" he asked.

Dr. Lewis Gann looked up from behind a tent of draperies. "Knocking along. I'm just marking time with a slow drip of succinylcholine and enough Pentothal to keep him quiet."

Greg glanced at the lines racing across the monitor tube and the chart on the small table beside Dr. Gann. "Everything seems to be holding up O.K."

"Physiologically, you're correct, but we could have a real philosophical bull session over that statement," said the anesthesiologist. "The patient is cold, his heart doesn't beat, he doesn't breathe. In fact, you could make a good argument that the only thing alive about him is that gadget there." He nodded toward the pump-oxygenator. "And a burnt-out fuse could snuff out what life is left in that."

"His brain is still working." Greg pointed toward the wavy line on the bottom of the monitor, where, almost alone among the body indicators, the even slow pattern of the electrical waves collected by terminals strapped to Guy Merchant's skull showed life as they moved across the cathode ray tube in a rhythmic progression.

"Reminds me of when I visited the cave paintings of Trois

Frères in France," said Dr. Gann. "They were made over twenty thousand years ago, but, when the artist wanted to depict motion in a herd of deer being hunted by Stone Age men, all he had to do was show a wave passing through a line of antlers. Maybe we haven't come as far as we think, in spite of all our fancy gadgets."

One of the nurses laughed and as the operating team relaxed visibly, Greg gave the gray-haired anesthesiologist an affectionate punch on the shoulder.

"If we didn't have a screwball philosopher like you in the operating room at a time like this, Lew, I guess we'd all explode with tension," he said. "Just at the right moment, you always come up with some sort of an oddball observation that takes off the heat."

"I have to be worth something," said Dr. Gann. "With this automation movement you're making yourself the apostle of, anesthesia will soon be nothing but a couple of bottles dripping solutions into a patient's veins and an electronic monitor watching over him to turn them on and off. Still, if the heart and lungs can be replaced by a machine, I suppose I shouldn't squawk."

"Were you able to get most of Merchant's blood out before you started using the perfusate?" Greg asked the head technician. Perfusate was the term used to describe the blood mixture used to charge the heart-lung pump before the metal discs began to spin.

"I'd say three quarters of it at least, Doctor," said the technician. "We couldn't risk taking any more for fear the circulation wouldn't hold up."

"That should help a great deal."

"Just what do you hope to gain by not using Merchant's own blood, Greg?" Dr. Gann asked.

"It's an idea of Helen Foucald's. She thinks that replacing Merchant's blood with another makes a severe rejection less likely soon after the transplant. Our work with dogs seems to support the theory."

"How about afterwards?"

"We'll save as much of Lawson's blood as we can and use that for transfusion later. That way, we'll theoretically be supplying the heart with a considerable percentage of the blood to which it was accustomed, and thus further decrease the possibility of a rejection."

"It's a clever idea," said the anesthesiologist. "But I never heard of it before."

"I wouldn't have thought of it myself if Helen hadn't suggested it," Greg admitted. "She works with cells all the time and thinks having a different set of lymphocytes circulating in the bloodstream from those of the person who's receiving the transplant might decrease the probability of rejection."

"You're going to use ALG, too, aren't you?"

"As much as we can get. I've ordered a fresh supply flown from Munich."

The newest—and potentially most valuable—weapon against the tendency of the human body to reject tissues other than its own, anti-lymphocytic globulin—ALG for short—was made by injecting human lymphocytes into animals, much as was done in producing tetanus antitoxin and other serums. When the animal reacted by producing antibodies in the blood capable of paralyzing and even destroying human white blood cells, it was then bled and the antibody-rich factor called globulin extracted. This in turn could be used to help prevent the white blood cells of the transplant recipient from attacking the new organ received from the donor— the physiological process called rejection, which had caused so much trouble in earlier transplant cases.

Still wearing his gown and gloves so it wouldn't be necessary for him to scrub again when he changed to resume surgery, Greg took a shortcut through the scrub room and the doctors' lounge beneath the surgical lecture room to enter the other operating theater and the adjoining anesthetic room. There, Herbert Partridge, the medical examiner and a nurse-anesthetist were watching the monitor that recorded Frank Lawson's brain waves, as well as his temperature, blood pressure and heart action.

Greg noted with approval, as he passed through the operating theater itself, that the tables against the walls had been covered with sterile sheets by the scrub nurses. Beneath them, he knew, everything was ready for the rapid opening of Lawson's chest in order to remove the heart and lungs; two nurses, scrubbed and ready, sat on stools at one side, their gloved hands protected by sterile towels.

"How's Merchant?" Herbert Partridge looked up when Greg came in.

"He almost went out on us, but I got him on the pump in time."

"How long can you carry him?" The medical examiner asked the question that was uppermost in all their minds.

"The most we've ever had a patient on bypass during surgery was a little over three hours," said Greg. "Beyond that—we're in unknown territory."

"Any reason why it couldn't be longer?"

"Prolonged cooling seems to decrease the chances of obtaining a satisfactory function of the heart afterward," said Greg. "In Merchant's case, though, we're not going to use it, so that factor doesn't hold. The thing we need to be concerned about most is the effect of cooling on the brain."

"It's getting an adequate oxygen supply with the pump, isn't it?"

"Yes. And as long as cooling keeps the need of the cells for oxygen down to a minimum while enough blood actually reaches it to maintain that small degree of vital function, I suppose theoretically a brain could be cooled indefinitely," Greg said as he moved over beside the table and stood looking down at Frank Lawson. "But that's only in theory, nobody actually knows."

The respirator still clicked away with its steady rhythm, inflating and deflating the injured man's lungs. The wavy lines registering the various components of the heart action upon the cathode tube of the monitor were as strong and regular as ever, too. Only the tracings of the brain waves showed any significant deviation from normal. Here the pattern was still as disorderly as before, and the height of the waves was distinctly less, hardly half of what it had been when Greg had last visited the room.

"His brain is dying fairly rapidly," said Herb Partridge. "It's been particularly noticeable in the last half hour."

"Suppose the heart keeps on beating spontaneously, even after the brain registers death?" Dr. Dennison asked. "What then, Greg?"

"The A.M.A. recommends that two doctors certify death in potential transplants and neither of them can be the operating surgeon, so that lets me out and leaves the actual decision to you and Dr. Partridge."

"Judge Sutler's order says death must be established unquestionably," said the medical examiner. "I have no choice except to wait until all indicators have ceased to function before letting you go ahead."

"We understand that," Greg assured him.

"A while ago it was a race between Merchant's heart and Lawson's but Merchant's faulted in the stretch," said Herb Partridge. "Now the race is between a machine and Lawson's heart."

"One thing is certain," said Dr. Dennison. "No race like this was ever run before."

iii

Ed McDougal poured a stiff drink for Dr. Timothy Puckett and handed it to the potbellied pediatrician. "Calm yourself, Tim, and tell me just what this guy said."

"He isn't just a guy. His face looked familiar to me in the lecture room but I thought it was because he'd been a Fellow here at one time. It wasn't until I saw him later at that telephone the reporters use outside the emergency room that I realized who he is."

"So it was a reporter. What did he say?"

"I think he's suspicious about the business of moving The Clinic." They were sitting in the extra suite Ed had rented to serve as headquarters during the campaign and to give him a base of operations away from Hannah and her querulous demands. Ed had been busy all evening entertaining a steady stream of influential doctors among the Members and trustees, lining up support for the campaign upon which he and Henry Anders had embarked.

Dr. Tim Puckett's news of his encounter with Jud Templeton was the first adverse happening of the evening, but Ed wasn't particularly worried about it. The smell of scandal could hardly be wafted as far as Texas, and, by that time, the whole thing would be locked up so tight that nothing could change it. Under other conditions, Ed wouldn't even have bothered about Tim

Puckett's fears, but, since the small man was chairman of the Board of Trustees, he had to keep him reassured and in line.

"Just how much do you think this fellow knows?" he asked. "You couldn't have been such a fool as to blab to him about the syndicate?"

"Of course not." The gulp of almost pure bourbon he'd taken when the glass was put into his hand was warming the little man's stomach and stirring his courage. "This guy's got extrasensory perception or something."

"Don't be a damn fool, Tim. How far had Greg gone with the operation when you left?"

"He's got the patient on the heart-lung pump."

"And the other one—the donor?"

"I don't know. He's in the anesthetic room outside the other operating theater, so they didn't have the TV cameras on him."

"Merchant's heart must have gone bad even faster than Greg expected. He can't carry him but so long on the pump and, if Merchant dies before the transplant can be done, this publicity gimmick could backfire. We can always claim Greg has given The Clinic a bad name and demand his resignation."

"Resignation?" Dr. Puckett looked horrified. "Who said anything about resigning?"

"Henry Anders insists on it. Don't tell me you didn't know that?"

"Of course I didn't know it! Greg and Jeanne are among our best friends." The whiskey was shoring up Puckett's self-confidence. "Do you think I want to preside as chairman of the board over the death of The Clinic?"

"The funeral—if it comes to that—won't happen during your term of office, Tim." Ed reached over to pour more bourbon into Puckett's glass and drop in some ice. "Besides, it doesn't have to happen just because Greg Alexander's not around any more."

"But—"

"Look at this thing sensibly, Tim. I know it sounds big to be a Member of The Clinic, when you're running for an office in the state medical association—I use it myself whenever it will do me any good. But have you ever stopped to think how much the doctors practicing here in town lose by having an institution close by that leaves it up to the patient to say how much of a fee he can pay—or none at all? Old Dr. Anders got a lot of free publicity out of that gimmick and it meant something in the old days, when so many people were poor. But with the average income per capita going up all the time, to say nothing of what it costs a doctor to maintain an office, what's the sense in letting a lot of people get the kind of medical care they can get across the street without paying a dime for it?"

"I—I never thought of that."

"Then it's time you did—along with rest of the doctors around here. The Clinic has been able to get by without changing its financial requirements because people like Sam Hunter and a lot of other patients of old Dr. Anders have been willing to ante up at the end of the year to cover its deficit. But that can't last forever with taxes the way they are."

"Greg's kept up The Clinic's reputation."

"Maybe he has; I never did say Greg didn't have ability. But he hasn't shown much sense by staying here at twenty thousand a year when he could have made a hundred in private practice. With Greg gone, The Clinic will lose a lot of its drawing power for people who can pay their way, which means more patients for you fellows who are right here on the ground and don't believe that idealistic crap Greg and old Dr. Anders were always handing out."

"But if this fellow Templeton is on to the syndicate—"

"He's not on to it—unless you told him."

"I said I didn't," Dr. Puckett squawked indignantly.

"Then all he's doing is putting two and two together. Maybe he did come up with the right answer, but you can be damn certain he won't print it in a newspaper without proof."

"Are you sure?"

"Of course I'm sure. Some pretty important people are in on this deal and one of them ought to be able to shut off Mr. Jud Templeton when the time comes. Right now, it's to our interest to let him keep on writing about the transplant operation. Obviously, Greg is feeding information to him, hoping to profit from the publicity, so we'll just let him go ahead and print it. If Greg had to put his patient on a heart-lung pump before he could even get Lawson's heart, this whole stunt is going to fail and we can use that against him at the trustees' meeting. Things are breaking just the way we want them, Tim. The first time Greg fumbles, we'll pick up the ball and run with it for a touchdown."

"Shouldn't we cancel that meeting Friday afternoon?"

"Sam Hunter demanded it to look into the question of Greg's building the hyperbaric chamber without consulting the board and we can't do anything to make Sam mad, so we'll have to go through with it."

"Suppose Greg succeeds with this operation? Won't that be proof that building the chamber was justified?"

"If the patient lives, Sam Hunter will have the rug pulled out from under him, but that's his hard luck. What we've got to do is to make Greg show these new plans there's so much talk about so we can get a crack at them before the regular meeting of the board on Saturday morning."

"How?"

"By going ahead with the Friday afternoon meeting, without any fixed agenda."

"Suppose Greg has already shown the plans to this fellow Templeton."

"He can hardly do that before the board sees them, and he thinks that will be Saturday morning. Once the board has nixed the plan, they won't do Greg or anybody any good."

"You may be right," said Tim Puckett. "I don't know."

"Stop worrying," Ed McDougal told him. "That automation speech of Greg's scared the hell out of a lot of doctors and we're gaining support steadily. By the time the banquet comes off tomorrow night, I'm pretty sure we'll have enough votes to squelch anything he tries to do. Right now, we want Greg to have all the publicity he can get on the actual operation; that's the rope we're going to hang him with."

When Dr. Puckett left, Ed McDougal switched off the lights in the suite and left it, locking the door. At the bank of elevators, he punched the "Up" button and, when the elevator came, rode up two floors to where his and Hannah's suite was located.

He always felt keyed up after one of these wire-pulling deals and was ready for a celebration. Besides, he owed Hannah something for not being able to take an active part in the cocktail party earlier that evening, and the best way to celebrate—as well as keep her happy—was for them to hang one on.

Hannah's belongings were scattered through the living room of the suite; her purse was on the chair, her shoes in the doorway leading to the bedroom—which meant she'd come in loaded. Hannah herself, in her slip, lay sprawled across the bed asleep, snoring gently. When he took her by the shoulder and turned her over, she didn't rouse and, leaving her there, he went to the bathroom and examined the shelf under the mirror.

The bottle of red capsules she carried with her everywhere was there, with the top off. But when he counted them and found only two missing from the two dozen that had been in the bottle when they'd left home last night, he was sure she hadn't taken enough to form the lethal combination with alcohol favored by declining movie actresses and fading members of the jet set.

Leaning over the bed, he straightened out Hannah's legs and turned her on her side so she couldn't swallow her tongue. Taking the bottle of amphetamine tablets she always carried with her out of her bag, he set it down on the bedside table along with a glass of water, knowing that, when she finally roused in the morning, she would need them to get herself wide enough awake to order coffee from room service. Then, locking the door behind him, he returned to the suite he had left a few minutes before and picked up the phone.

"Bell captain," he told the operator and, when a man's voice answered, said: "This is Dr. McDougal in suite four-forty. Any chance of obtaining some entertainment tonight?"

"It can be arranged, sir." The bell captain's voice was discreetly low. "But there's quite a demand and the cost may be high, say fifty for a top-quality performer?"

"Send her up," Ed said, and poured himself another drink. After all, entertainment at a medical convention was deductible.

iv

In Sam Hunter's suite, the financier sat in pajamas, robe and slippers, watching the TV screen but paying little attention to what was happening there. The afternoon paper lay on the table beside him, with Jud Templeton's story on the front page. Moto, the valet, had left a glass of warm milk and some crackers in a cellophane packet on the table; the old man opened one of the packets now and took out a cracker, crunching it between his teeth before washing it down with the milk.

He'd been having heartburn a lot at night lately and made a mental note to tell Dr. Connor about it when he had his physical tomorrow. Even the milk didn't help much, though, particularly since the break with Ted. He'd had to get up early every night and take a couple of antacid tablets to relieve the discomfort before he could get back to sleep.

Ever since his talk that evening with Peter Carewe and Helen Foucald, and later with Claire Anders, Sam Hunter had been filled with a vague discontent, whose source he couldn't immediately identify. However pragmatic his own point of view might be in his business, he could appreciate dedication and loyalty when he saw it and had recognized those qualities in both Helen and the doctor from the World Health Organization. He knew enough, too, about the world-wide operations of his companies to recognize that what Peter had told him about the Persian Gulf incident was true.

Whatever he might think of the United Nations as a whole, he could admire a man like Carewe. And there, he faced the truth at last, was the source of his discontent. In Peter Carewe, he'd seen many of the qualities Ted possessed, qualities of dedication and devotion to ideals, which, he recognized now, had been the source of most of the friction between them and had finally resulted in the break, when Ted had married the Italian girl and gone off with the circus.

Perhaps because the memory of the old is far more vivid for the distant than the recent past, Sam Hunter found himself recalling those carefree days in Italy when, for a few months, he'd even considered giving up the place waiting for him in his father's growing business back home. He had long since destroyed the few dabs he'd made at painting then, but now he felt once again, as if excavated from the remains of that long-distant but happy period, some of the pride of accomplishment he'd felt in them.

Obeying an impulse he had rigidly resisted until now, Sam Hunter went to the telephone and picking up the receiver, dialed the long-distance operator and gave her the number of his telephone charge card, followed by a number in Texas. When Mike Hawkins, chief of the security detail that guarded his properties and operations all over the world, answered, he said: "Mike, do you know where Ted is?"

"The weekly report from the people that check on him for us came over my desk only yesterday, Mr. Hunter. Just a minute and I'll get it from the file."

After a brief period, the security chief spoke again in the telephone. "Ted's not far from you, sir."

"I know that from the reports before I left. But what town?"

"Let's see. Tonight the circus is playing in Reisterstown, Maryland. Tomorrow night they'll be in small town not far from there." Sam Hunter copied down the name. "I'll have next week's itinerary in a few days, want me to call you?"

"Never mind. What about business?"

"The agency reports pretty small crowds at the circus. Are you going to see the boy while you're up there, sir?" Mike had been with Sam Hunter since before young Sam's birth and had often taken the boys on hunting and fishing trips when they were growing up.

"I don't know, Mike."

"I hope you will, sir. The agency says Ted and the girl have a real good act. They turned down a chance to audition for Ringling a few months ago."

"Then he's making a go of it?"

"You didn't think he wouldn't, did you?"

"No, I suppose not."

"The circus may not last out the season," said Mike Hawkins, "but I guess Ted and the girl plan to stay with the old man to the end."

"Thanks, Mike. Everything all right down there?"

"Fine, sir. Your checkup going okay?"

"They're ramming a tube in one end or the other every few minutes." Sam Hunter chuckled. "I guess it's when they start ram-

237

ming it in both ends at the same time that you really have to worry. Good night, Mike."

"Good night, sir. Give Ted my regards, if you see him."

Sam Hunter was thoughtful as he went back to the table and finished his milk and crackers. Then he went into the bathroom, removed his teeth and put them into a cup of water into which he dropped a tablet that fizzed. Rinsing his mouth out with water, he turned the light out and went back to the bed, where he removed his robe and lay down, pulling up the covers.

For a few moments, he lay staring up at the ceiling, then, with a purposeful movement, reached up and switched off the light, turned over on his side and was almost instantly asleep.

18

The audience in the lecture room had dwindled to no more than twenty-five people when Greg Alexander opened the door from the operating theater just outside which Frank Lawson lay. He was still wearing the gown and gloves he'd worn while making the incision into Guy Merchant's chest and attaching his circulation to the heart-lung pump. As he moved to the podium in the center of the room, there was a stir among those sitting upon the seats and a few who had fallen asleep were roused by the others. Jud Templeton came wide awake at the sound of Greg's voice but was careful to remain slumped down so as not to call the surgeon's attention to his presence.

"I'm not going to apologize for this procedure having taken so long, because it is beyond my power to shorten it," Greg told the waiting group. "I *can* report to you that Mr. Merchant is holding up well, now that his respiration and circulation have been taken over by the pump-oxygenator. We've not lost hope of being able to carry out a successful transplant, but I would be less than truthful if I didn't admit that the odds against success are increasing with every passing moment. That's about all I can say at this time."

"What about Lawson?" one of the watchers asked.

"His brain picture is growing steadily more chaotic, proving that the damage from hemorrhage is progressive. I wish it were possible to connect a monitor in here so you could see the electroencephalogram, but we didn't exactly anticipate this sort of a situation."

"Wouldn't it be better just to let Merchant die?" one man asked. "This seems only to be prolonging the agony."

"Would you want me to make that decision, if you were in his place, Doctor?" Greg asked.

"Well, no. But—"

"Actually, I can't even use what I would want done in my own case as a standard by which to make such a decision," said Greg. "Life is life and as long as I can preserve it, I have no choice. Are you familiar with the case of Dr. Smirnov in Russia?"

"No," the questioner admitted.

"Smirnov is regarded as one of the world's leading mathematicians. He was injured in an accident not long ago while on his way to an important scientific meeting and was rushed to a hospital, apparently dead. In the next twenty-four to thirty-six hours, he was clinically dead several times, yet, each time, he was revived by the same technique we use in this hospital for resuscitation when the heart has stopped. Today Smirnov is alive and at work."

"With no damage to his brain?" one of the onlookers asked.

"There has been some slight impairment of his faculties. But merely preserving most of such a brain is of incalculable value to science."

"How can you stand the strain yourself, Greg?" Abe Lantz asked. "Just watching it makes me want to go out and get a stiff drink."

"I'm sorry we can't serve it to you here, Abe. I don't mind admitting that once or twice tonight I could have used one myself."

The door to the operating room Greg had just left opened, and Herb Partridge spoke through it. "We need you in here, Dr. Alexander. Pronto!"

ii

Greg's first glance was not at Frank Lawson but at the monitor tube. The change he saw there warned him, far more accurately than any examination of Lawson could have done, that the critical moment was fast approaching. The heart picture still followed its regular pattern but the amplitude of the beat had markedly diminished, even since he'd left the room a few moments before. As for the electroencephalographic pattern, it was difficult to distinguish any movement there at all; only rarely did the flicker of an electric wave show upon the screen.

"There was a sudden change," said Herb Partridge. "I think we will have brain death at any moment."

"Get him into the O.R. and uncover the instrument tables." Greg was pulling off his gown over his gloves as he spoke. As he stripped off the gloves themselves and dropped them into a waste container, a scrub nurse was already holding up a fresh sterile gown before him. And while one of the two circulating nurses tied the strings of his gown, he thrust his hands into fresh gloves being held out for him by the scrub nurse.

"I'm going to prep him, Phil," he told the medical examiner. "But I'll not make an incision until you and Herb give the word."

Dr. Dennison nodded without removing his eyes from the monitor, where the rapidly dwindling pattern of heart and brain action were being portrayed. Moving swiftly, Greg painted Frank Lawson's chest with an antiseptic solution and, with the help of a resident who had been waiting, scrubbed and ready with the nurses, covered it with a broad sheet of transparent plastic. A second large sheet with a window covered the whole table, leaving exposed only the front of the chest. He did not look at the monitors while he worked, for the task of establishing death now legally belonged to the medical examiner, according to the order Judge Sutler had issued that afternoon, and to Herb Partridge.

"Test the temperature of the Tyrode's solution," he told the circulating nurse.

"It's four degrees Centigrade, Doctor."

"Bone cutters ready?"

"Yes, Doctor."

"Get ready, Greg." Dr. Dennison was studying the sweep-second hand of his watch as it crept around the dial. Upon the cardiac monitor, the heart wave had now flattened out to a straight line and there were no more waves on the brain monitor.

"One minute without heartbeat," the medical examiner said and Greg picked up the scalpel, ready to make the incision. "Frank Lawson is dead."

"I agree," said Herb Partridge and his words still echoed in the room as Greg's scalpel moved in a wide arc across the dead man's chest below the collarbones, cutting through muscle and down to ribs and breastbone in one stroke. It was the cut used by pathologists in the autopsy room, allowing maximum exposure of the organs in the chest. At the center of the arc, he made a downward stroke, splitting both skin and tissues beneath down to the breastbone.

"Dissect the flap outward on the right side, exposing the upper chest," he instructed the house officer who was assisting him, handing him the scalpel he had used and picking up a fresh one, with which he began to separate the muscles from the chest wall. In a matter of moments, sufficient exposure had been obtained to reveal the upper two thirds of the rib cage. And when a heavy bone-cutting forceps came into his hand, Greg inserted it beneath the ribs and began to cut rapidly across them, lifting up a flaplike window from the chest itself to expose the heart and the lungs beneath.

So swift were his movements, perfected by long practice to almost a stylized grace, that less than five minutes elapsed between the beginning of the incision and the complete exposure of the heart and lungs within the chest cavity. At what he saw there, Greg didn't break the rapid movement of his work; but he felt a sudden sense of impending disaster, nevertheless. For, where the ribs had been broken when Frank Lawson had crashed to the street below the underpass, the outer surface of the pleural covering over the lungs was dark with hemorrhage. And although the original X-rays had not shown any involvement of the lungs themselves, he had no way of knowing whether the hemorrhage had extended into vital lung tissue since the night of Lawson's accident, jeopardizing seriously the chances of success with the transplant.

No time could be wasted in conjecture now, however. In rapid succession, he clamped the great vessels connected to the heart: the aorta, from which blood was carried to the body other than the lungs, which had their own private circulation; the superior and inferior vena cava that brought blood back to the heart from the upper and lower part of the body, respectively; the bronchial arteries supplying the tissue of the lung itself with the blood necessary for life, as distinguished from the main lung circulation, whose function it was to expose the blood to oxygen.

He did not put clamps on the heart side of the major vessels, lest the walls be crushed by the instruments and thus interfere with the new connections, medically termed anastomoses, which would have to be made to place Frank Lawson's heart in Guy Merchant's circulation. And he left a section of the large artery called the aorta, perhaps two inches long, attached to the heart in order to facilitate its connection to Guy Merchant's own artery system.

Less than ten minutes had passed before Greg lifted the heart and lungs together from Frank Lawson's body and immersed them gently in a large basin filled with the solution called Tyrode's, cooled to four degrees Centigrade. A gasp went up from the instrument nurse holding the basin when the heart muscle contracted strongly from the stimulus of the cold solution, and Greg experienced the first spurt of hope he'd allowed himself to feel since he'd opened the chest and seen the dark stain of hemorrhage across Frank Lawson's right lung.

Carrying the basin with its precious contents, he moved by way of the adjoining scrub rooms to the other operating theater. There, warned of what was happening, Bob Johnson was working swiftly, removing Guy Merchant's useless heart and lungs from his body.

iii

Like magic, so rapidly does word of an extraordinary event spread through the corridors of a great hospital, the surgical lecture room had begun to fill with people. They clustered mainly in the lower right-hand seats, where the screen had suddenly become active after the brief scene on the left screen, when the closed-circuit TV tube had faithfully recorded the medical examiner's dramatic announcement and Greg's immediate action.

When Greg lifted Frank Lawson's heart and lungs from his body, Jud Templeton glanced at his watch, made a quick mental calculation and bolted for the corridor and the telephone. "How long can you hold the presses, Casey?" he asked when the voice of the city editor came on the line.

"An hour if we have to, maybe longer. What's up?"

"Dr. Alexander is starting the transplant. Give me a rewrite man and I'll dictate the first part of the story. Then I can keep feeding it to you in batches, until the deadline."

"Sounds like you're watching over his shoulder," said the city editor.

"It's almost that. Damnedest sensation I ever had, looking right down into an incision with a television camera."

"Any chance of pictures?"

"I'll try to snap the TV screen with a Minox and fast film, if I don't get caught, but they probably won't turn out. Anyway, we couldn't run them until tomorrow."

"O.K. Here's rewrite."

"I just watched a great surgeon carrying a living heart in his hands," Jud Templeton dictated tersely into the phone as soon as the rewrite man's voice spoke in his ear. "The heart had to be living, although the former occupant was legally dead, because the surgeon is now putting it into the chest of another man . . ."

iv

When word had come from the other operating theater that Frank Lawson was dead, Bob Johnson started at once on the final stages of preparing Guy Merchant to receive the new heart and lungs he needed so badly. He was busily at work when Greg came in carrying the basin of Tyrode's solution with its precious contents. Changing gown and gloves quickly, Greg stepped up to the table in Bob's place, surveyed the situation in one quick glance, and gave it an approving nod.

"You can start warming now," he told the anesthesiologist and the pump technicians.

Immediately, Dr. Gann stopped the circulation through the pad beneath Guy Merchant's body of the icy slush which had been helping to keep his temperature at a low level, while the pump technicians opened the heat exchanger to start warming the blood flowing through the heart-lung pump into Guy Merchant's body.

Working swiftly, Greg finished removing the now useless organs and dropped them into a basin held by the instrument nurse.

Almost in the same motion, he reached down into the basin of cold Tyrode's solution he had placed upon a stand beside the table and lifted out the heart and lungs which moments before had been inside Frank Lawson's body.

The most critical stage of the technique Greg had worked out in experimental operations on dogs involved breaking off the actual circulation of blood to the heart itself through the coronary vessels for the briefest possible period. To make that time lapse even shorter, he had devised a temporary coupling composed of a circular clamp and a Teflon gasket, with which to connect quickly the cut end of the recipient's aorta to that of the donor. In this way, blood under the force of the pump was allowed to surge through the arterial system of the body immediately and enter the small openings of the coronary arteries. Lying just at the beginning of the aorta itself, they could thus serve to maintain the vital circulation to the heart muscle while he rapidly completed the rest of the connections necessary before the new heart could begin to function.

While Bob Johnson applied the aortic coupling, Greg was using a very fine needle to place a row of sutures joining the right side of Frank Lawson's heart to the remaining cuff of Guy Merchant's atrium outside the mouths of the great veins and the tubes which still connected them to the heart-lung pump. So practiced was the entire team that no words were actually necessary as the step-by-step procedure moved through the familiar routine. When he finished the aortic coupling, Bob moved to connect the bronchial arteries and veins, using nylon mesh tubing which Greg had also developed for this purpose. And, by that time, Greg had finished his first row of sutures on the right side of the heart.

"Body temperature rising steadily," Dr. Lewis Gann reported as Greg started the second row of sutures to make the right-sided connection tight. More important, with an adequate supply of oxygen now in the blood surging into the coronary arteries, the muscle of the new heart had once again resumed its normal pink color.

It took a little while longer for Greg to place a row of sutures connecting the aorta and replacing the temporary connection made by means of the special clamp and the Teflon cuff. When that was completed, he made another incision in the notch just above Guy Merchant's breastbone and opened a space through which he drew the trachea from Frank Lawson's lungs, attaching the cut end to the skin with several sutures. He slipped a tracheostomy tube into this opening and, when Dr. Lewis Gann shifted the respirator connection to it, the new lungs were now ready for expansion.

When he heard a sudden gasp from the instrument nurse and looked at the chest incision, Greg saw that Frank Lawson's heart, now connected entirely to Guy Merchant's body, had already begun to contract of its own accord. The motion was not the rhythmic contraction of a normal heart, however, but the helter-skelter, purposeless sort of contraction known as "fibrillation," the usual response of a heart after chilling. On the cardiac monitor tube, the flat line indicating no heart activity had suddenly been seized by a crazy profusion of waves, somewhat similar to those that existed in Frank Lawson's brain just before death.

"You've done it, Greg!" Dr. Lewis Gann exclaimed from behind his tent of draperies. "Congratulations!"

"We've gone this far many times before," Greg warned quietly, but even those watching on the screen in the surgical lecture room some distance away could hear the note of quiet satisfaction in his voice as it came to them by way of the auditory part of the system.

"Ready to defibrillate," he said quietly, and the instrument nurse handed him two sterilized plastic rods to which were attached round platelike metal electrodes. From each of the rods, a rubber-coated wire ran to the Pacemaker defibrillator, standing close by the table where the supervisor stood ready to press the switch that would automatically send a measured single jolt of electricity through the heart.

Working very carefully, Greg slid one of the electrodes into place beneath the heart. Then, while Bob Johnson held it, he placed a second one in front, with the organ itself between the two platelike connections.

"Contact, please!"

The supervisor pressed the button upon the machine and Frank

Lawson's heart jerked in a powerful contraction as the momentary current went from one metal electrode to the other, passing through the muscle of the heart itself on the way. Except for a sudden sharp rise in the wave pattern with the introduction of the electric current from outside the heart, however, there was no change in the wild jumble of contractions. Tension rose perceptibly in the room, but Greg ignored it, intent upon what he was doing.

"Once again, please," he said, and the nurse pressed the button, sending a second charge of electricity through Frank Lawson's heart.

The sudden complete cessation of movement in the monitor pattern following the leap upward with completion of the circuit between machine-heart-machine was startling compared to the squirming "bag-of-worms" action the heart had been exhibiting before. Almost hesitantly, as if reluctant to begin, a faint single contraction occurred, then another, then another, in a steady rhythm that indicated a resumption of the normal beat. As it grew stronger with each contraction a cheer broke out from those in the operating room and from the crowd which now half filled the surgical lecture room watching the television screen.

"We're not out of the woods yet." Greg's eyes were on the monitor screen as he spoke. The heart pattern portrayed there was obviously growing stronger all the while, but only when the peaks marking the electrical impulses that initiated each contraction approached normal, did he turn back to the operative field to complete the closure that marked the end of the dramatic operative procedure.

"Do you want to try inflation, Lew?" he asked the anesthesiologist. If the connection between respirator and the new airway was not tight, now was the time to correct it, but, when Dr. Gann turned a valve on the respirator, inflating the lungs, the pressure held and the exhale valve tripped automatically, allowing them to deflate.

"We're ready to come off the pump," said Greg and tension gripped the operating room again at his words.

Actually, this stage was even more critical than had been the task of putting Guy Merchant on the heart-lung pump at the beginning of the operation. Any failure correctly to adjust pressures here could interfere easily with the rhythmic action of the heart, beating quietly now but not pumping blood, bringing it to a halt. Then another jolt of the electric current would be needed to start it, with possible damage to the delicate control network inside the heart itself, through which the nerve impulses controlling the beat were transmitted. Just as dangerous, a failure during the crucial moments of transfer from mechanical to physiological action could interfere with the vital circulation to the brain, leaving Guy Merchant a vegetable, even if the new heart and lungs functioned perfectly.

"I'm clamping the venous cannulae," Greg warned the technicians as he slowly began to close down the tubes which had been feeding blood from the body veins into the spinning heart-lung pump. One technician called out the steadily rising venous pressures indicated on the pump, while another read the arterial pressures as reported on the electronic monitor from the tiny tube of nylon inserted into an artery of the hand at the beginning of the operation.

"Loosen the snares," Greg directed.

Bob Johnson reached behind the heart to where the tapes that surrounded the inferior and the superior vena cava, with the cannulae still inside them, maintained a snug fit around the plastic tubes. With the snares loosened, blood flowed past the tubes into the right side of the heart, but at the same moment Greg loosened the purse-string in the wall of the atrium, which he had placed long ago, it seemed, when Guy Merchant had been put upon the pump. A faint froth of blood and air escaped around the tube, removing the small amount of air which had entered the heart while the connections to Guy Merchant's circulatory system were being made. When no more froth escaped, he slid the cannula quickly out of the superior vena cava, allowed the atrium to fill with blood and spill out through the purse-string opening, then closed it by tightening the ends of the suture. The tube in the lower of the great veins would be removed later through the common femoral vein, into which it had been inserted.

The pump-oxygenator, its steel discs still spinning, was now forcing blood into Guy Merchant's body through the tube in the artery of his upper thigh but was taking none from it. As the pressure in the right side of the heart rose from the blood now pouring into the atrium from the great veins, the valve that controlled its emptying opened and filled the adjoining muscular chamber on the right side, called the ventricle. Stimulated by the change in pressure, the ventricle began to pump blood through the lungs, from which it was returned to the left side of the heart, where the same sequence of events occurred.

Seconds ticked away while the vital pressure gradients recorded on the monitors and the gauges of the heart-lung pump rose steadily. Blood being forced into Guy Merchant's circulation was now passing through the tiny capillary vessels connecting veins to arteries in even the most distant parts of his body and pouring into the heart from the right side, while the surging force of the pump still filled the aorta and the rest of the arterial system. When the pressure gradients reached the desired level, the pump technician at the valves began to shut off the flow into the body. And as the pressure inside the now vigorously pumping left ventricle overcame the back pressure in the arterial system from the pump, the valve between ventricle and aorta opened and blood surged through.

"Femoral cannula closed, Dr. Alexander," said the pump technician as he turned the valve through which blood had been flowing to Guy Merchant's body from the machine. "He's on his own."

Greg was watching the monitors. When the arterial pressure recorded there continued to show a level that was obviously able to maintain the vital brain circulation, he began to tie the ends of the purse-string suture, closing finally the opening through which the cannula in the superior vena cava had carried blood from Guy Merchant's body to the pump. Only the click-click of the respirator filled the room now as the whirr of the pump ceased, and Greg reached for the wire sutures used to pull the two halves of the split breastbone together.

"The patient is now maintaining his own circulation without assistance," he announced to the watching audience and everyone there could easily hear the note of pride in his voice. When he looked up at the clock over the door, he was startled to see that barely an hour had elapsed since the medical examiner had given him the go-ahead to begin the epochal transplant.

v

In the adjoining lecture room, Jud Templeton blinked as he turned his eyes from the television screen. He looked at his watch, then sprinted for the telephone. When the rewrite man to whom he had been feeding elements of the story intermittently over the past hour came on, he said jubilantly:

"Pull out all the stops, Jeff! He's made it!"

"Give me a lead, Jud. The city editor's having a fit."

"How about this? *'Tonight a murderer atoned for his sins as no other man has ever done in history, when Dr. Gregory Alexander, a quiet, self-effacing surgeon at Baltimore's world-famous Clinic, successfully transplanted the murderer's heart and lungs to the body of a dying man.'*"

19

It was nearly midnight before Greg was finally able to telephone Jeanne. "Congratulations, darling!" she cried.

"How did you know?"

"You're all over the television. Half the eleven o'clock news was devoted to you."

"I can't leave the hospital tonight, but I would love to see you at least for a few minutes," he told her. "Could you meet me at the feet of Jesus?"

"I'll be there—in five minutes."

"Take longer if you need it."

"No. That will be enough."

She was waiting at the foot of the great statue when he came into the lobby after reporting the successful conclusion of the operation to Georgia Merchant. Visiting hours were long over and the rotunda was empty, save for an intern and a nurse whispering in the shadows and the telephone operators behind their grille.

"You look worn, darling," she said. "Was the operation so difficult?"

"Not the operation—but the waiting. We almost didn't make it."

"Then Merchant will live?"

"Everything's functioning well but we still have to watch for infection—mostly of the lungs—and rejection."

"After tonight, how could the trustees turn you down?"

"I'm afraid the operation won't really change things. It might even have the opposite effect."

"Why?"

"There's a great deal of jealousy among doctors. Some will

want to cut me down just because I had the courage to do something they wouldn't tackle."

"But it's they who should beg you to stay. You're still going to push your plan for The Clinic, aren't you? It's too beautiful to be lost."

Greg looked up into the dimness of the rotunda. The marble features of the Christ somehow seemed different. He thought his eyes were playing tricks on him, until Jeanne, whose gaze had followed his, suddenly cried, "He's smiling! It's a good omen, Greg! I know it is!"

"What you're seeing is most likely the effect of the shadows there under the dome," he said. But somehow he wasn't surprised at the feeling of assurance and peace that had suddenly come over him, as if perhaps He, too, had seen Keith Jackson's sketches and wanted to come out of the shadows into the sunlight.

"When can you come home?" Jeanne asked.

"Perhaps tomorrow night. I'm going to send Bob Johnson home. Lew Gann and I will take turns watching over Merchant." He glanced at his watch. "It's time for me to let Bob go off duty now. Thanks for coming over, darling."

"I—I'm glad you wanted me after—"

"That's all over now," he said quickly. "Forever."

"Go back to your patient," she told him. "I think I'll sit here at the foot of the statue for a while."

"Ask the night watchman at the guard post by the entrance to see that you get across to the apartment safely. There's been some mugging in this area." He bent to kiss her. "Good night."

"Good night, dear."

When he was gone, she remained standing at the foot of the great statue, recalling the times she'd met Greg there for a few stolen moments when he had been a Fellow and she a nurse. She didn't notice the presence of another person, until Georgia Merchant said, "Mrs. Alexander?"

"Yes." Jeanne turned to face her.

"I saw you talking to Dr. Alexander just now and the receptionist told me you're his wife. I'm Mrs. Merchant."

"I'm so glad your husband came through the operation safely,

Mrs. Merchant," said Jeanne warmly. "It must be a great relief to have it over with."

"To tell the truth, I don't know whether to be happy or guilty."

"But why?"

"I let my faith weaken for a while," Georgia confessed. "When it seemed that Guy had gone so far there could be no bringing him back, even with the operation, I kept asking myself whether I loved him enough to let him die and wasn't selfish in wanting him to live."

"I think that's a very natural way to feel."

"I'll always be grateful to your husband for taking the burden of decision off my shoulders."

"You must be exhausted," said Jeanne. "We have an extra room and I'll be happy for you to use it."

"Thank you, Mrs. Alexander, but I couldn't." Georgia's smile was wry with the pain of many years of rebuffs. "You see, I'm a stripper—a striptease dancer."

Jeanne Alexander looked up at the features of the statue, then back at the woman before her.

"I seem to remember reading that the leader of the women who followed Him was a dancer. If He didn't hold that against her, I'd be pretty small to hold your occupation against you, wouldn't I?"

Georgia Merchant's shoulders straightened and her chin lifted. "I *was* beginning to feel sorry for myself and Guy wouldn't want that. Your husband is one of the gentlest men I've ever known, Mrs. Alexander, as gentle even as my Guy. I guess we're two of the luckiest women alive; thank you for helping me not to forget."

"I'm glad I could help," Jeanne said quietly. "You see, I once came very close to forgetting myself."

"I'll be all right now," said Georgia. "Guy might wake up and want to know I was nearby. Thanks for being so kind."

As Jeanne was leaving the hospital, a newspaper truck pulled up the driveway and stopped at the entrance. The driver got down from the cab and lifted a package of morning papers from it. Going to a coin-operated rack beside the entrance, he unlocked it, shoved in a stack of papers, placed one in front and locked it back in a swift succession of movements, before leaping upon his truck and starting down the driveway again.

Across the top of the copy he'd slid into place in the front of the vending machine, Jeanne could see the bold headlines:

CLINIC SURGEON MAKES MEDICAL HISTORY
Performs Surgical Miracle

ii

Guy Merchant regained consciousness—if it could be called that—shortly after dawn. At first, he wondered whether he were alive and not simply a soul in transit, for he seemed to be floating between earth and sky. When his eyes were able to focus, however, he recognized the same dull white ceiling of the room where he had been taken, a long time ago it seemed now, when his breathing had become so difficult. And when he moved his shoulders, seeking a more comfortable position, the pain in his chest confirmed the fact that he was alive and in the flesh, instead of a random spirit on the way to whatever was its final destination.

"Mr. Merchant?" The face floating above him slowly cleared like a color slide being focused on a screen, and he saw that the speaker was a nurse. She was wearing a gown and mask but he could see enough hair escaping around her cap to determine that she was red-haired, reminding him that he hadn't seen Georgia for a long, long time. He tried to speak and ask for Georgia, but wasn't able to force air through his voice box, which seemed strange, for he could feel the rhythmic expansion and contraction of his chest with breathing, and the pain that went with it.

"Your wife's outside," said the nurse. "You're in isolation, so she can't come in for a while."

He tried to speak again and ask if the operation was over, but gave up because there simply wasn't any air to form the words.

"We're trying to keep infection away from you." Strange that he could see the nurse perfectly now and hear her, yet the words that formed in his brain wouldn't come from his larynx. "I'll send word to your wife that you're awake, and perhaps she can see you later today. You were operated on nearly ten hours ago, Mr. Merchant."

Another face appeared beside that of the nurse and he recognized the young surgeon who was usually with Dr. Alexander.

"You're doing fine," Bob Johnson assured him. "We gave you a new heart and lungs and they're working very well."

The younger man reached toward something that was out of Guy's sight beside the bed and the rhythmic clicking stopped. "Try to take a breath for me, please."

Guy concentrated on the act of breathing but nothing happened. Before he could suffer any apprehension, however, the clicking started again and, with it, the regular filling and emptying of his lungs.

"Dr. Alexander was up most of the night watching over you, Mr. Merchant," Bob Johnson explained. "He's getting some sleep now and you'd better get some more, too. The nurse is going to give you a hypo."

Guy could feel the sting of the needle as the drug was injected; then almost immediately he was floating downward again into the familiar pleasant void.

iii

Helen was wondering whether she would find Peter waiting when she came into the motel dining room shortly after eight. He was standing by the cashier's booth, however, and moved at once to guide her to a secluded table distinguished from the rest by a magnificent arrangement of red roses.

"How did you know they're my favorite flower?" Her eyes were warm as he pulled out her chair.

"They had to be. Roses are independent, yet beautiful—like you."

"No wonder women can't resist you. The charm stays on, like a light left burning."

"Let's talk more about this idea that women can't resist me," he said. "Are you speaking from experience?"

"Didn't you make me eat ham and eggs yesterday morning, when a protein cereal and orange juice is my regular menu?"

"I've already ordered for both of us. Want to know today's menu?"

"Ham and eggs?"

"Eventually—first we'll have a fresh honeydew melon, brought here from Florida especially for you."

"Don't tell me you had that flown in since yesterday—like the roses?"

"I would have, if the restaurant hadn't had them in stock."

"Is this part of the famous Carewe technique of whirlwind courtship?"

"You can't blame me if I work fast. I only have a few days."

"Has something new come up?" she asked quickly, and he nodded.

"A night letter from Lars Nordstrom, my chief at the UN section in New York. He wants me in Los Angeles no later than Monday afternoon to take charge of the search for that polio vaccine contaminant I was telling you about."

Both of them were subdued a little by the thought that their time together would be so short. Only when the waitress had poured a second cup of coffee for them did Peter suddenly ask, "Have I told you I'm in love with you?"

"Please, Peter." Helen put down her coffee cup with a hand that had suddenly started to tremble. "You mustn't."

"Why not?"

"Let's just keep this light and pleasant—the way it's been so far."

"That's only a front we've been using to cover the way we've really felt about each other since the moment I saw you at the airport yesterday. Don't deny it."

"I can't," she confessed. "But there are reasons why we mustn't be serious."

"Are you in love with someone else?"

"Oh no!"

"And are you in love with me?"

"I think I am." The moment of truth had come, she could no longer evade it. "Yes, I know I am."

"Is it Henry Anders then?"

"Why do you say that?"

"The way he acted last night toward you—like he owned you. I

256

never liked the bastard anyway, but even in medical school he had a formidable reputation with women." He took both her hands in his across the table. "Don't tell me you love him?"

"Oh no. You see I—"

"No details—please."

"I was going to tell you before this—this went too far. But then I was afraid of losing you and thought we could just enjoy the time you're going to be here together."

"What's happened to us isn't something you can just enjoy for a while and forget, Helen. I've had plenty of casual affairs and this is different."

"So what do we do—get married?"

"Are you sure enough of yourself for that?"

"Not yet—but I don't think I'm far from it."

"I'm nearer than that," he said. "Say the word and we'll head for Elkton this morning. Years ago you could get married there at any time of the day or night."

"I couldn't do that to you, darling." Her voice was sober. "You see, I know myself—and my needs."

"I figured that's what's been troubling you," he said. "And sometime around midnight I came up with what may be the answer."

"What is it?"

"Something like a physiologic test to distinguish between love and simply sex attraction, plus finding out just how well we're suited to each other physically."

"Room service?"

"Something more appropriate, I think, for us."

"I'm not the kind of woman who jumps into the bed of any man who asks me—no matter how attractive he is."

"We're both scientists, so why not a scientific experiment?"

"Experiment? That's a new name for an affair."

"We both know this wouldn't be just another affair. What we need is a chance to get to know each other and find out some things for ourselves. For instance, it's quite possible that with your—" He fumbled for a word and she supplied it—somewhat bitterly.

"Experience?"

"I didn't plan to put it so bluntly. The truth is, you might not find me quite the lover I seem to have the reputation of being."

"And vice versa."

"Since we're using such starkly realistic phraseology—yes. But however that part of it turns out, we could have a pleasantly comfortable weekend together, with no strings attached. Then Monday morning, I'll fly away for a while and you'll have time to think things out."

"You still haven't named the place for this—experiment. Shall it be my apartment or your suite?"

"Neither. Did you ever hear of the Chalet Julienne?"

"No."

"It's a typical Swiss-type inn located in the Catoctin Mountains not far from Frederick, only a couple of hours or so drive from here. Two old friends of mine, Carl and Julia Koenig, run it. They don't have many guests in winter and we'll be treated like royalty."

"It's an attractive prospect," she admitted.

"Nobody else need know," he assured her. "I have to leave for California Sunday afternoon, so you can drive your car to the airport Friday afternoon and I'll meet you there. We'll leave your car in the parking lot and I'll rent one. That way, I can abduct you, and shut you away somewhere—like Rumpelstiltskin."

20

Jeanne Alexander had been up an hour when Greg called at eight. She hadn't eaten breakfast, however, hoping he might have time to join her.

"Just thought you'd like to know Merchant seems to be doing well," he said. "Mainly, I called to tell you I love you."

"I couldn't blame you if you didn't."

"And I couldn't stop if I tried. I wish I could come over for breakfast, but I've called a conference for nine o'clock to evaluate Merchant's condition and I have to get all the information I can for it."

"I thought you said he's doing all right."

"He is—so far."

"You're worried about rejection, aren't you?"

"That's the next hurdle. Even with ALG, it can still happen, though that's our best weapon. I've got to run now—"

"Greg!"

"Yes, dear."

"Isn't there some way I can help?"

"You've helped already. Just knowing we're together again has made all the difference in the world."

"Will you be able to go to the banquet tonight?"

"I'm going to try. I'll have to call you later about that."

When he hung up the phone, Jeanne put on the percolator and made some coffee, while she poured cereal in a bowl and sat down at the kitchen table. She was eating when Ethel came in.

"The doctor sure has been making a name for hisself," the maid said proudly. "He's all over the newspapers, the television, everywhere. When's he coming home?"

"I went over to the hospital to see him last night," Jeanne told her. "He hopes to get home tonight. We're supposed to go to a banquet."

"Do you good to get out—with him. Just bein' yourself again is what he needs most."

The maid's wisdom, Jeanne thought wryly, was greater than her own. But she still needed to do something tangible to allay her feeling of guilt for having let Greg down at a time when he had been more troubled than during the whole period of their marriage —if only she could find a way.

Pulling on a heavy sweater, she stepped out upon the balcony that surrounded two sides of the penthouse. From this lofty viewpoint, she could see the whole of The Clinic, squat and ugly across the street in its brownstone dress.

California would be bright and cheerful, the sun warm most of the year. She had seen the medical school in which Greg would work there; it was all steel and glass while here everything was dingy and drab. Yet, however drab and uninspiring it might look now, she knew the complex of buildings across the busy Parkway was as much a part of Greg as his own heart—and something no surgeon could replace. More than twenty years of his life had gone into another man's dream, and now, with Keith Jackson's plan for a soaring tower of healing in place of the drab and the brown, he hoped to turn that dream into a flame brighter even than old Dr. Anders had ever conceived.

She didn't for a moment really believe he was as unconcerned as he claimed to be about the outcome of the controversy which would reach its climax Saturday morning. The Clinic was Greg's life and to give up the dream now of what it could be, would be nothing less than heartbreaking for him. There had to be something she could do and somehow she had to find it. The trouble was that time was so short; only two more days until the convocation would be over and the crucial session of the Board of Trustees would begin.

Then, when her spirits were at their lowest, she suddenly remembered something that sent her inside to ring Claire Anders on the telephone.

"Sorry I had to leave you to entertain all the men last night, when Greg started the operation, Claire," she said. "But I couldn't think of anything except what he was going through."

"You did me a favor, darling," said Claire. "Helen went to the laboratory and I had Peter Carewe to myself for a drink—but nothing else, worse luck."

"Did you mean what you said yesterday at lunch about our working together to keep The Clinic from being moved, Claire?"

"Of course, but things look bleak. Henry is sure Greg has overstepped himself in operating on Merchant and that they have him where they want him."

"I'm worried about the same thing," Jeanne admitted. "Greg claims the idea of going somewhere else doesn't bother him any more but I know better."

"The Clinic would never be the same without Greg," Claire agreed. "Lord knows I've tried to keep Henry from making a fool of himself, but he's hell bent on it this time. So where does that leave us?"

"There may be a chance of blocking Henry and Ed, if you'll help me."

"Say the word."

"Yesterday morning, when Hannah barged in while I was having breakfast, she let drop something about a syndicate being formed to develop The Clinic property when it goes to Henry after the move to the Beltway. She hinted that if Greg stopped opposing the move, they'd cut him in. Do you know anything about it?"

"Henry knows I don't approve of moving The Clinic, so he's pretty secretive about his plans," said Claire. "What did you have in mind?"

"From what Hannah said before she clammed up on me, some other people besides Henry and Ed must be involved in this syndicate. I was thinking that if we could possibly get a list of them, it might be useful."

"A little judicious blackmail?"

"Well—yes."

"Henry's got a desk upstairs in his study that he always keeps locked. If he's got a list of people in the syndicate, it will be there."

"But can you get it?"

"I learned to pick the lock a long time ago, hunting for *billets-doux* from Henry's girl friends, before he settled down with Helen. I think I still know how to do it. Give me a little while and I'll call you back."

"I'll be waiting," Jeanne promised.

The call came in less than half an hour. "We hit pay dirt, Jeanne," said Claire. "I found the list tucked away in Henry's desk. What do you have in mind doing with it?"

"Jud Templeton has been treating Greg well—"

"Jud's just the man. Get your pencil and write these names down. They're dynamite."

When Jeanne finished copying the list Claire read to her over the telephone, she sat studying the names written there for a long moment. It was an impressive array of men prominent in medical, political and business affairs, a truly formidable barrier for one woman to buck alone. Yet she knew Greg wouldn't use it if she showed it to him, so the job was hers. Finally, she leafed through the directory, found a number and dialed it.

"Mr. Jud Templeton, please," she said when the operator at the newspaper offices downtown answered.

ii

The conference Greg had called to evaluate Guy Merchant's condition was held before the Thursday-morning session of the convocation began. At his request, Dave Connor listened to the patient's heart and lungs and studied the laboratory reports, while Bob Johnson brought up the portable X-ray films of the chest taken that morning. The three of them, with Dr. Gann, gathered after the examination in the doctor's lounge between the two main operating theaters of the surgical building.

"Dr. Zenoff's busy with a fluoroscopic examination," Bob Johnson said as he flicked on the switch of a portable X-ray viewbox. "But I got an off-the-cuff reading on the film from the Senior Fellow in X-ray. All he sees is cloudiness at the bases of the lungs and he says that may be only a pleural reaction."

"You can't take out the heart and lungs and connect up another pair without roughing up the inside of the chest cage a little, so some cloudiness can be expected," said Greg. "What do you think from your examination, Dave?"

"He's in remarkably good condition," said the cardiologist. "Frankly, when I saw you putting him on the pump while the donor was still alive, I was sure you were way out on a limb that was half sawed off already."

"I felt a little that way, too," Greg admitted. "Do you agree that haziness at the lung bases may not have any real significance?"

"There's some moisture in the lower lobes of the lungs, too; I could hear râles in the stethoscope," said the cardiologist. "But there was a lot more of it yesterday before we gave him the diuretic."

"This is a new pair of lungs," Bob Johnson reminded him.

"I'm not forgetting that—and it worries me a little," said Dr. Connor.

"Do you think we should give him another injection of ethacrynic acid?" Greg asked, but the cardiologist shook his head.

"There doesn't seem to be enough moisture to justify hitting him with anything that strong at the moment, particularly since the kidneys seem to be functioning very well," he said. "I think the best procedure is to watch and wait."

"Meanwhile, we'll give him one or two transfusions with Lawson's blood," said Greg, "just in case the moisture in the lungs is the beginning of a rejection phenomenon. The transfusion should provide him with some fresh white blood cells, too, in case his infection-resisting powers have been knocked down by the six-mercaptopurine and methylprednisolone we're giving him to keep down the rejection, along with ALG."

"Do you see any suggestion of rejection in the cardiogram, sir," Bob Johnson asked Dr. Connor.

"Not at the moment. The first thing we'd expect, if his body tries to get rid of the transplant, would be a fall in the ECG voltage. But the R-wave of limb lead two"—he pointed to a wavy line on the electrocardiographic tracing—"seems to be as high as it has been at any time."

"What do you think about moving him to intensive care?" Greg asked. "We can watch the ECG a little better on the monitors there than we're able to do in the O.R. And we won't have quite so many people moving in and out with the possibility of bringing in outside infection."

"It sounds like a good idea," said Dave Connor.

"I'll vote for that," said Dr. Gann. "The chances of any virulent bacteria getting to him while his immunity is knocked down so severely by the drugs you're giving to prevent rejection will be considerably less on ICU than down here."

"Bob will help you move him, Lew," said Greg. "I promised to make a report at the opening of the convocation this morning on Merchant's progress."

From the lounge, he went into the surgical lecture room, which was gradually filling with Members of The Clinic in preparation for the morning presentations. Minutes before the clock struck ten and Dr. Timothy Puckett gaveled for attention, Ed McDougal and several others of his faction came in.

Ed looked a little hung over, Greg thought, but that wasn't unusual for him at medical conventions. He seemed to have lost none of his assurance, however, by which Greg judged that Ed and his cronies had been successfully lining up support on the Board of Trustees for themselves while he was busy last night with the transplant operation. Jud Templeton was lounging, as usual, at the back of the room.

"Dr. Alexander has requested a few minutes at the beginning of the session," Dr. Puckett announced. "Go ahead, Greg."

"Some of you have asked for a report on the heart-lung transplant patient we operated upon last night," said Greg. "Dr. Connor has just examined him with me and finds his general condition very good. The only possible adverse sign we see now is a little moisture at the bases of the lungs and we're not sure this is significant under the circumstances."

"Is he breathing without the respirator?" Ed McDougal asked.

"Not yet," Greg admitted.

"Then it sounds like your operation was a failure."

"Not necessarily." Greg contained his temper, recognizing the purpose of the question. "In some of our experimental transplants, respiration hasn't actually begun for several days following operation. In a few others, we've had to stimulate the phrenic nerves electrically to produce contraction of the diaphragm for some time before spontaneous breathing was resumed."

"What about rejection?" another man asked.

"That's our major concern," said Greg. "We're deliberately holding off using heavy doses of immuno-suppressive drugs, as was done in some of the early heart transplant cases, so as not to knock down his defenses against bacteria. Usually, this sort of an infection begins in the lungs, which is another reason why the presence of the moisture there this morning gives us some concern. We are, of course, giving him antibiotics to prevent infection and keeping him isolated."

"What are the chances of his living now?" Ed McDougal asked.

"I think it's too early to evaluate them yet," said Greg. "The fact that he came through surgery in satisfactory condition is a considerable plus value in his favor. The deciding factor in survival will no doubt be whether his body accepts the transplant or rejects it."

When there seemed to be no more questions, he started toward the door leading to the lounge, but Ed McDougal's voice stopped him before he left the room.

"There's been some pretty sharp criticism of your action in subjecting this patient to an operation whose results are so uncertain," he said. "What do you have to say about that?"

Realizing that the purpose of the question was to crystallize the opposition to him, Greg's immediate reaction was one of anger, but he controlled it.

"Anyone who dares to break through a new frontier is liable to get a few arrows stuck in him." He spoke directly to the questioner. "Usually from the rear, by people who are afraid to explore unmarked territory."

There was a wave of laughter and Ed McDougal reddened at the thrust.

"I've always considered that my major obligation to a patient is to keep him alive as long as possible," Greg continued. "This man was clinically dead by the time we were able to get the heart-lung pump in operation and bypass a heart that had failed—yet this morning he's alive. If you can figure out how that makes me guilty of negligence toward him, you're welcome to do so."

Turning on his heel, Greg left the room, but not before it was swept by a spatter of applause. At the podium, Dr. Timothy Puckett gaveled hurriedly for order and began to introduce the first scheduled speaker of the morning session.

iii

Jud Templeton was waiting in the corridor outside the lecture room when Greg came out. "You've won rounds one and two, Doctor," he said. "If you can keep up the pace, you'll get a TKO at the very least."

"You skipped one round."

"The smoke-filled room?"

"Yes."

"Maybe we ought to print that sketch sooner than we intended. The cut of it turned out beautifully."

"Not yet," said Greg. "We may not even get to use it Friday if the question of hospital plans doesn't come up at the afternoon meeting—"

"I wouldn't be too sure they won't."

"Why?"

"If Guy Merchant is still living Friday afternoon when the special meeting comes to order, any attempt to censure you because of your work in experimental surgery is liable to fall pretty flat, with the world applauding you for being a pioneer."

"I think we should stick to schedule. If we detonate our only bomb too soon, the effect may subside before Saturday. By the way, that was a nice piece you did on Mrs. Merchant."

"Georgia deserves all the kudos she can get. Her world might seem to be a pretty scurvy one to you, but it's a very human one nevertheless. And in it, she's a great lady."

Greg smiled. "I'm not quite so square as my predilection for work might make you believe, Jud. I've seen her perform and agree wholly."

"Do you happen to know where she is?"

"She told me earlier she was going back to her hotel for a few minutes to get a shower and a change of clothes. She ought to be back soon."

"A few telegrams came for her in care of me," said Jud Templeton. "Seems like a lot of other people aren't square either, Doctor. Where do we go from here?"

"Watch and wait is all we can do. Are you going to stick around?"

"I think I'll go back to the shop and write a follow-up, then get some sleep."

"I envy you," said Greg as he took the elevator to his office. "I've still got work to do."

"Mr. Templeton!" It was the emergency room nursing supervisor with a slip of paper in her hand. Since the play the newspaperman had given The Clinic's favorite surgeon, he was very popular with the staff. "That phone you've been using outside the emergency room was ringing just now, so I answered it. You're to call Mrs. Alexander at this number."

"Dr. Alexander's wife?"

"Yes. I recognized the number."

"Thanks," he said, and headed for the telephone, wondering why Greg Alexander's wife would call him here.

iv

Helen Foucald was busy at her desk Thursday morning, clearing it so she could attend the morning session of the convocation, when her secretary ushered Sam Hunter into the inner office.

"Did they send you down for some more special examinations, Mr. Hunter?" she asked. "We finished up the routine things yesterday."

"I've just finished in otolaryngology." Sam looked at the green routing sheet in his hand. "And I'm on my way to proctology. Reminds me of a book I read a long time ago, called *Through the Alimentary Canal with Gun and Camera*."

Helen Foucald laughed. "It's not so bad, as long as you can still smile. Can we do something for you here in the laboratory?"

"It's you I came to see. Can you have dinner with me tonight and go to a circus?"

"I had planned to go to the banquet," she said doubtfully.

"Your friend Carewe is going to be pretty busy with the banquet and I thought you might not mind helping cheer up a lonely old man." The odd intensity in his voice told her this was not a casual invitation, particularly when he added, "Besides, we'll probably be back by the time he finishes with the speech and the autograph hunters after it."

"That doesn't matter at all," Helen said quickly, sensing how anxious he was for her to accept. "I shall be happy to go. Did you say the circus?"

"It's only a small one that will probably play in a Shrine auditorium—if there's such a thing in the town we're going to."

"I'll wear something warm. Those places can get pretty drafty."

"How about six o'clock? The town isn't far away and we can have dinner somewhere along the road."

"Six o'clock will be fine," she assured him. "Shall I meet you in the lobby of the Inn? I live next door."

"If that suits you?"

"It suits me fine. I'll see you at six."

"I shall be desolate," Peter said when she told him of Sam Hunter's odd request as they were going in for the morning session of the convocation.

"You'll be basking in the limelight and enjoying it, with admiring women all around you. I'd be jealous if I were there."

"How about a nightcap when you get back?"

"I'd love it—provided some amazon hasn't abducted you by then."

v

"This is Jud Templeton," a male voice said when Jeanne answered her telephone shortly after ten o'clock.

"Oh yes, Mr. Templeton. I appreciate your calling so quickly."

"I would have made it sooner, but I'm at the hospital and the paper had to call me there. Just finished listening to your husband give a report to the convocation on that operation he did last night. It was a spectacular job."

"I need your help, Mr. Templeton—for my husband."

"Any favor I can do either of you is a pleasure, Mrs. Alexander."

"I suppose you've heard rumors that The Clinic may be moved."

"I've heard—and I don't like it any more than Dr. Alexander does."

"Did you know that a syndicate has been formed to develop the property if the trustees decide to move it?"

"I've heard the rumor, but I've seen no real proof."

"Would you consider a list of those in the syndicate real proof?"

"If some of the names on that list are vulnerable, Mrs. Alexander"—she sensed the rising excitement in his voice—"we may not need proof."

"They're vulnerable, Mr. Templeton. More vulnerable than you would believe."

Jud Templeton chuckled. "Newspapermen are like doctors, Mrs. Alexander. They see human nature at its worst more often than they do at its best, so I'm always ready to believe the worst of my fellow-men. When can I see the list?"

"I'm free right now."

"It may be just as well if we're not seen together near The Clinic," he said. "Where would you suggest that we meet?"

"I'll walk north several blocks along The Parkway," she said. "I'll be wearing a dark London Fog coat and a matching hat."

"Give me five minutes."

Jeanne often walked the central pavement strip of The Parkway, even in cold weather, so she was sure no one who knew her would think it odd for her to be there. Four blocks beyond the hospital, she turned back and almost immediately saw Jud Templeton approaching.

"You didn't waste any time," he said with a smile.

"I'm trying to help my husband, Mr. Templeton, and there isn't much time."

"Maybe we can gain some—if this list is all you say it is."

Jeanne handed him the sheet of paper and he ran his eyes down its length, pursing his lips once or twice in a soundless whistle.

"I never cease to be amazed at the avariciousness of human nature," he said finally. "Every one of these men is rich by any standard you name, yet they all succumbed to the possibility of making a fast buck. Who's the leader?"

"Dr. Ed McDougal—from Texas."

"He would be—this is a Texas-style operation. But I need to fire a round or two at targets nearer home. Believe me, it's going to be a pleasure to scare the daylights out of a few of our leading medical citizens."

"You're not going to publish the list in the paper, are you?"

"As a bunch of names, it means nothing, but if I bear down hard enough on some of these characters, one of them may just blurt out the whole scheme. Then I'll have something I can put headlines on and we'll blow this whole thing to smithereens."

"Where are you going to start?" she asked.

"Dr. Timothy Puckett seems to be the one who's got most to lose, I'd say. As chairman of the Board of Trustees, he's supposed to be like Caesar's wife, so I'll give him the first chance to repent of his sins."

"Promise you won't tell my husband about this."

"Your husband is the finest surgeon I know, Mrs. Alexander—but he'd probably be the worst conniver. You and I will handle this little hatchet job ourselves."

vi

Seen by day, the sleazy environs of the nightclub area were even shabbier-looking than Georgia remembered. After two days at the hospital with crisp-uniformed doctors and nurses everywhere, she shivered at the thought of going back into the world it represented. Yet she had good friends there, people who had stood by her and Guy before in times of trouble and would stand by her again, she was sure.

In the club where she had been working, the chairs were still turned upside down atop the tables as the early morning cleaners had left them after doing their work. A single bartender was polishing glasses behind the long bar and a lonely drinker sat at one end, nursing a beer.

"Hi, Georgia," said the bartender. "How's Guy?"

"He came through the operation O.K. The doctors say he's doing well."

"Must have been pretty exciting. You and him have been all over the newspapers."

"I've been too busy to read them," said Georgia. "Is Aaron in?"

"Sure. He's working on the books in his office."

The office door was open and she saw Aaron Schwartz bent over the desk. He was a rumpled bear of a man, so near-sighted that he had to wear thick lenses. He looked up when Georgia tapped on the door, then got up with surprising agility for his size and came around the end of the desk to take both her hands.

"Georgia!" He greeted her warmly, leading her to a chair by the desk. "You and Guy are famous! Have you seen *Variety?*"

Georgia shook her head. "I've hardly been out of the intensive care unit at The Clinic since the other night."

"*Variety* picked up Jud Templeton's piece about you." He handed her the newspaper that was the bible of show business. There in the middle of the second page, in a box where it could hardly be missed, was the article Jud Templeton had written. It was illustrated with a photograph of her, not as she was now, but as she had been as a burlesque headliner.

"I couldn't be more glad if it had happened to me," Aaron Schwartz assured her. "The booking agents will be on your trail any minute."

"I'm a little old for another career now, Aaron."

"Don't you believe it," he said. "You're too high-class for a rat race like this." The wave of his cigar took in the shabby surroundings of the nightclub.

"Are you firing me, Aaron?"

"Firing?" He looked at her with honest pain in his eyes, and she reached out to squeeze his hand.

"Forgive me. I've been under a terrible strain."

"Of course you have. I was going to wait until later to talk to you about this." Georgia understood what "later" meant—until she no longer had Guy hanging around her neck, like the millstone he had considered himself to be.

"I've got to face the future sometime, Aaron. What do you have in mind?"

"Traveling burlesque is coming back. Not the kind we have now with a bunch of young broads who don't know enough to even draw down a zipper without stumbling over themselves, taking off their clothes to canned music. In the old days, burlesque was an art, and the humor a lot better than the stuff you hear coming in on television these days. I've been thinking about putting together a traveling show, not to play the old burlesque houses, but regular theaters on one-, two- or maybe three-night stands, with a whole week whenever we hit a city that's large enough. A show like that will need class and that's something you've always had."

"What about Guy—if he lives?"

"If I put the package together, I'll need somebody I can trust to watch over it, a sort of traveling manager. Guy could handle that in his sleep."

"It might be the answer to our problems, Aaron—after I get me a new face." Georgia's eyes fell to the newspaper and the picture. "The rest of me still stacks up pretty well with what it was fifteen years ago, but you could check the bags under my eyes in any railroad station."

"Don't give that part a thought. It will take a while to put this package together and there's a surgeon out at The Clinic who's remodeled some of the most famous faces in show business. How about it?"

"Don't ask me to make a decision now, Aaron, but you're a sweet guy to think of it. I just came by to say hello and pick up my check."

"I made it out last night and was going to send it over to the hotel this morning." He handed her the check and, when she saw the amount, tears suddenly came into her eyes.

"It's too much, Aaron," she managed to say.

"The check? It's your regular salary."

"That—and everything." She blew her nose with her handkerchief and dabbed her eyes. "You don't owe me all this—the week wasn't half finished when I had to stop the other night."

"Call it an advance, then, until we can get started on this new project. Besides, you kept those Teamsters from wrecking this joint."

"It may be a long time—months even—before Guy's back in shape."

"You won't have to be at the hospital all that time, will you?"

"I wouldn't think so, why?"

"I'm going to need some expert help in putting this package together and nobody's more of an expert in this business than you are. You can help me find some of the old burlesque comics, the real greats, and a couple of young strippers with class that you can train as you go along. That'll be the toughest part of all, and where I'll need the most help from you."

"It sounds interesting. And I could certainly use the weekly pay check."

"Whatever happens to Guy, he'd want you to go on working, Georgia. You're one of the few aristocrats in this business—"

"A gone-to-seed aristocrat."

"Not on your life. You're still better than ninety-nine per cent of the others and with the right kind of show, you'll be back on top again in a few months. That would be the best present you could give Guy, wherever he'd be."

"Thanks, Aaron—for the check and the vote of confidence."

"Don't worry about anything except Guy. You're on the payroll right along, and, when he gets to where you aren't worried about him all the time, start remembering some of the old routines. You know: Cleopatra and the Asp, the new patient in the hospital —skits like that. You're still the best straight woman in the business."

When she left the club, Georgia went to the hotel nearby where she and Guy had been living. The clerk put down the copy of *Variety* he was reading and gave her a big smile.

"Good morning, Mrs. Merchant," he said. "How's your husband?"

"He's holding his own, Mike." Georgia handed him Aaron Schwartz's check and he counted out part of the money, shoving it beneath the grilled cashier's window.

"Take out the rest, Mike, we owe it to you," she said, but he shook his head.

"We'll put that on the cuff until Mr. Merchant is so you can work again," he said. "About the only class this joint has any more is from people like you two. Judging by the piece in *Variety*, though, you won't be staying here much longer."

"That picture was taken over ten years ago, Mike. Better take your money while I've got it."

"I'm betting on you, Mrs. Merchant; so's the boss. He told me to tell you not to worry about the rent. The fact is, we ought to pay you to stay in a dump like this."

21

"That son of a bitch!" Ed McDougal was pacing the living room of the suite where he'd spent the night, a half-filled glass of bourbon and water in his hand and his beefy face still suffused with anger. "He'll find out what it means to cross me."

"Greg did more than cross you, Ed," said a doctor from Boston who was pouring himself a drink before lunch from the array of bottles on a nearby table. "He spitted you right through the gizzard this morning—before everybody."

"He'll regret it before I get through with him," the Texan snapped. "Until then, I was willing to work out some sort of a compromise that would let Greg at least retreat with honor. Now it's dog eat dog."

"I told you that was the way it had to be in the beginning," said Henry Anders.

"Where the hell were you last night when I was lining up support, Henry?" The Texan finished the contents of his glass in a gulp. "Seducing somebody's wife who'd heard what a great lover you are?"

"Of course not." Henry Anders looked away quickly lest his guilty flush betray him.

"We've got to change strategy," Ed said suddenly.

"What do you mean?" squeaked Dr. Timothy Puckett, who had been talking to the Boston doctor in one corner of the room.

"All along we've figured that this transplant patient would die and we could nail Greg with a vote of censure in the board Friday afternoon on two counts: building the hyperbaric laboratory without approval and tarnishing the reputation of The Clinic by a bad choice of patients in operating on Merchant. But since it looks like the fellow's going to live for a while, those arguments may not hold water."

"When did you decide that?" Dr. Puckett's face was now creased with anxiety.

"Just now, when I realized that Greg wouldn't have torn into me like he did this morning at the convocation if he wasn't pretty sure he's in the driver's seat."

"That makes sense," said the Boston doctor. "So what do we do now?"

"For Christ's sake, do I have to spell out everything for you fellows?" Ed threw up his hands in disgust. "We let old Sam press his charge against Greg and maybe be voted down. Then we drop a bomb by demanding that Greg produce the secret plans we've been hearing about." He turned to Henry Anders. "Will Keith Jackson have them ready by then?"

"I imagine so. When he phoned me right after Greg first saw them, Jackson said Greg flipped over them and wanted him to get out as detailed a set as he could in a hurry."

"Any way you can check up?"

"Jackson and Greg are working pretty closely on this thing and everybody knows I'm against Greg," said Henry doubtfully. "It might tip them off if I asked about the plans now."

"Guess you're right," Ed McDougal agreed. "If we raise enough of a squawk at the special meeting, he'll have to produce something. And if this thing is as far out as you say it is, old Sam will hit the ceiling."

"The plan's far out, all right," said Henry. "It's not like anything you ever saw in the way of a hospital."

"Guess that's all we can do at the moment then," said the Texan.

"And no more of this retreat with honor business for Greg," Henry Anders insisted.

"He's your meat, Henry," said Ed. "I'll even help hold him while you carve him up."

ii

Georgia Merchant woke from a nightmare in which she'd watched Guy's slowly beating heart pressing down upon her until it had seemed that it would smother her. She remembered lying down in the room for a moment to rest after taking a shower, before going back to the hospital. Her watch told her now that it was after one o'clock, which meant she'd been asleep about two hours.

She knew the meaning of the dream: some rebellious part of her mind, which she had denied access to consciousness, had taken advantage of her sleep to remind her that Guy's living might well mean the failure of the plan Aaron Schwartz had outlined to her a few hours ago. And the vision of Guy's beating heart pressing down upon her and threatening to kill her had been a symbol from her unconscious mind of its rebellion against what his living could mean. Overcome with guilt that such a thought had somehow managed to reach consciousness, even through the back door, so to speak, of a dream, she reached for the telephone and dialed the hospital. When the operator answered, she gave her the extension number of the operating room suite.

"This is Mrs. Merchant," she told the nurse who answered. "Is my husband—"

"Dr. Alexander had him moved back to the ICU about two hours ago, Mrs. Merchant."

"Are you sure he was all right?"

"He's doing fine, Mrs. Merchant. I went with the stretcher up to intensive care. Dr. Alexander wanted him where they could watch him a little more closely with the monitors and where so many people wouldn't be going in and out as they do here."

Georgia dressed quickly and drove to the hospital. When she came to the small intensive care waiting room she saw Bob Johnson talking to the charge nurse. While she waited for him to finish, her eyes moved along the banks of cathode ray tubes above the desk of the nurses' station until they found the one upon which was flashed the closed-circuit TV picture of the room Guy was in.

She could see his chest rise and fall with the forced respiration, but the bandage about his neck, where the tracheostomy tube had been put in, made it impossible for her to see his face. And when her eyes dropped to the monitor tube just below the picture of the room, she saw that the flashing pattern of his heart was strong and regular, far different from the irregular pattern that had characterized it before he had been taken to the operating room yesterday afternoon.

"I hope you got some rest." Bob Johnson had finished writing an order and came over to where she was sitting. "We looked for you to tell you we were bringing him back here, but someone said you'd gone back to the hotel to change clothes."

"I took a shower and fell asleep."

"It was the best thing you could have done. You must be thoroughly bushed."

"Is Guy all right?"

"There are some signs that he may be developing a slight rejection reaction, but we're taking measures to combat it." They had warned Georgia about this most dangerous of complications, so she knew what he meant.

"Is there something I can do—give blood or anything?"

"We're taking care of that. Why don't you come down to the cafeteria and have something to eat with me? The nurse will call me on the beeper if there's any change."

"I think I will," said Georgia. "I can't even remember when I've had anything except coffee and danish pastry."

"Those mechanized waitresses off the main corridor don't have much imagination," he agreed. "Some real food will do you good for a change."

When they were eating in a corner of the big cafeteria, Georgia asked: "If my husband comes through, Doctor, what shape will his heart be in?"

"Excellent—from our experience."

"I seem to remember reading somewhere that cutting all the nerves makes a change."

"A lot of investigators worried about that in the beginning and so did Dr. Alexander," he said. "You see, the heart is normally controlled by two sets of nerves belonging to what is called the automatic, or autonomic, nervous system, enabling it to respond immediately to demands upon it from exercise, emotional tension and the like by speeding up the rate. Naturally, those nerves are cut during a transplant operation and, since they're very small, we make no attempt to bring them back together."

"Would they grow back if you did?"

"We think they do grow back to a certain extent, but we can't be sure, because the heart also responds to the amount of adrenaline and other hormones in the blood. In fact, we're putting a small amount of a drug resembling Adrenalin into your husband's bloodstream in order to step up the heart rate, since it tends to be a little slow immediately after these operations. In our dogs, we find that after a few weeks to a month—sometimes a little longer—this hormonal control is able to make a transplanted heart respond to change almost as quickly as the normal one would do."

"So he should be able to live a normal life?"

"Except for strenuous activity—though I wouldn't promise that he'll ever dance again."

"We may have a chance to form our own traveling troupe and Guy would be the stage manager."

"A heart as strong as Frank Lawson's should be able to stand that."

They ate in silence for a while. When he brought a second cup of coffee to the table for each of them, she asked: "Isn't there a famous plastic surgeon here at The Clinic?"

"Dr. Pinzon?"

"I don't know his name."

"Dr. Pinzon is probably the most famous cosmetic surgeon in the world."

"Face lifting and that sort of thing."

"Much more than simply that sort of thing," he assured her. "He's a real artist."

"When Guy is all right, do you think he would see me?"

"You have only to make an appointment, but I think you're worrying unduly."

"In show business a woman needs to look at least ten years younger than her age, Doctor."

"Dr. Pinzon can do better than that easily," he assured her. "Just speak to me when you're ready and I'll take care of the appointment for you."

"You're very kind."

"Nice people deserve nice treatment. Besides, when I tell my wife I had lunch with Georgia Merchant, she'll flip her lid."

iii

Jud Templeton timed his arrival at the Clinic Inn to coincide with the exodus of the Members of The Clinic from the afternoon session of the convocation. Most, he knew, headed straight for the bar, so he wangled a table for two near the door and sat sipping a gin and tonic while he watched the stream of prosperous looking men pouring into the bar and the adjoining lounge. He hadn't been waiting long when he saw what he was looking for—the plump form of Dr. Timothy Puckett. Fortunately for Jud's purposes, the chairman of the board was alone.

"How about my buying you a drink, Dr. Puckett?" he called. When the pediatrician came over and sat down, he signaled a waitress, who took his order.

"You've certainly been faithful at the convocation, Doctor," said Jud. "I saw you there this morning."

"I'm chairman of the Board of Trustees, so I feel that I ought to help out as much as I can." Puckett's eyes were searching the crowd.

"That's a pretty responsible position," said Jud. "Especially with the new hospital being built and everything."

"We haven't decided on a new hospital." Puckett spoke with some severity.

"I understand that it's not definitely settled. But there are rumors all over the place."

"Rumors?" Jud didn't miss the sudden flash of anxiety in the little man's eyes.

"Everybody seems to have his own ideas about what should be done. Some want to keep The Clinic here and just renovate the old buildings, but I understand that would cost as much as building a new one."

"It's a very expensive process."

"Another faction's behind Dr. Alexander and his plans for the highly automated hospital and clinic on the present site he spoke about at the opening session yesterday. You know—one of these places where they have computers doing everything except sticking you in the tail."

"You seem to be well informed on the subject, Mr. Templeton." Puckett's voice was a little frosty now.

"I make it a point to keep abreast of what's going on around town, Doctor. Confidentially, though, I hear the third faction has the upper hand right now."

"Third faction?"

"You know, the one that wants a brand-new hospital and clinic built out on the Beltway."

"There's something to be said for all the proposals," said Dr. Puckett cautiously.

"Naturally, as chairman you have to stay uncommitted," said Jud. "The most interesting thing I've come across yet involves what use will be made of the present property if The Clinic is moved to the new location."

"It goes to Dr. Henry Anders II under his father's will," said the pediatrician. "I thought everybody knew that."

"I mean afterwards," said Jud. "There's a rumor going around that a syndicate has already been formed to develop this section into a whole new city, with high-rise apartment houses, shopping centers—the whole works. If that goes through, the men in the syndicate will certainly make a killing."

"It's legal, isn't it?" The plump doctor was beginning to sweat a little.

"Oh, I guess it's legal. But from what I hear, a number of doctors are in that syndicate and, if it should come out that some of them are members of the board and voted to have the hospital moved, it would make one of the hottest scandals this town has ever seen."

"I'm sure there's no truth to that rumor, Mr. Templeton." Puckett was a little pale now.

"I'm thinking of doing a piece on it, just the same." Jud calmly removed from his pocket the list Jeanne Alexander had given him shortly before noon. Spreading the sheet out on the table as if he were going to use it for notepaper, he searched in his pocket for a pencil while, from the corner of his eye, he watched Dr. Puckett's eyes freeze upon the list, like a bird dog pointing a covey of quail.

"Wha—what's that?" he whispered.

"Just a list of names somebody gave me. Men who might be in the syndicate to develop The Clinic property."

"Who—who gave it to you?"

"A woman. I'm always getting suggestions from anonymous sources, but it sometimes turns out that they're quite valuable. I've only had a chance to glance at this one," he added, pretending to study the list. "Good Lord, Dr. Puckett! Your name's here, too."

The pediatrician started to push back his chair. His hands were shaking and, in his agitation, he knocked over his glass. But before he could rise, Jud Templeton's left hand closed about a flabby wrist, muscling him back into his chair.

"A lot of people are going to be pretty indignant if the trustees vote to move The Clinic and I decide to publish this little list, Doctor," he said.

"This is b—blackmail."

"Call it whatever you will. It's still not as bad as the deal you and your friends are planning to pull Saturday."

"But I—"

"Your Texas friend won't give a damn when the scandal breaks because he'll be safely away from the stink. But can *you* ignore what people will say to a headline like this?" With a pencil he printed in bold block letters across the top of the list:

LEADING DOCTORS IN ON CLINIC STEAL

"For God's sake, keep that covered," said Puckett.

"Even if you don't go to jail, you're a little old to start practicing again somewhere else after your license is taken away, Doctor." Jud released Puckett's wrist and the little man shot from his chair. As if propelled by a rocket he fairly raced for the elevator.

"What did you say to him?" Peter Carewe dropped into the empty chair across from Jud. "I never saw Rabbit move so fast before in all my life."

"Was that what you called him in medical school?"

"That—and worse. He went into pediatrics because grown people couldn't stand him."

"I'm looking forward to your speech tonight, Doctor," said the newspaperman. "The paper's even buying my dinner."

"I still want to know what you said to scare old Puck like that. Maybe I could use some of it on African witch doctors when they get into my hair."

Jud Templeton took his hand off the list he had covered when Peter Carewe sat down at the table. "Know any of these? Besides Dr. Puckett, I mean?"

The doctor from WHO studied the list for a moment, then shoved it back to Jud. "I know most of the doctors on there."

"Several of them are on the Board of Trustees. If things go to suit them Saturday morning, they'll vote to move The Clinic. Then, one fine day, when everybody's forgotten about that, plans will be announced for a big project here. And lo, the gentlemen on that list will profit much by being silent stockholders in said corporation."

"Verily a scheme worthy of Mephistopheles himself." Peter Carewe whistled softly. "Where do I enlist?"

"Here and now," said Jud Templeton. "Just make a point of seeing as many of those men as you can and casually mentioning a rumor you've heard that a newspaperman is busy running down a story about a group of doctors belonging to a syndicate. You won't have to include Dr. Puckett; I'm not sure his heart would stand a second scare."

Peter Carewe stood up and looked around the room. "I can see three of them here now," he said. "Good hunting."

Jud Templeton raised his glass. "Tally ho!"

iv

In Ed McDougal's suite, the Texan was trying to calm Tim Puckett down and not succeeding very well.

"I tell you, Ed, Jud Templeton knows everything," the little pediatrician babbled. "He's going to blow the whole story in the papers."

"What can he blow, when we haven't even incorporated yet? The guy's playing you for a sucker, Tim. Twice he's fished for a story and this time you may have given it to him."

"I didn't say a thing—not a thing."

"Go dry yourself, Puck. You're wetting your pants."

"We've got to call this thing off, Ed. Scandal won't bother you down in Texas, but I'm right here in the middle of it."

"Did this fellow remind you of that?"

"We—l, yes."

"Like I said, the guy's playing you for a sucker. And you fell for it all the way."

"You really think so?" Puckett quavered.

"I know so."

"But where did he get that list?"

"Somebody talked, probably when he was drunk—or with a woman. If I find out who it was, I'll break him with my own hands."

The door to the suite opened and Dr. Jake Geiger came in. Like Puckett, his practice was in Baltimore and he was sweating, though the room was cool.

"Ed," he said. "I've got to see you privately."

"Not now, Jake. Puck here is upset."

"I'm upset, too. Did you know that a newspaperman downstairs has got the syndicate list?"

"Who told you that?"

"Peter Carewe."

"You see," Timothy Puckett squalled. "They're spreading the word around already."

"Who told you?" Jake Geiger demanded.

"Templeton, the newspaperman."

Ed McDougal started for the door, with Timothy Puckett close behind him. "Where you going, Ed?" he demanded.

"To throw that son of a bitch out of the motel. I'll teach him to threaten honest people."

"That's what he wants," Puckett squeaked. "You say he's got no proof of what that list means, so he can't print anything about us. But if you go down there and beat him up, the publisher of those papers is going to want to know why. Then they can print anything they like."

"You may be right at that, Puck." Ed McDougal stopped with

his hand on the doorknob. "Down in Texas, we'd do it different, but up here I guess we have to play it close to our chests."

"What can we do?"

"One thing I can do is go see Greg Alexander. He let this man in on the operation yesterday, so he must be working hand and glove with Templeton."

"I don't see Greg doing a thing like that," Jake Geiger objected.

"By now Greg knows he's fighting for his professional life," said Ed. "When the chips are down, a man will use any weapon he can get."

"What are you going to do?" Timothy Puckett asked.

"Ask for an armistice, what else?" Ed said with a grin.

"Why an armistice?"

"Were you in Korea, Puck?"

"No."

"If you had been, you'd know that an armistice is a time when you persuade the enemy to lower his guard so you can stick a knife in his back."

v

Greg was in his office dictating answers to the morning mail into a Dictaphone when Ed McDougal came in. It was a few minutes after five o'clock, so his secretary had already left, but his days were so filled that he usually had to handle his correspondence at odd times.

He had hoped to take Jeanne to the banquet that night to hear Peter Carewe but was wondering now whether he shouldn't call and tell her to go on without him, for he was worried by a gradual change in Guy Merchant's condition during the day. When the door of his waiting room slammed shut and he saw Ed McDougal coming through the office suite, he put the Dictaphone back on its cradle.

"You look upset, Ed," he said.

"I am upset. This is a hell of a crummy trick you're playing, Greg."

"Like what?"

"Setting that bastard Templeton to blackmailing trustees."

"I don't know what you're talking about."

"Don't give me that!"

"This is my office, Ed." Greg's voice was cold. "Suppose you leave now before this goes any farther."

The Texan controlled himself with an effort. "All right," he said. "Let's talk it over."

"That's better. Now what is Jud Templeton doing?"

"He's helping you by spreading rumors."

"A lot of people happen to think what you and Henry are trying to pull is a lousy deal, but I don't know many who would go out on a limb for me. Whatever Templeton's doing, he's doing on his own."

"He's got a list and claims it's the names of members of a syndicate that will develop the property here after we move The Clinic."

"So you're the brains behind that scheme?" said Greg. "I couldn't see Henry thinking it up by himself. When did you work it out? Last year, when he went down to the Southern Medical in Dallas?"

"Of course not," Ed McDougal blustered, but the sudden flash of guilt in his eyes betrayed him.

"I'm disappointed in you Ed." Greg made no attempt to hide the contempt he felt for the other man. "All the time, I thought it was Sam Hunter's money you were after, so you could build a new medical school in your hometown and be the big shot professor of surgery. But you were just looking to make a killing for yourself by gypping poor Henry out of his inheritance, weren't you? I'm ashamed of you Ed, really ashamed."

"I don't need your shame!" Stung by Greg's tone, the Texan came out of his chair. "I'm telling you now. Call off your dog before he gets hurt."

"I haven't any dog. I told you that."

"Then telephone this fellow Templeton and tell him to stop meddling in things that are none of his business."

"Is Templeton at the Inn?"

"He was a few minutes ago."

Greg dialed nine for outside and then the number of the Clinic Inn. "Please call Mr. Jud Templeton to the phone," he asked the operator. "You'll probably find him in the bar. It's urgent."

"This is Dr. Alexander," he said when Jud answered. "I'm told that you've been threatening people over there in the mistaken belief that you were helping me."

"So that's where the big bull went." Templeton said. "I saw him go out of the door here just now like a Sherman tank."

"Have I your promise not to continue what you're doing?"

"You've got it, Doctor. If the leader's that scared, I've already done all I can do."

"Thank you, Mr. Templeton." Greg hung up and turned to Ed McDougal. "He won't bother you any more, Ed."

"Why don't we call an armistice, Greg?" Ed's tone was ingratiating now. "After all, we both want what's best for The Clinic."

"How can I call an armistice when I'm not fighting? The board asked me to prepare a plan for a new clinic and hospital and that's what I'm going to do."

"All right—if you don't want to meet us halfway."

"I've slept about four hours in the past thirty-six and I've got a patient who needs help, Ed. My only concern right now is to find out how I can help him."

"I gave you the choice," said the Texan. "Don't say I didn't."

"What happened to you, Ed?" Greg's voice halted him at the door, not so much by what he was saying but by the note of genuine concern in it.

"What do you mean?"

"You were a better than average surgeon when you were here at The Clinic. I know you have a big practice at home and you probably give your patients their money's worth. That should be enough for any doctor, but you had to sell your soul for money. Tell me why, Ed."

"Because money's important. Why else? Maybe I am just another surgeon in a middle-sized Texas town like you say, but my wife wears an ermine coat. What does Jeanne wear?"

"A rather old mink stole, I believe."

"How much have you got stashed away? A hundred thousand?"

"Rather less than that the last time I looked."

"I've got my first million behind me and enough oil leases to bring in a couple more."

"And yet you have to plan crooked schemes with people like

287

Henry Anders to make more." Greg shook his head. "I really feel sorry for you, Ed."

"*You* feel sorry for me!" For a moment the balloon was pricked and Greg looked away so as not to see its collapse. But it lasted only for an instant and Ed was his old blustering self again when he swaggered out of the office.

For a long moment, Greg sat immobile. In the moment of the big man's deflation, he'd had a glimpse of the small shriveled soul inside him. And no matter what Ed McDougal had said about him, done to him, or might yet do, he could find no pleasure in it.

Finally, he picked up the telephone and, when he was connected with Dave Connor, said: "Could you join me on the ICU, Dave? I don't like the way things are going with Merchant and I think we might profit from another council of war."

The examination didn't take long. The portable film of Guy Merchant's chest, taken late in the afternoon, plus the carefully kept hospital records and laboratory reports, told them everything they needed to know that was not revealed by Dave Connor's careful stethoscopic examination of the air being forced in and out of the sick man's lungs.

"It's the rising fever you're worried about most, isn't it?" the cardiologist asked while they were studying the hospital record at the nursing station.

Greg nodded. "Lawson's lungs were damaged from the accident when his chest was crushed; I didn't realize how much until I removed them. They're the weakest part of the whole picture here, but I had to use them or Merchant would have died of emphysema before long—even with a new heart."

"Nothing here definitely indicates pneumonia—yet," said the heart specialist. "The X-ray film does show some deeper shadows at the bases of the lungs than it did this morning, which could mean a spreading infectious process—or congestion."

"Any idea which?"

"I doubt if it's congestion; the heart is functioning well, the output is excellent and the T-wave complex in the ECG doesn't suggest any major rejection symptoms as yet."

"So it all boils down to keeping infection from developing in the lungs—or controlling it if it has already developed," said Greg.

"As I see it, we've got to cut down on the anti-rejection treatment and hope his normal immune response plus the antibiotic he's getting will keep down whatever infection is already there."

"The two-pronged attack is probably best," Dave Connor agreed. "I wish I could help more, Greg."

"You confirmed my own thinking, Dave. Thanks for your trouble."

"You and Jeanne going to the banquet tonight?"

"I promised her I would. You get around; how's the sentiment on the new hospital running among the Members?"

"I haven't exactly taken a poll but I'd say it's pretty close to fifty-fifty. There's a lot of interest in this bold new plan of yours, whatever it is. I think you've got the opposition worried."

"That's what I want them to be."

"Still going to keep it under wraps until Saturday?"

"My guess is that somebody's going to demand to see the plans at the special meeting Friday afternoon. I hope to have at least the sketches ready by then."

"Don't underestimate Ed McDougal and his crowd, Greg. That could be disastrous." Dave Connor looked across the narrow corridor to the glass-fronted room where Guy Merchant lay. "And losing him just when the board is about to meet could be an even worse catastrophe."

"Whether or not I lose a patient shouldn't affect the future of The Clinic."

"Nevertheless, it will. If Merchant dies, they'll use his death as proof that you jumped the gun and operated, hoping to impress the board. That's bound to go against you, even if it isn't true."

"I'm not trying to impress anybody," Greg said wearily. "Five minutes before I called you, I finished telling Ed McDougal that."

"He came to see you?"

"Yes—and mad as a hornet. Somebody's threatening to expose that little scheme he and Henry have cooked up so Henry will get the property here and they can develop it. He wanted me to call off my dogs."

"Were they your dogs?"

"I haven't had time for that sort of thing, even if I would have tried it."

"Which you wouldn't have," the cardiologist said with a sign. "Did it ever occur to you that you're your own worst enemy, Greg?"

"Not until lately. Jeanne's been telling me."

"You'd better listen to her."

"I'm too old for conniving, Dave. Being the best surgeon I'm able to be is about all the job I can handle effectively."

When the other man had gone, Greg wrote new orders on the chart, cutting in half the dosage of the immuno-suppressive drugs being given to lessen the likelihood of rejection of the organ transplant and doubling the dose of the broad-spectrum antibiotic they were giving Guy Merchant to keep down infection. He was taking a calculated risk, but this sort of decision making had become so much a part of his everyday life that it didn't occur to him to doubt his own judgment.

Transferring the hospital beeper to the breast pocket of the sport jacket he hadn't had on for, it seemed, eons, he took the elevator to the street floor and The Clinic lobby. Bob Johnson was on duty and he trusted the younger surgeon's judgment implicitly, so he might as well take Jeanne to the banquet. Besides, if there were an emergency, the beeper in his pocket could reach him across the street in the banquet room as easily as it could in the hospital.

22

Sam Hunter was standing in the lobby of the motel when Helen Foucald came downstairs from the crossover to the apartment building a few minutes after six. She wore a fur coat and cap to match over her dark auburn hair.

"Glad you're dressed warmly," he told her. "The TV predicts a heavy snow tomorrow but we should be all right tonight."

"Sorry I'm late," she said. "I had to run some last-minute blood chemistry studies in the laboratory."

"On Dr. Alexander's patient?"

"Yes."

"How's he doing?"

"His blood chemistry is definitely improved over what it was before the operation, so the heart seems to be functioning well. Greg's worried now about possible lung complications."

Sam Hunter took her arm and guided her through the door to the marquee-covered driveway outside, where a Continental limousine stood with the engine running to keep the interior warm. The uniformed chauffeur opened the door for them and, when they were inside, guided the car out onto The Parkway.

"The chauffeur tells me there's an excellent restaurant about ten miles out of town," said Sam Hunter. "I usually hire limousines when I'm away from home and the drivers always know the best places to eat.

"Want to take off your coat?" he asked as she settled back in the luxurious car. "When you're as old as I am, cold sort of gets to your bones. The car may be too warm for you."

"The laboratory radiators are pretty old, so it's usually on the cold side there in weather like this," she said. "I'm happy just to relax and be warm."

"That wouldn't be a bit of propaganda for a new hospital, would it?"

Helen smiled. "We have to get in our licks whenever we can. Greg has promised that in the new one I'm to have probably the most advanced laboratory in the country, if not in the world. Naturally, I'm doing everything I can."

"Thank you for passing up the banquet," he said. "I know what a sacrifice it was."

"On the contrary, Mr. Hunter, I think it's time I got away—for a little perspective."

"Not letting yourself be rushed off your feet, eh?"

"At thirty-five, a woman has to be sure. At twenty it's different; there's a long time and a lot of opportunities ahead."

"You've never been married?"

"No. I only came close once—in France."

"That why you ran away?"

"What gave you that idea?"

"You don't employ as many people as I do without getting to be a pretty good judge of character. You're a very intelligent and strong-minded woman who might take a man as a lover that wasn't your equal—except as a lover. But you could only marry a man you respected."

"You're very perceptive—and frank."

"It's as much a tribute to a woman to praise her mind as it is her figure—and you have both."

"I consider that a real compliment."

"You don't have to answer, if you'd rather not," he said. "Is it true that you're having an affair with Henry Anders?"

"It's true. You wouldn't have to ask many people to find that out."

"But neither you nor Claire could possibly respect Henry's intelligence. The man's a pompous fool."

Helen's eyes twinkled. "Henry has, shall we say, other attributes, which Claire and I both appreciate."

"What about Carewe? Or am I asking too much?"

"No. I'm glad of the chance to talk to somebody about the whole thing. Until yesterday morning, my world was pretty orderly. I had my work, which I love—"

"And which you're very good at."

"Have you been checking up on me?"

"I check up on everybody who interests me—both friends and enemies."

"Whatever happens about the hospital, I don't want to be your enemy," she told him. "I was impertinent yesterday in my office and I apologize."

"You were merely looking after your own interests and what you think is right," he corrected her. "I would have less respect for you if you'd done anything else."

"Actually, I wasn't quite myself," she explained. "I had just come from meeting Peter Carewe at the airport, the first time I had ever seen him."

"And he bowled you over?"

"Frankly, yes."

"Did you ever stop to think that he's probably bowled over a lot of other women in the same way?"

"I'm sure he has and at first I told myself it's nothing but the sort of physical attraction a strong man has for a woman like me."

"What about Henry?"

"He has no more right to expect faithfulness in me than I do in him. Claire and I understand that perfectly." She smiled wryly. "As you said, Henry isn't the most intelligent person in the world, but I'm a woman of strong needs."

"And you doubt that one man could satisfy both your mind and your body?"

"No one has—yet. But Peter is hard to resist."

"Then why resist?"

She took a deep breath. "I guess because I realize how tragic it would be for both of us if either failed the other."

"You could always exercise a woman's prerogative and leave the whole question undecided, you know." Again she was surprised by his perceptiveness.

"Why do you say that?"

"Even if you thought your world was safe before Carewe came along, it really wasn't. Claire isn't going to give Henry up and you've admitted that you don't want him as a husband, so all you've done is make a temporary arrangement like the one you'd probably made before you left Paris. That can't possibly be the final answer for you, so what most people would call your promiscuity is merely an attempt to rationalize the adjustment you've tried to make, even though you know it can't last."

"You should be a psychoanalyst," she said, a little shakily.

"It's nothing but logic. Is Peter Carewe the first man you ever met that you're willing to admit may be your equal in every respect?"

"Yes."

"Then there's only one answer."

She nodded slowly. "I guess I've been avoiding it because I'm afraid I might discover he has a weakness. But that's the chance I have to take, isn't it?"

"I would call it a calculated risk."

"Peter wants me to go away with him for the weekend. I wasn't sure before, but I am now." She put out her hand and squeezed the wrinkled but still strong one lying on his knee. "Thanks for setting me straight."

"All I can do any more is advise," Sam Hunter said with a sigh. "But I don't mind telling you I'd give half of what I possess to be that young doctor for the next few days."

"You're a dear." Helen leaned over and kissed him on the cheek. "How did you ever get the reputation of being such an ogre?"

"Oh, I can be tough, all right," he said. "And don't think that just because you're buttering me up I'm going to be any softer on your friend Dr. Alexander."

"I'm sure even Greg doesn't want you to do anything except what you decide is best for The Clinic," she said. "After all, you were a close friend of the elder Dr. Anders and Greg was like an adopted son to him, so your feelings about him must be the same."

"That's what troubles me most," Sam Hunter admitted. "I keep asking myself what Henry Anders would want and I can't be sure. The way I see it, the present Clinic is a monument to him. He largely designed it himself and practically built it with his own hands. Whatever else is built here could never really be the same, so I can't help feeling that changing the old building may be almost the same as pushing over Henry Anders' gravestone."

ii

Jeanne opened the apartment door before Greg could turn the lock with his key. She was wearing a silk dressing gown he'd given her for Christmas so long ago that he couldn't remember when it was and the sight of her slender loveliness made some of his weariness evaporate. She came into his arms and clung to him for a long sweet moment, but when he would have guided her toward the bedroom, she laughed and pushed him away.

"Be good now, darling," she said. "We're supposed to be at the head table and the serving starts promptly at eight."

"I'd much rather stay here."

"You can't have people saying you know you're already licked and are afraid to show your face," she said firmly. "Now, go get your shower while I lay out your dinner jacket."

"A boiled shirt after all I've been through?"

"I bought you a new one; it isn't starched and has ruffles all down the front and at the cuffs." She was guiding him toward the shower. "I'll fix some drinks while you're getting your bath."

The shower was scalding hot and he let it soak away some of the tiredness from his body before turning it to cold for a stinging moment of change, then stepped out and began to dry himself with a big nubby towel.

"Ed McDougal jumped me this afternoon," he called to Jeanne through the partly opened door. "He claims somebody put Jud Templeton up to blackmailing him and his gang."

"I know." Jeanne came over as he came out of the bathroom for him to zip her short evening dress up the back. "I did it."

"You?" he asked, startled. "How did you manage that?"

"Hannah let something drop at breakfast yesterday morning that made me suspicious, so I checked with Claire. She found a list of those in Henry's syndicate in his desk and gave it to me. I was the one who turned it over to Jud Templeton." She turned to face him. "Are you angry?"

295

"No—but I wish you hadn't."

"Why?"

"I guess I'm male enough to want to fight my own battles."

"And I'm female enough not to want to see my male clobbered by a bunch of skunks that aren't fit to touch the ground he walks on." She returned to her dressing table. "That's your one big fault, darling—probably your only one. You're too easygoing and trusting, so people are always taking advantage of you."

"As long as it doesn't hurt anybody but me, I can stand it," he said.

"But I can't, Greg. I've loved you so long I can't remember when I didn't. And when I see you letting other people run over you just to get their own way, it makes my blood boil—at them and sometimes at you."

"There's always more than one way of accomplishing the same purpose." He came over for her to adjust his tie and she stood on tiptoes to kiss him when she finished.

"That's what I decided this morning," she said. "So I'm taking a hand in your affairs, even if you won't do it."

"What changed you?"

"I think it was Hannah McDougal's ermine coat—and her unhappiness. She rooked Ed in, when we were all here together years ago, by deliberately getting herself pregnant so he'd have to marry her. Everybody in the hospital knew it."

"Except me."

"You were busy being a boy scout even then. I can remember crying myself to sleep a lot of times, so lonely I could hardly stand it, while you were over there working on dog operations and not even remembering you had a wife at home. I guess Hannah did the same—for a while."

"What do you mean—for a while?"

"Every doctor's wife has to learn pretty soon to occupy herself—else she turns into a self-pitying whiner or ends up on the short end of a divorce."

"Surely it isn't as bad as that."

"Even the most undramatic woman likes to think of the man she marries as a Galahad or a Lochinvar. But unless her husband is a Quasimodo, a doctor's wife soon learns that a lot of his women patients are in love with him and a few quite willing to do something about it. If he's out in private practice and has any ability at all, his income begins to zoom about that time, too, and he joins a posh country club, where an even larger percentage of the women are on the make."

"I'm beginning to be sorry for what I've missed," said Greg.

"I'm serious," she insisted. "Lots of times doctors marry secretaries or nurses—like me. They hardly ever have the background most of the women their successful husbands meet have, and pretty soon the wife feels herself suffering in comparison."

"When did you start studying your fellow doctors' wives so closely?" he asked.

"Only recently. If I'd started sooner, I might have been able to diagnose my own symptoms before they almost went beyond the point of no return. A book I'm reading says a woman's personality from day to day is as much a part of her hormone pattern as it is of her early upbringing. I don't have to tell you that there are times each month when I'm morose, easily hurt and quick to resent snubs that aren't really snubs at all."

"Like my working late."

"That—and other things that seem important at the time. When she's feeling sorry for herself, it's pretty easy for a wife to decide she's deserted and from there to go on imagining things her husband may be doing—particularly with other women. A lot of times, she's got good reason to imagine them, too."

"You're not painting a very good picture of my brother physicians."

"They're no worse than any other professional group that goes up rapidly—and neither are the wives. If they can learn to stay with their husbands in maturity and find outlets for their energies after the children start leaving the household, they can make a fine adjustment and get along well. For a lot of them, though, it's easier to start feeling sorry for themselves and nagging when there's no real reason. Then one day the husband starts pursuing a younger woman with the inevitable result in so many cases—a divorce."

"You said just now that Hannah had solved her problem—but she's still with Ed."

"Maybe I should have said she's found a placebo that lulls her into not worrying about it. Ed has affairs with other women, so she has affairs with other men. She's still pretty decorative and Ed likes to boast of his success by hanging jewels and ermine coats and that sort of thing on her, all of which bolsters up her feeling of self-esteem."

"That's twice you spoke about the ermine coat," he reminded her.

"When she came into the restaurant with it yesterday morning, I expected any moment to see her start dragging it across the floor like an old-time Hollywood actress. I'll admit that I felt a little sorry for myself at first, but when I saw what's really happened to Hannah, I got a little scared. Nothing's more pitiful than a woman whose husband has deserted her for a younger one, leaving her nothing except to stare into the mirror every morning and face the fact that she's a day older—and looks it."

"At least you know there's never been another woman as far as I'm concerned."

"Maybe not one you would take to bed with you—but she's there just the same."

"Who?"

"Why do you think health is always depicted as a female goddess called Hygeia? She's always there in the form of a doctor's dedication to his profession, competing with his wife for his affections."

"Where is that drink you promised me?" he asked. "You'll have me crying into it any minute."

She went to the small bar just off the living room and brought back two glasses of bourbon and ginger ale, which she knew was all he ever drank.

"You can't escape the facts of life, darling." She sipped her drink while he finished dressing. "After I saw Hannah, I decided that I'm not going to be a victim of the Doctor's Wife Disease. That's why I got the list from Claire and gave it to Jud Templeton."

"What I don't understand is why Claire would give it to you."

"She wants things as they are—like any other wife who's satisfied with the status quo."

"The status quo in that household wouldn't seem to be very satisfactory from what I hear."

"On the contrary, Claire is perfectly happy with it as it is. Henry's no Lochinvar and never will be, but Claire can easily find a substitute every now and then. Meanwhile, her own ego is amply fed by the knowledge that she's a lot smarter than Henry can ever hope to be."

"After what I've been hearing for the last ten minutes," Greg conceded as he put on his dinner jacket and straightened the cummerbund, "you'll never have any reason to lack for self-esteem. I guess the happiest marriages are where the wife is a lot smarter than the husband and right now I'll admit to being even more of a clod than Henry."

"In some ways—yes." Her eyes were dancing now. "But you're a loveable clod, even if something of a clod as a lover."

"Have you been taking hormones?"

"Hannah advised it this morning, but I'm not quite ready for the pasture yet. Come on or we'll be late for the banquet."

"After that last crack of yours, I'd be willing to be late. One superiority of the male at least is at stake here."

"Maybe you'll feel more superior after the banquet."

"Why?"

"I prepared the menu. You're starting off with bluepoints on the half shell as an appetizer."

iii

The auditorium where the Tarentino Circus was performing in a benefit for the local P.T.A. was, appropriately enough, the high-school gymnasium. Chairs had been arranged along either side to serve as box seats, but, to Helen's surprise, Sam Hunter purchased seats in the bleachers, scaffold-like rows of planking that rose in a staircase pattern.

"We can see better up here," he explained as they made their way to seats not far from the top row in the center, the only part of the bleachers that was in any way crowded. Actually, hardly half the seats were filled, a mute commentary on the financial status of the struggling circus. It was obviously a small outfit, too, for Helen had seen only a few trucks parked outside the building, one of them a large red van that, judging from its

299

curtained windows, also served as living quarters for some of the performers.

"I'd think you were pinching pennies if I hadn't just finished one of the best dinners I ever ate," she said. "I like small circuses. We had a lot of them in Europe when I was a little girl."

"I doubt if this one will come up to the standard of those you saw there," said Sam Hunter.

Looking at the shabby equipment, the frayed costumes of the two clowns who were warming up the audience before the show began, Helen could believe he spoke the truth. All of which made her wonder once again why he had gone to the trouble of bringing her here, but she made no attemppt to draw him out, sensing that something intensely personal was involved.

The performance began with a parade around the single ring by the clowns, a small herd of elephants, a few performers and the calliope. As the wheezing strains of the old music machine shook the rafters of the high-school gymnasium, Helen relaxed in her seat and let memory carry her back to the days of her childhood in France and the small circus that had played once a year in the village where she had grown up before going to school in Paris. Lost in memory, she hardly noticed the opening acts of the performance, until the calliope burst into a rock-and-roll tune and the pudgy little ringmaster in the high silk hat announced:

"Introducing the Flying Tarentinos!"

The spotlight silhouetted a lovely small girl in white tights at the ringside. Then a lithe six-footer with dark hair appeared beside the girl and they started across to where the ropes for ascent to the trapeze, anchored high up among the trusses supporting the roof of the gymnasium, were being held by a roustabout.

Sam Hunter's sudden intake of breath beside her made Helen glance at him. Startled by what she saw, she looked again at the male member of the acrobatic pair and realized suddenly that she might have been seeing a younger version of Sam Hunter himself. Understanding now why they were there and why the old man had avoided calling attention to himself, she gave all her attention to the two young performers.

The music took up its blaring beat again as the two moved to the center of the ring. The girl was hoisted up to the trapeze with the spotlight following her. But when the young man started to climb up hand over hand, Helen thought she detected a slight hesitancy every time his right hand closed upon the rope, very much like a pulse skipping a beat. It was barely noticeable, however, and as the two young acrobats went into their routine, she saw that they were very good.

Once, as they neared the climax of their act high in the air, the boy's right hand appeared to slip, and, for an instant, the lovely figure of the girl hung by one arm. It could have been deliberate, but, noticing how the ringmaster and the roustabout handling the rope suddenly tensed themselves, Helen wasn't sure and felt a vague sense of apprehension—and puzzlement.

At the climax of the act, when the girl went flying out like a lovely white bird, Helen found herself gasping like the rest of the crowd, until the nylon rope checked her fall and she swung like a pendulum spinning at its end, before seizing the climb rope and sliding to the floor of the ring.

The boy came down much more slowly than the girl had, and, as he stood beside her with the spotlight upon them, taking their bows, Helen thought once that he seemed to stagger. But the girl put her arm protectively through his and they walked from the ring while the spotlight swung to the next performer.

"Do you mind if we don't see any more?" Sam Hunter asked.

"Of course not."

At the foot of the row of seats before they were leaving the auditorium, she put her hand upon his arm and asked: "Don't you want to speak to him?"

"Who?"

"Your son. They're really very good and both of them are beautiful." For a moment, she thought he would deny the relationship and added quickly, "They're married, aren't they?"

He nodded but still did not speak.

"Without your permission?"

"I'd rather not talk about it." His voice was harsh for the first time that evening. "If you don't mind."

"I didn't mean to pry. But he's such a fine-looking young man that I'm sure you must be very proud of him—and of such a lovely daughter-in-law."

Sam Hunter didn't speak until they were in the car again and headed back toward Baltimore. When he did, it was not about the circus or his son.

iv

"That hand's bothering you again." Vivian's face was concerned as she and Ted slipped their feet into the clogs they'd left at the edge of the ring and started toward the large red van where they had their quarters. "I saw you hesitate as you went up the rope. And when you almost dropped me, I knew it was hurting more than you've been admitting."

"I couldn't let the audience think I'm a weakling." Ted managed to smile although the pain that had been throbbing in his hand for the past twenty-four hours had now begun to extend up the arm. "Don't you know the women come to admire your handsome husband as much as the men come to see you in tights?"

"Be serious, darling. It's really more painful, isn't it?"

"A little. Maybe I used it too much getting the equipment into the auditorium."

"We're going to see a doctor about it tonight," she said firmly.

"It can wait until tomorrow when we get to Frederick."

"You've been putting off doing anything too long already." Vivian closed the door of their mobile apartment behind them and, stripping off her tights, pulled on slacks and a jersey. "I noticed a public phone in the hall across from the principal's office. Get dressed while I see if I can locate a doctor."

"You'd never find one at this time of night."

"All towns have hospitals these days. Somebody has to be on emergency duty."

"My husband has an infected hand," she told the woman who answered the telephone call to the hospital. "Do you have a doctor on duty who can see him tonight?"

"The resident physician is here. When can you come over?"

"Right away. Ask him to wait for Mr. and Mrs. Hunter."

"Drive out Main Street until you see the neon sign," the woman directed her. "You can't miss it."

"I've located a doctor," Vivian said when she returned to the truck. "We'll take the jeep."

They found the hospital without trouble and followed a neon-lit arrow to the emergency entrance. Inside, a small dark-skinned man in a white uniform was bandaging the head of a child.

"Dr. Fernandez will be with you in a minute," a nurse told them. "Just have a seat."

"A Filipino?" Vivian said doubtfully under her breath.

"They have them in a lot of hospitals now," Ted told her. "Most American interns are used up by teaching hospitals or by Army service, so Filipinos have been coming over in large numbers to serve as resident physicians."

Dr. Fernandez was pleasant and spoke fairly good English. "You have a beginning infection here," he said when he finished examining the swollen hand. "Is this a wound perhaps?" He pointed to the red spot where the splinter had entered.

"A splinter several days ago," Ted explained. "But I pulled it out."

Ted couldn't help flinching from pain as the dark-skinned doctor squeezed the loose tissue between his thumb and forefinger, tense now from the swelling. "There seems to be some accumulation of pus here," he said. "We must open it wider and afterward I shall give you an injection of penicillin."

"Do you think some of the splinter might still be in there?" Vivian asked.

"It is possible; we will see when we open it." Dr. Fernandez turned to the nurse. "I shall need a tray with a hemostat, a sharp-pointed scalpel and some ethyl chloride, please."

It took a few minutes to prepare the tray. The ethyl chloride was in a container with a spray nozzle somewhat like the tubes containing dessert topping, but with a much finer and quickly evaporating spray. When the doctor directed a stream of it upon the skin of Ted's hand between the thumb and forefinger, frost formed upon the skin almost immediately as the tissues beneath it were frozen in an area perhaps as large as a quarter.

"This will prevent most of the pain when I open the wound," he explained and Ted felt very little discomfort even when he used the sharp-pointed scalpel to widen the tiny wound where the splinter had gone in. But when he thrust the forceps deep into the tissues and spread its jaws apart, Ted almost came off the stool where he was sitting. Dr. Fernandez probed the wound briefly for a depth of perhaps half an inch but found no sign of a splinter, and only a small amount of thin red purulent fluid escaped.

"I shall put in a drain to keep the wound open," he said, and pushed a small bit of gauze into the wound, again causing Ted considerable pain. It lasted only a moment, however, and afterward the doctor covered the area with several squares of gauze and bandaged it into place. Only a few minutes longer were required to inject the penicillin and give him a dozen brownish tablets for pain.

"I feel a lot better," said Vivian as they returned to the jeep after paying the bill. "How about you?"

"My tail hurts where he shot that penicillin," said Ted. "What's worrying me now is that I won't be able to go on tomorrow night."

"I can do the solo bit I did at F.S.U. before I fell in love with you," said Vivian. "Of course, the women in the audience won't get to admire your manly beauty, but we'll make out somehow."

"The doctor seemed to think this would take care of everything, so I shouldn't be out but a few nights."

"If that hand needs any more treatment," said Vivian, "I'm going to take you to Baltimore to The Clinic."

"I can have it dressed day after tomorrow in Cumberland," said Ted. "Do you think Papa Gus will be able to get us any farther than that? We had a mighty thin audience tonight and with snow expected in Frederick tomorrow, it could be even worse."

But Vivian couldn't answer that question any more than he could.

v

Peter Carewe was sitting at a table in the Falstaff Tavern having a drink with several Members when Helen came to the door after saying good night to Sam Hunter at the front of the elevators. Peter came to her at once and she felt a warm tide of happiness flood through her at this proof that he had been watching for her.

"Back so soon?" he asked, taking her arm and guiding her to a secluded table in the corner.

"We left before the circus performance was over. He went there to see his son."

"Sam Hunter's son in a circus?"

"He's an acrobat or an aerialist—and married to a lovely young girl. They have a very good act."

"Imagine turning down all that money to become the daring young man on the flying trapeze. No wonder the old man was burned up."

"He was very sad tonight. I'd heard something about his disinheriting one of his sons; but I think he realized for the first time tonight that the boy and the girl he married are very, very good, even if the circus is almost on its last leg."

"The kid probably inherited enough of the old man's tenacity to succeed."

"Probably. But I've got the strangest feeling that something is wrong with him."

"What?"

"I can't put my finger on it, maybe because I don't practice clinical medicine. But I'm sure it's something physical."

"Did old Sam say anything about it?"

"No. I didn't mention it to him, either."

"What's the kid like?"

"Sam insisted on leaving as soon as the act was finished. I wish I could have persuaded him to talk to them but he wouldn't hear of it."

"How was your dinner?"

"Wonderful."

"You'll fare even better at the Chalet Julienne. The weather report on the six o'clock news forecasted a heavy snow tomorrow afternoon. We might just be snowed in up there for a week or two with no way to reach the world outside."

"What if I say no?"

"I'd only find a reason to come back to Baltimore and ask you again, after I finish tracking down that vaccine contaminant in California."

"Would you give up going to California if I promised the week-end as a reward?"

"You'd be driving a hard bargain."

"But would you?"

"I'm afraid not. If a few more batches of that virus go bad, half the oral polio vaccine scheduled for next year's immunization programs will be no good. That means maybe a thousand kids will have polio who wouldn't otherwise have it, and some of them will walk with braces the rest of their lives, if they manage to walk at all."

"But why is it so important that *you* work on that particular project?"

"I've had more experience with this sort of detective work than any other doctor in the world," he explained. "It's my job."

"Then you'd turn me down if I attached that condition?"

He nodded. "What was it some poet said about that? '*I could not love thee dear so much,/loved I not honor more?*' By now you know I'm not really the hard-hearted sophisticate I pretend to be. Beneath this hairy chest beats a heart of purest gold."

"Don't start waving the flag." Helen reached out to take his hands. "I intended to go with you all the time; Sam Hunter convinced me."

"And you deliberately put me on the griddle? I ought to withdraw my invitation just to punish you."

"You still can."

"And lose what I've been looking for all my life—a woman with a brain *and* beauty. The airport at noon?"

"All right."

"Better bring along a few extra things. I just might get so attached to you that I'll drag you off to California with me on Monday—like young Lochinvar."

23

Greg awoke sometime after midnight, troubled by a vague uneasiness he had experienced more than once when he had a seriously ill patient in the hospital. It would have been logical to attribute the feeling to extrasensory perception, but on at least half the occasions when he'd felt it before, there had been nothing to worry about, so he'd put it down as a by-product of the concern that was always uppermost in his mind whenever a life hung in the balance.

Jeanne was asleep beside him, the first night she'd been there in many weeks. It had been a long time since they'd known the rapture they'd experienced after their return to the apartment, following an excellent dinner and Peter Carewe's humorous account of his adventures and misadventures as a roving knight fighting against disease.

Greg sat up, being careful not to disturb Jeanne, and swung his feet to the floor. Although there was a telephone extension beside the bed, he moved quietly to the den so as not to awaken her. Dialing the hospital, he asked for the ICU extension. To his surprise, Bob Johnson answered.

"Oh, it's you, sir." The younger surgeon's relief was apparent in his voice. "I've been debating calling you for the past hour."

"What's happening?"

"I think the lung involvement is spreading, sir. Merchant's temperature has been rising steadily since around midnight."

"I'll be there in ten minutes."

Pulling a sheet of paper from the desk, Greg scribbled:

> "Gone to the hospital. Merchant worse.
>   All my love."

Then, putting the note on the bedside table, where Jeanne would see it immediately when she awoke in the morning, he dressed quickly and took the elevator down to the ground level.

It was cold outside with gray clouds hiding the sky and the wind whipping up from the harbor sent a chill into his bones even through a heavy coat. The weather report, he remembered now from the bedside radio on the eleven o'clock news, had predicted snow for the entire area beginning sometime that day. Looking at the sky now, he could well believe the forecast would be correct and the snowfall early.

The hospital lobby was deserted except for the night operator and the cleaning women who were mopping the tiled floor around the foot of the great statue. The corridors, too, were empty as he made his way to the intensive care unit on the third floor of the surgical building next-door to the experimental surgery laboratory.

In a few more hours, the place would teem with life when the shifts changed at seven, and even before that the wards would be busy with morning care. At this hour, though, a stillness gripped the great hospital, a healing stillness of pain- and disease-racked bodies at rest.

Georgia Merchant was asleep, curled up on the single couch in the waiting room of the intensive care unit. He didn't disturb her but went directly to Guy Merchant's room, where he could see Bob Johnson standing beside the bed, adjusting the rubber tube connecting the respirator to the tracheostomy.

Greg listened briefly to the back of the sick man's chest, since the adhesive strappings holding the dressings on the incision where his sternum had been split made it impossible to listen from the front. Afterward, the two doctors went to the nurses' station, where the banked monitor tubes continued to register their graphic patterns of life.

"We taped an ECG reading from the monitor right after I talked to you just now, sir." Bob handed him the strip of paper with the record. "The pulse volume remains constant and so does the blood pressure. There's no appreciable change in the T-wave segment either, but his temperature has been rising steadily."

"That means he's absorbing toxic products from an inflammation in the lungs," said Greg.

"Do you think it's spreading?"

Greg nodded. "Maybe half of each lower lobe is involved now on both sides."

"The antibiotic doesn't seem to be touching it either. And we're giving him the maximum dose."

"As long as he continues to get plenty of oxygen into the blood through the lungs, we're in fairly good shape," said Greg. "But if this inflammation continues to spread and restrict the amount of lung available for respiration, we could be in trouble. How much of Lawson's blood do you think we still have in storage?"

"I'll find out." Bob Johnson dialed the hospital blood bank extension and spoke to the night technician. "About two thousand cc., sir," he reported.

"I'm going to discontinue both the Imuran and methylprednisolone," said Greg.

"How about ALG?"

"We'll stop that, too, for the time being at least; right now he's in more danger from a spreading lung infection than he is from rejection. If we start a slow transfusion with Lawson's blood, the new white blood cells might help fight the lung infection."

Bob Johnson gave the order to the blood bank and hung up the telephone. "How fast do you want it given, sir?"

"Set the drip to inject the first five hundred cc. in an hour, then have the nurse cut it down until we run out of Lawson's blood or it looks like Merchant's circulation is getting overloaded. If this inflammation isn't stopped in the next few hours, it may get out of control."

"I'll get things going right away," Bob Johnson promised.

"You might as well go home then," Greg told him. "I'll be in my office and can get here in a minute."

"I'll be happy to stay, sir."

"I couldn't sleep any more anyway. I'll see you in the morning."

"Good night, sir. Do you think we should tell Mrs. Merchant?"

"There's no need yet. She already knows what the situation is and his condition isn't liable to change that rapidly."

In his office, Greg surveyed the shelves of books against the back wall on either side of the window, seeking something to read. They contained only technical medical books or journals, however, and finding nothing that promised calm to his restlessness, he went to the desk, unlocked the center drawer and took from it one of Keith Jackson's sketches for the hospital central tower.

The drawing was on thin tracing paper, and, obeying a sudden hunch, he took it to the X-ray viewbox that stood on a table at one side of the office, fixed the sheet before the ground glass and switched on the light. Immediately, as he had thought it might, the sketch took on a three-dimensional quality, giving it a fullness and a grandeur that was literally breathtaking. With the outlines of the statue sketched in lightly, he was sure the whole effect would be that of seeing the structure as it would actually exist, if built, with the massive statue dominating the glass-walled center section. He couldn't risk ruining the sketch by trying to pencil in the statue himself, however—that would have to wait until he could call Keith Jackson about seven before the architect went to his office.

Keith, he was sure, would be able to see, as he had, the potentiality in such a presentation when he faced the Board of Trustees that afternoon and a preview of the new plan was demanded by Ed McDougal and his followers—as he had every reason to anticipate that it would be.

About the meeting itself, Greg felt no apprehension. With the technical difficulties of transplanting a human heart and lungs successfully behind him, and with Jeanne close to him once again, even Sam Hunter's threat of censure was only a minor irritation. The undeniable fact that he had done something no one else had done before and, through it, opened up new vistas for surgical progress, made his position in the rapidly expanding field of organ transplantation more than secure. A half dozen medical schools, he knew, would welcome him warmly and supply everything he would need in his work.

He would hate to leave The Clinic, it was true, just as he had hated to leave his childhood home every September for four years to board the hot and dirty train for Baltimore. But a few days after he registered for classes again each year and became occupied with the engrossing subjects of the medical curriculum, his loneliness had departed. And as far back as he could remember, he had been able to shut out the world outside and bury himself in his work, so he had no doubt that this surcease would be available to him again.

Not that he had any intention of giving up without a fight before the board. He was convinced that the new plan was the logical answer to the future role of The Clinic and its ever-expanding field of influence upon the people here, as well as what it had always been, one of the finest training institutions in the world for young medical men. No matter what might happen to him personally, he still felt too much of a sense of loyalty to old Dr. Anders to let what The Clinic's founder had worked so hard to build—and in which a considerable part of Greg's own life was invested—be destroyed until every possibility for preserving it had been exhausted.

A glance at his watch told Greg it was only six o'clock, although he could hear the manifold sounds of the hospital's early morning activities meshing into gear. Keith Jackson had been getting precious little sleep lately and Greg hated to awaken him before seven at the earliest, so, leaving the office, he visited Guy Merchant's room to be sure the blood was flowing satisfactorily and that there had been no major change in his condition, then stopped in the lobby, where the night telephone operators worked behind a grilled partition.

"I'm going over to my apartment for about an hour," he told the operator on duty there. "I'm not going back to bed, so you can get me on the beeper if they need me on intensive care."

"Don't worry, Doctor," the operator said. "If I have to, I'll send an orderly over there to ring the doorbell of your apartment."

Jeanne was still asleep, looking like a lovely little girl sprawled out on the bed under a sheet. She'd always taken two thirds of the bed but he'd been happy to have her where he could touch her when he woke up in the night or press a foot against hers and feel the reflex response, even though she didn't awaken.

Pulling up a chair beside the bed, he sat engrossed in the sheer joy of having her back in the big bed and the memory of her arms about him last night. He had been sitting there for perhaps half an hour when she opened her eyes and, seeing him, sat up in bed clutching the sheet about her breasts.

"What are you doing up, and already dressed, darling?" she asked.

"I went to see Guy Merchant about four this morning. Came back only a few minutes ago."

"Why didn't you wake me to get you some breakfast?"

"I was just sitting here looking at you and wondering how I could have neglected you the way I've done the past two years."

"No woman is neglected who knows she's loved." She leaned over to kiss him. "I just forgot it for a while, but all that's behind us now. Hand me my robe, will you? I feel like a hussy with nothing on but a sheet."

"For a while last night you didn't even have that on, but you certainly didn't look like a hussy—or act like one."

"How would you know? Or were those only lies you used to tell me about my being the only girl you ever loved?"

"They're the truth. I guess I'm just hopelessly square."

"Believe me, I wouldn't want you any other way. When I look at Ed McDougal—" She shivered. "Men like that give me the creeps. He really doesn't have any chance of beating you, does he?"

"He may. When it comes to money, most men react according to a predictable pattern, and there's a lot involved. But when the heart I took from Frank Lawson started beating in Guy Merchant's body the other night, I knew I had reached a height from which no man could drag me down."

"It can be lonely up there. You need people to help you."

"That's the main reason why I came home—besides seeing you. I'm going down to Keith Jackson's apartment, as soon as I'm sure he and Mary are awake. The hospital sketch needs one final touch. When that's done, I'll be ready to face the trustees."

ii

For a while Friday morning, it seemed that the measures Greg had taken during the night would give Guy Merchant enough weapons—mainly in the form of fresh white blood cells from the man who had also furnished him with a new heart and lungs—to fight a winning battle against the infection that was filling his lungs with the swelling of inflammation, slowly shutting off the

312

rhythmic expansion and contraction of the tiny air sacs, called alveoli, whose thin lining membrane allowed oxygen to pass freely into the bloodstream and carbon dioxide out of it.

Shortly after eleven, Helen Foucald came into Greg's office. He was staring morosely at the desk blotter while he racked his brain for some new way to attack the deadly process.

"Can I bother you for a moment, Greg?" she asked.

"Of course. What's troubling you?"

"I'm planning to go away for the weekend, leaving about noon, but if you think you'll need me here, I'll stay."

"Your idea about using Lawson's blood helped a lot, but we've done everything we can, so there's nothing to do now but wait it out." He glanced out of the window, where skiffs of snow had already begun to fall. "Are you driving?"

"Yes."

"Then you'd better get going. The view out there doesn't look very promising."

"We're only going a little beyond Frederick. Peter knows—" She stopped, then shrugged. "I don't imagine you would approve."

"I'm as fond of you and Peter Carewe as I am of anybody I know, Helen. Nothing would please me more than to see you happy—together." He hesitated, then added, "Does Peter know about Henry?"

"Yes."

"And you're going away together to see whether or not it might still work out?"

"You think it's hopeless, don't you?"

"I think you're both adults and entitled to the sort of happiness Jeanne and I had—have together."

"I'm glad you found it again, Greg."

"So am I," he said. "Now, whatever happens with The Clinic and with Merchant, I'll come out ahead, even if Sam Hunter does manage to conk me this afternoon."

"Don't be too angry with him, Greg," she begged. "Last night I went with him to a performance of the circus his son Ted and his wife are with. Sam Hunter is really a lonely old man."

"Why does he have to take his loneliness out on me?"

"It's not you personally; it's what you represent, what you're making him face."

"How do you figure that?"

"The old have an instinctive fear of tomorrow, knowing that every passing day increases the odds in favor of the next one bringing death. Because of that, Sam would naturally be suspicious of anything that represents a sharp change from the status quo."

"Sir William Osler once said everybody over sixty should be chloroformed—or something like that, but I'm getting too close to that age myself to be much in favor of it."

"There's another side to Sam Hunter's opposition to you, I'm sure," she said. "He really worshiped Henry's father."

"We're kindred spirits there."

"And he sees you as a threat to the image he holds of Dr. Anders."

"Nothing could be farther from the truth," Greg protested. "Dr. Anders was a visionary—ahead of his time. I only want to make The Clinic what he would make it himself, if he were alive today."

"I tried to tell Sam that, but I don't think I succeeded very well. Good luck, Greg—with the trustees."

"Give my regards to Peter. I'm sorry we got to see so little of each other this time, but I've been a bit busy."

"Nobody could deny that," she agreed.

When Helen was gone, Greg went to the intensive care unit and looked in on Guy Merchant, but there was no change for the better. The brief period of improvement with the transfusions had only been temporary; now his temperature was slowly climbing once again. His color was good, however, indicating that enough of the lungs were still functioning to provide an adequate supply of oxygen for the red blood cells to carry to the rest of the body. But how much longer the balance would be in his favor, with the amount of functioning lung tissues being gradually encroached on by the progress of the infection, was problematic.

Greg ordered another portable X-ray of the chest for noon and went to the surgical lecture room, where the last paper of the morning session was being given. Seeing Bill Remick there, he nodded to the Washington roentgenologist and fellow trustee to follow and left the room. Remick joined him moments later in the corridor and they went into the doctors' lounge between the two main operating theaters.

"Why the cloak-and-dagger atmosphere?" the X-ray man asked.

"I need to talk to you about the strategy for this afternoon's meeting."

"That's the best news I've heard yet."

"What?"

"That you're hitting back at last and not letting people push you around."

"You sound just like my wife," said Greg.

"It's true. You're my friend, Greg, but I've got to tell you just the same."

"What you don't realize, Bill, is that when people appear to be pushing me around, it's usually because I've already decided the course I will follow. In the end, things usually work out the way I want them to."

"This thing is too important to take a chance on," the X-ray man insisted. "If it's moved somewhere else, The Clinic will never be the same."

"I agree with you there. That's why I've decided on a little nudging."

"It may take more than a little."

"Perhaps, but I think I can manage that, too—with your help. What do you think will be the opposition's plan of attack?"

"They know I'm behind you, so they don't confide in me."

"How do you see the situation then?"

"If I were Ed McDougal, I would play down this attempt of Sam Hunter's to censure you. The old man called the special meeting this afternoon to press the charge, so they'll have to go through with that to humor him, but your success with the transplant has pretty well spiked their guns. I'm sure Ed recognizes that, even if Sam Hunter might not."

"Any chance that Ed will persuade Sam not to insist on the special meeting?"

"Not the way I see it. By letting a vote to censure be taken, they can see who's wavering and who needs to be worked on before tomorrow, so it will help them, even if they lose. The most important goal they have right now is to make you reveal your hospital plans prematurely, so they'll have time to plan ways to combat it before the final meeting tomorrow morning. I've tried to figure out some way to forestall a demand for the plans at this afternoon's meeting, but so far I've had no luck. No specific agenda has been announced—"

"That's why I came to see you," said Greg. "If you'll help me, I think I can steal a march on them."

"How?"

"Jud Templeton has a copy of the main drawing I'm going to show the board and his piece on it is already written, ready to be published in this afternoon's final editions, after the special meeting. Jud also has a list of the people who will join with Henry and Ed to develop this property after The Clinic is moved, but he can't publish it because they haven't actually started yet."

"Suppose Ed and his crowd become wary and don't demand to see the plan."

"Then I want you to do it."

"How?"

"Even if they don't ask to see it, I'm going to show the sketches anyway," said Greg. "As soon as I start the presentation, I want you to call Jud Templeton." He handed the roentgenologist a slip of paper. "Here's his telephone number. All you have to say is that you're calling for me and that he's to turn loose his dogs."

"It's a smart trick. Ed and his crowd will be fit to be tied."

"That's the idea," said Greg. "I figure that, by showing the new plan before anyone from the opposition has a chance to demand to see it, we'll be sowing confusion in their ranks."

"It couldn't happen to a more deserving crew of scoundrels."

iii

Peter Carewe was waiting at one of the car-rental booths at the airport when Helen came in, carrying a small overnight case.

"The weatherman says the snow's pretty heavy toward the Catoctins," he said, taking her arm. "If we're going to get through we'd better get started right away. They're putting up some sandwiches and a thermos of coffee for us in the lunch room."

It was barely one o'clock when they pulled away from the front of Friendship Airport and took a country road that connected with U.S. 40 near Ellicott City.

"I'm more accustomed to driving a jeep in the tropics," said Peter. "But my work takes me into some pretty rough country, so I hope I can still cope with a snowstorm. How about breaking out the sandwiches and coffee?"

They ate on the move, for the snow was already pelting down. The going became steadily more difficult on the narrow back road and it took them almost two hours to reach the four-lane arterial highway westward. When they did, visibility was almost nil and ahead they saw a line of blinking red lights marking a highway patrol barricade.

"We're only letting emergencies through westward," said the patrolman who stopped them. "How far were you going?"

"We have reservations at Chalet Julienne in the Catoctins."

"They've been snowed in since midnight. Frederick is pretty well blocked, too, unless it's a very grave emergency. My advice to you is to go back to Baltimore while you can still make it and wait until we can get snowplows through."

"When is that liable to be?" Peter asked.

"The forecast says the snow will end before midnight and we'll have plows going immediately."

Peter looked questioningly at Helen. "What do you think?"

"Let's go back," she said. "There's no point in risking our lives."

He turned the car around and they started back toward Baltimore but the going was bad even then. An hour had passed when Helen suddenly started to laugh.

"What's so funny?" Peter asked.

"It looks as if even heaven is trying to protect the working girl."

"You'll not escape my clutches that easy, me proud beauty," he said with a chuckle. "I'm taking you back to my suite."

Helen made no objection; here in the warm car close beside him with the falling snow a fleecy white curtain outside, Henry and the rest of the world seemed far away.

317

"Anyway," she said contentedly, "I'll get to see what this room service you recommend so highly is really like."

iv

The brown tablets given Vivian and Ted by the Filipino doctor at the hospital had relieved the pain in his hand and enabled him to get some sleep while the circus was moving to Frederick that night. But when morning dawned to a dull and lowering sky with the promise of snow, Vivian could see that Ted was much worse.

The swelling, which had been confined to the hand itself until the splinter wound was opened the night before, now extended well up the wrist and was apparent above the bandage. Ted complained, too, of a severe headache, which even the tablets didn't entirely relieve, and the feverish look in his eyes, plus his hot, dry skin, told Vivian their visit to the hospital last night had not helped control the infection in his hand.

Snow had begun to fall in Frederick well before noon and the half-hourly weather reports were now predicting an even heavier fall as the front moved eastward toward Baltimore and the coast. At 3 P.M. the police canceled the evening performance of the circus to avoid the danger of people being marooned in the auditorium where it was to be held. When, shortly afterwards, Ted began to shake with a severe chill and talk wildly in delirium, Vivian sent for Papa Gus, who was busy preparing the circus for the full onslaught of the storm.

"Ted's much worse than he was this morning, Papa," she said. "We've got to take him to a hospital."

"I'll tell Joe Califino to get the jeep. There's certain to be a hospital here in Frederick."

"Ted's too sick to be treated by just any doctor," she said firmly. "I'm going to take him to The Clinic and ask his father to see that he has the best doctors there."

"Mr. Hunter has a right to know Ted is sick," Papa Gus agreed. "It is the right thing to do."

"We'll use our van," she said. "Joe has driven it through snow before and that way Ted can lie down all the way."

318

"They're wary, Greg," said Bill Remick as the members of the Board of Trustees began to file into one of the meeting rooms of the Clinic Inn for the Friday-afternoon special session Sam Hunter had demanded. The convocation had officially ended with the final paper at four o'clock and it was now nearly five. Glancing at the large flat package Greg carried, the X-ray man added, "I doubt that they're going to ask for the plans this afternoon."

"Then we'll make them." Greg kept his voice low so only the roentgenologist could hear. "I have everything set up."

He nodded toward a viewbox which had been pushed back against the wall so it wouldn't be noticeable, yet could be seen by everyone in the room once the light was switched on.

"I'll take care of that as we planned," Bill Remick promised.

The tactics the opposition had decided upon were obvious from the first words of Dr. Timothy Puckett, after he gaveled the meeting to order.

"This special meeting has been called for the purpose of taking up a charge made against Dr. Gregory Alexander by Mr. Sam Hunter," he said. "Namely, that he constructed an addition to the present hospital without the authority of the board. No other—"

"Mr. Chairman," Bill Remick interrupted. "Did I understand you to say that this is a special meeting?"

"You know it is, Bill," Timothy Puckett said testily. "The regularly scheduled meeting is tomorrow morning."

"Have you read the bylaws recently, Mr. Chairman?"

"Well, I—"

"Obviously you haven't, so I will read from them in order to bring you up to date." Taking a typed sheet from his pocket, the roentgenologist read:

> *When a special meeting is called, the trustees shall be notified in writing no less than five days in advance of this meeting concerning the matters to be taken up at that time.*

"I protest the failure of the chairman to follow the bylaws in calling this meeting," Bill Remick added, "unless you consider this only a part of the regular annual meeting of the Board of Trustees."

"We'll call it that, if you wish." Timothy Puckett missed seeing frantic signals from Ed McDougal. "The regular meeting is now open for business."

"Mr. Chairman." Bill Remick spoke quickly again before anyone else could gain the floor. "I move that Dr. Gregory Alexander, chairman of the building committee for the Board of Trustees, give a preliminary presentation of the plan he has developed for a new building complex to be constructed upon the site of the present one."

Dave Connor seconded the motion, and, stunned by the swift action, Timothy Puckett asked automatically, "Is there any discussion?"

Ed McDougal was rising to his feet when, pretending that the motion had already passed, Greg moved to the corner of the room where he had set up the viewbox.

"Dr. Alexander." Timothy Puckett was groping for some way to stop him. "You are—"

"It was my intention to present plans in some detail to this body at the meeting tomorrow," Greg interrupted firmly, drowning out the chairman's protest. "But since Dr. Remick has made the motion, I shall show you some preliminary sketches."

Ignoring the clamor of voices demanding to be heard, Greg placed the transparent preliminary sketch for the high-rise ICU tower on the viewbox. He and Keith Jackson had spent a busy hour together early that morning and the outline of the statue was now drawn in place in the center of the ground glass front of the viewbox.

"This is a sketch of the proposed new hospital and diagnostic clinic building drawn by architect Keith Jackson at my request." Greg flipped the switch to illuminate the sketch.

A hush fell over the group of shouting men; as if seen in three dimensions, both the statue and the surrounding glass-walled enclosure of the tower stood out in all its startling beauty and grandeur.

"As all of you know," he continued, "one of the provisions of Dr. Anders' will was that, should any alterations in the structure of the present Clinic be necessary, the statue of Christ in the lobby should never lose its position of pre-eminence. This requirement posed a considerable architectural problem but I am sure you will see, even in this preliminary sketch, that Mr. Jackson has completely fulfilled Dr. Anders' provision."

From the corner of his eye, Greg saw Bill Remick leave the room to call Jud Templeton. As he scanned the faces before him, he could see that the sketch was affecting many of the trustees in the same way that it had affected him when he'd first seen it, with a feeling of awe and reverence far transcending whatever preconceptions they might have had. Only the most prejudiced could fail to see that he and Keith Jackson had brought forth a new creation, a new concept in hospital construction combining beauty and effectiveness in a perfect amalgam.

"Mr. Chairman." Ed McDougal's voice sounded a little stunned.

"Dr. McDougal."

"I move that consideration of this matter be tabled until tomorrow morning at the regular session."

Henry Anders quickly seconded the motion and Dr. Puckett spoke before anyone else could intervene.

"A motion to table cannot be discussed," he announced. "All in favor say 'aye.'"

There was a chorus of "ayes" and, when he called for the "nays," about an equally loud negative vote, but the sweating chairman chose to hear only the former, and announced that the motion had carried.

"Do I hear a motion for adjournment?" he asked, and, when that, too, came quickly, the meeting was over.

24

At first, the state police hadn't wanted to let the big red van from the Tarentino Circus move eastward toward Baltimore because of the storm. But when Vivian pleaded that Ted must be taken to The Clinic for treatment immediately, they finally agreed to let it through. Even though the truck was equipped with snow tires and Joe Califino was a skilled driver, the going was slow and more than two hours were required for the some forty-odd miles to Baltimore.

It was six o'clock when they finally reached the emergency entrance to The Clinic and Ted was lifted out and placed on a rolling stretcher. Vivian went inside to make arrangements while Joe parked the truck in the adjacent lot, planning to remain there until Vivian came to give him further orders. While she was giving the necessary information to the emergency room nursing supervisor, Vivian could see that the hospital routine was meshing smoothly into action, for a young doctor in crisp white ducks began examining Ted immediately.

"Do you have any idea how I could reach Mr. Sam Hunter?" she asked the nurse.

"Is he a relative?"

"Mr. Hunter is my husband's father." Vivian's voice shook a little as she spoke the words that might end her marriage, if Sam Hunter managed to get his way. But saving Ted's life was more important now than either her pride or her love for him.

"Mr. Hunter comes to The Clinic every year at this time," the nurse said. "I believe he's at the Clinic Inn."

"Would you telephone him, please? Tell him Ted is seriously ill and I need help."

"I'll call him right away, Mrs. Hunter. Do you want to speak to him yourself?"

"N—no, thanks."

"Dr. Adams is already examining your husband," the nurse told her as she dialed. "You can be sure he'll be well taken care of."

Vivian was sitting on a bench outside the waiting room drinking coffee when the tall old man, whom she had never actually seen but whom she recognized from his picture, came charging out of the elevator followed by Ed McDougal and Henry Anders. He didn't even give her a glance but moved to the door of the emergency room, where Ted was lying on a treatment table, with the young doctor in a white uniform bending over his arm.

"Ted!" The cry of agony penetrated momentarily through the curtain of delirium that threatened to shut away Ted's mind from reality.

"Hello, Dad." The words were slightly slurred. "Where's Vivian?"

"I'm here, darling." Vivian had moved to the doorway, where Ted could see her. "It's all right, you're at The Clinic."

Sam Hunter wheeled upon the small figure. "What have you done to my son?" he demanded angrily.

Vivian stiffened at his tone, but worry about Ted during the long ride from Frederick to Baltimore through the snowstorm had almost used up her strength.

"You turned him out, Mr. Hunter," she said with all the dignity she could muster. "Now I've given him back to you. His life is worth more to me than anything else."

"Dr. Anders," the young doctor said, "this looks like an anerobic infection."

"What?" Henry Anders asked, frowning.

"There's crepitation in the tissues of the hand and lower arm. I'm sure we're dealing with gas"—he broke off, not wanting to speak the dread words "gas gangrene" where Sam Hunter and Vivian could hear—"with a gas bacillus infection."

"Do something, Henry," Sam Hunter demanded, and Henry Anders moved to the table where Ted lay. The dressings had been removed from his hand and the strange odor of the infection, dank and repelling like the air in some freshly opened funeral crypt, reached even into the corridor outside the room. Henry examined the arm briefly, running his fingers along the skin, then turned to Ed McDougal.

"You'd better take a look at this, too, Ed," he said doubtfully. "I don't treat this sort of thing very often."

"What is it, Ed?" Sam Hunter demanded when the Texas surgeon finished a brief examination.

"The prognosis isn't good, Mr. Hunter."

"What does that mean?"

"The boy has a gas bacillus infection of his hand and arm. It appears to be progressive."

"Well, do something about it."

Ed McDougal hesitated, reluctant to speak the words. "Ted's very sick," he said at last. "Unless his arm is amputated quickly, there's little hope of saving him—and not much at that."

Sam Hunter staggered and it was Vivian who took him by the arm and led him to a bench.

"But, Dr. Anders—" the house officer started to say in a tone of shocked protest, only to be cut off by Sam Hunter's strangled cry:

"Amputation? You can't mean it."

"Are you saying the only treatment that can save my husband is to cut off his arm?" Vivian asked incredulously.

"I wish there were some other way except amputation." No one could doubt that Ed McDougal meant what he said. "God knows I wish it."

ii

Helen and Peter were crossing the parking lot after depositing their luggage at the Clinic Inn and leaving his rental car at a nearby garage to be picked up. She stopped when she saw the big red van with the letters TARANTINO CIRCUS emblazoned across its sides parked beneath a lamppost so the light would shine into the cab.

"Look, Peter!" she cried. "That truck is from the circus I saw with Sam Hunter last night."

"Are you sure?"

"There would hardly be two Tarentino Circuses in this area at the same time."

"Let's see if anyone's inside."

When Peter tapped on the glass of the door, Joe Califino sat up in his cubicle and swung his legs down so he could slide into the seat and run down the glass of the door.

"Are you here with someone from the circus?" Helen asked.

"What's the matter?" said the roustabout. "Ain't I supposed to park here?"

"I don't have anything to do with parking," said Helen. "I saw the circus last night in Frederick and recognized the truck."

"Vivian and Ted—they're inside."

"Those are the names of the young acrobats." Helen gave Peter a quick look and turned back to the roustabout. "Is anything wrong?"

"It's Ted, ma'am. He's got this trouble with his hand."

"I knew something was wrong!" Helen cried. "He almost dropped her last night."

"And scared the daylights out of me and Papa Gus," Joe Califino said.

"Are they in the hospital?" Peter asked.

"Ted got worse last night so Vivian decided to bring him here to his old man," said the roustabout.

"That boy is Sam Hunter's son, Peter," Helen said quickly. "We've got to go in and see about him."

"Of course."

They came into the corridor outside the emergency room in time to hear Ed McDougal's words, and Helen gave a cry of protest as she realized their significance. But it was Peter who spoke.

"What's this, Ed?" he asked.

"Mr. Hunter's son Ted has a gas bacillus infection of the hand and arm."

Peter moved into the emergency room without invitation and touched the skin of Ted's arm above the now puffed and angry wound in his hand. Ted himself had lapsed into delirium again and was muttering incoherently.

"Look here, Carewe," Henry Anders blustered, "you're not on the staff."

"Neither is Ed McDougal, but it looks like he's in charge," Peter said curtly.

"He's in consultation with me."

Ignoring The Clinic director, Peter continued his examination, but a third-year medical student could have diagnosed the nature of the infection and traced its course from the brief history Vivian had given the house officer for the admission record and which he had written on a card.

The germ of gas gangrene, a common inhabitant of the animal —and often the human—digestive tract, had obviously been introduced into Ted's hand by means of the splinter when he'd picked up the stake a few days before to fend off the stampeding elephants. Growing in the body tissue, the virulent organism had been fairly well localized in the hand around the original wound by the body's own defenses, until the incision the night before had broken down the wall of tissue resistance that held it in check. With the wall thus breached, noxious bacteria had been able to break out, like an enemy escaping from a trap, and spread into the surrounding tissues, where they were rapidly overwhelming the body's defenses and would soon become a fatal septicemia. The crinkly feeling beneath Peter's fingers, a certain indicator that gas was being formed there by the rapidly spreading infection, was enough in itself to make the diagnosis.

"Ed's in charge here at my request," Henry Anders started to splutter, but Peter cut him off sharply.

"Did you say amputation, Ed?" he demanded.

"I don't like it, Peter," said the Texan. "But nothing else can save the boy."

"Dr. Adams." Peter spoke to the house officer, who wore a nameplate over the pocket of his duck coat.

"Yes, sir?"

"How would you treat this infection?"

"With hyperbaric oxygen," the younger doctor answered unhesitatingly. "Dr. Alexander's experiments . . ."

"Experiments!" The strangled cry came from Sam Hunter.

"Hyperbaric oxygen treatment for this type of infection is more than an experiment, Mr. Hunter," said Helen. "You can't let them amputate."

"You mean there's another treatment that might save Ted's arm?" Vivian spoke for the first time since Peter and Helen had come in.

"His arm and his life," said Peter. "The experimental work done by Dr. Alexander here proves that these infections can be controlled by the special treatment Dr. Adams mentioned."

"Is that true, Henry?" Sam Hunter demanded.

"Well, it is still experi—"

"I had forgotten that The Clinic had a hyperbaric chamber, Mr. Hunter." Ed McDougal's relief at the avenue of escape opened to him by Peter's words was quite apparent in his voice. "It should certainly be tried first."

"I'll call Dr. Alexander at once," said Helen, seizing the opportunity Ed McDougal's strategic retreat had offered her.

"I'm not sure I can give permission for my son to be experimented on," Sam Hunter objected. "There's been too much of that here already."

"You don't have to give permission, Mr. Hunter," said Peter. "Your son's wife is here and her legal rights come before yours, where Ted is concerned."

Every eye was suddenly upon Vivian, small and still partially frozen with the horror of what had been first proposed for treating Ted. In her need for help and assurance, she turned instinctively to another woman.

"Is what they're saying true?" she asked Helen.

"Yes, Vivian," said Helen. "Amputation might save Ted's life but his arm would be lost. The treatment Dr. Carewe and Dr. Adams suggest has a good chance of saving both."

"Then let him have it," she said firmly. "I give my permission."

"Go call Greg, Helen," said Peter. "I'll stay here."

iii

Greg was working in Guy Merchant's room on the ICU when Helen found him. He had slipped a needle between the ribs to the left of the sternum, seeking to enter the pericardial sac surrounding the heart. As he pushed it slowly inward, a reddish fluid suddenly spurted into the syringe attached to the needle.

Busy with what he was doing, Greg hadn't noticed Helen standing in the door of the room and she hesitated to interrupt him in anything so delicate and dangerous as tapping the space around the heart with a needle.

"The fluid doesn't look purulent, Bob." He spoke to the Senior Fellow, whose eyes were also on the syringe. "That means there's no infection in the pericardium and relieving the pressure of the fluid ought to improve heart action."

"It gives us a chance," Bob Johnson agreed. "I guess maybe our last one."

"As soon as I finish removing the rest of the pericardial fluid, I'll tap the pleural cavities to give the lungs all the room we can," said Greg. "Then we can put him in—"

"Greg." Helen spoke from the door, and he looked up in surprise."

"I thought you were out of town, Helen?"

"It's a long story," she said. "Could you possibly see a patient for me in the emergency room right away?"

"Of course," he said. "Bob can finish up here. But what's so urgent?"

"Sam Hunter's son was just brought in with a far-advanced gas gangrene of the arm."

The sudden silence in the room surprised her, but Greg broke it almost immediately. "I'll come right away," he said. "Wait for me."

"Tell me what you can about the case," he said as they were waiting for the elevator to take them to the ground floor. Helen gave him a brief rundown on the events that had transpired since she and Peter had recognized the red circus van in the parking lot outside and had come into the emergency room. Long before she finished, his face was grave.

"You say Ed and Henry have seen him already?" he asked.

"Yes. Ed recommended amputation."

"Most surgeons would—particularly if a hyperbaric chamber wasn't available. We've only realized recently that these anerobic infections can be tackled more successfully with the use of oxygen under high pressure."

"Henry tried to stop Peter from recommending it," she said. "But

328

Ed McDougal was smart enough to see that it got him off the hook."

"And me on it," said Greg soberly. "The first treatment will take at least four hours, including decompression. If it doesn't stop the infection, that's four hours we will have lost when we have to amputate, as a final resort."

"I'm sorry, Greg. The girl trusted Peter and me and refused to let Ed and Henry go ahead. We can't let her down."

"More than that's involved, Helen." At the odd note in his voice, she gave him a quick appraising glance.

"What do you mean?"

"I planned to take Guy Merchant directly to the hyperbaric chamber when we finished taking off the fluid."

"Oh, Greg!" she cried. "I didn't know."

"How could you?"

"Do you think he has a chance outside the chamber?"

"I doubt it—we were hoping the extra oxygen might make the difference—in his favor."

"And now I've robbed you of that."

"You and Peter had no alternative," he assured her. "It looks like we're all having hard choices today."

"How did the special meeting come out this afternoon?" she asked.

"When Ed McDougal and his gang realized how close the vote would be, they managed to table any action until tomorrow morning."

"Did you show the new plan?"

"Yes. I did manage that."

They were just outside the emergency room, and, noticing a newspaper vending rack, Greg stopped before it.

"Got a dime?" he asked. "My money's in my wallet in the dressing room."

She fished out a coin and he dropped it into the slot. Taking out a paper, he handed it to her, pointing to the front page, where the sketch of the proposed central section of The Clinic occupied a full half of the space.

"It's beautiful!" she cried. "Truly majestic!"

"Just thought you might want to see what we're risking."

329

"Oh, Greg, I'm sorry. Truly sorry."

"We aren't licked yet." He held open the door to the emergency room for her to pass through ahead of him. "But wouldn't it be ironic if Sam Hunter succeeds in censuring me tomorrow for building the chamber that saves his son's life?"

iv

The tableau in the emergency room was like a Greek tragedy halted in mid-scene. Peter Carewe stood at one side of the room with Vivian Hunter beside him; ranged against them were Ed McDougal, Henry Anders and Sam Hunter. The girl was pale and looked very small compared to her antagonists and her single protector, but she had obviously not given ground, for the expression on Sam Hunter's face was one of angry bafflement.

"There's a question of ethics involved here, Greg." Henry Anders hadn't yet given up, in spite of Ed McDougal's wish to retreat.

"We can settle the ethical question at once," Greg said mildly and turned to Vivian.

"I'm Dr. Alexander, chief surgeon of The Clinic, Mrs. Hunter," he said. "Did you engage Dr. McDougal and Dr. Anders to treat your husband?"

"I certainly did not." Vivian looked defiantly at Sam Hunter. "Mr. Hunter brought these other doctors and now they say they have to amputate Ted's arm."

"Do you wish me to take charge of your husband's case?" Greg asked her.

"Yes. I certainly do."

"I think that takes care of the ethics question, Henry," said Greg. "Let's see the patient, Mrs. White." He spoke to the nurse who appeared at his elbow, and moved to the cubicle where Ted was lying upon a treatment table.

No one spoke during the five-minute examination. When he came out of the cubicle, Greg went directly to a basin at one side of the room and washed his hands carefully, then rinsed them with antiseptic from a bottle on the shelf over the basin.

"Dr. McDougal has already made the diagnosis." He spoke to

330

Vivian. "If what we call hyperbaric oxygen wasn't available, I would recommend immediate amputation, as he did."

"Can you guarantee that this experiment of yours will succeed?" Sam Hunter demanded.

"I can only tell you that in your son's condition even an amputation might very well not save him, Mr. Hunter," Greg said quietly. "Oxygen under pressure is the only thing that offers any hope."

"Please go ahead, Doctor," Vivian begged. "We've lost too much time already, while these others were bickering."

"I'll take him into the chamber immediately," said Greg.

"H—how soon will you know, Doctor?"

"The first exposure to oxygen will take about three hours, all told. We ought to know something when it's over."

"You'll stay with him?"

"Of course. As soon as we obtain the pressure we need in the chamber, I shall open the wound in his hand more widely."

v

At the nurses' desk, Greg rang the experimental laboratory and Hans Werner. "I'm bringing a case of gas gangrene over right now, Hans," he said. "We'll put him into the hyperbaric chamber instead of Mr. Merchant. Please call Dr. Gann and ask the operating room to send over a sterile incision and drainage tray."

"Very goot, Doctor."

"This is a severe case," Greg added. "We'll be in the chamber for two hours at four atmospheres, perhaps longer."

"Do not worry, Doctor," said Hans. "Everything iss ready."

While Ted was being moved by means of a portable stretcher, Greg found Georgia Merchant in the ICU waiting room.

"You have bad news for me, Doctor," she said when she saw his face.

"Not about your husband's immediate condition," he said. "In fact, removing the fluid from the pericardium has improved his heart action."

"What then?"

"I planned to treat him in the pressure chamber after I took off the fluid, but I shall not be able to do it."

"Why not?"

"Another patient has just been admitted who needs oxygen under pressure very badly."

"It's the only treatment with a chance of saving Guy, isn't it?"

"I think so—yes."

"Then how could anyone need it more than he does?"

"This is a young man with a rapidly progressing infection that can be controlled only by means of the chamber."

"Couldn't you treat him later—and give Guy this added chance?"

"We may not be able to save the young man as it is. If we wait, all chance would be lost."

"Are you asking my permission to let the chamber be used for this young man instead of my husband, with the knowledge that not using it for Guy may mean his death?" Georgia asked.

"I've already made the decision, but I wanted you to understand why," Greg told her. "We'll do everything we can, of course. Dr. Johnson will be with your husband all the time and I hope things still turn out for the best. I must go now; they're waiting to close the chamber."

25

Besides Ted Hunter, muttering and picking at the covering sheet in his delirium, Greg took only Hans Werner, the doyen of the experimental laboratory, and Dr. Lewis Gann into the chamber with him, along with the sterile tray of instruments and dressings he had ordered prepared. Hans had helped with hundreds of operations and was as skilled as any nurse; besides, there was barely room inside the steel-walled tank with its glass-covered ports for the three of them and the cushioned operating table to which Ted was transferred.

The small hyperbaric chamber, which was all Greg had been able to get funds for, was very much like the pressure tanks used for many years in compressing and decompressing divers and caisson workers, whose jobs took them underwater, as well as in treating those who developed what was called "bends" from too rapid decompression. The actual operation of the tank itself was in the hands of specially trained technicians, all of them former Navy diving experts; one or more of these constantly watched the activities going on inside the chamber through one of the glass ports, so as to be ready to take whatever measures might be necessary in an emergency.

Since the air pouring into the tank, as the pump began to raise the pressure, was only one fifth oxygen and the highest possible concentration in the blood was desired, Dr. Gann placed a mask over Ted's face immediately and began to administer pure oxygen, saturating the body tissues quickly as the pressure rose and surrounding the oxygen-hating germs of the infection with a medium in which, hopefully, they would no longer grow and thrive, as they had been doing in the tissues of his hand and arm.

Fortunately unusual, except in wartime, gas bacillus infections did not come into the hands of the average doctor often. Relatively little progress had therefore been made in treatment over amputation, which had been used for centuries, until this method had been devised of putting a high concentration of oxygen, with its powerful dampening effect upon the growth of this particular type of bacteria, into the patient's body through the use of the hyperbaric chamber.

"Think the bug has invaded the bloodstream yet, Greg?" Dr. Gann asked as he added a weak mixture of nitrous oxide to the oxygen flow to achieve the very light anesthesia Greg would need in order to open the wound widely in search of a foreign body and to remove any gangrenous tissue that would encourage the further growth of the invading bacteria.

"I doubt it." Like the others, Greg was sweating profusely as the pressure rose, for the concentration of air into a smaller volume with each stroke of the pump also concentrated its heat and the chamber lacked the elaborate cooling system that marked larger and newer ones. "It's certainly galloping now but I hope we can still get ahead of it."

"Strange the doctor who treated him last night didn't notice the gas. Your nose usually diagnoses these infections."

"There may not have been much last night; it hadn't really started spreading then." Greg had put on sterile gloves and was painting Ted Hunter's hand with an antiseptic, while Hans Werner held it above an arm board extending out from the table. Draping the arm with a sterile sheet, he nodded to Hans, who lowered the hand upon it and held it tightly so Ted would not be able to draw it back if he were able to feel pain through the light gas anesthesia.

Laying another small sterile drape across the arm over Hans Werner's hand, Greg took a scalpel and cut in both directions through the inflamed incision, laying the small wound open widely. Bits of dark, unhealthy-looking tissue he trimmed away, until there was a fresh flow of blood, bright red now from the high concentration of oxygen. And in the depths of the wound, he lifted out with a forceps a broken splinter of wood about a half inch long.

"There's the culprit," he said with a ring of satisfaction in his voice. "We should be able to keep the situation under control now."

It took only a few minutes more to trim away some remaining damaged tissues around where the fragment of splinter had rested. When he finished, Greg put a loose dressing over the wound, allowing it to bleed rather freely in order to wash out as many of the invading bacteria as possible, as well as any remaining bits of damaged tissue, before the bleeding stopped of its own accord through the normal process of clotting.

"Pressure is three atmospheres." Hans Werner was watching a dial set against the wall of the tank. The glass ports had filmed over with moisture with the sudden rise of temperature as the pressure increased. They were beginning to clear now and one of the technicians watching them from outside raised his hand with thumb and forefinger joined to form the letter O, indicating that all was well with the chamber mechanism.

"How high are you going, Greg?" Lew Gann asked.

"Four atmospheres for two hours or maybe a bit longer—if you think it's safe."

"That's close to the danger level for oxygen convulsions," said the anesthesiologist. "But I guess you want to hit those bugs as hard as you can the first crack."

"It's the possibility that a few of them may have been seeded into the bloodstream by the treatment last night that I'm worried particularly about," Greg explained. "But we'll hold it at three, if you're worried about him, Lew."

"He's young and strong," said Dr. Gann. "Besides, I can always control an oxygen convulsion, if it comes, by cutting off the O-two and letting him breathe air just as we're doing. Go on to four atmospheres."

"Is the transplant case lost already, Doctor?" Hans Werner asked.

"I'm afraid his lungs are filling," said Greg. "The infection seems to be under control and after removing the pericardial fluid that was cramping the heart we might have carried him with hyperbaric

oxygen on the small amount of lung tissue still functioning. But—"
He didn't go on.

"Did Georgia Merchant take it hard?" Lew Gann asked.

"She's a trouper, but it hit her, of course. One of the hardest
things I ever had to do was tell her we wouldn't be able to use
the chamber for her husband as I had planned."

"Life is always a matter of choices," said the old Austrian
technician. "If you had not chosen Johns Hopkins, Dr. Alexander.
If you had not come to the attention of Dr. Anders when you
were a student." He shrugged. "When so much of life depends on
chance, you can only believe in a pattern beyond chance, a power
that controls even the throw of the dice."

"I wonder if I offended that power by daring to push death
back too far," Greg hazarded.

"It's a question to be discussed late at night, over steins of cold
beer," Hans said with a smile.

"When the conclusions of the night are to be forgotten in the
headache of tomorrow," Dr. Gann agreed.

"Night is the time for doubting," said Hans. "Day is the time
for decision—and for work."

"There will be those who say I should not try again," said Greg.

"Will you listen?" Lew Gann asked.

"No."

"Goot!" said Hans. "It works on a dog, so it will work one day
with a man. The differences between them are not so great—
except in the dog's favor."

"Why do you say that, Hans?"

"A dog is faithful. Can the same be said of all men?"

"No. We're proving that right now in the controversy over the
new hospital."

"A dog is also grateful—an emotion that quickly turns to hate
in men."

"You're right." Dr. Gann had shut off the anesthetic and Ted
Hunter was breathing only oxygen now. "But I could never understand why."

"In Vienna, long ago, I once heard Dr. Freud lecture," said
Hans. "I was only a student then and much of what he said I

336

did not understand. But one thing I remember well: he was quoting, I think, from Schiller's play *Wallenstein*, where one actor said of his eyes:

> *'He has now opened mine*
> *And I see more than pleases me.'"*

"Are you saying that gratitude begets hate, Hans, because the grateful one eventually sees his gratitude as an admission of his own inadequacy?" Greg asked.

"I could not have put it so well," the technician admitted.

"If that theory is true," said Dr. Gann, "Henry Anders II has always hated you, Greg, because his father trusted you more than him."

"Not exactly," the old Austrian demurred. "The old doctor learned soon that his son never would be the man he was and turned to Dr. Alexander here to carry on his work. To the junior Dr. Anders, Dr. Alexander is a symbol of his own inadequacy. He sees in the present controversy a chance to remove that symbol, so he works against him."

"I would be willing to be the loser if it would make Henry the doctor his father hoped he would be," said Greg.

"Since that is impossible, it is better to leave him as he is," said Hans.

"How do you think this will all end, Hans?"

"Until this boy came upon the scene, I was prepared to see you defeated, Doctor," said the old man. "I don't know why but somehow I think he may be an omen of the future, though, as always, much will still depend upon the throw of the dice."

"It's a long-shot gamble but the only chance for Ted," Greg agreed.

"Others would be willing to settle for the less hazardous course—and bury their mistake," said Hans. "But take heart; already the oxygen seems to be having an effect."

"That, or removing the splinter," said Dr. Gann. "Upon such a slender thread hangs often a human life."

"Who said that?" Greg asked.

"Me!" said the anesthesiologist with a grin. "Profound, ain't I?"

337

Georgia Merchant was in the intensive care waiting room when the others came there from the emergency room at Helen's suggestion. Now there was nothing for all of them to do but wait: Georgia for Bob Johnson to bring her word that Guy was dead; the others for Greg Alexander to come out of the chamber at the end of the first treatment, and report on Ted's condition.

"Can I get any of you some coffee?" Peter Carewe asked the room. "We have several hours yet to wait before we can get a report on Ted."

No one wanted coffee except Helen and Peter, so he went to the vending machine on the first floor to get it. While he was bringing the coffee, Georgia moved over beside Vivian.

"You did the right thing in letting Dr. Alexander take care of your husband, Mrs. Hunter," she said. "I'm Georgia Merchant."

"Oh!" Helen caught herself immediately and looked at Vivian— but the name meant nothing to the girl.

"We were hoping things would turn out differently from the way they have, Mrs. Merchant," said Helen.

"I guess I was just kidding myself that there was really any hope, Doctor."

"Your husband has already proved that the operation is technically possible with a human being. In the next case—"

"You mean Dr. Alexander would try again?"

"Of course."

"What she's saying"—Sam Hunter's voice was harsh with pain and bitter anger—"is that your husband was another of Dr. Alexander's experiments—just like my son."

"Are you the boy's father?" Georgia asked. "The one who's in the pressure chamber now?"

The old man nodded, but didn't speak.

"I know how concerned you must be, sir, but you're wrong about the experiment part. Dr. Alexander explained to me before Guy was operated upon about the hazards involved, but there was no other chance for my husband—except death. Then tonight—"

Her voice broke for a moment. "Tonight he told me he had to remove Guy's last chance of pulling through this so your son could be placed in the chamber. If Dr. Alexander was what you say he is, the last thing he would have done would be to make certain the failure of an operation that could make him world-famous—even to save your son."

iii

The two and a half hours Greg decided upon for the first hyperbaric treatment had ended and the occupants of the chamber were waiting for the pressure of air within the steel tank to be reduced gradually to normal. Because of the high pressure Greg had dared to use initially, decompression would take nearly an hour and already the air in the tank was perceptibly cooler as its heat was dissipated, the reverse of what had taken place during compression. Of the effect on the patient, there could hardly be any doubt now; Ted was sleeping quietly and his skin was almost as cool as Greg's own.

"I heard about the meeting of the Board of Trustees this afternoon, Dr. Alexander," said Hans. "What will happen tomorrow morning?"

"We've only postponed the end, I'm afraid," said Greg. "If I had been able to keep Guy Merchant alive even through tomorrow, enough people might have been impressed by the operation and the new plan for the vote to go in favor by a close margin."

"Do you think you could have kept Merchant alive?" Dr. Gann asked.

"I don't know. But at least we had a chance of winning—until this boy turned up with an otherwise fatal anerobic infection."

"I'm glad the decision wasn't mine to make," said the anesthesiologist.

"You would have come up with the same answer, Lew. How could you balance the life of a man more than sixty years old, with advanced arteriosclerosis throughout his body, against that of any young man in his prime?"

339

Bob Johnson had been at Guy Merchant's bedside ever since Greg had gone to the emergency room to see Ted Hunter. For a while the improvement brought about by removing fluid from around his heart gave some promise of holding, but, as the hours passed, it proved to be only temporary. The respirator continued to pump pure oxygen into Guy Merchant's lungs, but the duskiness of his fingertips, ear lobes and lips slowly deepened, mute proof that not enough oxygen was reaching the tissues through the severely crippled lungs to preserve life.

Knowing that the heart was the heaviest user of oxygen in the body, Bob was surprised that the gift Frank Lawson had given Guy Merchant continued to beat as strongly as it did in the face of the steadily diminishing supply of the vital element. Finally, however, the pulse rate, visible upon the flashing pattern of the electric monitor over the nurses' station, began to increase as the heart strove to answer the call of oxygen lack in its own tissues. Like a fire whose fuel is curtailed, the amplitude of the heartbeat slowly diminished and was barely distinguishable when Bob went to the door of the waiting room and called Georgia Merchant.

"Is it over?" she asked as he led her into the room.

"Not yet, but it can only be a few minutes more. He hasn't been conscious since early this morning."

Gradually the wavy lines on the monitor tube flattened out, then failed altogether and, switching the controls, Bob ran a brief record of the electrocardiogram upon a moving strip of paper. When the delicate pen that normally recorded the tiny electrical current emanating from the heart while functioning failed to move, he reached over and turned off the respirator.

"I'm sorry, Mrs. Merchant," he said. "We almost succeeded."

"Nobody could have done more than Dr. Alexander and the rest of you did," she said. "I'd like to stay long enough to thank him, if I may."

"He should be out of the pressure chamber in about another hour," said Bob. "The way it's snowing outside, you couldn't even get to your hotel before morning anyway, so why don't you just stay here?"

"I think I will, thank you. After all, it has almost become like home."

"Is there anything we can do, Mrs. Merchant?" Peter Carewe asked when she came back into the waiting room, but Georgia shook her head.

"No. Dr. Johnson says I can stay here until morning."

"Of course you can," said Helen, and drew Georgia over to sit beside her. "You and your husband were a team for a long time, weren't you?"

"We were together over twenty-five years. It will be rough without Guy, but I'm still going to do what we were hoping to do together, organize a traveling show of my own. Guy's insurance will help to launch it."

"I'd like to help, too, Mrs. Merchant." Sam Hunter's voice startled the others in the room.

"I appreciate your offer, Mr. Hunter," she said. "But the man whose statue stands in the hospital lobby once said: *Greater love hath no man than this, that he lay down his life for a friend.'* So I guess Guy played his greatest role tonight. Your helping me now would be like paying Guy for what he did for your son, and I know he wouldn't want that."

No one spoke in the room for a long moment; then Sam Hunter stood up suddenly and went to the telephone at the nursing station. "Do you know the number of the Clinic Inn?" he asked the nurse there.

"Certainly, sir," she said. "Shall I dial it for you?"

"Please."

She dialed quickly, then handed him the phone.

"Ring Dr. Edward McDougal's suite," those in the waiting room heard him say, and, after a brief pause, he spoke again:

"I want you to call off your dogs when the trustees meet in the morning, Ed."

There was another pause, apparently while Ed McDougal tried to argue, but the old man cut him off sharply:

"Never mind why, just give up your opposition to Dr. Alexander's plan or there'll be none of my money in that new medical school

341

you want to build down home. And tell Henry Anders I'll expose that real estate scheme of his, too, if he so much as opens his mouth at the meeting tomorrow."

Sam Hunter hung up before anything else could be said and came back into the waiting room to his chair. After a moment, Helen went over and pulled up a chair beside him.

"I was sure you would do the right thing, when you knew the truth," she said.

"My son may still die."

"At least he's had the only possible chance there could be of saving him. I've been doing the cultures for Greg Alexander's research with this type of infection; it's really miraculous the effect that a hundred per cent oxygen in the pressure chamber has upon them. Greg had everything to lose by not taking the transplant case into the chamber but he took Ted instead, because he knew there was no other way of saving him."

"It seems that I've been wrong about a lot of things lately." Sam Hunter turned toward where Vivian was sitting near Georgia Merchant and Peter Carewe.

"Young lady," he started to call.

"Her name is Vivian," Helen said quickly and moved to another chair.

"Vivian," he said.

The girl hesitated, then rose and came over to where the old man was sitting.

"You have every reason to hate me," Sam Hunter began, but Vivian interrupted quickly.

"Ted didn't and neither do I, Mr. Hunter; it's just that he wanted to make his own way. He would have, too, if that splinter hadn't caused so much trouble. Did you know he's already enrolled at the Harvard Graduate School of Business in the fall?"

The old man shook his head.

"I've been taking lessons in stenography and typing, too, so I could work to help. He was going to surprise you by sending you an invitation to his graduation."

As he fumbled for her hand, Sam Hunter suddenly looked every day of his sixty-eight years. When Vivian smiled and reached up

342

to take it in hers, he moved his chair closer to her and put his arm about her shoulders. With the old and the young strengthening each other, they waited for whatever was to come.

v

It was almost eleven when the elevator door opened in the corridor outside the waiting room and Greg Alexander stepped out. He glanced once at the monitor which had been recording Guy Merchant's heartbeat and, when he saw that it was dark, needed no other confirmation that his first heart-lung transplant was dead— and with him, his hopes. Straightening his shoulders, he went to the door of the waiting room.

"Ted's going to be fine," he told the small group sitting there.

"Then he's not dying?" Sam Hunter asked.

"The infection is under control. He'll need a few more treatments with oxygen under pressure, of course—"

"But no amputation?" Vivian asked.

"No more surgery. I found the rest of the splinter and removed it."

He turned to Georgia. "I'm sorry, Mrs. Merchant. I hope you see that I had no other choice."

"I understand, Doctor—and so would Guy."

vi

The rotunda of the hospital was empty when Helen and Peter paused in the shadows at the foot of the great statue shortly after midnight.

"I guess Georgia Merchant was right about her husband playing his greatest role tonight," said Peter. "But my plans for this evening certainly went to pieces."

"'Oh what a tangled web we weave, when first we practice to deceive,'" said Helen with a smile. "Except this wasn't your first practice, was it?"

"I refuse to answer on the grounds of self-incrimination. But you could end my deceiving by marrying me—now."

"Are you absolutely sure?" Her eyes were shining.

343

"From this day forward. Will you be my wife, Doctor?"

"This afternoon, I was prepared to go away with you for the weekend and let it end—"

"It couldn't end there," he interposed quickly. "Surely you know that now."

"What I'm trying to tell you, darling, is that being with Vivian—and with Georgia Merchant—has given me a different viewpoint on marriage. If you're willing to risk your freedom, I'll risk my independence."

"Sounds like an even swap," he said, tucking her arm beneath his. "The snow has stopped and it's not far to Elkton; if people can't still get married there at any time of the day or night, we'll sit in an all-night diner drinking coffee and holding hands until the marriage license bureau opens. How would you like to fly with me to California and hunt viruses on your honeymoon?"

"It sounds exciting. But are you sure you want to give up being the Doctor from WHO?"

"I won't call him until tomorrow but Lars Nordstrom will be happy to learn then that he's about to acquire a top-flight laboratory specialist for his staff. From now on, we'll be the Doctors from WHO—the hottest team of bacterial troubleshooters in the field."

vii

Greg had walked with Sam Hunter to the rotunda. They arrived just as Helen and Peter went hand in hand out into the night.

"I owe a lot to those two—and to you," the old millionaire said.

"Forget about me," said Greg. "I was only doing my job as a doctor."

"Even if it means I still fight you tomorrow?"

Greg glanced up at the marble features of the statue and was not surprised when it appeared to be smiling again.

"I've got an idea that even you couldn't defeat me in the long run now, Mr. Hunter," he said. "This hospital was built by a man with a dream that's lived on after his death. I suppose it could be called a form of immortality."

"No man could wish for greater," Sam Hunter agreed.

"You and I both lost sight of the truth of that dream for a while," said Greg. "You, in the fear that the spirit of the man who conceived it might be lost in the new; I, by not having the courage to let the new dream speak for itself and taking what might be called less honorable measures to advance it."

"The new hospital isn't built yet," Sam Hunter reminded him.

"It will be; I stopped worrying about that yesterday morning at dawn, when I realized that Dr. Anders knew exactly what he was doing when he put the provision in his will that the statue must remain the center point of any new hospital. You see, he knew any surroundings that preserved this"—he put his hand upon the marble and could almost believe it was warm with life— "would also preserve the true spirit of his dream."

"I guess you and I have been concerned about the same thing," Sam Hunter admitted. "We just went about it in different ways."

"Ted's going to be all right, and as a doctor I'd advise you to get some rest," said Greg. "I'll be expecting you to do battle with me tomorrow if I come up with something unworthy of The Clinic and the man who founded it—as I seem to have done two years ago when this controversy first began."

"We may not always be on the same side, Doctor," said the old multimillionaire. "But I've got an idea that we're working for the same goal—and that's what really counts. Good night."

"Good night, sir."

Greg looked at his watch as the spare, erect figure disappeared through the front door. In two more hours he would have to take Ted Hunter back into the hyperbaric chamber, but he'd still come out well before dawn.

And he knew Jeanne would be there, flushed and rosy from sleep, when he came home.